PARKS AND PROVOCATION

Green Valley Heroes Book #2

JULIETTE CROSS

www.smartypantsromance.com

Copyright

Made in the United States of America

Print Edition
ISBN: 978-1-949202-85-4

Dedication

For my beloved daughter, Noelle,
who locked her keys in the car with it running at the Walmart gas station and inspired this book idea. Love you, princess. XO

Chapter One

-LOLA-

"My college crush DMed me yesterday, but I'm scared to answer." @SuzyQ
"As Whittier said, 'Of all sad words of tongue or pen, the saddest are these, it might have been.' Take a chance, Suzy." @kiss-n-tell

"You've *got* to be kidding me."

I jerked on the car door handle three times, slinging my weight back and forth like a maniac, and prayed I'd suddenly discover dormant superpowers to get me out of this mess. Releasing the handle on a frustrated growl, I felt the stare of the frightened middle-aged woman pumping gas one slot over. Peering at me over her hood, she looked on the verge of dialing 911 to help the *poor lady* having a seizure against her ten-year-old Honda Accord.

I gave a little wave and a smile to reassure her that I wasn't a lunatic or in need of medical attention—though the jury was still out on both—then she creepily disappeared below the roof of her car. Pretending I wasn't making a scene, I stared back through my driver's side window, hoping I was mistaken.

Nope. I'd actually locked myself out of my car...with the radio blaring... and the engine running. Who the hell does that?

Thankfully, I had my phone in my hand before I'd made the stupidest mistake in my recent history. I was too frazzled. Too out of sorts. You'd think that four months of living back home and developing a new routine would be enough to get my head screwed back on straight. Apparently not. I was still a huge, hot mess.

The thing is, normally, this wouldn't be that big of a deal. I could just call my Aunt Polly and ask her to bring my extra key. Voila! Problem solved. But somehow, in the move, I'd lost the spare. I also would've called Roadside Assistance. That is, if I hadn't cancelled the service three months ago because it was just too damn expensive. Waitresses didn't make nearly the same amount of money as mid-level marketing associates, which is what I was when I had luxuries like someone on-call to come fix a flat tire. Or say, when I locked myself out of my own damn car, which—I swear—had never happened before. I could also call Pop-A-Lock if I had an extra few hundred dollars to waste, but I didn't.

Exhaling a sad, despairing sigh that I was in the eye of the perfect storm of shame, I unlocked my iPhone and hit Marly's number. One hand on my hip, I swiveled around, hoping no one I knew was in the parking lot. Admitting my moment of stupidity to my best friend was one thing. Having someone I knew witness it live and in vivid color was quite another.

"Hey." Marly answered, perky as usual, the ringing of an office phone in the background.

"Sorry to bother you at work, but I need your help."

Marly was manager of a local moonshine distillery, the Green Valley Shine Company. Unless she had a tour group to entertain with shots and her wild personality, I could always count on her picking up the phone. Thank goodness she did today.

"Sure. You okay? You sound weird."

Blowing out an exasperated breath, I knew my next command would go unheeded. "Okay, don't laugh at me."

She was already laughing. "What did you do?"

"I locked my keys in my car."

More laughing. Hysterical laughter, to be more precise.

"It's *not* that funny."

"Oh, no. It totally is."

"It's not, Marly." I ignored the fact I sounded like a two-year-old titty baby.

"How did you do this?" Snickering. "Don't you take the keys out of the ignition when you get out of your car?"

"Shut *up*. I just wasn't thinking, okay?" I yell-whispered, feeling a mild anxiety attack coming on. I hated embarrassing myself like this. "Seriously, Marly, I'm starting to panic here. We're recording tonight, Jason will be at my house in a few hours, and I have to shower off a greasy layer of Bucky's before all that. And now I'm locked out of my own damn car on the edge of town."

"Calm down." She exhaled a deep breath, finally squashing her giggle-fest. "Just tell me how I can help."

"Well, I was hoping your brother could come to get it open for me."

She snorted. "He works at Jiffy Lube, changing oil and wiper fluid all day. I can pretty much guarantee that ding-dong doesn't know how to jimmy a locked car door. But wait a minute."

Then nothing. "Don't tell me you learned to pick locks from one of your exes."

"Nah. However, that might've been in Bobby's wheelhouse. That man was good with his hands." There was a pregnant pause. Her wheels were turning way too fast. "I *think* I might know someone who can help you out."

"Why did you say it like that?"

"Like what?"

Playing coy wasn't Marly's style. "I don't know, like you're high or something."

"I'm not high."

But I could hear the outrageous smile in her voice. "You're up to something."

"Chill, Lola. You're so paranoid. I was just thinking one of my co-worker's brother is a fireman in town and probably knows how to do that sort of thing. Hang on!" That weird, freaky elation was back in her voice.

Muffled phone, footsteps, and a door creaking open. "Hey, Bekah, do you think your brother could do a favor for my friend? She's in *desperate* need."

Jesus, Marly. She didn't have to make it sound like I was asking for him to do more than jimmy my lock even if I could use a little jimmying in other places.

She popped back on the phone.

"All good. Tell me where you're at. She'll get him *right* over there." She dragged out the word "right" in a weird, sing-song voice.

"Okay, I'm at that Quick-n-Go on the Green Valley city limits heading to Merryville. Thank you!"

"Kisses. We'll talk later," she said with a demonic giggle. What the hell? "Gotta go. A new group of tourists just rolled in."

"Thank you! Bye."

Whew. Okay. This wasn't going to be so bad after all. Hopefully, this fireman was a nice enough guy who could break into my car and then wave me off with a kind smile, and a *have a nice day, ma'am.*

Beck's "Loser" vibrated against the windows from inside my car. Thanks. As if I needed the reminder. This day couldn't get any worse.

I hated being in the wrong and looking like an idiot. I loathed it with the passion of a thousand suns. I mean, obviously, no one wanted to look like an idiot. But for me, it was a bone-deep fear. I wasn't a big risk-taker, because taking risks meant there was a greater chance of failure. I'd never taken many risks, and yet, I was still failing at life. Though I was totally winning for a while there.

I'm just not the kind of girl who stumbles over her own feet or forgets where she put her purse or locks her keys in her stupid-ass car. I'm orderly and organized and usually brilliant at making my way through life in a successful, albeit micromanaged, fashion.

My senior year, I was actually voted "most likely to succeed." And I had been for a long time. Earning my degree in a double-major of marketing and mass communications in under four years, then landing a mid-level position at Clarks and Taylor Marketing in New Orleans, had made me a rising star in my parents' eyes. And in my own, for that matter. All my life goals were being achieved on my pre-planned schedule, like clockwork, until they weren't.

As for my other little dream, things were looking up there. And then days like today reminded me how out of whack my world was. How my life had taken a sharp left off my highway of success ever since Clarks and Taylor. Actually, I was beginning to think I'd careened off every paved path, and was now bumping along a dusty, gravel road to nowheresville. And *that* was horrifying.

It had been under ten minutes when an SUV with the Green Valley Fire Department logo emblazoned on the side swung into the parking lot. I glanced down at my denim mini-skirt and white polo shirt with the Bucky's Bar & Grill emblem on the chest. There was a dribble of fajita grease on my left boob, and I smelled like deep-fried dog poop after my long day-shift, but I plastered on my flirty smile anyway.

Chin up, Lola.

Facing west with the sun behind his SUV, I braced my hand on my forehead, squinting in his direction. A giant of a man unfolded out of the vehicle. Whoa. Mr. Fireman looked like one of those hot officers with bulging biceps and visible arm tattoos who posed with puppies on Instagram and had fifty-thousand followers as he swaggered toward me.

And I do mean swaggered. I knew the difference because I used to watch old movies with my dad on Sundays while growing up. His favorites were John Wayne westerns. Now that man knew how to enter a room. Or a saloon. Or a showdown at noon. He moved leisurely but also with unwavering confidence and masculinity.

That's how the hot fireman was heading my way. A man with purpose who knew how to get the job done. No matter what job it was. Including keys inadvertently locked in cars.

Breathless from the mere silhouette of his magnificence, I wished I didn't smell or look like a grease pit. But I clearly didn't plan on meeting one of Green Valley's absolute *finest* post-shift. I'd have to really turn up my sparkling personality.

"Hi," I chirped as he drew closer, finally moving my ogling gaze up to his face though the sun was still in my eyes. Flashing him a big smile, I said, "Thank you so much for coming out."

He didn't respond as he came straight for me, carrying a small duffle bag in one hand. He froze mid-step for a split second before strolling toward me at a much slower pace. His broad upper torso shifted and blocked out the sun behind him as he said, "Well, well, well. If it isn't Coca-Cola Lola."

My heart froze in fright before taking off at breakneck, runaway speed. I actually thought I was hallucinating that voice until the owner came fully into view right in front of me.

You've seriously *got* to be kidding me, Universe! I recognized that voice. It rumbled deeper and darker than it did in high school, but I'd know it anywhere.

I gawked, soaking in the ridiculously handsome face of my long-ago nemesis. While my smile slipped, his grew in immense proportions, that far-too-adorable and aggravating left dimple popping. Still quite visible above his trim beard. I couldn't freaking believe this. How was this happening to me?

His hazel-brown eyes punched me with a wave of nostalgia. The kind you get when you hear a song you haven't heard in years, and yet it brings you back to a moment in your life that's imprinted in your brain like it's a link in your DNA.

That's what happened when I stared into his familiar gaze. One that was wholly fixed on me, the same way it used to be in high school when his penetrating stare made my heart pound and my neck sweat and my hands shake. Then that intense gaze slid down my rumpled clothes, all the way to my dirt-smudged Converse shoes. I refused to fidget. I refused to show any signs of weakness in front of Jedediah Lawson.

Planting my hands on my hips, I sighed in despair and frustration, along with complete and total humiliation, then replied the only way I possibly could.

"Jockstrap Jed. This is...surprising."

Stay calm. Stay cool.

You'd think the nickname I'd cursed him with back in our sophomore year would make him flinch or scowl or growl at me, but no. The ass smiled bigger.

And how the hell was he a fireman in Green Valley? Last I'd heard, he was playing football for UT in Knoxville. I assumed he'd be pro by now. I mean, just look at him. He was high school Jed times ten. He definitely looked like he belonged on a pro football field somewhere, smashing helmets, crushing quarterbacks, kicking ass, and taking names.

"I didn't know you moved back," he said casually, dropping the duffel bag on the ground next to my car.

Adrenaline-spiked laughter burst out of me like a jacked-up hyena. "It wasn't in the plans."

Not even in backup plans B, C, or D. He needs zero information, Lola! Shut your *trap*.

His head lowered for a brief second, and another slap of memory hit me hard. His straight black hair, longer on top, fell forward. Though it was much shorter on the sides than when I knew him, he always had that wayward piece that wanted to misbehave and cover one of his eyes.

"So," he enunciated with all the levity of a nuclear bomb, "it seems you've gotten yourself into a jam."

Kill me now. *Kill me now!*

"Just a bit."

Unzipping the duffel, he pulled out what looked like a rectangular, flat whoopee cushion. I thought he didn't know what he was doing for a second because that's not how they did it on the TV shows. But then, Jed slid the rubbery contraption into the crack between the door and the car and started inflating it with a small hand pump. While he worked, he slid his sideways smile back to me. Something fluttered in my tummy.

Oh, hell no. There would be no flutters of any kind regarding Jockstrap Jed. None!

"When did you get home?" The low, deep baritone that matched his physique rumbled down my spine.

"About four months ago."

"Weren't you in New Orleans?"

"Uh, yeah." Why does he know that? Was he asking about me since I've been gone?

"Graduated early at LSU and stayed in Louisiana, huh?"

"Yeah?"

I hadn't intended it to sound like a question, but I was kind of confused, verging on excited, that he'd asked about me.

He seemed to understand my reaction, tilting his head and focusing on the door. "Small town."

Ah. Of course.

"Right."

He'd just caught the news on the Green Valley gossip circuit. That made more sense, of course. Why did I suddenly feel disappointed?

I swiped a loose curl away from my temple, terrified that my hair was puffing up far too fast in the afternoon humidity.

I kept my chin up and refused to fidget, even though I looked and smelled like an oily Tex-Mex nightmare. He scanned my face with an intense sweep. I stared right back, refusing to let him see I was in any way uncomfortable or embarrassed by the situation.

"You don't wear glasses anymore?"

"*Nope*," I answered with too much emphasis.

His mouth ticked up higher on both sides. "You finally started wearing contacts."

"No," I enunciated slowly and clearly. "I actually got Lasik surgery last summer. I don't need glasses or contacts anymore."

I would never in a million years admit to anyone, especially him, that my insecurity about wearing super-thick glasses started with his name-calling back in high school. Yes, I was an adult and should've been able to move past it. But that, in addition to my phobia of touching my own eyeballs in any way, prompted me to finally look into the surgery. I went ahead with the procedure for more than cosmetic reasons, so I wasn't ashamed. As a matter of fact, I hadn't even thought about those days or the way he'd made me feel until this very humiliating second.

Strangely though, he wasn't teasing, more like just asking. All polite and stuff. So weird. Maybe he had grown up?

He measured me another second before blowing my mind with, "I like seeing your green eyes better. Still have those freckles, too, I see." His crooked smile was all playful, but his eyes were so somber.

I touched my nose as if I could feel them or I'd forgotten they were there. While I had light brown hair, my mom, like my Aunt Polly, were both redheads. I'd inherited the pale skin with a dappling of freckles. Nothing I was ever self-conscious about until Jed was sweeping those hazel-dark eyes across my face. I didn't know what to say, completely thrown off by my typically-controlled demeanor.

He leaned over the duffel bag and pulled out a long steel rod with a loopy hook at the end. As he maneuvered the rod, hook first, into the crack he'd created with the inflation device—clever, that—he glanced at me, still staring like he was waiting to find some fault he could exploit like he used to back in the day.

But when he turned his attention back to the window and jimmied the rod down toward the lock, he said in that low, solid tone, "You look fantastic."

My knees wobbled.

Was he being serious?

I did NOT look fantastic. I was covered in grease, my curly hair was puffed up like a Bob Ross Chia-pet, and I had zero makeup on. Considering he'd once told me I should join a vampire coven because I was so pale, I knew how he felt about my au naturale status. Back then, anyway.

"So you didn't want to go pro?" I changed the subject, still unsure whether he was mocking me or not with his *fantastic* comment. "I figured that was your plan." Everyone assumed he would. He had the physique and the discipline to go far in the sport.

Clearing his throat, he kept his focus on my car door. "I didn't finish at UT. I was needed here."

The somber admission seemed to mellow his mood significantly, giving me the strange sensation to comfort him. "Oh. Sorry to hear that."

"Nothing to be sorry about." He flashed me a brilliant smile, his gaze dropping to my legs for a fleeting second before turning back to the car. "This is right where I want to be."

"In Green Valley? Opening stranded girls' car doors?"

He laughed, the deep, masculine sound giving me the sweats. "Not everyone needs to leave here to find happiness, Cola."

"I didn't *need* to leave," I protested, smarting a little at the nickname again. "It's just—" I heard the snick of my lock disengaging. "Oh, thank goodness!"

He whipped out the rod and the inflatable, then opened the door for me, gesturing with a sweep of his hand. I maneuvered past him and slid inside to turn off my radio that had been tuned into an older pop station, now blaring Lady Gaga's "Bad Romance."

Remembering he'd just saved me quite a bit of money and that I was a decent, mature human being most of the time, I swallowed my aggravation and my pride, then swiveled in my car seat, my feet on the concrete. I shot out my hand for him to shake.

"Thank you for your help."

While I ground my molars together, holding my hand out in an offer of thanks, I reminded myself that I was no longer Coca-Cola Lola, that insecure girl who he loved to pick on back in the day. The famous football player on Green Valley High's championship-winning team who made more of an impression on me than I cared to admit. To anyone. Even myself.

I stared up—way up—at him and waited. He squatted and took my hand in both of his. It didn't escape me that we were even in height with him squatting on the ground. He really had put on the extra height in inches and mass since high school. I'd thought him ginormous back then.

"Let's say we get together and catch up," he suggested, flashing me that stupid, adorable, dimpled smile.

To avoid his freaking face, I stared at where he kept my hand captive between his giant, calloused paws. "Um, I'm super busy."

"Waiting tables at Bucky's?"

"Yeah." I shot him a glare, knowing this had to be a dig. But his gaze was even and warm, his expression calm and confident. Where the hell was the hot-tempered Jockstrap Jed? He seemed totally sincere. Maybe this was all just a trick and the old Jed would come prowling out the second I let down my guard. "And other stuff. Just busy."

"Okay then," he said, releasing my hand and standing.

Why in the name of all things holy did I suddenly want to leap up like a maniac and snatch his hands back? The afternoon heat was apparently melting my brain cells.

He braced one hand on the car door, the other on the top of my Honda.

"I think you should take a break from your busy schedule and go to dinner with me."

I blinked. "Like a date?"

"Not *like* a date," he clarified with confidence. "An actual date."

"I work a lot of night shifts," I answered calmly while there was some kind of crazy circus act going on inside my tummy.

"Lunch then," he pushed.

I opened my mouth to make up an excuse because this entire encounter had rattled me down to my toes, and I needed to escape with my dignity intact.

"I don't think that's a good idea."

He drummed his long fingers on the top of the car door for a few long seconds, then he only nodded, seeming to have some grand epiphany. "I see."

He backed up and released my door, but I just sat there, staring up at him. "What do you think you see?"

He crossed his arms over his uniformed chest, biceps bulging, accenting the black ink roping down his bronzed forearms.

"I think you're embarrassed that I had to bail you out of this little predicament, and you're too proud to admit that you might actually enjoy spending time with me."

Wait. *What?*

"Of course, I'm embarrassed! This is the worst. But...too proud? I'm *not* too proud."

"Then have dinner with me." He was grinning like mad now, and I wondered where that wash of heat over my chest was coming from.

"Maybe I just don't want to have dinner with the guy who nicknamed me Coca-Cola Lola in high school."

"Yes, you do."

I snorted. "You're unbelievable."

He gave a slight shrug of one shoulder, arms still crossed. "Some say so."

"Wow. Just...wow."

"Some say that, too."

My jaw dropped in complete disbelief, but then he belted out a laugh, a swathe of pink flushing his cheekbones. Was he blushing? I figured that was a phenomenon he only experienced in high school.

"You owe me." He arched a superior brow, dipping his chin low, drawing my attention to his dark, close-cropped beard. I stared at it like it was a new revelation, because seriously, Jed 2.0 was a force to be reckoned with. My eyeballs were hurting from jumping all over the place. I didn't want him to see me staring at one place too long. He probably thought I had a facial tic.

"I'll pay you back some other way." An idea snapped to me. "Cookies!"

"Cookies?"

"You still like snickerdoodles, right?"

His smile fell, a puzzled expression scrunching up his wide brow.

What are you doing?

He was now recalling how I knew he loved my cookies. This catastrophe had to end.

"That's what I'll do." I beamed up at him, grabbing my car door handle as he backed away. "Cookies it is," I said all casually, as if I hadn't just admitted I still remembered a very sweet memory of the two of us and the stadium bleachers and snickerdoodle cookies. Like I could ever forget it.

Slamming the door shut, I fastened myself in, shifted into drive, and tore out of there in 1.7 seconds like the devil was chasing me. I glanced in my rearview, his giant form still there, arms crossed, watching me go.

No, the devil wasn't chasing after me. And why did that somehow make my stomach sink with disappointment?

I raised my hands to the sky before banging them back on my steering wheel, crying, "Why!"

As my pulse slowed, my brain finally began to catch up, putting puzzle pieces together. That's when I realized it had nothing to do with the heavens cursing me at all. This was no sadistic act by the universe against me. This was the wicked work of my so-called best friend.

"Marly."

I was going to kill her.

Chapter Two

-LOLA-

"Even your ride-or-die bestie may one day make you contemplate where to hide her body." @kiss-n-tell

"You're dead to me."

Marly spat out her gulp of coffee she'd just sipped from her to-go mug as she walked into my Aunt Polly's kitchen.

"I'm serious. We're broken up," I said flippantly, still typing on my MacBook. "Divorced."

The fiendish laughter commenced as she wiped the coffee dribbling down her chin with her sleeve. Then she set down a second coffee-to-go cup in front of me and plopped with an undignified thump. Not that Marly gave a damn about being dignified.

"You're such a lady, too. You know that?"

"Here. A peace offering. Your favorite."

She slid the cup toward me. Just like Marly to use my cappuccino addiction to gain forgiveness.

"You're not even going to say you're sorry?"

She just grinned.

"Because you're not sorry, are you?" I clarified.

"Nope. Not even a little. But oh, my *God*, I would've done anything to have seen your face when he walked up."

"Why do you hate me?"

"Did you go all ice-queen Lola or deer-in-headlights Lola?" She dropped her purse on the table where I was taking notes on my laptop for our soon-to-arrive podcast guest.

"I have no idea what you're talking about." I'd kind of gone ice-queen, actually.

She laughed, eyes glittering with the glee of my humiliation, or her caffeine high, or maybe both. I wasn't sure. "I was hoping for silent horror."

"What are you babbling about?" I asked while revising one of my questions for Jason.

"You know. When you're so freaked out you can't even form a sentence."

"And why would you wish that on me, exactly?"

"That way, you wouldn't scare him off this time."

I scoffed so loud, I almost choked on my own spit. "What the *hell* are you talking about, Marleen Marie?"

"The fact that you two have always had it bad for each other, but you never gave him a chance." Then she rapidly blinked at me sweetly and sipped her coffee like she hadn't just let the most ludicrous lie escape from her mouth.

"You're remembering it wrong. He was a jackass to me, and I was equally unpleasant in a completely understandable recompense of his bad behavior."

"Right." She rolled her eyes. "Well, amidst all your tit for tat, sparks were flying."

"Yeah. Sparks of hate."

"Uh-uh." She sipped her coffee with mischief and mayhem in her eyes. "Sparks of delicious, lusty—"

"Stop it right now, Marly. That weird ship sailed over five years ago at graduation. Wasn't even a ship. More like a leaky canoe."

Her sea-blue eyes twinkled with devilry. "You are such a drama queen."

"Me? You're the one imagining some long-lost romance. You obviously have rewritten history in your own crazy head. Do you know what kind of torture he put me through in high school?"

"Perfectly. You were in love with him and wanted to have all his babies."

"Not after junior year, I didn't." I pointed a finger at her. "And you know why."

I can still remember the day that had caused me a water-well-deep amount of heartache. I overheard one of his asshat friends from the football team, Trey Baxter, laughing at Jed when he said he was asking me to the prom. Trey had said, "That would be hilarious. I dare you." Jed had grunted in reply and hadn't denied he was asking me as a joke. So, when he caught me in the school parking lot the next day and asked me, I replied in Trey's words, "That would be hilarious." When his eyes sharpened with a flicker of pain, I added that I already had a date, then got in my car and fled the scene like a bat out of hell.

I was never sure if he'd asked me as a joke or not, but after our tumultuous and antagonistic relationship since freshman year, I refused to take a chance of looking like a fool.

The worst part was I ended up dragging Marly's cousin as my date. He was from another school and spent the whole night flirting with all my friends. And I'd had to watch Jed dance all night with his date, the beautiful and kind-hearted class president, Amanda Higginbotham. Amanda and I were also on the Speech and Debate team together. What made it worse was that I *really* liked her. When that old song by Jewel, "You Were Meant For Me," came on and they danced together, it had crushed my teenage heart.

"Newsflash," said Marly, snapping me back to the present. She pulled the ponytail holder from her wrist and twisted her straight dirty blonde hair up into a messy bun. "That was a hundred years ago. And he's all grown up now."

"Tell me about it," I mumbled into my coffee cup before setting it down and typing one last question.

Marly kicked me under the table.

"Ow! What is wrong with you, crazy?"

"You just admitted it!" she squealed with delight.

"What? That he's hot?"

"You do still like him."

Squinting my eyes at her, I shook my head then returned my attention to my laptop screen, though I completely forgot what I was about to type.

"First, I have not spent my years absent from Green Valley pining over Jedediah Lawson. And second, I'm not blind, for Pete's sake. I mean, he's obviously..."

"*Hot.*"

"Sure. Yes. Whatever."

"Now stop stalling. What did he say?" She propped her elbows on the table, leaning forward.

Still typing, I shrugged. "He told me I looked good, and he wanted to take me to dinner."

"Get *out*!" She banged a hand on the table, wobbling my coffee.

"Marly, you've got to dial it down by at least a thousand. We've got a podcast guest coming in the next half hour, and you're making me nervous."

Marly and I had been on the Speech and Debate team as well as the Drama Club together in high school. We'd often fantasized about starting our own podcast. Back then, our biggest idea had been a review podcast of musicals on Broadway, because of course, we'd have all the time and money in the world to jet to New York and see musicals on the regular.

And even though I went off to school at LSU in Baton Rouge and she stayed here and went to UT in Knoxville, we'd never lost touch. Nor did we ever stop dreaming about our podcast that we'd eventually start someday together. In college, our ideas shifted to things like affordable fashion for college kids and the breakdown of college professors with God complexes. Needless to say, we never intended to host podcasts on these things, but it was a fun game we liked to play.

The first weekend after I returned to Green Valley, Marly had me over to her house for dinner and lots of margaritas. We shared all our horrific dating stories over the past few years and laughed our asses off. It was Marly who first said, "We should totally do a dating podcast."

We'd laughed at the idea, and then I'd sobered in a split second and said, "Marly, we're one hundred percent doing it."

From that day on, I researched, planned, and then launched our podcast, Kiss-n-Tell. It was actually more mine than Marly's since I'd been putting in most of the work hours and investing in the recording equipment and software. It was the perfect project to get my mind off of the fact I was no longer employed by a marketing firm. The podcast allowed me to flex my marketing skills as well as my creative ones.

"So what!" Marly got wild googly eyes, not caring in the slightest that I needed to focus on our upcoming podcast recording. "This is amazing! So when is Jed taking you out?"

"What? I'm not going out with him."

Her mouth literally dropped open so far I could see her uvula. Strangely, I'd never noticed how perfect her teeth were. Not one cavity that I could see from where I was sitting. After she snapped out of her shock-and-awed daze, she pointed a purple-painted index finger at me. "You are *going* on a date with him."

"No, I'm not."

"Yes, you are."

I sighed and kept typing.

"Lola Elizabeth Landry. Yes. You. Are."

"If you think he's so great, you go out with him."

"He doesn't want to date me. Trust me, I'd climb that mountain of a man, stake my flag, and set up camp."

I rolled my eyes, clamping my jaw at the thought of Marly waving her flag from up on top of Mount Jed.

I typed a string of question marks just to type something, in the attempt to get my brain back on track, which wasn't working. "Well, I'm not going on a date just because he opened my locked car door. I thought I'd just bake him some snickerdoodles or something. Isn't that the always-appreciated gift of Green Valley residents? Baked goods?"

"Woman, you are not baking him freaking cookies. Unless you're using that as a euphemism for something naughty."

Time for a subject change. "How did you know he was a firefighter anyway?"

She arched her eyebrow with a salacious grin. "He came in one day to drop off his niece to his sister, Bekah, in his uniform. Jesus." She fanned herself. "The other girls and I almost fainted. I thought Bekah was going to have to hit Patricia with a glass jug of our new flavor *blueberry bombshell* that we were unpacking onto the display table."

I didn't know Patricia, but right now I didn't particularly like her.

"But seriously. Listen, Lola." Then she got that look of deep concentration that was so rare for Marly. She usually looked like she was about to commit major mischief. Or she just had. "I think you should go on this date. I mean, hell, you could do it for the podcast and satisfy both your curiosity and protect your fragile ego at the same time."

I frowned, wanting to deny that my ego was fragile. But I wasn't that big a liar. Ever since the layoff, my ego had been suffering from severe fracture lines, splintering into a million spiderweb breaks. I was holding it together with duct tape and a prayer, the most reliable of southern adhesives.

"What do you mean exactly?"

Marly didn't laugh but tilted her head with that sincere expression that reminded me how much she loved me. "You might not have been pining over Jed all these years, but once upon a time, you wanted a date with him. Think of this opportunity as a check on your bucket list. And if it doesn't go well, then you've got a great episode for the podcast."

"What if he doesn't want to do the podcast?"

I'd had two of the twelve guys refuse to do it so far. They'd been offended at the end of the date when I asked them to be on the show, thinking it was all just an experiment. And quite frankly, it sort of was. I wasn't interested in dating anyone seriously while I was here in town, only for the podcast.

"If he doesn't want to do the podcast, then so what. You finally got your date with Jed, and that's that," she said matter-of-factly.

Except there wasn't anything matter-of-fact about going on a date with Jed, the guy I'd fallen in love with on my first day of freshman year. Okay, infatuation. The love came by slow degrees of mooning over him in English class, in the cafeteria, on the football field. And especially when he stood at his locker right above mine on class schedule breaks.

Then he'd turned into a total asshole sophomore year, twisting that deep, teenage longing kind of love into furious spite—kind of. I couldn't make my heart stop yearning, even after his mean nickname Coca-Cola Lola caught on to the rest of our class like freaking wildfire. Even my retaliation nickname didn't alleviate the pain he'd carved with words.

Sticks and stones, my ass. Words always hurt more.

Ding-dong.

Saved by the doorbell. Thank the Lord!

"There's Jason. Grab my MacBook. Your questions are all ready to go."

I leapt up and headed toward the front door. "Got it." I heard her standing behind me.

Jason Hoffman was two years ahead of us at Green Valley High and was one of the elite on the football team. I'd ran into him at Daisy's Nut House two weeks ago, and we struck up a conversation after he unashamedly flirted with me over what was better, pecan or chocolate pie.

Of course, he didn't remember me from high school because we didn't run in the same circles. But he was certainly interested in post-high school Lola. So when he asked me on a date, I excitedly accepted, preferring dates that I hadn't gotten on the dating app for the podcast.

Marly was essential in playing moderator for the date interviews on the show, keeping the conversation going, and also fielding questions and comments from followers on my YouTube channel since we recorded the interviews live. The fan interaction was paramount on D-day, what Marly had dubbed date interview day. It's what really got followers buzzing.

I swung open the door to the handsome figure of Jason Hoffman, dressed nicely in dark jeans and a starched button-up, his face clean-shaven and doused with cologne. I hoped he understood that the podcast interview wasn't a second date.

His eyes widened as Marly shoved herself into the doorway, holding my MacBook.

"Hi!" she said cheerily.

He grinned. "Uh, hi."

"Jason, this is Marly." I gave him my business-professional yet welcoming smile. "As I mentioned on the phone, she'll be moderating the interview and helping me out."

"Sounds cool," he said, head bobbing in understanding.

"Come on in then," I stepped to the side of the entrance and waved him to go first.

"Let's get this party started, kiddos," said Marly, leading the way.

Chapter Three

-LOLA-

"Do you believe in second-chance romance?" @TaraLee
"Once a douche, always a douche." @kiss-n-tell
"Kylo Ren changed back to Ben, so..." @marlypants
"Truth. I guess there's always hope. #Reylo4Ever." @kiss-n-tell

"So, how'd I do?" Jason placed the headphones on the table and combed his fingers through his hair.

"You were great," I answered honestly, taking the MacBook from in front of Marly and saving the file in the correct folder. Not that Marly couldn't do it. I was just that much of a control freak.

Marly popped up out of her chair with a wide smile. "You were awesome. Listeners are going to love you. You've got that whole handsome but friendly, puppy-dog vibe going on."

"Puppy dog?" He scratched his head with an expression halfway between concern and amusement.

"Don't mind her," I assured him. "It's a compliment in a Marly sort of way."

"Okay. I'll take your word for it," he answered with an embarrassed laugh as he followed me back downstairs. "Well, I hope your podcast followers like the show."

"I'm sure they will."

We'd broken down the pros and cons of the date. Pro: bowling was the perfect setting to cut loose and get to know each other. Con: Italian food can be messy and not a great choice for the self-conscious eater. But overall, Jason had scored well on the date-o-meter. A higher-than-average 8 out of 10. I rated each date based on dinner, venue, conversation, and rapport.

"Thank you again for agreeing to be on the show," I added over my shoulder as we rounded into the living room. "I sometimes know that guys think I'm going to dissect them to death on the air."

The point of *Kiss-n-Tell* wasn't for me to rate or demean the person I went on a date with. I'd never do that. It was to analyze and rate the date itself, to share the good and the bad. My mission was to not only offer entertainment for all the singles out there, but also to hopefully provide some guidance and good advice for those on the front lines. That's what Marly and I thought would appeal the most to our audience.

Dating these days was a warzone, riddled with the pitfalls of social media hyper-awareness, among a million other things. Singles often spent an inordinate amount of time scrutinizing a potential date's social media sites for all of their flaws and/or potential, making a predetermined judgment before they ever even took a seat at the table across from them for coffee or drinks or dinner, wherever the first date was set.

That's why one of my biggest suggestions to my listeners was to withhold from stalking a date's social media sites until *after* the first date. Get to know them in person first. Give them a *real* chance before you decide you'd never date a guy who wore a neon green sweater, or who posted too many pictures of his cat, or who shared too many TGIF memes. Some people were just social media awkward and might surprise you in real life.

"I didn't feel that way. It was fun." Jason stuffed both hands in his pockets. "And, I just have to say one more time what a good sport you were and how cute you looked rolling all those gutter balls."

We both laughed. I had no problem laughing at myself over trivial embarrassing things like being a horrendous bowler. It was just the big ones that bruised my ego.

"I appreciate you being a good sport about me having an ulterior motive for our date."

A few guys felt like I'd tricked them at the end of the date when I asked them to be on the show.

Okay, I suppose I *did* trick them. But I genuinely put myself out there on these dates. I wanted it to be awesome just as much as they did because that's what got my listeners all aflutter, buzzing around on social media. The good dates brought me higher reviews and more subscribers. I wasn't out to hurt anyone. But I'd never gone on a podcast date with someone I knew.

That made me think about Marly's suggestion to go on that date with Jed for the podcast.

I more than knew Jed. We had a solid history of teenage animosity. And maybe one or two good moments. I don't think he'd be upset about it. I mean, he practically insisted we go to dinner, didn't he?

"Let me walk you out." I led Jason toward the foyer to the front door, then spun and held out my hand. "Thank you again. I greatly appreciate it. Do you mind if I tag you when the podcast goes live?"

"Not at all." He shook my hand, holding it a tad longer than expected. "So, I have to admit. I was hoping that I might be able to coerce you into a second date. Since I scored an eight on your dating scale and all."

His charming smile captivated me for a second or two. But dating—real dating—wasn't on the agenda for me in the near future. And though Jason Hoffman was considered quite the catch in the pool of Green Valley bachelors, I couldn't lead him on.

"Jason, I one-hundred-percent enjoyed our date. But I'm honestly not looking for a relationship right now."

He bobbed his head, biting his bottom lip. "I understand."

"Coming through!" Marly rushed out of the house with her cell phone in hand with the speaker on and someone yelling in Spanish on the other end.

"What's going on? Who's that?" I called as she jogged toward her pick-up truck.

"The dachshund is having her babies! Could be a record-breaking litter!" Then she yelled back toward her phone, "Get my pink pillow! The *pink* one!" In seconds, she was hopping in and tearing out of my driveway like her house was on fire.

Jason turned to me, confusion written all over his face, probably mirroring mine. "What the hell was that?"

"I have no idea."

"Does she have a pregnant dachshund?"

"No. She doesn't even like dogs. She's a cat person."

"Isn't she your best friend?" he asked on a laugh.

"Yep." Shaking my head at whatever insanity Marly was up to now, I turned to him. "Anyway, thanks again." I tried to say it with finality.

He seemed to get the point. "Well, if you change your mind about that second date, just give me a call."

"Will do," I said politely, knowing full well that was never going to happen. But I kept my sweet, southern politeness in place as he got into his sedan and drove away.

Heading back into the house, I went upstairs and closed down my laptop. It was Pokeno night for Aunt Polly. Her friend Helen was hosting, and she'd likely be gone till I was fast asleep. I had another lunch shift tomorrow.

After eating some leftover chicken spaghetti, washing my face, and brushing my teeth, I changed into some sleep shorts and a tank top, then crawled into bed. It had been one long-ass day.

I'd just plugged my phone into the charger when it started vibrating with an incoming call. I didn't recognize the number, but it was local, so I answered. "Hello?"

"Hi, Cola." His rumble-deep voice and intimate greeting sent a zap all the way down my body, ricocheting somewhere between my thighs.

"How'd you get my phone number?" I congratulated myself at only sounding slightly breathless.

"I have my ways." He cleared his throat. "I was calling to tell you I don't want your cookies."

"My cookies?"

"Well," he laughed, all husky and warm. I could picture that flush of pink crawling up his neck. "Actually, I'm pretty sure I'd enjoy them quite a bit." Were we literally talking about cookies? "But what I really want is a date. With you."

I couldn't speak. I could barely breathe. Jedediah Lawson had tracked me down to ask me out. If high school Lola could see me now! She'd probably have a panic attack then pass out. But grown-up Lola was far too mature for that.

And why shouldn't I go out with him? Like Marly said, I'd finally check off that bucket list item, and he'd make a good candidate for next week's podcast.

"Okay."

"Okay? As in yes, you'll go?" The earnest hopefulness in his voice actually made me smile.

"Yes, I'll go." Then it was his turn to go silent. "Are you there?"

"Yeah, yeah. I'm here." He laughed with a deep, raspy roll. "Great. How is Saturday at 6:00?"

"That sounds perfect. I'm off Saturday."

"Perfect."

More silence thickened the line. I think we might both have been in shock.

"Right then. Have a good night," I said, all mature and natural-sounding.

"See you Saturday. Night, Cola."

Then he hung up, and I set my phone down, staring at it in complete and utter shock.

"I'm going on a date with Jockstrap Jed," I muttered to no one.

After squishing my spare pillow and hugging it in a fetal position, I stared at the wall, realizing only minutes later that I was grinning like a crazy person. Butterflies were doing some kind of ballet akin to Tchaikovsky's "Swan Lake" in my tummy as I imagined him picking me up for our date.

My phone vibrated with a text message. My heart rate skyrocketed and my stomach plummeted in a Pavlovian response to the sound of the buzz. Not good. This was not a good reaction to messages from Jed, who I was fake-dating.

I jerked my phone off the nightstand, but it was from Marly. It was a meme of Will Ferrell as Ron Burgundy with the words: *I call my penis Batman...bitches love it when the Dark Knight rises.* I snorted.

Just Marly sending me my nightly naughty meme. As crazy as it sounded, Marly's perverted mind had become part of my bedtime routine. I'd feel lost without it.

ME: Bitches need some sleep. Goodnight.

THOUGH I WAS curious about her great escape while screaming about dachshund puppies, I was too tired to ask. And too wrapped up in the newest development. I also wasn't even remotely prepared to tell Marly about what I'd just agreed to. She'd go all psycho on me, so I was putting a pin in that conversation for now. Setting my phone back down, I stared at the ceiling, wondering how I'd gotten here.

Six months ago, I was living in an upscale apartment in New Orleans, making an excellent salary as a young professional, working out three days a week at the gym, going on the occasional date, and climbing the career ladder at Clarks and Taylor. My life was perfectly ordered and on the track I'd foreseen for myself. Then...*boom*! Downsizing, cutbacks, a monumental disastrous mistake, then my savings evaporating while I blasted New

Orleans with resumes and went on so many fruitless interviews that I came home and cried in my pillow. Literally.

Now, I was living in my aunt's house back in Green Valley for some indeterminate amount of time, waiting tables on an ever-changing schedule, never working out because being healthy was exhausting right now, and working on my podcast every chance I got. Basically, my life was a topsy-turvy, chaotic mess.

The only thing that kept me sane was maintaining my spreadsheets for podcast episodes and my lists for social media promotion posts. It was the one area in my life where I had some organized control.

Also, I had secret high hopes that the podcast became big enough to lure in some advertisers. Maybe even a podcast network where this could make real money. I couldn't very well imagine it supplanting a position with a marketing firm, but it could become legit supplemental income.

Our social media presence was rising. Last week's pic of me and date #14, Ben, at the dance club where he'd taken me after dinner had received sixty-two comments on Twitter. Of course, it had more to do with the fact that the selfie caught some photo-bomber behind us making a lewd gesture with his tongue. I'd gotten more replies about the rude douchebags of the world than I did about the date with Ben. He was nice. That's about it.

He'd received a seven on the date-o-meter, mainly because a nightclub really wasn't the best place to take a girl out and get to know her. I had strict criteria and a detailed rubric in judging my dates for the date-o-meter. Marly laughed at how seriously I took the judging process, but if this was the only thing in my life I could keep orderly, well then, so be it. She could laugh it up.

I rolled over on my pillow, wondering where Jed planned to take me.

Would it be fancy? Should I wear a dress? Maybe I should buy a new one.

Nope, nope, nope. *Stop it.*

This was a podcast date. Anything already in my closet will do. I wasn't spending one extra dime than I needed to for a fake date. Not even for Jedediah Lawson.

Chapter Four

-JED-

"Lola! Your date is here!" Ms. Polly yelled from the kitchen where we were standing. She smiled at me while checking out my suit. "Looks like y'all are going somewhere nice."

"Yes, ma'am. Taking her to Knoxville tonight."

She glanced toward the hallway with a conspiratorial glint in her eyes, then she turned to me and whisper-yelled, "Good thing she bought a new dress."

I laughed, pleased to think that Lola had cared enough to buy something new to wear on our date.

Yet again, a flash of heat made my neck break out into a sweat. I couldn't believe I was standing here about to go on a date with Lola Landry. I wanted to shake myself to remind me this was real. This was happening.

Remembering the bottle of chardonnay I held in my hands, I offered it to her. "I brought this for you, Ms. Polly."

"Oh, Jed. You're so sweet. You always were the sweetest boy in high school. And you can just call me Polly. You're a grown man now."

I chuckled with a nod, trying to wrangle my nerves. Ms. Polly had worked as a guidance counselor at Green Valley High up until her husband died of a heart attack a few years ago. My sister Caroline had told me she'd struggled with the loss and had decided to retire early, able to live off her husband's inheritance. From what I understood, she dabbled in some kind of crochet business she sold at arts-and-crafts shows. At least that's what my sister Sally had said.

Yeah, I'd done a little snooping ever since I found out Lola had moved back into town. If I'd thought my sisters didn't already know how bad I had it for her back in high school, I would've been stealthier about my investigation. But they knew. They *all* knew—all four of them. And I was sure they'd make me miserable over it.

They already had been, actually. Interrogating where I'd planned on taking her, criticizing my date choices, then reminding me to wear protection. That last was from Bekah. For Christ's sake, this was our first date.

Not that I hadn't thought about having sex with Lola. Countless times. Hell, I'd had fantasies in high school that would make the devil blush.

I heard Lola's footsteps on the stairs and coming up the hall to the kitchen. I kept my game face on when she appeared in the kitchen, doing my damned best not to show what was happening on the inside. Because holy hell, seeing her in that pretty rose-colored wrap dress, accentuating her sweet curves and exposing her delicate collar bone and slender neck with her curls piled on her head, had my pulse jackhammering against my ribs.

I couldn't explain it. The spark that lit between us in high school had never left. Not for me anyway. If anything, there was a maturity to that subtle burn. Slowly smoldering into something much bigger, much better.

Back then, I was a stupid kid, unable to admit my feelings when she'd wounded mine. So I kept her at a distance, not wanting to experience more rejection from this wisp of a girl who tied me into knots.

Like graduation day. I was relentless that day, picking on her left and right, knowing it was the last day I'd ever see her. After we'd gotten our diplomas, walked down the aisle side-by-side, then thrown our caps in the air, I'd picked her up and spun her around in a moment of celebration. And desperation. I'd whispered in her ear, "Good luck, Lola Landry," then set her on her feet before staring down and adding, "Have a nice life." I hadn't intended for it to sound so cavalier, but she'd seemed to take it that way. After a lingering inspection of me, she'd given me a dismissive response, "You, too, Jedediah."

I still remember her sauntering away, her long honey-brown curls bouncing in her wake, waving me goodbye.

But now, here she was, standing in her Aunt Polly's kitchen, smirking at me with that sassy mouth and looking like a goddess, knocking the wind out of me with a flick of those grass-green eyes.

"I see you met my Aunt Polly."

"We remember each other from high school," I reminded her.

"Oh, right," she nodded, clutching her purse tightly. Nervously?

Maybe I wasn't the only one dealing with a touch of anxiety.

"And he brought me a bottle of wine," said Polly, blushing to the roots of her red-orange hair. "Isn't that the sweetest?"

Lola narrowed her gaze on me. "How did you know what wine she liked?"

"I have my ways." Lola had forgotten what a small town this in actuality was. My sister Sally was in Polly's Ladies Pokeno Night group, the youngest of the troublemakers who gambled, drank, and even smoked cigars on occasion once a month.

Lola tilted her head as if she was going to fight me for the information. I got a little hard just thinking about it, wishing she would. But she just headed for the door, tossing over her shoulder, "Goodnight, Aunt Polly. I won't be too late."

"Oh, you be as late as you want, baby girl." She gave me a wink. I winked back and caught up to Lola.

I beat her to the passenger door of my Yukon and opened the door for her.

"Thank you," she muttered, sliding in and belting herself.

Once I was buckled and backed out of the drive, I caught her glancing in the bucket seats in the back where I had a baby car seat strapped in.

I could see those big wheels turning in her head as I maneuvered out of the neighborhood toward the highway. "What are you thinking?"

"I was just wondering, is this your SUV or your sister's?"

"Mine," I answered evenly, heading toward the highway to take us to Knoxville. "I pick up my baby niece, Tessa, on Wednesdays from school. Caroline teaches at Green Valley High. She stays late to grade papers on Wednesdays, so I get Tessa and keep her out of her hair for a while."

"Oh," she said quietly, pausing a few seconds before she asked, "You running for the best uncle award or something?"

I chuckled lightly. "Just doing what I can to help out. When Caroline's husband works the graveyard shift, I give her a hand."

"I see. So not all the time, just when he's working nights?"

"Nah. I still get her. That's when Wednesdays turn into a date night for my sister and her husband, Thomas."

She didn't respond, just stared at me, frowning.

"What?" I asked on a huff.

"Who are you?" She sounded completely baffled.

I flashed her a quick smile, then focused as I maneuvered onto the interstate. "That's the whole point of this date, isn't it? To find out."

She frowned again, glancing away quickly like I'd reminded her of something unpleasant.

"What's wrong?" I asked.

"What do you mean?"

"You just made a weird face."

She laced her fingers tightly in her lap then asked, "So tell me, why'd you move back to Green Valley? I thought you were playing football at UT."

Quick subject change.

"You remember that?" I asked, a little surprised.

"Pfft. How could I not? They had that extravaganza of a signing party in the library that day. I couldn't print out my research paper."

Definitely a note of bitterness in her voice.

It was my turn to frown as I drummed my fingers on the steering wheel. "Bet that pissed you off."

"What? You signing with UT? Not at all. I mean, look at you. That's what you were meant for."

Wow. Still thinking of me as Jockstrap Jed. Pushing aside the flare of frustration, I answered evenly, "No, I wasn't. And that's not what I was talking about. I'll bet you were furious that the signing party got you kicked out of the library that day."

She shrugged. "A little." She looked out the window. "So what happened at UT? You didn't like college ball?"

"It wasn't that. Football was always easy for me. I mean, I had to work hard at it, but I enjoyed it."

"Then what happened?"

I paused a minute, passing someone on the left before veering back over. "My dad had a stroke."

She gasped and jerked her head toward me. "Oh, no. I'm so sorry."

I gave her a reassuring smile, the kind that told her it was genuinely okay and not to worry. "Believe it or not, it was the best thing that could've happened to me. I came home my sophomore year and moved in with him. He needed round-the-clock care at the time."

"None of your sisters could do it? You had to give up school?"

Her voice had taken on a desperate tone. I'm not sure why.

"They helped out. Sally, especially. She'd always been our caretaker since mom had passed on. But someone needed to live with him. And...I wanted to come home."

"To Green Valley?" She seemed utterly aghast. "*Why?*" She squeezed her eyes shut. "Wow, that sounded so rude. I mean, you had to drop school and football. That's a lot to ask."

I shrugged a shoulder. "It was the right thing to do."

"But didn't you want to stay in school?"

"To be honest, it wasn't a hardship to leave."

"Oh. College ball wasn't what you thought it would be?"

"Not that. I had other reasons." And they certainly weren't ones I was prepared to share with her. Not yet anyway. Some wounds never heal, and where she'd cut me a time or two in high school had left their mark.

We rode in silence a while longer, veering off the interstate into Knoxville. We wove through traffic, drawing closer to the restaurant until I finally flipped on the blinker and turned into the restaurant parking lot.

I'd thought the conversation over when she asked lightly, "A girl?"

I pulled into a parking spot and turned off the engine so I could give her my full attention. Her pretty eyes widened and measured me with such thoroughness, I tightened my hand still on the steering wheel. "Not a girl," I answered with a smirky smile.

She didn't respond. Just gulped hard, drawing my attention to the soft skin of her throat. Before I gave in to the disastrous urge to lean over and taste the sweetness of her, I popped out of the truck. I went around to open her door, but she was already on the pavement. I gave her a disappointed look but wiped it away quickly enough as we walked toward the door.

"So I'll bet your dad was happy you came home," she continued.

I let out a rough laugh. "Not at first. He was mad I left football and school. But then once I'd moved in, he was glad I was there, even if he was too stubborn to say so. And a pain in the ass most days."

She laughed, poking me in the bicep. "Your dad is a pain in the ass? The apple didn't fall far from the tree then."

"Still is," I smiled. "I bought the house across the street so I wouldn't be far, even though he said he didn't need me hovering anymore." I kept my expression soft and warm, not wanting her to be uncomfortable. This wasn't the light and fun first-date conversation I'd thought we'd have. I smiled brighter and added lightly, "But I still hover, so maybe I'm the pain in the ass now."

She smiled back. With that, I opened the door of the restaurant and ushered her inside.

"I don't know this restaurant," she said. "Do you come here a lot?"

I rubbed the back of my neck with my palm as we walked inside. "No. Never been. But a friend told me it was a nice place."

My high school buddy Grant was still single and seemed an expert in dating. He'd recommended this as the place to take a girl I really wanted to impress.

Getting my first look around, it was pretty posh. Soft mood lighting, deep maroon carpeting, and candle-lit tabletops. I gave my name to the hostess, who then led us to a corner table.

I pulled out Lola's chair for her.

"Thank you."

Once seated, we both started to pore over the menus, an awkward silence stretching. I should've taken control of the conversation, keeping it away from the sadder topics of my father, of leaving school. But then again, I wanted her to know that I was happy in Green Valley. I never regretted returning home. I wanted her to see it as I did, not as she once did in high school. As the place she had to flee in order to prove to the world what a success she was.

The menu was pricey, but I'd known that. I wanted to show Lola that we could still dine in nice restaurants, even living in Green Valley. That was my aim for our more cultured night out following dinner as well. If she could see that she could have it all while living in Green Valley, maybe she'd change her mind about her hometown. And those of us who stayed.

Our waiter popped up before things could get too uncomfortable and greeted us warmly. His name was William.

"Would you care for something to drink while you look over the menu?" he asked.

"I'll have a pinot noir," she said.

"We have an extensive selection for you to choose from."

He pulled a wine list from the middle of the table and presented it to her. Her eyes widened, perhaps overwhelmed by the extensive list.

"Um. Just the house pinot is fine," she finally said, putting the menu back.

"And you, sir?"

I was still pretending to read the dinner menu, glancing at her over the top. "I'll have the same. That's fine."

"I'll have that right out." Then the waiter disappeared.

"I never would've pegged you as a wine guy," she teased.

I licked my lips, a nervous movement, my gaze skating to her, then back to the menu. "Sometimes."

We both settled into a rather uncomfortable silence while we perused the menu. I was too nervous to focus, so I was content with myself simply watching her from across the table.

"So much to choose from," she said, a stray curl falling against her cheek.

"Sure is."

We remained quiet till William reappeared with our wines. "May I take your order or would you like more time?"

"I think I'm ready," she said. "I'll have the sugar cane lacquered duck."

"Excellent choice." He smiled warmly. "And you, sir?"

I tried again to calm myself enough to read the menu, but it was no use. A cold sweat broke out across my neck. That familiar anxiety that had plagued me all my life threatened to engulf me. "What's your special tonight?"

"Oh, I apologize," said William. "I should've told you that already. Let's see. Tonight, we have andouille-crusted sea bass with grilled vegetables, shoestring potatoes, glazed pecans, and Creole meunière. We also have a grilled beef tenderloin with roasted oyster mushrooms and broccoli, Swiss chard, and a green peppercorn horseradish crème fraîche."

"I'll have the beef tenderloin," I said quickly, snapping the menu shut and handing it over.

"Very good, sir."

Lola handed over hers then William disappeared again, leaving us in yet another awkward silence. This wasn't going as planned, and I was on the verge of a minor freak-out since it seemed my duty to get us back on solid ground. Ever since she'd mentioned my father and we'd come into this place, a mood-killer had doused our easy conversation earlier tonight. It was Lola who finally broke the silence.

"So, tell me what it's like being a firefighter."

"What would you like to know?"

"Well, what do you do on your average workday?"

"Different things on different days. But we keep track of campers with the park rangers, check in, make sure they're safe, and follow the rules of open fires and whatnot. Not starting them where they aren't supposed to. Definitely have to keep an eye on the teenagers heading into the park during the summertime. In May and June, we pay particular attention to thunderstorms."

"Why May and June?"

"That's when we're most likely to have a lightning-sparked wildfire."

"Really? That happen often?"

"In the Smokies, it happens twice a year on average, so we watch closely when the storms come up. Oak and pine can catch fire in a lightning storm like a match in a bucket of gasoline."

"Seriously?" She sipped her wine. "I can't believe I grew up here and didn't know that."

"Most people don't realize it, unless you need to know."

"I'll bet it's dangerous too." Her brow pinched, and her voice dropped to a somber tone.

I nodded. It could be deadly dangerous, but I didn't want to talk about that. Not tonight. Again, kind of heavy conversation for a first date. "We've had to deal with some crazy stuff too."

Her eyes lit up. "Like what?"

"The craziest thing had nothing to do with a fire actually."

"What do you mean?"

I brushed my hand over my close-cropped beard, smiling at the memory, wondering if I should actually tell her this story.

"Well, I had checked in with the park ranger, Jethro Winston. Back before he left the park and became a stay-at-home dad. You know him, right?"

"*Everybody* knows the Winstons," she said a little dreamily.

I tried not to get jealous of that look and went on.

"Anyway, I'd driven by the ranger cabin to drop off some new medic supplies and first-aid kits that Green Valley funded but that we shared to keep our local rangers well-equipped. As I was leaving, he got two calls at once. One was about a bear venturing down into the valley close to Bandit Lake, and the other was about some hikers that had gotten lost."

I paused, remembering that day. I took a sip of wine and cleared my throat, trying to figure out how to say this politely. I mean, our high school conversations never ventured to the X-rated territory.

"Are you blushing? Tell me, Jed. Right *now*."

My name on her lips did it. I angled my body toward her, one leg shifting under the table till I accidentally bumped her thigh. I wanted to keep the connection, but also didn't want to push it.

"You're sure you want to know?" I teased, lifting one eyebrow.

"One-hundred percent," she urged with glee, taking a deep sip of her wine.

"I told Jethro I knew the territory where those hikers were, so I'd take care of the hikers while he tended to the bear. I met up with the hiking party to find out one couple had broken off to find a waterfall. They hadn't returned since lunch." I held my glass by the lip and swirled the wine. "It was sunset by the time I'd found them." I bit my lip a second before going on. "I heard movement and, uh, something, halfway up the trail. I ventured off into the woods a few yards toward the sound and saw them easily enough." I glanced up and held her curious gaze. "They were spread out on a blanket. Enjoying each other."

"Oh, Lord! You walked up on them having sex? That must've been so embarrassing for them."

"For them? If it was just sex, they might've disentangled quickly enough, and it wouldn't have been so embarrassing. But they were, uh, experimenting."

Lola's devious laugh shot straight to my cock. The wicked gleam in her eye didn't help. "Explain yourself, Firefighter Lawson. What did you catch them doing exactly?"

I swallowed down the rest of my wine. "Sixty-nine. And even my flashlight and heavy throat-clearing didn't catch their attention. They were fully focused on each other." I couldn't help but drop my gaze to her full lips. "*Fully* focused. If you know what I mean."

"No. Way." Her throaty laugh was so infectious, I couldn't help but laugh too.

"Totally serious," I continued lightly, clearing the rasp from my throat. "I had to shout as I approached before they realized they were no longer alone. The girl was on top, and she scrambled so fast she belted him in the eye with her knee, rolled off their blanket onto a log, and scratched her butt on a rough knot of the wood."

It was Lola's turn to blush as she continued to laugh. The flush of pink filled her cheeks, making me lean closer to enjoy the pretty view. "I can't believe that."

"Believe it. I had to administer first aid on this girl's butt cheek while her boyfriend hurriedly put his clothes back on. And then, once we'd made it back to their party, they had to explain how he got a black eye since the group thought they were hurt or injured on the trail somewhere."

"They didn't tell their friends how he got the black eye, did they?" Lola's eyes rounded with shock.

"Oh, no. He said he hit a branch and fell and got lost, and that's why they were so late. I let them say whatever they wanted, because I sure as hell wasn't going to explain to anyone what I saw."

"You didn't tell anyone?"

"Hell no! Except for Jethro. The guys I work with would never let it go if they knew. But I called it into Jethro afterwards and told him he could keep his ranger job. I'd rather fight fires than deal with randy hitchhikers."

She laughed again, the husky sound stirring hot things in my chest.

My gaze skirted down to her neckline, lingering around her collarbone, then skated back up to her shoulder. I could just make out the unusual reddish birthmark she had that had tortured me throughout high school.

I used to stand above her while she was at her locker, obsessed with the delicate line of her throat and that birthmark I wanted to press my lips to. I wanted to lick and kiss it until she fell back against me, into my arms where she belonged. They might've been a boy's fantasies, but it was a man who sat here now, still wanting the same thing. Ready to make it a reality.

I locked gazes with her, sensing her breath quickening. There was no way in hell she didn't sense the heatwave building between us. Lola Landry was many things, but she wasn't oblivious or ignorant. The question was, would she ignore this thing between us like she did in high school? Or finally give us a chance?

Chapter Five

-LOLA-

"Remember, even in the face of first-date jitters, smile and power through like the Super Woman you are." @kiss-n-tell

I couldn't breathe. And my heart threatened to crack open my chest and sprint for the door.

That story he'd told was hilarious. But then the tone shifted suddenly. His brown-eyed gaze had darkened, sweeping over my neck, lower, and I'd felt it like a hot caress. Of his tongue.

I was about to excuse myself to the restroom just to get out of range of his intense, predatory expression.

"So tell me about you," he said, glancing away. "How'd you end up coming back to Green Valley?"

So thankful he'd broken the tension, I scoffed and wrangled my wits. "Not a great story. You sure you want to hear it?"

"Of course, I do."

I sure as hell didn't want to retell it again. It was hard enough to confess the awful truth to my parents when it all happened. And telling it to Jed Lawson, my date, was about as pleasant as getting a Brazilian bikini wax.

"Not too much to tell, honestly. After my internship, I got a great position at Clarks and Taylor as a marketing associate."

"Sounds fancy. And fitting for you." His tone was light, but his gaze was heavy and penetrating.

"I guess. Until it wasn't." I drank down the rest of my wine. "I'd been there several years. Had served as a copywriter in one of the corporate departments. I worked a lot. I mean late hours, weekends, you name it."

His brow puckered. "So why would they let you go? Such a hard worker."

"That's just it." This is the part I hadn't told my parents. "I screwed up an account presentation. *Bad.*"

I winced at the memory. Rubbing my forehead, I decided to tell it all. Might as well at this point. It's not like I was trying to impress Jed. This wasn't going anywhere beyond tonight anyway. He waited patiently, not saying a word. I refused to look at him as I spilled my failure out onto the table.

"It was a big account presentation. I'd worked till midnight, making sure everything was in order, copying the zip files to our mainframe so that we could access it from the conference room. So the next morning, when the bigwigs were all gathered, my boss took the presentation clicker from me, clicked on the files and—" I made a poof gesture with my hands—"they were gone."

Jed blinked, concern all over his face. "What do you mean gone?"

I snorted. "Just gone. Somehow, I'd deleted them. Maybe I turned off my computer before they transferred. Maybe I just dumped them in the trash bin. I don't know. I hadn't slept in over twenty-four hours. Who knows? But even when I ran frantically back to my desktop in my office, the files had vanished. I finally found them in my trash bin after panicking for a full hour."

"Wow." He shook his head.

"I know."

His stern expression softened into something like concern. "And they fired you for that?"

"Not exactly. It was all bad timing. Fate, I guess. My boss was furious because the corporate guys had flown in from Dallas, and I'd made them wait over an hour to get the presentation going. Besides making them look totally unprofessional. Then, two days later, they received the notice that Clarks and Taylor were downsizing due to the loss of a massive account."

Jed nodded, clenching his jaw. "And you were an easy target after the deleted files incident."

"Yeeeep." The wine was really warming me up, but the sting of being *fired* due to incompetence, rather than simple cutbacks, was more humiliating than I could bear. "Fate hates me."

He leaned forward, his dark gaze snagging mine, holding me there. I couldn't pinpoint the emotion behind those eyes, but I could admit it gave me a rush and heated my blood, more so than the wine.

"I think maybe fate just had other plans for you, Cola. Maybe you were meant to lose that job because something better is waiting for you down the line."

I narrowed my eyes at him. "Still calling me Cola? You do realize I no longer wear coke bottle glasses."

His gaze skated from my eyes to my brow, down to my mouth, and back again. "I'm well aware."

Whoa. And that hot look sent a sizzle down my spine, inflaming my thighs. Trying not to focus on the way his deep, sonorous voice vibrated through to my bones and made my skin flush with heat, I said rather haughtily, "You can stop calling me Cola."

"Uh-uh. You like it."

"I do not."

Then William showed up with our dinner, and I was saved from contemplating all the swoony breathlessness that Jed's attention gave me.

My meal was freaking delicious. We fell into silence again, devouring the food and absorbing the night's revelations. I couldn't get over the selflessness of his choices since high school. He'd left a promising football career to return to Green Valley to care for his ailing father. He'd given up school, the scholarship he'd earned, everything for family and small-town life. To become a firefighter. Basically an unsung hero. And yet, he seemed completely content with his choices. It baffled the mind.

William returned with more wine, which Jed had ordered for us. My usual at home was a $10 bottle from Piggly Wiggly or the Thrifty liquor store. This high-priced food and drink were outside my comfort zone. Even when I made a good salary back in New Orleans, I'd always pinched my pennies, even when I was making lots of pennies. An old habit that died hard. And I worried about Jed spending his hard-earned money as a fireman —which I was pretty sure wasn't a high-salary position—on a meal for me. And our fake date.

Guilt threatened to topple me out of my chair, realizing how seriously Jed had taken this date. And while conversation had been awkward and stilted at times, I was enjoying every solitary second in his magnificent presence. That alone was sending off alarm bells.

Once we left, Jed didn't tell me where we were headed next, keeping me in suspense, which I strangely found thrilling. I usually liked to know every detail of plans that involved me, but Jed's mysterious ways had my heart pumping faster for no reason other than anticipation of the unknown.

I was impressed when we pulled into the Knoxville Civic Auditorium, the digital marquee displaying that the Knoxville Symphony Orchestra was playing Tchaikovsky tonight. However, my *Kiss-n-Tell* brain reminded me that this was a bad first-date move. It was equally as awful as going to the movies. Why? Because no one can talk in the movies. Same for the symphony. These kinds of dates should be reserved for somewhere around the fifth or sixth dates, when you've really gotten to know each other and are content just to *be* in each other's company.

Jed was polite throughout, asking me if I wanted wine at intermission, but I wanted to keep a clear head for the rest of the night. I caught him glancing at me, staring as a matter of fact, a few times during the symphony performance. I especially liked how he looked at me when the violins slowed to a haunting, romantic melody. I wanted to know what thoughts put that penetrating expression on his face, but I didn't ask. And I certainly didn't mind, even though his hot looks made me wish this was an actual date.

I spent the majority of the night fighting my inner turmoil. The time to tell him about *Kiss-n-Tell* and ask him to be a part of my podcast was quickly drawing near. This part never bothered me before, so why did it now?

If he noticed I was being overly quiet on the way home, he didn't say anything. As a matter of fact, he seemed to be brooding about his own issues all the way back to Aunt Polly's.

Once parked, he walked me to the door, and like he'd done all night, he kept his hands to himself. *Dammit.* He'd only touched me twice the whole night. When his knee had grazed my thigh under the table at the restaurant. And when some guy bumped into me while leaving the theater. Jed pulled me by the shoulders back into the shelter of his body, the thumb of one hand brushing over the curve of my bare shoulder. It was an exhilarating and magnificent all-too-brief experience.

But now, he kept his hands in his pockets, and his brow pursed as something seemed to be bothering him when I walked up the porch steps and turned at the front door.

"So—" I started to say, but he cut me off.

"I don't know why I didn't say this at all tonight, but I should've." His hands still in his pockets, he huffed out a heavy breath. "You looked very beautiful tonight."

"Oh." A shock of electricity buzzed under my skin at the one-and-only Jedediah calling me beautiful. I swallowed, once again having zero saliva due to my nervous dry mouth at realizing what was coming next was going to be hard as hell. "Thank you."

"And I'm not sure how tonight went exactly. Sometimes it felt..."

"Awkward?"

"Yeah." He let out a laugh. "But even then, I was glad to be with you."

I sighed and agreed inwardly.

"I'd like to take you out again." His expression was so hopeful, my stomach turned into a cauldron of acid at what I was about to say.

"I don't think that's a good idea."

His soft expression blanked, his eyes searching mine.

"You see, there's something I need to tell you."

"You have a boyfriend?" His honeyed voice had gone all raspy and gruff.

"No. Nothing like that. The opposite actually."

His frown deepened. "A girlfriend?"

"No. Just listen a minute. I, so...one thing I've always wanted to do is start my own podcast and see if I could use my marketing abilities to create a business out of it." He didn't move or speak, just watched and listened like I'd asked him to. "So when I moved back here, I started my podcast *Kiss-n-Tell*. It's a podcast on dating. Half of my episodes are Marly and me interviewing my dates on the show, discussing what was good and maybe not so good about the date. I just pose a few questions, and we talk. That's it."

Okay, now his frown had furrowed into deep crevices.

"So I wanted to know if you'd be a guest on my podcast. I record on Thursday."

No response. Just literally crickets chirping in the yard. Actually, a shit-ton of buzzing was going on. This was freaking Tennessee, so yeah, lots of lively insects filling up the black hole of silence yawning between the burning star that was Jed and the dwarf planet that was me trying to shrink away and escape into the vast unknown. Otherwise known as the front door.

"And if you don't want to, I understand."

"You agreed to go out with me just for your podcast?"

There it was. Genuine hurt in his voice and anger simmering in those dark eyes that had looked at me with so much admiration only sixty seconds before. I honestly hated myself for earning that look. I hadn't wanted to hurt his feelings, but yes, this was all this was. I wasn't up for dating because I wasn't going to be here long. Even if this was my high school obsession turned super-hot firefighter.

"Yeah. I mean, I did want to catch up with you." That wasn't a lie. "But I'd hoped you'd agree to be on the podcast."

"So you're not interested in a second date."

A statement, not a question. Licking my lips which drew his full attention, I answered truthfully. "I don't do second dates. Not right now." The standard response fell from my lips, feeling sad and stupid and untrue.

He stood there, his chest heaving just a tad heavier than normal, but his eyes were blazing. He looked off into the night. I never noticed how full his bottom lip was until he was biting on it. And why was I staring at his mouth? *Stop it.*

It didn't matter anyway. He wasn't looking at me. He was staring into space, somewhere very far away, planning something monumental. He looked like he was drawing up battle plans and contemplating who should go to the battlefront first. I hoped it wasn't me.

Finally, he turned his focus back to me and said one clipped word. "Okay."

"Okay?" My heart somehow climbed up my throat and lodged there, trying to get closer to him.

"Okay," he repeated with so much weight I felt the word hit me with force.

Since I'd lost my ability to speak trying to swallow my heart back into my chest where it belonged, I just stared at him and waited for him to say something else. He didn't. The intensity of his stare and the clenching of his jaw resembling some kind of ancient warrior staring down his opponent had me about to pee in my panties. I suddenly felt very sorry for all of those football players on opposing teams back in the day.

"Thanks," I said, or actually whispered in a breathy voice, shifting in place from one foot to the other.

But it seemed like he hadn't heard me. He continued to stare me down, all dark eyes and grim expression. A millennium passed by, then he finally gave me a stiff nod, seemingly satisfied. Strangely, it wasn't as if he was nodding to me, but more to himself. As if he'd had some internal conversation and come to a satisfying conclusion.

As he turned and walked away, a prick of guilt washed over me for the hundredth time. The mood had turned sour because of me, and I really did appreciate all he'd done tonight.

"Thank you for tonight." I couldn't tell him I had a fabulous time since that would be a lie. I had an interesting and memorable time, highlighted by moments of chivalry and lust and clarity about who he truly was. But it was far from fabulous.

He paused and turned beside a column on the porch, one hand propped against it. He stared, absorbing me like osmosis, soaking in my molecules through the air. Determination decorated every line of his face. My skin tingled, goosebumps spreading up my bare arms, dancing behind my neck. The kind of goosebumps you get right before a thunderstorm. Or something equally electrifying.

"I'll see you on Thursday." His voice had lost the heaviness yet was no less forceful. No less intense. "Be ready for me."

With that cryptic farewell that made my knees wobble, he strode down the stairs and to his SUV, started it up, and backed out of the drive without one more glance in my direction to where I still stood on the doorstep, scared out of my ever-loving mind.

As his brake lights disappeared down the street, I knew only one thing. I needed to gird my loins and prepare for battle between now and Thursday. Because a storm was definitely coming, and his name was Jed.

Chapter Six

-LOLA-

"My dad always said, 'if you're not nervous, you're not ready.'" @kiss-n-tell
"Mine said that means you're in deep shit." @marlypants
"They could both be right." @kiss-n-tell

"By the way, we need to do another minisode for this month," Marly said as she scrolled through the questions on my MacBook at the kitchen table.

"Mmhmm," was my terse reply while pacing and trying not to throw up.

Marly and I often recorded shorter episodes about general dating topics in between interview posts. Right now, I couldn't focus on anything except the dwindling of the hour toward the arrival of a certain swaggering—and last I'd seen him, steaming—fireman.

"What's the theme this month?" she asked.

"What?"

Marly snapped the laptop shut behind me and crossed to the window where I was now hovering, peering through the blinds like a stalker.

"The theme," she repeated.

I heard the smirk in her voice, so I finally glanced her way. Sure enough, she was grinning, thoroughly enjoying my mini-meltdown. Fortunately, I've always been able to fake bravado, even when my insides were twisting in a tornado of high-velocity angst.

"Theme? Theme. Oh, yeah." I licked my lips and spun away from the window toward the kitchen counter. "Be a safety girl." I took a swig from my glass of ice water.

"Niiiiice. Love the sex talks."

"Mmhmm." I drank my water, wondering if I should go to the bathroom one more time. When my nervousness rode high like this, I tended to go to the bathroom every few minutes with nothing at all to release. However, I didn't want to excuse myself to the bathroom when Jed got here because I didn't want him having visions of me on the toilet. Not that he'd be thinking of that, but I honestly wasn't even making sense to myself right now. I was definitely on the verge of a panic attack. And I had no idea why!

It was just another podcast interview. Right?

No, it really wasn't. All the guys who came before were just that: "podcast dates." But a date with Jed had been my poor decision-making in live action. I couldn't think of him as just another podcast date on account of him being my high school obsession for a year or two.

Okay, *fine*. For pretty much every year, even when he was mean to me. (And I was mean to him.)

"Oh, my God! There he is!" screamed Marly, peering through the blinds. "And look at him!"

I jerked my water glass, splashed my face, grabbed a kitchen towel, then bolted for the window while wiping myself off. "What? What do you mean!"

By the time I skidded to a stop, Marly had tossed her head back and cackled like an evil witch. If I tilted my head just right, she looked frighteningly like Cruella from *101 Dalmatians*. No one was in the driveway.

"Your face," she blurted through laughter.

I swatted her with the kitchen towel. "I honestly have no idea why I'm friends with you."

"You are sooooo worked up over this. I just can't help myself. It's like—" Her gaze snagged out the window.

I followed her gaze to catch Jed *actually* pulling up into the driveway. He parked and stepped out of his Yukon in well-worn jeans and a black T-shirt, looking like a delicious man-cicle. And I so wanted to lick it.

"Gracious," whispered Marly. "Green Valley living has been so, so good to him."

"Yeah," I exhaled on a shaky breath before making my way to the front door. Clearing my throat and pasting on a smile, I swung open the door just as he reached it. "Hi, Jed. Thank you for coming. Coming on in." I shook my head. "I mean, come on in."

Jesus! Stop saying *come* and *coming*.

His full mouth tipped up in a smirk as he walked past me, wafting some amazing masculine scent in his wake. "Thank you, Cola."

I shut the door and squared my shoulders, raising my brows and giving him my serious face. "You can*not* call me Cola on the podcast."

His smile only widened. "Just on the podcast?"

"I mean, never. Actually, ever. Because never would make that statement a double negative."

His grin stretched at my inane word-vomit, though he didn't comment. Thankfully.

I stared at him a second longer—possibly because his biceps were highly distracting in that T-shirt—then muttered. "Well, come on in then."

"You said that."

I was still standing there like an idiot, so I turned and sashayed into the living room where Marly was holding my laptop.

"You know Marly," I said, gesturing.

"Hey, Marly. My sister behaving at the distillery?"

"No way," she teased. "That girl's always up to no good."

"I believe it," he shot back without hesitation. "I used to worry about her working with you, you being a bad influence and all. But these days I'm more worried about the other way around." His words might've been scornful, but his affectionate smile said something else entirely.

"Oh, yeah? She tells lots of stories about you torturing her when she was little. Maybe the bad influence is all on you."

"Not me. I've always been an angel. Model big brother." His grin was anything but polite or civilized.

"Looks like you've grown into a very big brother."

"*Marly*," I hissed. She was such an embarrassing flirt.

Jed chuckled, hands in his front pockets. "Eating my Wheaties."

"I see that."

"Okay then," I cut in. "Let's get rolling. Upstairs."

I led the way to my Aunt Polly's third bedroom. She'd turned it into her crochet studio between my graduation and now. My parents had often worked late after school, and Aunt Polly never had any kids of her own, so she took care of me on weekdays till Mom or Dad picked me up.

This room had been my personal playroom back then. But gone was the Barbie dreamhouse that I'd pretended was Lola Incorporated. I'd replaced the furniture in my Barbie house with my own miniature office desks made of cardboard. I'd spent many an hour sitting on the handwoven rug, scolding Beach Barbie for improper work attire and sending her to

HR. Or leading business meetings with my favorite brunette Barbie that looked the most like me, who was *always* wearing her business best, mind you.

But now, the playroom was a studio split between Aunt Polly's business and my podcast. Along with her wall of bins of yarn, which I'd helped organize, she now had a separate table we used for product photographs. I took the photos for her and uploaded them to Etsy under her shop name, *Creature Cozies*. Aunt Polly had started crocheting the cutest tea and toaster cozies for family and friends a few years ago, but then she couldn't stop making them. They were super cute animal shapes, like bunnies, turtles, raccoons. Anything she could think of.

She had a unique passion to which she'd turned into a small business for arts and crafts fairs. And a few local businesses sold them on consignment out of their shops. However, I'd wanted to expand her business with an online presence, trying to put my marketing degree to good use for her. And it worked. She'd had a bin-full of cozies built up and had never sold, but within a month, they were all gone. Now, she was doing preorders only, having sold every cozy she'd had in storage.

She only had one complaint, and it was a local order via her Etsy shop. The order had come through for a dozen armadillo cozies to be delivered to Jackson James, the sheriff deputy here in Green Valley. The complaint had come from Jackson himself, because he'd said he hadn't ordered them. But the order had been prepaid, and we couldn't return the money for some reason. A glitch in the payment system prevented us from contacting or even seeing who the payee was.

So strange.

Anyway, the third bedroom was now half *Creature Cozies* headquarters and half *Kiss-n-Tell* studios. I'd even put some soundproofing material on the walls to help reduce the echo while recording.

"Have a seat right there," I told Jed, pointing to the seat next to where I always sat.

Two mics and headsets were in their places and ready to go with one more set on the opposite side of the round table where Marly always sat. She popped open the laptop while I reached over and tapped the waiver agreement which I had all my podcast interviewees sign.

"If you could read over this please, and sign at the bottom. It just basically gives me the right to use the recording of your voice today."

No one had sued me yet or had even remotely threatened to, but Marly's dad, an attorney in Knoxville, said it was always better to be safe than sorry.

Especially in legal matters. So I took the advice to heart and had a waiver drawn up that covered me legally for using the recordings.

I explained briefly the show's set-up, where we'd do some quick rapid-fire questions, then we'd break down the date, and I'd score each section out of ten. Jed didn't respond as I yammered on. He looked down at the paper for a brief minute, frowned, then picked up the pen to sign it.

"Don't you want to read it?" I asked.

"I trust you," he said, though his voice was a little gruff, reminding me of his anger at the end of our date.

"Also, I won't include your full name or anything, so don't worry about that. Just to keep stalkers away, you know."

He finished signing in a long, bold scrawl then pushed the paper back to the center of the round table before shifting his gaze to me.

Marly had hooked up the laptop to the mic and was putting on her headphones as she said, "And if you don't want us to tag you on social media, we won't. Sometimes, the poddie hotties like to join in the conversation after the episode goes live. But I warn you, Jedediah, we've got lots of thirsty listeners out there." Then she turned on the video camera on the tripod right next to her. "And viewers." She winked.

"Thanks for the warning," he said amiably, putting his headphones on.

And how he looked so hot with giant, puffy headphones on, I'll never know. I knew what I looked like with my wild curly hair making my head look even more ginormous. Not attractive.

"Okay." Marly angled her mic close and tapped on the laptop one more time. "Y'all ready?"

When we both nodded, she clicked the camera feed on, which would go live on YouTube. That was my cue to get us started.

"Hey, everyone. Welcome to another episode of *Kiss-n-Tell,* a dating review podcast where I interview my first dates and dish on the good, the bad, and the ugly. This is your host, Lola, and I'm here with my co-host, Marly."

"Hey, you guys," Marly chimed in her sing-song voice.

"And today, we have Jed with us," I added, my voice squeaking a little too high. Marly arched a brow at me, but I plowed ahead with enthusiasm. "Please say hello, Jed."

"Hello, everyone," he said in his deep timbre, as natural as you please.

"So glad to have you, Jed," I added, keeping my attention on Marly across the table. Due to every time I felt his gaze land on me, a flicker of heat crawled up my neck. "As always, we'll start with some rapid-fire questions so our listeners can learn a little about you first. So all I need is super short answers. Sound good?"

Finally, I glanced his way.

His warm gaze was steady and heavy. On me. "Fire away."

"Alrighty then. Age?"

"Twenty-six."

"Profession?"

"Firefighter for the Green Valley Fire Department."

"Zodiac sign?"

"Scorpio."

"Oh, ladies," interjected Marly, reading from her Zodiac list of traits which she used to add tidbits for listeners. "Just a reminder, Scorpio is one of our top dominant-in-bed signs." She winked at Jed. "Good for you, Jed."

He chuckled, and a touch of pink tinged his cheeks above his immaculately groomed beard. Also, I wanted to crawl under the table and hide. Or onto his lap, I wasn't sure.

Before reacting too wildly, I remembered this was being captured on video and quickly gazed down at my rapid-fire questions.

"Moving on. Beer or cocktail?"

"Whiskey."

"And a rule bender," I added with a snarky smile.

"Your categories should've been broader there."

"You drank beer in high school," I accused.

"So did you," he bit back, all while a smile teased his perfectly sensuous lips. "But I'd say that isn't your drink of choice anymore. Now that you're all grown up." The drop of his gaze down my body made my neck start sweating. It hadn't missed my attention that this man often made me a bumbling, sweaty idiot in his presence.

Clearing my throat, I straightened in my seat. "Touché."

"Now might be a good time," interrupted Marly, "to let our listeners and viewers know that Jed and Lola have a little bit of history together from high school."

I shot her a death glare which only made her beam pearly whites at me.

"That we do," added Jed.

"We haven't even finished our rapid-fire questions," I snapped.

"I'm ready when you are." His relentless grin told me he knew good and well that he was rattling me.

"Next question. What was your childhood dream job?"

I wanted to take it back immediately. Terrified of the answer, knowing his pro-football career came to a sudden, sad end. But then he surprised me.

"A cowboy." He smiled sheepishly.

Marly leaned forward, lowering her voice to porn-star sultry. "Oooo, Cowboy Jed. Come on over here and rope my cattle."

The laugh he belted out zinged down my spine then back up my legs, where it swirled in my chest in a hot ball of loveliness. I'd forgotten what an infectious laugh he had. I couldn't help but join in. Leave it to Marly, the only person who could make a double entendre with cattle.

"Any pets?" I asked, still laughing.

"A yellow lab named Joe."

"Awww," cooed Marly.

I laughed again. It was Marly's job on the show to interject entertainingly while I kept the questions moving and the show clipping at a good pace. But I wanted to stop and ask him a million questions about Joe all of a sudden. For some reason, I couldn't imagine Jed with a dog. Maybe that's because I'd labeled him "the enemy" over the years. And enemies couldn't have adorable Labradors named Joe.

In the end, all I said was, "Cute," before turning back to my list and asking, "Jog in the park or gym rat?"

"Jog in the mountains?"

"A serious jogger then," said Marly. "Does Joe go with you?"

He chuckled. "Yeah, he does."

I forced my brain not to imagine him running down a trail in the woods in sweaty gym shorts with his cute dog trotting alongside him.

"And last one," I said, "favorite book."

"Hmm." He shifted uncomfortably, rubbing his palms along his jeans. It was the first time today I'd seen him look uncomfortable, which struck me as strange. He cleared his throat. "I'd have to say *Dune* by Frank Hubert."

A memory flashed to me of him in homeroom with that book on his desk as he ignored the world around him. Including me in the seat behind him.

"Weren't you reading that senior year?"

His gaze locked on mine, some elusive emotion swimming in the deep brown. "I was."

An awkward tension had suddenly crept into the space between us, and I wasn't sure why.

"I love sci-fi," said Marly. "I've got a list of some great books in that genre if you want."

"Sure," he nodded sharply.

"Okay, guys," said Marly with a single clap of her hands. "Now that we've gotten to know our lab-owning, mountain trail-jogging, whiskey-drinking fireman, it's time to get down to business." She rubbed her hands together gleefully. "The date!"

Chapter Seven

-JED-

The one thing that had always mesmerized me about Lola Landry was her eyes. They were always bright with emotion and intelligence, broadcasting her anger or excitement, embarrassment, or joy. Everything she was thinking or feeling was amplified through those emerald eyes. As a somewhat shy kid, her outgoing nature and bursting-with-life demeanor had entranced me. Even now, her gaze flicked from me to Marly, an animated sparkle shimmering as her thoughts spun.

"As previous listeners know," she said, "Marly will guide us through the pros and cons of our date last Saturday night and I'll give my scores."

"You score the date?" I asked.

"Of course." She frowned.

"I'll bet you've got a rubric and everything, don't you?" I couldn't help but jab at her. She was notorious for her spreadsheets and following the teachers' rubrics down to the word back in high school.

"Of course, I do." She arched a slender brow, daring me to challenge her. "I have the date broken down by dinner, event venue, conversation, and rapport. I award points out of a rating of 1 to 10 in each category and average them for the final score."

"Wow." I chuckled. Because this was not shocking at all, but I'd forgotten how over-the-top she was with organizational things.

"Is something wrong?" A twinge of irritation leaked into her voice.

"Not at all." I gestured toward Marly. "Ready when you are."

"Okay, cowboy. First up is dinner." Marly glanced down at what must have been notes from Lola. "Whoa. So Jed took Lola to Chez Louie, a very nice restaurant in Knoxville. I've never been, but I've heard the food is amazing. Seems you spared no expense on this first date, Jed. Except before we get your thoughts, we'll hear from Lola first. What did you think of the dinner?"

I couldn't help but stare at her as she barreled ahead with what I could only imagine was a well-rehearsed answer.

"What you heard is correct, Marly. The food was absolutely amazing. The wine, too. But I have to admit, the ambiance was very formal. At times, I felt even a little awkward. I'd never been presented with a wine menu so extensive. And truthfully, I'm not a sommelier or even a connoisseur really...I just like red wine. So I felt a little nervous trying to make a decision."

She peered at me for a brief second, before charging ahead again.

"And though I appreciate the effort Jed made in taking me to such a nice place, I think it's actually not the best for a first date." Her expression softened to an apologetic one, squinting one eye. So cute. "I mean, I think a more casual dinner setting is better where there's noise and distraction, and the couple can feel at ease rather than worry about having perfect table manners or how to read the menu."

Ouch. I winced at the last part.

"Hmm, interesting," said Marly. "I can see where she's coming from. Jed, did you feel the same way? Or was the dinner all you expected it to be?"

I leaned forward, bracing my elbows and forearms on the table in front of the mic. "Actually, I think she's right." I laughed a little, a wash of heat crawling up my neck. "I suppose it would've been easier to relax and open up at a more casual place."

"I'd save the fancy dinner for someone you've been dating a while," Marly added. "Someone you know well and can relax around, even in a formal setting like that."

"I'll remember that," I said, catching Lola's sideways glance.

"So what score did you give dinner, Lola?" asked Marly.

"I gave it a seven."

That stung, but also...she was so right. I'd chosen Chez Louie hoping to impress her. To show her I wasn't the dumb jock she once knew and that I had more sophistication now.

"Moving onto the main event, which was, as I see here, a night at the Knoxville Symphony! Wow, Jed. You were without a doubt pulling out all the stops."

Again, that flame of heat brushed up my neck. I couldn't help but be a little embarrassed that it showed how badly I'd tried to impress Lola with my elevated tastes. Since I couldn't find my voice, Lola went ahead, her voice softer than earlier.

"The symphony was so beautiful. Honestly, I'd never even seen a live symphony before, so it was a lovely experience."

"But?" asked Marly pointedly.

"But again, this atmosphere didn't allow us time to talk and get to know one another. Like you said earlier, Marly, this is a great date idea for a couple who already know each other well." Again with that apologetic look that had my stomach sinking. "As I said, for a first date, you really want a place where you can try to become more acquainted."

"And how about you, Jed? Did you agree?"

I couldn't help but be totally honest. "No, not at all."

Lola's head snapped in my direction.

My heart hammered faster, but I couldn't hold my tongue. I wanted her to know exactly how I felt, and I didn't care if all her podcast followers heard it.

"I'll admit we didn't have much time to talk, but I could see the joy on your face when you watched the orchestra play and listened to the music. Watching you," I paused to lick my lips, "seeing you enjoy the experience made my whole night." I watched her expression morph from business-Lola to surprise then to something akin to fear. "Besides," I added, "we had lots of time to talk to and from Knoxville. And at dinner."

Lola seemed a little stupefied. Good. Let her marinate on that. I wasn't playing games here. I had plans for us, to see if there could be more between us.

"Very interesting," said Marly with a bit of wickedness in her voice. "So, Lola, what score did you give the venue?"

She blinked a few times before muttering, "Five."

"It was a ten from where I was sitting," I said, my voice dropping as I leveled her with a more intimate gaze.

She swallowed hard before turning back to Marly, sucking in a deep breath. "Okay, let's talk about the conversation and rapport, shall we? That was very good, actually. Wouldn't you say it was good, Jed?" However, she didn't wait for me to respond, speed-talking her way through a one-way conversation. "Yeah, we caught up on what's been going on since high school. That was very nice. Didn't you think so? So, um, definitely, yeah, I gave this a solid seven. Only because we had moments of lag and a little awkwardness, which wasn't his fault, of course. It was a reflection on me just as well, so, anyway, the lower rating is more my fault, really."

Marly and I were both staring at her like she'd lost her mind.

"So that gives the final dating score of 6.3." She nodded emphatically, her cheeks flushed. "How about we move on to some questions from our YouTube viewers, Marly?"

If I wasn't mistaken, Lola was growing increasingly more uncomfortable and was trying to finish up this podcast as quickly as possible.

"That's a great idea," said Marly, staring at the laptop with a fiendish grin. "One of our regular followers, Belinda, is tuning in. Hey, Belinda! And her question is for Jed. She asks, *'Were you attracted to Lola in high school?'*"

I grinned, wanting to reach through cyberspace and hug Belinda. "Yes, I was. Very much so."

Lola coughed spastically. And kept coughing. I reached over and patted her on the back while Marly pushed a glass of water across the table. She gulped the water, her eyes watering by the time she set it back down before glaring at me.

"Are you being serious?"

"Dead serious."

"So...so prom was for real?"

"Of course, it was."

"You actually wanted to go with me?"

Frowning, I angled so she could see how serious I was. "I definitely wanted to go with you."

"Ooo, now this is getting interesting," Marly interjected. "So now Belinda is asking what happened with prom?"

We stared at each other for a moment. I raised my brow. "Do you want to share, or shall I?"

"I can't believe we're airing this all out right now," she grumbled before turning to the mic. "So, Jed asked me to prom. But I'd overheard one of his friends make fun of me."

"Who?" I snapped.

"I don't want to out your friend on the air," she said with a bit of disdain, "but he definitely made it sound like asking me out would be a total joke. So that's why I said no."

I felt the punch in my chest as hard as I did that day in the school parking lot, watching her reject and dismiss me so easily. Actually, it hurt more because now I knew it was all Trey's fault. I remember him making some stupid remark in the hallway, which was his norm. He was always talking out of his ass. I didn't straighten him out because I didn't care what he thought. I had no idea that she'd overheard. The pain pierced harder, thinking she might've gone with me otherwise. Especially when I remembered the red dress she wore with some other guy and how it gutted me.

"And did you want to go with him?" asked Marly, apparently reading my mind.

Clearing her throat and straightening her spine, she said, "Yeah."

I couldn't even speak, letting that sink in. I'd envisioned senior prom being my last chance to show Lola how I felt about her, to show her what we could be together. Because even then, as a kid, I knew there was something there. I wasn't so much a fool to think she'd stay in Green Valley for a high school relationship, but I'd still longed to see where our chemistry led us the summer before she left.

If she thought this was ending here, after this podcast, she was incredibly mistaken. I wasn't giving up so easily. Not fucking now.

"Wowza," said Marly, totally gleeful as Lola and I stared at each other with equal amounts of shock and awe. "So time is getting away from us today, but we have time for one more question from a viewer. Mary says, '*Jed is super hot. Lola, why don't you go on a second date to give him another chance to up the score?*'"

Lola opened her mouth to protest, but I beat her to it. "Thank you, Mary. I agree."

Not to mention the fact that burning jealousy lashed at my insides even thinking about her going out with another guy for this podcast, I was seriously determined to get my second shot at this girl. This was happening.

Lola stammered, "Well, we don't usually, I mean, I don't—"

"I challenge you to a second date, Lola," I stated, knowing full well my voice was more of a command than a request.

"I don't think that's a good idea."

"I bet I can raise the score, and your YouTube viewers can be the judge at the end of the show this time." She didn't respond, so I added fuel to the fire. "Unless you're scared."

Her pretty brow furrowed exactly as I expected. "I'm not scared."

Tough as balls, this girl. She'd never back down from a challenge, and I knew it.

"Great. So, this Saturday. Date number two."

Her eyes widened with surprise as she realized what she'd just agreed to.

"Awesome!" exclaimed Marly on a throaty laugh. "Well, that wraps up today's episode of *Kiss-n-Tell*, you guys. Please subscribe to our YouTube channel and the podcast @kiss-n-tell. Join us next week for our next minisode, "Be a Safety Girl," and for date number 2 with Jedediah."

"Thanks so much for watching and listening," said Lola into the mic in a bit of a daze.

"And remember, singles, they don't have to be a perfect date, as long as they're perfect for you." Marly clicked off the video camera, tapped the laptop, and then pulled off her headphones, cackling with laughter. "Epic." She shook her head at Lola.

I pulled off the headset and set it on the table, then stood and offered Lola my hand. She took it robotically, gazing up at me.

I gave her delicate hand a soft squeeze, brushing my thumb over her knuckles before I let her go. "I'll see you on Saturday."

She nodded dumbly as I headed out the door. I heard her mumble "fuck" as I jogged happily down the stairs, feeling like a king.

Chapter Eight

-LOLA-

"When should I let the guy see the real me—embarrassing quirks and all?"
@coffeequeen
"The second you meet him. If he doesn't like the real you, he's not yours." @kiss-n-tell

"Watch that pothole, Lola."

Aunt Polly was the worst side-seat driver, but I'd admit she had reason to co-pilot me at every turn on the drive to my parents' house for Friday night supper. I'd worked the day shift and was eager to stay busy. But truthfully, nothing was successfully distracting me from the podcast recording yesterday.

My brain was on repeat, replaying every hot look Jed gave me and every word that dripped from his pretty lips. And now my brain was spinning with where we were headed on our date tomorrow.

He'd texted this morning, saying he'd pick me up at 9:00 a.m. A day date? That was unusual, and he had my curiosity thoroughly piqued. So much so that I hadn't been able to help myself from trying to get answers when I'd texted him before Aunt Polly and I had left for my parents.

ME: Where are we going on our date?

JED: You'll fine out.

. . .

I ALMOST TEASED him about his typo, but I was too determined to get answers.

ME: I know that, but I want to know ahead of time. I like to be prepared.

JED: I'm well aware that you do.

ME: Why all the secrecy? I want to know.

JED: Cola. Didn't anyone ever tell you that anticipation heightens the pleasure?

JUST THE WORD *pleasure* in a text from him made my mouth go dry. I stared without responding till the little dots appeared as he typed.

JED: I'll pick you up at 9:00 a.m. Wear something comfortabel for outdoors.

SO HERE I WAS, losing my damn mind because...Jed.

Discovering that he had actually wanted to go to prom with me for real, and I'd blown it due to my own insecurities, had rocked my world. It had me yet again overanalyzing my impetuous and often reactionary nature. Yes, I was one of those who was well-prepared for every plannable event. Mostly in my professional life. However, when thrown for a loop in personal situations, I tended to overreact and make snap decisions that were the wrong ones.

Like eons ago when Jed had asked me to senior prom, and I'd shut him down with a mean-spirited slam of my car door in his face. The very thought of it now made me sick. Not just because of what could've been back then, but also because it was my own damn ego that had gotten in the way. Wasn't the first or the last time that had happened, for damn sure.

And then, and *then,* him telling me he thought our date to the symphony should've been a ten, because watching me enjoy myself had *made his night*. Then challenging me to a second date, which he *knew* I couldn't turn down.

What I couldn't deny, especially after Marly texted me Thursday night, was how well our YouTube viewers enjoyed Jed on the show. Now I couldn't wait to get the episode edited and posted on Tuesday, which was our regular scheduled day for podcast episodes.

I wasn't mad, mind you. I was flustered and feeling out of my depth. This out-of-control sensation had subsided only mildly since I'd moved back to Green Valley. Like on the days I'd gotten paid and boosted my savings account for when I made my next move into a new job and a new city. Or when the podcast got exceptional listeners or a fabulous new review.

"Girl, slow down," said Aunt Polly. "Are you feeling okay?"

I glanced at the speedometer and immediately relaxed my foot. "Yeah, sorry. Just lots on my mind."

"Mmhmm. Well, if it has anything to do with a six-foot-four fireman, I can completely understand you acting so crazy."

"I'm not acting crazy."

"If you say so. Just don't kill your mother's gardenia bushes."

I was pulling up the driveaway and had been veering dangerously close to the edge of the lawn, but I was nowhere near my mother's gardenia bushes. Not really. Aunt Polly smirked at me as I jerked us into park.

"Don't forget the potato salad in the trunk," she said, carrying the grocery bag of chips and dip.

I unlocked the trunk and retrieved Aunt Polly's famous potato salad, which my dad demanded every time we had burger night. Or barbeque chicken night. Or pretty much anything that paired well with potato salad. He'd even tried to request it on spaghetti night, but my mom said he was being ridiculous. Ordinarily, I'd agree with Mom, but Aunt Polly without a doubt did have some kind of magical recipe with her creamy, tangy potato salad.

I trudged up the drive and into the house, hearing my Mom's voice greeting her sister, then my Dad, "Where's the potato salad?"

"How about where's my daughter?" I said, stepping through the back door.

Dad strolled from the kitchen and squeezed my shoulders with a peck on my forehead. "You always come first. Now let me take that off your hands."

"Mmhmm." He was going to try to sneak a spoonful, or four, before we even had dinner, no doubt. "I'll just put this in the fridge myself," I told him.

"I thought I was your favorite," he whispered.

"I heard that, Frank," Mom said, heading into the kitchen. "Come put these burgers on the grill now."

I followed her and Aunt Polly into the kitchen, where we always tended to gravitate. My gaze quickly landed on the dining room table. "Holy cow, Mom! Where'd you get this new table?"

We'd had the same brown, square table my entire life growing up. Mom had craftily covered its scarred and worn top with pretty tablecloths over the years that Aunt Polly made for her. But the old table, along with the well-worn chairs, was long gone. In its place was a pretty, round, oak table with an ornate beveled edge, a shiny, pale veneer, and pretty matching chairs.

Dad beamed. "Pretty, huh, Lola bug?"

Mom barely concealed a smile. "Your father has taken to woodworking in his retirement."

"Semi-retirement," he corrected her. He'd reduced his hours at the Eager Beaver's Hardware and Lumber because of his arthritis. He just couldn't stand all day the way he used to. He was only sixty-four, but the arthritis was brutal on his joints.

"Yes, yes." Mom waved her hand like shooing a fly. "And I have to admit, I'm pretty dang glad he did. I've got new cabinets in mind next." She eyed the kitchen cabinets that did indeed need an overhaul. Hell, our whole house pretty much required an overhaul.

"It's beautiful, Dad," I said, running my hand over the smooth top. "You could do work on commission, it's so good."

He puffed up his chest a little as Mom passed him the tray of raw hamburger patties. "I was thinking the same."

"Not till my cabinets get done," said Mom. "I've waited long enough."

"I know, I know," he said, heading out the back door to the grill.

"Definitely get him on your cabinets next, Mom," I added, genuinely happy she was finally getting to do some of the things she'd wanted to do for years.

It's true. My parents never had much extra money or time to fix up the house. They both worked hard, but Dad's salary at Eager Beaver's and Mom's as a secretary at the dentist's office didn't bring home a lot. It was one reason I worked so hard in school and studied like crazy to get the scholarships I had. And why it infuriated me when others didn't take their education seriously.

I remember catching sight of Jed's third F paper in English our sophomore year. I remarked that if he worked harder on his studies like he did with football, he could get better grades. Come to think of it, that was the very day he'd turned to me with a scowl and told me to mind my own business, *Coca-Cola Lola.* My crush dissolved that day, mostly, and our antagonistic relationship began.

However, it was just dumb to squander opportunities. Watching my parents struggle had instilled that fire in me. Growing up, anything "extra" went to me. You name it; from braces, eye doctor appointments, leadership camp fees, speech and debate competitions, used car note, and insurance.

And then helping me with room and board once I got to college at Louisiana State University, since my scholarship only paid for tuition and books.

So yeah, the house renovations had always taken a backseat.

This was also the reason I made damn sure I didn't have to rely on them for anything after I graduated. That included after I'd gotten fired and came home. It was bad enough to admit I'd lost my job. I wasn't about to let them think they'd have to pay for a single thing while I was back in Green Valley. I'd even managed to coerce Aunt Polly into at least letting me split the grocery bill with her. I tried to pay her rent, but she refused, saying my help setting her shop up online was an even exchange.

I sure as hell planned to get another great job soon so Mom wouldn't worry so much. I noticed the slight pinch in her forehead any time we talked about my next step. Even though I told her I had feelers out there already, which I did, she couldn't help but worry. And I couldn't stand the thought of being a burden on my parents, even emotionally, especially after all they'd sacrificed so I'd have everything I needed growing up.

Dinner went as usual. Terrific food, loud talking, Dad's grunts of pleasure over everything, mainly over the potato salad, then Mom and Aunt Polly retiring with their wine on the porch. Dad and I had kicked up in the living room together like always, watching one of our favorites on the Classic Movies channel, *Arsenic and Old Lace*. I was giggling at Cary Grant when my phone buzzed on the coffee table.

I unlocked it to find a text from Betty, my best friend from college, a Louisiana girl I kept in touch with. Fortunately, she was my first and only roommate in the dorms. And though we had very different majors—her in education, me in business—we had so much in common. Small town girls with lots of ambition and no-nonsense attitudes.

Betty: Hey. I've got some good news for you.

Me: Hey, Beebee! I love good news. ;)

Betty: My cousin works in Houston. He has a connection to a cool, growing marketing agency. They have a new opening for a creative director & they're looking for someone experienced but with fresh, progressive ideas. That's you, girl!

"Oh, my Lord," I mumbled.

"What is it, Bug?"

"My friend Betty has a job possibility for me."

"Really? That's great, baby. Where is it?"

"Houston," I said, texting her back with *yes, please send me all the details* so I could apply.

Then she shot back another text.

BETTY: Also, look who's a homeowner!

SHE'D TOLD me she was moving out of the city of Baton Rouge where she'd been teaching to her hometown of Beauville, smack dab in the middle of Cajun country. I hadn't spoken to her much, though, since I'd come back to my own hometown.

A few dots scrolled at the bottom of my message app, then in came a selfie. Her mouth was open wide with excitement, fire-red hair flying across her face, as she stood in front of a cute gray house with white trim and an adorable front porch.

"What is that?" I giggled, noting the tiny animal on her doorstep.

ME: Is that a goat on your porch?

Betty: Dammit. That's Gilbert! A pygmy goat. My neighbor's. Don't ask. I'll send you the details for the job soon. Ciao, girl.

"IT'S REALLY hot in Houston, isn't it?" asked Dad.

I snorted. "Not any hotter than it was in New Orleans, I'm sure."

"If that's what you want, then you should go for it," he said before popping up and heading into the kitchen. I sent Betty my reply, then watched Dad walk away. Like clockwork, forty-five minutes after dinner, he needed something sweet. But I was pretty sure that sour look was due to me.

Mom was more supportive of me going away to school with the full ride on tuition, but Dad never was. Don't get me wrong. He was always happy for me in my accomplishments, but I knew he was also sad to see me go.

The cabinets banged open and closed. "Lola! Come make those snickerdoodle cookies for your Daddy."

I was too stuffed to even think about cookies. But I'd do anything for my Dad, especially after upsetting him with my news.

Houston. A new city. That would be exciting. I started to text Marly then decided against it. She was so happy I was home, even if for only a little while, that I didn't want to upset her. I tossed my phone on the coffee table and ventured into the kitchen.

"Y'all have peanut butter?"

He opened the pantry and pulled out a jar.

"No. That's crunchy. I need the smooth for my recipe."

"Come on, then." He grabbed his cap and his car keys off the hook. "Let's go to the Piggly Wiggly."

I couldn't even argue. The Piggly Wiggly was a three-minute drive from the house, so I followed him out the back door.

"Where are you two going?" Mom called.

"Piggly Wiggly. Need peanut butter."

"Snickerdoodles," mumbled Aunt Polly.

"Frank, there's peanut butter in the pantry."

"Not the right kind, Mom," I argued, standing shoulder to shoulder with him. Mom could never handle a united front.

"See? We need the other kind," he said with a wave over his shoulder, tugging on my sweatshirt sleeve.

"You don't need snickerdoodles. I'm going to tell Dr. Hudson. Your sugar levels were high last time."

"Still need my daughter to bake me cookies, Ellen," he said, stopping under the carport. "She'll be moving away again soon, and I won't get 'em as often."

He looked and sounded so pitiful, making his puppy dog eyes. Like this was a life or death situation not to have me bake him snickerdoodles.

Mom tilted her head and huffed out a laugh. "Fine! But when Dr. Hudson puts you on diabetes medication, don't complain to me."

He hurried toward his truck with a wink at me. "Hurry, before she changes her mind," he whispered.

My dad liked to pretend he lived in fear of my mother's wrath, but he secretly loved it. Mom showed her affection by complaining about your health. For example, when she told me she was worried my unemployment might cause me stress, which could lead to other ailments such as depression and diarrhea—not sure why she emphasized those two together, but she did—I knew that she loved me.

After hopping in the truck, we were hopping right back out three minutes later. Not many cars in the parking lot, but it was a Friday night.

"Maybe we should get some vanilla ice cream, too," said Dad as he tucked his keys in his jeans pocket.

"Sure. Why not?" Because there in reality was no arguing with the man when he had a craving. "Do you know if Mom has real butter or only margarine?"

His brows squished together.

I laughed. "Better get some just in case." We ambled around the cashiers. "You go get the ice cream," I told him, heading for the peanut butter aisle.

"I'll grab the butter, too."

I gave him a salute in the air as I strolled down the coffee aisle, crossed the middle aisle to the condiments, then slowed down to find what I needed.

"Sorry, Peter Pan. I'm a Jiffy girl." I scanned to find the jars of smooth when it hit me what song they were playing.

You know how there are some songs you just can't resist dancing to? Well, "Low" by Flo Rida was one of those songs. I bobbed my head, my curls bouncing in my messy half-ponytail, half-bun on top of my head. I mumble-sang "apple bottom jeans" and the rest until I slid my bum *low, low, low* to the bottom shelf for the Jiffy smooth peanut butter.

I grabbed a jar and stood with a little shimmy of my hips, then turned to find Jed standing in the empty middle aisle, frozen, watching me. I jumped and gasped, almost dropping the Jiffy. His goofy grin widened, but not before I caught a flash of heat in those expressive eyes.

I took inventory of his faded jeans, Sound Garden T-shirt, and brown cowboy boots. His black hair was messily rumpled, his beard perfectly trimmed as always. How the hell did he manage to look so damn good in his casual clothes when I knew my well-loved Converse, hot pink yoga pants with a ketchup stain from dinner, and green sweatshirt reading *House Slytherin Slays* was in no way remotely equal to his current state of hotness? Still, his hazel eyes dropped down my body with interest.

Chin up, I tugged on the hem of my sweatshirt, well aware he had gotten a nice show when it rode up past my hips during my grocery aisle dance number.

"Hi." I waved. Why was I waving? "What are you doing here?" I cradled the peanut butter with two hands, noticing the bottle of white zinfandel he was holding.

"I'm here with my Gran."

"Your grandmother?" I tried not to sound skeptical, but he looked sinfully hot and held a very girly wine.

He smiled even bigger, kicking my heart into the next gear. "Come and meet her."

I arched a brow. "Okay." Sure, I'll play. "Let's go meet your Gran."

I followed him around the corner. Because there was no way that Jedediah was spending his Friday night looking like that, taking his grandmother to the Piggly Wiggly.

"Gran. There's someone I want you to meet."

The white-haired woman squinting at a jar of fruit with her glasses on the bridge of her nose wore stylish pants and a floral blouse. She turned her head and dipped her chin down so that she peered over the rim of her glasses at us approaching.

Feeling as foolish as I possibly could for doubting him, I stared wide-eyed, trying to wipe away every preconceived notion I ever had about Jed.

"This is my good friend, Lola Landry."

Her hawk-like blue eyes might not be able to read a label's fine print, but they sure as shit could measure me in two seconds flat. "Your Momma still working at Dr. Henagan's office?"

Unsure how she made the connection since we'd never met, I answered politely, "Yes, ma'am."

"Hmph. Well, she shouldn't. My root canal cost an arm and a leg. That man is committing highway robbery. She oughta up and leave him."

"Uh." I glanced nervously at Jed. "Well, she's been working for him for twenty-six years."

"I know that. I've been going to him for thirty. She should retire early. No sense in working for a criminal."

This whole time, her intense gaze swiveled from me to Jed, back and forth, in a way that made me feel jittery.

"Gran, Dr. Henagan isn't a criminal," argued Jed, trying not to laugh.

"Says you," she snapped, handing him the can of pears. "Put that in my buggy, Jedediah. Make yourself useful and stop telling your older and wiser grandmother falsehoods."

Jed dropped the can in the shopping cart, half-full with mostly canned fruits and veggies, a ton of toilet paper, and a giant bag of Kibbles 'n Bits. He also set the bottle of wine next to the eggs in the top of the cart.

"If you're convinced he's a criminal, why don't you go to someone else?"

"Because I'm a creature of habit, Jedediah.

He just smiled at her. "I'm going to walk Lola to the front. I'll be right back."

"Nice to meet you—" Hell, Jed didn't tell me her name! And I wasn't about to call this ornery woman I'd just met Gran.

"It's Louise, sweetheart," she said, her gaze softening when it landed on Jed's hand at the small of my back.

"Nice to meet you, Miss Louise."

"I'll be seeing you around, Lola Landry."

I walked faster, giving Jed my enlarged scaredy eyes. "I almost peed my pants," I whispered.

He laughed. "She's not that scary."

I stopped by the front cash registers, glancing around for Dad. He wasn't in sight yet. "Have you met your grandmother?"

He faced me, tucking his hands in his pockets. The smoldering smile spreading across his face made my bones feel soft. "The indomitable Cola afraid of a little, ole Granny."

Indomitable?

"You think I'm invincible, do you?" I arched a superior eyebrow at him.

"Unassailable. Unconquerable." He edged closer, dipping his head closer to mine. "But I've always loved a challenge."

"Jedediah Lawson! Look at that." Dad walked up with an armful of vanilla, strawberry, and mint chocolate chip ice cream. Oh, and the butter.

"Mom is going to kill you." I took one tub off his hands.

"You just keep getting bigger and bigger, son," said Dad, ignoring me. "I still remember that block you made in the championship game. Wouldn't have won without that hit, I'm telling you."

Not this again. Dad played on the offensive line when he was in high school, too, so he always bragged about what a fantastic job they did after that state championship game our senior year. And of course, he had pointed out to me over and over back then that we wouldn't have won without Jed's game-changing block of two defensive players so our quarterback could get the ball into the end zone. Dad never knew that Jed was the only player I watched on the field anyway. I'd seen him manhandle those two behemoths all by himself so Trey could make the winning pass.

"Yes, sir," agreed Jed.

I was unsure if he was agreeing with my Dad that he kept getting bigger or that he made the winning block. What I did know was that Jed was blushing all the way past his beard, tinging the tops of his cheeks pink. Jeesh, he was adorable.

"Last play of the game. Stopped 'em on a dime, like a solid brick wall. And we won the game with that pass." Dad shook his head admiringly before he peered at me, suddenly remembering that he had a daughter. "So, you ran into Lola Bug?"

"We better get going, Dad." I hip-bumped him toward the register.

Jed's grin spread wider. "Yeah, me and Lola Bug were catching up."

I was going to kill my father. "If you want those snickerdoodles, we better get going." I gave him my serious face.

"Oh, yeah, yeah." He dropped his gallons of sugar on the first register. "See ya, Jed!"

"Snickerdoodles, huh?" he asked, glancing at the peanut butter, smiling sweetly, no doubt remembering that day on the bleachers.

"Dad loves them," I whispered, a little shy now.

"Bet he does." His gaze locked on mine, his smile sliding and eyes darkening, sending my pulse galloping off into Never Never Land.

"Well, I better go." I turned and took a quick step away.

I was almost out of reach when I felt a warm hand wrap entirely around my bicep and hold me still. He dipped his head low from behind, his breath tickling the wispy hair on my neck. "Tomorrow morning. 9:00 a.m. And wear something warm for the outdoors."

Then he let me go just as I'd decided I was giving into temptation and going to lean back and feel his hard body against mine. Instead, I inhaled a deep breath and walked over to drop my goods on the conveyor belt before glancing sideways to get a view of Jed walking away. Damn, that was an awfully pretty sight.

That's when I knew I was in trouble. This was no upcoming podcast date or even a bucket-list date. This was an I-like-the-shape-of-your-ass-you-wanna-touch-mine kind of date. Yep. So much trouble.

Chapter Nine

-LOLA-

"What if the conversation takes the wrong path on your date?" @BitsyBee
"Ask a question about him. If he's a good guy, he'll reciprocate." @kiss-n-tell
"That goes for the bedroom, too." @marlypants

I dropped my Boho purse on the bed and stood in front of my full-length mirror. Deep breath in...and out. Then I moved into position. Forming fists, I propped them on my hips in a Superwoman pose.

My college bestie Betty, who had more sense than anyone I knew, taught me this trick. She instructed me to do the Superwoman pose whenever I was about to do something big that required confidence and a great outcome.

I'd done this before my comp exams for grad school, for my internship position post-grad, for my interview with Clarks and Taylor, and for most of my interviews after I was fired. And though I hadn't landed a job post-Clarks-and-Taylor, I'd gone into every interview completely confident and sure of myself. Perhaps the best outcome I'd hoped for was not getting those jobs so I could come home for a while. Hmph. Hadn't thought of that till just now.

Anyway, this date with Jed warranted a little manifesting the best of myself, because I was edgy as all hell. I needed to calm down and get a hold of myself. I tended to get diarrhea of the mouth when I was nervous.

I looked into the mirror, chin up, and admired my outfit—dark skinny jeans and a form-fitting green sweater. I'd even pulled out my favorite brown boots, which gave me a little height. I needed it next to giant Jed.

My phone buzzed on the dresser. Marly.

I tapped to answer. "Hey."

"What are you wearing?"

"Jeans, green sweater, favorite boots, and some bangle bracelets, I think."

"Wait. The v-neck or the one with the black ribbing around the end of the sleeves?"

"The v-neck."

"Good choice. That one makes your boobs look fantastic."

"My boobs need to mind their own business and stay out of trouble."

"If the girls want to have some fun, then let them."

"Marly!"

"Lola!"

"Come on," I huffed, trying to reason with her, which was equivalent to wrangling a greased piglet. "You and I both know that this is just Jed trying to beat me at this dating game."

"Says who?"

"Me. Because he was always competitive, and he thinks if he gets a higher dating score, then he wins."

"What does he win?"

I shoved my favorite gold bangle bracelets on my left wrist, while holding the phone between my shoulder and ear. "He wins the Jed-beat-Lola competition."

Marly sighed. "Oh, you sweet summer child."

Hell, she was quoting *Game of Thrones*. Prepare for profound wisdom.

"Jed doesn't want to beat you." She laughs. "He wants to win you. Kiss you. Take you to bed. Honestly, I think he wants to keep you."

"You have lost your mind, Marleen."

"I'm right. I'm so fucking right, and that scares the bejeezus out of you. That's why you're all defensive and your voice is getting all screechy."

"Lola!" yelled Aunt Polly from downstairs. "Jed is here!"

My stomach did a triple flip then sank like a boulder.

"Gotta go," I whisper-yelled.

"Wish the girls good luck for me!"

I cut her off and stuffed my phone in my purse. Standing back in front of the mirror in my Superwoman pose, I eyed my perky rack, narrowing my gaze before staring straight down at them. "There will be no misbehavior, ladies. This is a business date." Sort of.

I blew out a breath, one of my soft curls flying to the side. At least my hair had been agreeable, probably because the weather turning cooler.

Remembering Betty's phrase she made me memorize, I stared back at my reflection and recited, "I believe in myself and my abilities. I'm capable of much more than I imagine. The only limitations are the ones in my mind. And I'm a confident, kickass woman."

The last part I added in myself, of course. Smiling at my reflection, my brown hair draped past my shoulders in perfect waves, I hauled my bag onto my shoulder and headed downstairs.

Aunt Polly's soft laugh and Jed's rumbly voice carried down the hallway as I headed up front. I'll bet he was just throwing all his southern boy charm her way, making her laugh at anything and—

Dear Lord in heaven above.

I caught myself before I actually stumbled at the sight of Jed. A chambray button-down that fit so well, tucked into his dark jeans, highlighted his broad chest and shoulders and the peek of tan skin at the neck.

On one of our margarita nights, Marly and I had argued over the sexiest parts of a man. One of my top favorites was the suprasternal notch. Also called the jugular notch, or more plainly, the neck dent—that dip at the base of the throat between the collarbone. Marly called it the tongue slide because it was the perfect place to let your tongue have some fun on the playground. Right now, my eyes were held entirely hostage by Jed's suprasternal notch. The man was all muscle and height and girth, which made that delicate part of his neck somehow beyond intriguing.

"Lola?" Finally breaking from my hypnotic thrall, I found him gracing me with his rockstar smile that said *I'm a good boy and a bad boy* all at the same time and in all the right ways. "You ready to go?"

"Totally." With a swift kiss on Aunt Polly's cheek, I said, "I'd give you a time when I'm returning, but my date won't tell me where we're going."

"It'll be tonight," he told her, "but not too late."

"Keep her as long as you like, Jed."

I gave Aunt Polly my wide-eyed, are-you-kidding-me face, then zipped out before she could say anything else embarrassing. Why was everyone around me so pro-Jed?

As I got in his SUV and belted, I wondered why I was still anti-Jed. Or if I truly was. Maybe Marly was right, and I was just scared.

Jed glanced at me with a curious smile as he fastened himself and backed his SUV down the drive.

"What?" I asked.

"What-what?"

I rolled my eyes. He laughed as he wound down the road toward the main highway, but he didn't tell me what that look was for. I side-eyed him, that smirk still firmly planted on his handsome face.

"So, do you take your grandmother grocery shopping every Friday night?"

He steered us out of town, piquing my curiosity of where we were going again.

"Just once a month when her social security check comes in."

I shook my head.

"What?" he asked, his brow pinching a little.

"What-what?" I tossed back at him.

He let out a bark of laughter, the sound so infectious I couldn't help but join him. I don't remember him laughing much in high school. Around his friends in the hall sometimes, but never in class or anything. He always seemed so serious, actually. Broody. This Jed was lighter, content. I liked being around him. Quite a lot, I realized.

"I just figured you'd have a hot date every Friday night," I teased.

"In the metropolis of Green Valley?" He chuckled again. "Not really." He turned onto the interstate, heading west. "That actually reminds me of something I wanted to ask you." He tapped his fingers on the steering wheel, seeming to consider something. "I checked out your podcast."

"Oh?" I grinned, shifting to face him more fully. "Which episode did you listen to?"

He cleared his throat. "All of them."

What? "That's...shocking." I laughed nervously. "What did you think?"

"I wondered where the hell you found all these young, single men in Green Valley," he said lightly, seeming to be downright baffled. And just maybe a tad jealous.

"Most aren't from the *metropolis* of Green Valley," I said pointedly. "I usually use a dating app."

"Even Jason Barfman?"

"Who?" I tucked my hands between my legs, the temperature in the car a little chilly since the weather just turned. "Do you mean Jason Hoffman?"

He turned the heater on and reached over to angle a vent toward me. "No, I definitely meant *Barfman*. I couldn't stand that guy back in school."

"Okay, okay. I give up. Why did y'all call him Barfman?"

"You warm enough?" He glanced at where I had my hands tucked between my legs.

"Oh, yeah. All good. I'm just one of those people with poor blood circulation as soon as the weather turns. My hands and feet are always cold." He frowned at my lap like my hands had done something to offend him. "Don't try to get out of it. You brought it up. Explain Barfman."

He shook his head. "He was older than us and a defensive lineman. I remember he used to pound on my friends and me at practice when we were freshmen. Irritated the hell out of me."

"Only freshman year?"

He smiled, blessing me with one of those smoldering sideways glances that did tingly things to my insides. "Summer before tenth grade, I hit a growth spurt. And that ended the pounding on the field." He turned back to the road, flipping his blinker and veering at a junction, following the signs to Nashville.

"We're going to Nashville?" I asked.

Instead of answering that question, he went on about Jason. "Somehow, that made us cool in his book, so he'd invite my friends and me to their parties. And every single time," he emphasized with a wrap of his palm on the steering wheel, "he'd drink till he was puking in the bushes."

"Thereby creating *Barfman*."

"You got it." His fingers drummed again—nice long, strong fingers. Fingers, I shouldn't be ogling and wondering what marvelous things they could do to me. "So, how was he on a date?" he finally asked, eyes on the road.

"You listened to the podcast, so you should know."

"All I know is that you gave him an eight on your date-o-meter." His tone was offended, but he shot me that killer smile before focusing back on the road.

"If you're so insulted by his high rating, then why are you grinning like that?"

"Because he didn't get a second date."

"No one gets a second date."

"Except me," he snapped quickly, his expression serious and seriously sexy.

I turned away, feeling the tell-tale heat flushing up my neck. "You bullied me into it."

That loud laugh filled the cabin of his SUV again, drawing my attention with a magnetic jerk. "I'd love to see the day Lola Landry is bullied into anything."

"Fine then. *Maybe* I agreed because it would be great for ratings on the podcast."

"Maybe," he agreed doubtfully.

"Are we going all the way to Nashville?" It was a good three hours from Green Valley.

"I decided you were right."

"Wait. *What?*" I beamed at him. "Say that again. And what was I right about?"

He shook his head, that wayward lock of dark hair falling forward. "The setting for date number one wasn't a great way to get to know each other."

"So you decided to trap me in your car for six hours to ensure that long, deep discussions would take place."

"I'm enjoying the drive. Aren't you?"

His heartfelt, quizzical expression shut down any sarcastic remark I might snap back with. "I'd say you're definitely getting high points for pleasant conversation." I smiled. "So far, that is," I added quickly.

He nodded. "I'm taking you to one of my favorite places. I'm also giving you an education."

"I'm a strong advocate for education. Let me guess. Country Music Hall of Fame?"

He grinned. "Nope."

"I've been there a hundred times anyway. Aunt Polly is obsessed with Johnny Cash and Dolly Parton. The Frist Art Museum then?"

He chuckled and shook his head.

"Hmm. The Lane Motor Museum?"

Another delighted shake of his head.

"You're enjoying this, aren't you?"

His gaze swept to me, those hazel eyes scaling down to my lips, then farther south over my body, leaving a trail of heat, before rising to meet mine again. "Every single second."

Chapter Ten

-JED-

Being with Lola was electric. Did she feel the intense energy the way I did? I remembered the way it felt to be around her in high school. I'd wanted her then, before I even knew what it truly meant to want a woman. Now, the desire had morphed into a hungry beast, twitching his tail and biding his time.

The fun, light conversation we had on the drive to Nashville did nothing to douse the heated tension building between us. I was attuned to every movement of her hands, every shift of her body, every lift and fall of her chest with every breath she took.

"Oh, my heavens," she said, laughing as we drew closer to the stadium. "We're going to a Titans game?" She glimpsed at my shirt, realizing I was wearing the team color. "You could've told me so I could've worn the right colors."

"We're not playing Green Bay, so you're good. If you'd come out wearing purple, then I would've. We're playing the Baltimore Ravens, and you look great, so don't worry."

I couldn't help but flick my gaze over her, admiring the way her sweater and jeans hugged her curves just right. Lola in a dress was beautiful. Lola in *this* was downright torture. My hands itched to touch her. I choked back that urge, determined to be a gentleman and not the horny caveman making grunt noises in my head. I swear, if I let myself indulge and stare and touch the way I really wanted, I'd be reduced to a nonverbal, brainless, hard-on.

She looked out her window at the stadium as I parked, a giant smile plastered on her pretty face. "Football. That's the education I'm getting?"

I put the truck in park. "You said once you never understood the big appeal of football. I'm going to show you."

"When did I say that?" She frowned, hopping out of the car.

I got out and locked the truck as I wound around the front to meet her. "In Mr. Brown's Social Studies class."

"What?" She laughed, slaying me with the sparkle in her emerald eyes. "You remember something I said in Mr. Brown's class from high school?"

"Oh, please," I said, taking her hand and guiding her in the direction where my friends always tailgated. She glanced down at our joined hands but didn't pull away. "I'll bet you remember a lot of things I said from high school."

"Why would I bother to remember anything you said?"

I pulled her to a stop to face me, pressing close. The wind kept lifting her curly hair. I tucked a thick strand behind her ear, relishing the silkiness of her cheek and neck, the soft whorl of her ear, wanting to reach back and fist my hand in her hair. Her merriment morphed into surprise and something hotter.

"Come now, Lola," I crooned softly. "Let's not pretend you weren't obsessed with me."

Her mouth opened in a gasp, and she jerked her hand from mine before marching away. Laughing, I caught up and took her hand again. She tried to pull away.

"I'm just *kidding*. I'm sorry."

She glared back and tugged less forcefully on her hand, but I held on.

"We both know I was the one obsessed with you."

"We do?"

"I confessed that whole thing about prom to you. My most painful rejection of adolescence. It shouldn't be a surprise that I wanted to be with you," I said sincerely, lacing our fingers. "I *want* to be with you."

A look of surprise flashed in those green eyes, and I wondered if I was coming on too strong. I couldn't help myself. Lola Landry did crazy things to me, like make me want to rewrite our history, where I didn't give in so easily, where I told her how I truly felt about her rather than let her walk away from me at graduation, where I proved to her I was more than just the Jockstrap Jed she knew in high school.

Her cheeks flushed pink as she glanced toward the stadium. "So, where are our seats?" Changing the subject. Not surprised.

"We have a stop first. My friends tailgate over on this side. You'll remember some of them."

"Wait. Your high school football buddies?"

"Yeah. We hang out before. Grant and I usually share my tickets since he and I are the only singles left in the group. Well, we were anyway. Wade is in the middle of a divorce actually. Anyway, I told Grant my extra seat was taken today." She went suddenly quiet, a scowl puckering her brow. "Is that okay?"

She paused for a few seconds. "Sure. Why not?"

But there was hidden anxiety behind those few, flippant words. I squeezed her hand. "We can go grab a bite on our own, then head to the game if you want. The game's at 3:00."

"No, no. This is your date. Let's follow your plan."

Sighing, I tugged her in the right direction. "I can see it now. You're subtracting points and tabulating my lesser score already."

"We'll see," she teased, finally smiling back. "The date isn't over yet."

The giant blue tent was in its regular spot on the south side of the parking lot. Trey's blonde head shone in the sun where he stood near the grill outside the tent. Grant tilted a beer back, listening to Trey carry on about who knows what.

I slowed as we approached, my pulse racing for some strange reason I couldn't quite figure out. Wade saw us first, sitting in a chair next to Trey's wife, with his four-year-old son Jake propped on his knee. Jake was a miniature version of his dad, same auburn-capped head, same dark eyes, and same broody frown most of the time. In high school, Wade was the only o-lineman bigger than me. Same was true today among our group.

Lola pulled her hand loose from mine as we drew closer, but I didn't let it bother me. Staying near her, I guided her under the tent with a gentle brush to her back.

"This is a fascinating sight," said Wade, his mouth tipped up in a lopsided smile as he surveyed Lola.

"Uncle Jed!" Jake launched off his dad's lap and charged for me.

I swept him up and tickled his ribs with a squeeze on his sides like I always did. He squirmed and squealed with laughter, yelling, "Stop, stop!"

"Not until you say the magic words."

I kept tickling while he said through laughter, "Uncle Grant is the best in the world."

Propping him on my hip, I kept tickling with the other. "Wrong."

Jake threw his head back, half-yelling, half-laughing, "Uncle Trey is the best!"

On a heavy sigh, I turned to Lola. "Excuse me a minute." I propped Jake under one arm and carried him like a sack of potatoes outside the tent, then tossed him straight up about six feet into the air. Lola gasped behind me. I caught him, then turned him upside down and held him by his legs in the air, swinging him like a pendulum. This was our typical greeting, so no one else seemed bothered or amused. Except for Jake, and that's all that mattered.

"The magic words, Jacob Matthew."

His face turned red as he grinned at me upside down, his little chest heaving. "Uncle Jed is the best in the world!"

I swung him right side up and planted him on the ground. "Yes, he is," I assured him with a wink and tousled his hair.

He wobbled off, making a zig-zag line in his dizziness. Trey's twin girls giggled and trailed after him.

"I'm Wade Kelley. And you are?"

I sauntered over to where Wade was already flirting with my girl.

My girl? Damn. My possessive urges were already rocketing a bit high.

"Lola Landry," she said, shaking his hand.

Wade's expression puckered into a frown. "Wait. You're—?"

"Yes," I said, standing close enough to brush her shoulder. "Lola from our class in high school."

"Whoa," said Grant, sauntering up into the conversation. Impeccably dressed in a starched pale blue shirt and black slacks, he eyed her from top to bottom.

And that's when I realized why I'd grown suddenly nervous when we'd approached the tent. My friends were ridiculous flirts. And Grant was a professional lady's man, having dated half the single women in Knoxville where he ran his IT analyst business.

He took Lola's hand in both of his and shook it slowly. "It's a pleasure to see you again, Lola."

He might as well have said, *May I pleasure you in bed, Lola.*

"Ease up, Baxter."

He winked at her and grinned at me.

"You remember Grant Baxter?"

She nodded, a nervous smile brightening her face.

"No way." Trey broke into our circle with giant grill tongs in one hand. "*Coca-Cola Lola?*"

"Drop it, Trey," I warned, wrapping an arm around her waist, resting my hand on her opposite hip. "It's just *Lola*."

No one called her Cola but me. No one understood where that name came from and why but me. It might've been spawned out of adolescent hurt, but it had become synonymous with the brilliant, beautiful girl whose locker was below mine, who I dreamed about and yearned for. And now, though that boy and his stupid words were a distant memory, that name was still mine. And mine alone. A small proprietary hold till I could claim the woman herself.

"Alright, alright, Lawson. Relax." Trey shook her hand with his free one. "Damn, you look *good*, girl."

Wade made an agreeable grunt, and I frowned at him. He just simply grinned back.

Why did I bring her here again?

"Thanks," she laughed, easing closer to me, her shoulder blade brushing my chest, which made me feel about ten feet tall. It was the first time she'd voluntarily moved into my personal space, and I don't think she'd even realized it.

"How the hell did you two hook up?" asked Trey.

I winced. "We met up again in Green Valley."

"Yeah," agreed Lola, smiling up at me. "He saved me from, well, a car problem."

I wasn't about to correct her that it was a car owner problem. I simply nodded.

"You're living back in Green Valley?" asked Wade. "Weren't you living down south or something?"

She didn't bother asking how he knew. Wade's mother was notorious for being the information highway or the gossip pipeline of Green Valley. She rattled on and on about anyone and everyone if she held you hostage for even three seconds in the Piggly Wiggly parking lot.

Lola didn't want to talk about that with these guys, and I damn sure wasn't going to let her feel uncomfortable about her current work situation.

"You guys are the rudest hosts," said Trey's wife, breaking into our party. "Hi, I'm Candice. Let me get you a drink. Come with me."

Candice tugged her toward the cooler for a drink, and I exhaled a heavy breath.

"I can't believe that's Lola Landry," said Trey, as we watched the ladies walk over to the table where Candace started setting out plates and napkins on the fold-out table. "Damn, she looks good."

"Mmhmm," murmured Grant, sipping his beer while watching the ladies.

"You already said that, Trey. And can y'all please stop ogling her like a piece of meat?"

"Holy fucking shit," said Wade.

We all swiveled to him at his sudden outburst, then stared and waited until his attention moved from the ladies back to us. Actually, me, to be more precise.

"It's finally happening, Jed." He clapped me on the back. "You're going to get your shot with the one that got away."

Then he laughed in that deep, rumbly way of his.

"What?" Trey was clueless as always. "Lola Landry?"

"Damn, Trey." Grant shook his head. "You're the only one who never figured out how bad Lawson had it for her?"

"You did?" Trey's blue eyes bugged out at me, then narrowed in betrayal before swinging back to where Lola and his wife were laughing at something.

Lola glanced my way, her secret smile finding its mark straight through the flesh and bone of my ribcage to that softer organ beneath.

"Well, hell, Jed," said Wade, taking a swig of his beer. He was my closest friend in the world, and the only one who knew the extent of my feelings for Lola. The only one who knew I carried that torch beyond high school. He lowered his voice so that only I could hear. "Don't let her get away this time."

The warning hammered home, morphing into a call. A command. To take hold of my own destiny. To follow that internal compass, pointing me in the right direction. The one that drove my gaze toward the pretty woman by the food table, where the wind was lifting her curly hair in the breeze, and who wore a smile that stalled the breath in my lungs.

Finally, I answered Wade, but it was really a declaration to myself. "I don't intend to."

Chapter Eleven

-LOLA-

"When should I go for the first kiss?" @johnblue
"When she starts looking at your mouth like it's a chocolate éclair." @kiss-n-tell

"I didn't mind staying longer, you know."

"I minded," Jed grumbled, ushering me through the gate after getting our tickets scanned.

"Why are you so growly?"

He shook his head with a smile, holding my hand again and tugging me up the ramp. I couldn't put into words the sublime sensation I experienced with Jed's giant, calloused hand holding mine. And when he brushed the pad of his thumb over the back of my wrist, heat pooled in lovely, lower places. I had no idea that the wrist was an erogenous zone. Or maybe it was just me. Or Jed. Or me with Jed.

"Sure you want to know?"

"Oh, now I *have* to know. This sounds juicy."

He shook his head, biting back a laugh as we walked through the portal and down a few steps. Our seats were close to the fifty-yard line in the lower section. We squeezed past a few people till he gestured toward one of two empty seats.

As soon as we sat, he asked, "You want something to drink?" Then started to get up.

I dug my claws into his bicep and jerked him down and closer, unable to hold back my laughter. "*Tell me*," I demanded in what sounded more like a Marly-demon voice.

He chuckled and turned his head to face mine, making me realize how close we were. His smile slipped, and those hot hazel eyes blazed a trail over my face, down to my lips, leisurely coasting back up to hold mine again.

"I didn't like the guys flirting so hard with you."

"Come on." I squeezed his arm playfully. "I'll bet those guys flirt with all the girls you bring."

"It's been a long time since I brought one around." The goldish-green of his eyes heated as he held me captive. "And none of them were you."

His volcanic stare was tempered with an intimacy that rang warning bells. Even so, it took everything in me to drag my gaze to the football field where the game hadn't started yet.

"I have a confession to make," I said lightly, pulling my hands back into my lap and away from his tight muscles. "I've always thought your friends were kind of, uh...sort of...you know."

I glanced at him to find his brows raised in question and accusation, a smirk telling me he already knew this.

"I have no idea what you're implying. Please spell it out for me."

I slapped his arm. "You're being stubborn on purpose."

"Yes, I am. Spill it. What is it that you always thought about my friends exactly?"

"Just that they were kind of douchey back in high school. Except for Wade. He was always pretty nice. But now they seem so...mature."

He belted out a laugh. "They *were* kind of douchey in high school. So was I, I'm sure. We were teenage boys, too full of testosterone and arrogance and our own sense of self-importance and invincible place in the world." His laughter died as he angled toward me. "But people grow up, Cola. And change."

I nodded, feeling silly for my foolish observation. "Of course, they do."

He stood. "How about something to drink before the game gets started?"

I beamed up at him. "A Coca-Cola, please."

He laughed and flicked his index finger under my chin, trailing and lingering for a brief two seconds. But he might as well have used a lit match. The shocking heat of his touch on my bare skin was doing crazy things to me. And it was so, so shockingly wonderful.

He held my gaze without blinking for a moment, then nodded. "Be right back."

I took the time he was gone to do some people-watching and try to get ahold of myself. Being with Jed felt familiar and fun in a way I'd never expected. Sure, we knew each other years ago, but like he said, people grow up and change. And so, we both had. Yet being in his sphere, even hanging with his friends who were surprisingly fun and cool guys, felt so natural. Like I belonged here. And that was terrifying.

Not to mention how my maternal instincts jotted down copious notes when he interacted with Wade's little boy Jake and when Trey's twin girls circled him and beamed and giggled at his every attention. And I couldn't stop smiling. What was going on here?

Jed returned with cokes in a holder, a tub of popcorn, and something wrapped in tiny white paper bags. He handed me my coke when he sat down, then put the tub between his legs and held out the white bag between us.

"Dessert." His smile grew across his face, scattering the butterflies in my stomach like a shotgun blast.

I peered inside and pulled out a chocolate chip cookie. "Mmm, they're warm."

He pulled one out and halved it in one bite. "Good," he hummed. "Not as good as your snickerdoodles." He watched me intently as he chewed.

My heart leaped at the mention of that day our sophomore year. When we'd shared an intimate moment, we never mentioned it again after that day. Until now.

Our Speech and Debate team celebrated our district victory with a feast after school that day. I'd made and brought my famous snickerdoodle cookies but had a few left over. I practically skipped to my car that day, high on sugar and team camaraderie and being a winner, when I'd glanced across the lot to the empty practice field, seeing the back of someone sitting in the bleachers. I'd know that broad back anywhere. It was the same one I stared at all the way through English class every day. He wore his football workout gear, his pads sitting next to him, and still in his cleats. His head hung low, his posture reeking of anguish.

I stood beside the driver's side of my car for three minutes before I decided and walked over to the bleachers. This was not long after we'd created nasty nicknames for each other, so there was still animosity coursing between us, but this boy was my weak spot. I couldn't just walk away.

He'd glanced up when I made it to his row as if he didn't realize he was no longer alone till I'd come so close. His eyes were ringed red, heartbreak marking every line of his handsome face. I asked him, "Are you okay?"

He'd looked away and shook his head. I couldn't just walk away, so I took a seat next to him and rummaged for the Ziplock bag of leftover cookies in my backpack.

"Here," I said. "My cookies make everyone feel better, I promise," I teased.

He'd stared at my outstretched hand for a minute. Just when I thought he'd stand up and walk away, he reached out and took the bag. "Thank you."

His voice was rusty with emotion.

"Go on," I'd said, "take a bite."

He'd opened the bag and bit into one, then stuffed the rest in his mouth before he'd chewed and swallowed the first bite. He'd closed his eyes and grunted, then smiled.

"Feel better, don't you?" I said, nudging his bicep with my shoulder.

He nodded, sliding a shy look my way. "It's my Mom's birthday."

My heart had plummeted. Instant pain staked me in the chest. Everyone knew that his mother had died in a car accident when he was in elementary school.

"I miss her," he'd whispered, staring out at the empty practice field.

"I'm so sorry." I'd wanted to wrap my arms around him and hug him, but that was way too out of character for our tumultuous relationship.

So I'd reached back into the plastic bag, took a cookie for myself, and handed one to him. I tapped mine to his like I was making a toast, "Happy Birthday, Mrs. Lawson."

His warm smile had reminded me that it was always better to be kind, even to your enemies. But we weren't enemies at that moment. Not at all.

He'd tapped my cookie with his. "Happy Birthday, Mom." Then he glanced heavenward as he took a bite, and my heart melted out of my chest and pooled onto the bleachers.

We'd left without another word after that. I'd gone home and baked two dozen snickerdoodles in a frenzy, then left them on his desk in an unmarked plastic container on his desk the next day. All I'd left was a sticky note on the inside of the lid that read: *For your cookie emergency needs. –L*

Snapping back to the present, I blinked at his admiring gaze. "I thought you forgot about that," I said, forcing myself to swallow the bite of the cookie.

"Forgot?" He huffed out a laugh. "I never forgot." He gave his head another definite shake. "Never," he whispered.

His gaze swept away from me to the field, but the connection didn't break. Like tumbling back through time, the boy and girl on the bleachers at

Green Valley High were floating on a parallel plane with the two of us. The strange, hypnotic link wove and merged between us. It felt like...fate.

"You have such a kind heart, Lola. Always have."

Said heart was racing a mile a minute. "I'm mean sometimes," I confessed. "Just ask Marly."

He smiled back at me, sitting back in his seat, his shoulders pushed against mine. So he stretched his arm along the back of my chair. "I'd love to hear about mean Lola," he said in that disbelieving tone.

"Are you kidding me?" I asked, incredulous. "I'm a total tyrant when it comes to business. My co-workers at the agency called me Lola Lenin behind my back."

He laughed, lifting one of my curls with the hand draped near my shoulder. "I have no doubt you're cutthroat in business. You've always been ambitious, Miss Most-Likely-to-Succeed." He wrapped that curl around his index finger and tugged lightly. "But your heart has always been tender." His warm gaze dropped once again to my mouth. The cocoon of sweet words and warm breath and hot looks coalesced into the fact that he was about to kiss me. My heart stuttered at the thought of his mouth on mine, waiting. Even hoping.

Then the crowd roared and leaped to their feet. Jed practically lifted me out of my own as we cheered for the Titans, making their way onto the field to loud, booming music. Adrenaline pumped through my veins with the excitement of the game and the thrill that, for one fleeting second, I knew that Jed Lawson was going to kiss me.

We settled into the game, cheering and yelling with the crowd. Jed took his time pointing out what the penalties meant, which I didn't know in all honesty. But then he pointed out the goal of the offensive line and was detailing positions.

"Yeah, the left side of the quarterback was the position you played, right?" I said, popping popcorn into my mouth.

"I thought you said you never paid attention to the football games." His grin told me I was caught.

Knowing my eyes were round with guilt, I stuffed a whole handful of popcorn in my mouth and mumbled, "Don't know what you mean," in mouth-chewing gibberish. "Oh, look! The mascot is dancing!" I jumped up and cheered.

Jed stood with me, reaching around to grab my hip and pull me into his body. He whispered close to my ear, "I'm onto you, Cola. You had it as bad as I did." He brushed the shell of my ear with his nose. Whether by accident or not, it sent a wave of arousal barreling south.

"This coke is so good," I sipped from my straw, blinking innocently up at him.

He laughed and squeezed my hip playfully before letting me go, then clapping at a catch on the next play. But all I wanted was to feel his large hand back on my hip, squeezing me close again.

The game was tight, but the Titans pulled it out in the last quarter.

"I love winning!" I yelled up into the afternoon sky as we walked back to his SUV.

He laughed and took my hand, our arms swinging like school kids as we strolled through the lot. "Did you have a good time?"

"Absolutely." I couldn't be coy or pretend otherwise. My joy had to be written all over my face.

"I'm glad," he crooned softly, but his expression beamed bright and loud and lovely.

We gabbed all the way home, laughing about more antics he'd experienced on the job. Like the time this lady called and said her house was on fire. They loaded up the truck and the extra van. Jed said he was on call at the firehouse and had to pee so bad when the alarm rang through the firehouse, but he didn't go because he didn't want to waste time with a little old lady's house on fire. So they hightailed it down there—every bump in the road pure torture for Jed—only to find her house was not on fire. Her dog had been stuck under the house, but she didn't think they'd come if she told the truth.

I laughed so hard at his facial expressions and cheeks flaming with embarrassment in retelling the story that I almost peed my own pants.

We talked about the things I loved about living in New Orleans. The food, the people, the unique culture. And how I didn't miss working for Clarks and Taylor, but I missed the city.

"You should definitely go some time," I told him as he pulled up into my driveway.

It was fully dark now. Aunt Polly had left the porch light and her bedroom light downstairs on.

"I'd need a tour guide. Maybe someone who's lived there."

I laughed nervously as we both opened the car doors and headed up to the porch. This was it. He was going to kiss me. Definitely. No way could we let all that sexual tension today go to waste.

I turned at the door. "Thank you for today. It was really a lot of fun." I couldn't keep the goofy grin off my face.

He tucked his hands into his pockets and stared down at me, a crooked smile teasing his sensuous lips. "Really glad to hear it. Can't wait to find out my score this Thursday." He shuffled a step closer, hands still in his pockets. "You wanna show a little mercy and tell me what it is now?"

"No mercy, Lawson. You'll just have to show up and see."

My smile fell when he took another step closer, mere inches between us.

"I'll show up," he said with some heat and determination behind the words. "You can't scare me away, Cola." He lifted one hand and cupped the side of my neck as he leaned in. I froze, breathless, closing my eyes. His warm lips brushed my cheek, his beard tickling my skin as he whispered, "Not this time."

Before I could catch my breath, he released me and sauntered away down the steps. "See you Thursday," he shouted over his shoulder before climbing into his SUV and backing down the drive, giving me one last look before driving away.

I stood there, staring, long after his taillights had disappeared, wondering about those gravel-deep words, *not this time*. Had I scared him away before? I was still pondering this revelation when my phone buzzed in my bag.

I pulled it out to find my nightly meme from Marly. It was a guy walking his rooster on a leash. The caption read: *Rock out with your cock out*.

My phone buzzed again.

MARLY: DID JED "ROCK OUT" tonight?

I SNORTED, pushing the front door open and ambling toward my bedroom.

ME: It was our second date!

Marly: Officially, yes. But in your fantasies, and I daresay his, it's like the one-hundredth date.

Me: Goodnight.

Marly: This bedding is long overdue.

Me: Talk tomorrow.

Marly: When it happens, I want details.

. . .

WHEN IT HAPPENS. As if it's inevitable. I tossed my purse on the bed and walked up to my wall mirror, touching my neck where the firm grip of his hand had branded me with warmth and promise. A shiver sizzled through me. The man hadn't even kissed me, and I was on fire.

He hadn't mentioned going out again, but there was no mistaking Jed was a man on a mission. And I was the mission.

Somehow, between tailgating and cookies and a long ride home, I was one hundred percent okay with that.

Chapter Twelve

-JED-

I was greeted much like the first time we recorded last week. Lola looked alarmed, on the verge of hysteria, and Marly looked like a devil planning someone's demise. I just hoped it wasn't mine.

I sat in the same spot, headphones on, while Marly and Lola greeted guests with their opening spiel.

"So this is unique for us, everyone," Marly declared from behind the laptop. "This is the first time we have a returning guest, so we're going to skip our typical rapid-fire questions. After all, you've already heard Jed's answers during last week's episode. Instead, I have a list of fun questions for both Jed and Lola to start us off today."

"For me, too?" asked Lola, surprise evident in her tone.

"Yep." Marly smiled, tapping on the laptop keyboard. "You guys ready?"

"Shoot," I said, glancing at Lola, who scooted closer to the mic, a frown puckering her brow.

Marly had been a hell-raiser in high school. Seemed her mischievous nature hadn't diminished at all. Lola didn't like surprises. She wanted to always be prepared for everything. Marly had sprung this on her, knowing she couldn't refuse since we were live on YouTube.

"Jed, you first. Favorite dessert?"

Easy.

"Cookies." I slid my gaze to Lola. "Snickerdoodles, to be exact."

She laughed out loud before containing it quickly, shaking her head at me, a pink blush filling her cheeks. I wanted to reach over and brush the back of my knuckles over them and feel the soothing heat.

"That's very precise," Marly teased, knowing full well who baked those cookies all the damn time. "Okay, Lola. Speaking of desserts, favorite pie?"

"Pecan," she answered quickly.

"Wait, I thought it was chocolate. You always used to get chocolate from Daisy's on Friday afternoons."

"In high school, yeah. But like someone recently told me," She arched her brow, a twinkle in her eyes. "People grow and change."

I stared, completely bewitched, as Marly went on. "Alrighty then. Jed, I know you're a football fan, but do you prefer college or pro?"

"Pro," I said at the same time Lola did.

We glanced at each other, both of us chuckling.

"Sorry, listeners," Marly said close to the mic. "They're sharing a private joke. We'll just wait it out."

Lola rolled her eyes at Marly. "I just know because of our date."

"Just because I took you to a pro game doesn't mean I prefer it over college," I challenged.

"Yeah, but the way you just lit up when the Titans came out on the field. You looked like a cute little boy on Christmas morning," she teased.

It took everything out of me not to reach over and kiss the woman.

"No spoilers on the date, guys," warned Marly. "Next question." She looked at Lola. "PDA, yes or no?"

"Yes," she said the same time I did.

Lola whipped her head toward me and laughed. "Let me answer my own question, please."

"You started it." I leaned across the space between us, blocking her mic with my hand, and whispered, "Besides, you let me hold your hand all night. And you liked it."

She bit her lip, trying to hide another smile as I straightened in my seat.

"If you two are finished having your own conversation," said Marly, "we'll move on to some more interesting questions."

Lola's smile fell as she stared wide-eyed at Marly.

"Jed, would you rather take a romantic getaway to an exotic beach far away or to a cozy mountain cabin?"

"It doesn't matter as long as I have the right girl."

Lola had her hands sandwiched between her jean-clad thighs, and her knees were bouncing ninety miles an hour. I could barely take my eyes off of her while she was studiously refusing to look my way.

"Nice answer, cowboy. Okay, Lola. With your man, would you prefer dancing the night away or a quiet night at home?"

She straightened, tucking a curly lock behind her ear. "Quiet night at home."

I could easily imagine us curled up together in front of my fireplace, stretched out on the sofa, watching whatever she wanted on the TV—or not watching anything at all but her.

"You're definitely a cozy girl," agreed Marly before turning to me. "Kissing. On the mouth or on the body?"

Pausing a second to take in that image, I cleared my throat. "Sorry," I laughed nervously, sliding my gaze to Lola, who had her eyes on her lap. "To be honest, I'd want to kiss her everywhere."

"Good man!" Marly tapped on the keyboard. "Yep, our YouTube viewers unanimously approve of that answer. And now, Lola. Which do you prefer? Cowgirl position or doggy style?"

"Okay, then," said Lola, her cheeks flushed cherry pink, "I think we can move on to the date breakdown now."

Damn that girl, Marly. She now had me imagining both positions with Lola. Not that I hadn't a million times before, but it was pretty inconvenient in the middle of a recorded video and podcast. Hopefully, by the time I stood up from the table, I wouldn't embarrass myself with the obvious bulge in my jeans.

"Oh, no. You can't get away that easy," reprimanded Marly. "Viewers want to know."

Lola shot her a death glare. "I'm not answering that question."

"Okay, a substitute question then? Less personal?"

"Fine."

"Fine."

"Well, ask it," snapped Lola.

"So impatient." She tapped on the keyboard. "Okay, here we go." Her mouth curved up into a wicked grin. "Ready?" She glanced over the laptop.

"Just ask it, Marly." Total exasperation. Professional Lola had left the building. I didn't blame her.

"Would you go on a third date with Jed?"

"Yes."

I nearly swallowed my tongue. Lola whipped her head toward me, her bright eyes screaming her embarrassment. She hadn't meant to answer that. All of a sudden, I loved Marly's interfering ways.

"I mean, if you want to," she whispered, though the mic still picked it up.

"I definitely want to."

She huffed out a nervous giggle, running her hands along her thighs before turning back to Marly.

"Viewers are absolutely loving that answer, Lola. And they have questions of their own, but before we get to that, let's talk about date number two. Where did you guys go for dinner?"

"We had more of a late lunch, early dinner." Lola's expression softened, her embarrassment sliding away. "It was at a tailgate party with Jed's friends."

"Oh, so the venue was the Titans football game in Nashville?" asked Marly, though I was pretty damn sure she had gotten full details of the date prior to the show.

"It was a day game, so we stopped at my friends' tent to eat and hang out," I said, turning to Lola. "How would you say Trey's famous burgers and hotdogs were? Five stars?"

"No doubt," she laughed. "And the dinner entertainment of Trey's twin girls fighting to sit on Uncle Jed's lap was pretty adorable."

"What can I say? The girls love me."

"So dinner and pre-game date sounds like it ranked high, Lola," interjected Marly.

"Definitely. We had fun."

"A lot of fun," I added, holding her gaze.

"And the game? How would you rank that part of the date?"

She seemed to catch herself, her sweet smile slipping a bit as she blinked and turned to the mic. "To be honest, I thought it was brilliant. It was the perfect place for a couple to talk and laugh, get to know one another, but also have a good time watching the fans and the game."

"Wow," said Marly. "Sounds like you're saying that Jed more than made up for the failure of date number one."

"Ouch." I rubbed at my chest.

Lola laughed at me, once again turning her attention back to me. Like she couldn't look away now. And damn, did I know that feeling.

"Let's move to a few questions from our live viewers on YouTube. Mandy has a question for Jed: '*Do you work out? Because you definitely look like it.*'"

Ignoring the heat crawling up my neck, I leaned forward. "Not really, no. I mean, my job requires a lot of physical activity and training that keeps me in shape. I do some hiking and jogging on my own sometimes, but I'm not really a gym guy."

Marly cackled at her screen. "Well, our viewers are impressed with your physique. You can check out the comments later."

I wasn't so sure I wanted to. Lola blew out a frustrated breath, sending a lock of hair flying into the air.

"Don't feel left out, Lola. Cherie has a question for you." Marly blinked innocently over the laptop. "She says: '*You're smiling a lot more than I've ever seen on Kiss-n-Tell. Is there real chemistry between you and Jed?*'" Marly glances back down to the screen. "Oh, actually, this question is for either of you," she corrects.

"Um," Lola started, then looked at me.

"You want me to answer?" I asked, loving the hopeful hesitation in her voice and in her eyes.

"Yeah, you can answer first," she said with a nonchalant wave of her hand.

"Mandy, I think I can answer this for both of us actually. *Yes*, there is definite chemistry between Lola and me." I turned to Lola. "Would you agree?"

She nodded her head slowly.

"I'd agree," added Marly, "from where I'm sitting anyway."

Lola's mouth gaped open in response, looking ready to tear into Marly, but then she snapped it shut as Marly continued.

"We have time for one last question, and this one is definitely for Lola, from Patsy. She says: '*You always have the greatest advice for first dates and dating in general. Now that you've agreed to another date with Jed, what would the perfect third date entail?*'"

"I'd love to know the answer to this question," I said, propping my jaw on my hand and waiting for her answer.

"Feels a little like cheating," Lola teased, smiling while trying not to.

"Feels more like research from my end."

She cleared her throat and scooted her butt farther up in the chair, leaning her crossed forearms on the table. "Patsy, that's an excellent question. I'd definitely say that date number three could be something that requires less talking and more physical contact." She gave me a sidelong teasing glance. "To see if that spark of chemistry you *think* you feel is actually there and not just a flickering flame."

Oh, Cola. I was going to show her that our chemistry was one hundred percent real. I leaned back in my chair, chuckling.

"Thank you for your questions, everyone," said Marly, looking between us. "What I'm gathering from all the eye-locking and goofy smiles between you two is that this was a very successful date."

"It was," agreed Lola.

I nodded.

"One last question from me, Lola. Was this a nine or a ten on your date-o-meter?"

Perfectly confident that this was a touchdown, I couldn't mask the shock when Lola let her curtain of curly hair fall to block her face when she leaned in and answered, "Nine," into the mic.

I might've even gasped. "Really?" I shook my head with a disbelieving laugh. "You certainly are a tough critic." I couldn't help growling.

"Oh, no!" She reached out and gripped my forearm, branding me with that delicate touch. "It's nothing like that. The date was perfect. You were perfect." She squeezed her eyes shut and shook her head. "I mean, I truly had a perfect time."

"Then I'd have a ten."

"Sorry, cowboy," said Marly. "Lola has a *Kiss-n-Tell* policy that no date, no matter how amazing, can get a ten on the date-o-meter unless there was a sizzling, swoony kiss by the end."

I swear, Lola was blushing all the way to her roots. She removed her hand from my arm and gulped hard.

"Is that so?" I leaned back in my seat and tapped my fingers on my thigh.

She had no idea how hard I restrained myself from moving in on her on the front porch. I had a decade of pent-up Lola fantasies, many of which were nothing more than long, hard kisses.

She finally looked my way, her expression broadcasting that she thought she knew what I was thinking. But she didn't. She had no idea.

My fantasies extended well beyond me mapping her body with my mouth. They ventured far into the future where afternoons on the porch, nights on the sofa, and mornings in a nursery peeking into a crib, existed.

I was well aware that my infatuation with this woman was far more than what she realized. Or perhaps even desired. But Lola and I matched. We fit. And some people might call me crazy, but, hell, I realized it during our day in Nashville. The second she let me take her hand, sending an alarming charge through my whole being and slapping me with a glimpse of a future I wanted. Longed for.

Before we'd become enemies in high school—for reasons I still had to work up the courage and confess to her—we fit perfectly the same way. The light that flared between us when we were kids was now a blazing inferno. And hell if I didn't want to light a match and burn with her.

"Yes-siree, cowboy," Marly interjected into my thoughts. "A ten will require a super hot kiss on your part. If you can deliver such a kiss."

I tore my gaze from Lola's to catch Marly giving me that devilish grin of hers. I turned my attention back to Lola, then leaned in nice and close. She had the arms of her chair in a death grip, white-knuckled, and I didn't think she was even breathing.

"Well, then," I murmured lowly. "I can't wait till our next date."

Chapter Thirteen

-LOLA-

"What does it mean when a guy you just started dating shows up at your work?"
@WinnieB
"Get ready, girl. He's got it bad." @kiss-n-tell

"That's right, bitches. Nobody puts baby in a corner." I sipped the last of my iced tea.

Aunt Polly laughed from her side of the L-shaped sectional, her head on a pillow at the point, and legs stretched out under her quilt. My head was on the opposite end, my feet tucked under her pillow. I loved these lazy days with her. Unfortunately, I had to work the night shift, so I had to exchange our usual margaritas with iced tea.

"Jeesh. I just love that Patrick Swayze." She exhaled a swoony sigh. "Look at the way he moves those hips."

"Not going to argue with you there. He knows what he's doing."

"That man left us far before his time." Another sigh from Aunt Polly. This one sadder.

My attention flickered away from the big finale dance number where they were having *the time of their lives* to look at my sweet aunt. Her husband Gene had died too soon, too. He was only fifty-six when he had a sudden heart attack. She was ten years younger than him, but she hadn't planned on being a young widow in her mid-forties.

I crawled from under my quilted throw to sit cross-legged closer to her at the end of the couch. "I'm sorry, Aunt Polly."

I never knew quite what to say or how to soothe someone at times like this. I'd never lost anyone close to me, except Uncle Gene. And I didn't know him all that well since he moved to Dallas with Aunt Polly when I was in seventh grade.

Aunt Polly had doted on me before then, always bringing me to arts and craft shows and dragging me to Dollywood and fun festivals when I was little. She'd never had any children and married later in life, so she spoiled me rotten. I wasn't complaining. Even though I was an only child, my parents didn't have that kind of time or energy, always working hard and late hours to make ends meet. So when my aunt left, a piece of me went with her.

She reached over with her freckled arm and gave me a playful slap on the leg. "No reason to be sorry, silly." She watched the rolling credits with a soft smile. "I had some wonderful years with Gene. And I was blessed to have 'em."

"You were one lucky gal. He was a sweetheart," I agreed softly. I pulled on a lock of hair near her temple and sectioned the long curl into thirds, then started braiding. "Do you remember when you two were dating, and Uncle Gene brought me a new Barbie every time you two came to Mom and Dad's for dinner?"

She chuckled. "He was trying to woo me by sweetening you up. He knew you were the way to my heart."

"Smart man. I was the most popular fifth-grader in school that year. Everybody wanted to sleepover at my house."

We both laughed as I finished up the braid, then tucked it behind her ear.

"What are you doing? Trying to make me into a hippie?"

"Too late." I snorted. "You're already a hippie."

Totally true. Since Uncle Gene left her a substantial inheritance from his insurance business, she was able to be the free spirit she always wanted to be. She moved back here, bought a rustic but roomy home on this quiet plot in Green Valley. The house was decorated in her eclectic style with homemade glass art that hung in the windows. She even had an actual, genuine cuckoo clock. But her little customized crochet business was what she loved the most and what identified her fun-loving spirit most of all.

"I just want you to find your own Gene one of these days." She glanced sheepishly from the rolling credits back to me. "Maybe that Jedediah Lawson would serve well."

"Aunt Polly," I stood, gathering our snack plates and my empty glass. "Jed and I are just, you know."

"No, not sure I do know. You've gone on two dates now and are gonna go on a third. And the smile you get when you talk about him."

"What smile?"

"The one you're wearing right now."

I scurried away to the kitchen. "Gotta get ready for work, Aunt Polly! No time to talk."

"You can run all you like, darlin'. But your heart catches up to you eventually."

"My heart?" I whispered to myself as I left the kitchen and hurried upstairs to slip on my work clothes.

I wasn't going to pretend, not even to myself, that I was beyond attracted to the man. But my heart wasn't involved. Was it? My hormones? Yes, indeed. But my heart had other plans. Ones that involved expanding my podcast business, finding a new job in a big city with a big salary and even an bigger benefits package so my parents wouldn't have to worry about me. So that *I* didn't have to worry about myself. I could finally prove to myself that I was the successful woman I always intended to be.

I opened my dresser and pulled out my clean denim mini-skirt and tossed it on the bed. I'd showered and everything, so I just needed to slip on my clothes and get going. I pulled my phone from the charger, noting quite a few notifications on *Kiss-n-Tell's* Twitter feed. I pulled off my t-shirt and tapped open Twitter. Then my mouth fell open.

@Belinda326: @kiss-n-tell OMG. Episode 53 rocked. Jed the fireman has a dreamy, delicious voice.

@JedRed: Thank you, @Belinda326. I didn't know voices were edible, but glad to know mine meets dreamy status.

@Belinda326: @JedRed On a scale from 1 to 10, it's fiya. DYING to hear about that hot kiss after date #3!

Instantly, my thighs went up in flames. "That man!" Pacing in my bedroom, half-naked, I scanned the many other comments on Twitter as well as Instagram, my body igniting with both embarrassment and lava-level arousal. Fans were saying things like "Lay it on her, @JedRed," and "I bet you're a 10...in bed." The balls of some people. And then the worst one, "If Lola passes on a 4th date, @SassySara is available. 😉"

"Look, Sassy Sara, you can just step *off*."

I threw my phone on the bed and stripped off my yoga pants, almost face-planting when I got the leg wrapped around my ankle. I stared at my phone like it was a viper as I tossed my dirty clothes in my hamper.

"Ugh! Sassy Sara can suck it," I muttered, pulling up my text messages before furiously sending one off to Jed.

ME: You can't hijack my podcast!

I JERKED my clean work shirt off the hanger and threw it on the bed when I saw the ellipses moving with a reply text. I grabbed my phone again.

JED: Hijack? Ma'am, that sounds a little hostile. Is someone overreaching?

"OVERREACHING?" I paced while texting. Oh, it must've been autocorrected.

ME: I am NOT overreacting. You're all over my Twitter and Instagram feed!

Jed: All over it, am I? In my defense, they tagged me first. Couldn't be rude to your fans.

Me: They seem to be more like *your* fans.

Jed: Are you jealous?

Me: No!

MAYBE. Okay, yes. But I wasn't admitting it.

JED: Have I broken some law that I'm not aware of, ma'am?

Me: Laws of social media etiquette, sir! Stop ma'aming me.

Jed: I apologize. I'll make it up to you. Saturday night. I promise.

. . .

I GLANCED at myself in the mirror in my bra and panties, suddenly feeling naughty talking to him about Saturday night in my underwear and thinking about his promises, imagining where he might put those promises. I threw my phone back on the bed and hurried to get dressed, twisting my hair into a messy bun and dabbing on some light make-up and chapstick.

Grabbing my phone and my purse, I jogged down the stairs, yelling, "Headed to work, Aunt Polly!"

"Drive safe, sweetheart!"

"Yes, ma'am!"

I pulled the door closed and jumped into my car. "Ma'aming me," I grumbled, backing out of the drive and heading to Bucky's. It was along the highway halfway between Green Valley and Merryville, a good ways away from Aunt Polly's outside of town. I sped just a tiny bit over the speed limit, knowing I'd make it by the skin of my teeth.

My phone vibrated where it sat on top of my purse, but I kept my eyes on the road and hands on the steering wheel until I came to the red light at the highway junction.

JED: Don't be mad at me. I thought it would be good for your ratings.

SIGHING, I glanced up at the light. Still red.

ME: Not mad. Just took me by surprise.

Jed: That women find me entertaining?

Me: That so many women now want to...light's grn

I DROPPED the phone and focused on the road the rest of the way to Bucky's even though my phone vibrated twice and tried to tempt me like the serpent in the garden. Swerving into the parking lot, I pulled into the back where the employees parked.

Grabbing the half-apron from the backseat, I tied it around my waist while standing outside the car, then pulled my bag on my shoulder and checked my texts as I walked toward the back entrance.

. . .

JED: Don't text and drive, Cola!

Jed: You're late for work, aren't you?

HOW WOULD he know my work schedule? And I was only five minutes late.

No time to ponder, I put my phone in my purse and tucked it in my employee cubby by the office.

"Hey, Mack!" I called out to our fry cook as I passed through the kitchen.

"Hurry, girl. Harold was looking for you."

"Shit," I muttered.

Harold was the night manager and a nice enough guy, but he was also a stickler about the rules. Tardiness was one of his pet peeves.

Bending down at the counter by the back register, I grabbed a pen and pad and stuck them in my apron, heading out to station three, my section for the night.

I crossed Jolie at the hostess station. Her eyes rounded as she whisper-yelled, "You've got a table."

"Couldn't you have waited till you saw me walk in?"

We weren't even busy yet. She could've sat another table till she saw me.

"Sorry! Harold sat them."

Dammit.

Pasting on my professional smile, I walked around the corner to my section of four-tops and almost tripped when I saw Jed sitting in one of my booths. No wonder he knew I was late for my shift. Some guy sat across from him with his back to me, but I didn't bother looking, unable to stop devouring Jed with my eyes.

Slowing my gait, I caught my breath as I walked toward him. That might've been a bad decision, because it gave him a nice long time to leisurely check me out from top to bottom and then back up again. I was a little breathless by the time I arrived at his table.

"Hi, there, Mr. Firefighter." I pulled out a pen and pad from my apron. "You off work?"

He had on what I gathered was his casual uniform—cargo pants and a navy blue t-shirt with the Green Valley Fire Department logo in one corner. Casual or not, it still made my chest sweat and knees shake.

"Thought I'd come check out Bucky's famous Tex-Mex burgers."

"Mmhmm," I nodded, tapping the back of my pen on the pad.

"You remember Wade," he gestured across the booth, his eyes never leaving me.

I turned politely to the auburn-haired behemoth that I'd met at the tailgate party. "Hi, Wade."

Then I noticed he was wearing some kind of uniform as well. I got a closer look at the emblem on the upper left corner.

"Didn't know you worked for the Wildlife Resources Agency. Wow." I smiled between them. "Two men in uniform. That's a treat."

Okay, I'd fallen into *crazy rambling* territory. Needed to calm myself down.

"Good to see you again, Lola," he said amiably, wearing a melty sort of smile that I'll bet scorched the panties off a number of Green Valley singles. Fortunately, the only one my panties wanted to fall off for was the man sitting across from him.

"Where's Jake tonight?"

"With his mama. I'd planned to have a quiet dinner at home, but this guy begged me to come with him to Bucky's for some strange reason. Now I know why."

Jed glared for all of two seconds at his friend before turning to me. "Fine, you caught me," he admitted casually. "I wanted to see you." Again, his eyes flickered down my bare legs before returning to my gaze. I suddenly found myself wishing date number three was right this flippin' second.

Clearing my throat, I tapped my pen nervously on the pad. "So, can I get you guys some drinks or do you want a minute?"

"Actually, we had a few minutes already," said Wade. "He wanted to be sure and get a spot in your section, so we've been here for fifteen minutes."

"Oh, I'm so sorry," I apologized.

"Shut up, Wade. It's fine." He turned to me before telling his friend, "Order, you rude asshat."

"Thank you. I will." He opened the menu back up. "I'll have the Texas Twister with extra jalapeños. And whatever domestic you have on draft."

"Got it. How about you, Jed?" He'd already put the menu back by the ketchup caddy.

"The bacon burger, hold the mayo, please. And whatever is on draft sounds good to me, too."

I scribbled it down then stopped suddenly. "Wait a minute. You don't like mayonnaise?"

"Hate it." He shook his head with a shiver.

"I'll take his mayo," said Wade. "Just slather it all on."

Jed curled his lip in disgust at Wade.

I couldn't help but laugh. "Mayo is awesome, Jed."

"No, Cola. Roller coasters are awesome. Chocolate ice cream is awesome. You are awesome. Mayo is, in fact, a repulsive gelatinous substance."

I shook my head, tucking my pen and pad back in my apron. "I think I might be Team Wade on this one." Then I sauntered off, hearing Wade chuckle and say something low under his breath.

I put in their order at the cook station, then waited at the bar for their beers.

"Nothing like two hotties to start off the night, eh?" The bartender Tara set the two frothy mugs in front of me.

"Yeah," I said with a smile, glancing across the restaurant at Jed's handsome profile as he listened to his friend Wade carry on about something.

"You oughta get some numbers off that one, then share with a friend." Tara winked.

"I'm actually dating one of them," I said, almost defensively.

Where was this anger coming from?

No. Not anger. Jealousy. I seemed to be laying claim to Jed all over the place this morning. I wanted Tara and Sassy Sara and everyone else to know we were dating. But, were we "dating"? That was an exclusive term, right? I should know. I was the dating podcast queen, and yet here I was, confused and wondering what we were doing.

We shouldn't be "dating" anyway. I'd received an email from the secretary of the CEO of Optimum Media in Houston yesterday afternoon. They wanted an online interview and would be contacting me soon with the date and time options. Their company focus was heavy on branding and social media marketing, which was right up my alley.

Honestly, from my recent success with the podcast and starting to monetize my YouTube channel, I had a lot of personal accolades to add to my resume, along with the experience at Clarks and Taylor. This was an exciting opportunity, and I honestly couldn't wait for the interview.

Then again, my mind was totally wrapped up in Jed. I figured he knew my stay in Green Valley was temporary, but then when he looked at me the way he did as I walked up to his booth a few minutes ago, there was something more there than blazing desire. I felt it pulling on me like a tug-of-war, and he was winning. I didn't want to ruin whatever this was while I was here, so I'd just keep the interview to myself. No need to worry about what-ifs at this point.

"Lucky girl," said Tara as I picked up the mugs then headed back to their table.

"Here you go, guys." I set them down, leaning a little to Jed's side of the booth. "It's Miller High Life. Hope that's okay."

Wade was already chugging his.

"That's fine," said Jed, drumming his index finger next to his mug. "What time do you get off?"

"I'm closing tonight, so it'll be around midnight by the time I get out of here."

He frowned and glanced toward the kitchen. "Someone walks you out, right? You don't walk out alone."

I bit my lip, trying not to smile at his obvious concern. "No, we always walk out with a buddy. The fry cook Mack could scare Bigfoot away."

His frown disappeared then he nodded. "Good."

Jolie sat me with a little elderly couple, her eyes bugging from behind Wade before she fanned her face like she was sweating.

I smiled. Yeah, they were hot. Got it, *loud and clear*.

"I'll be back in a bit."

I spent the next half hour tending to my new table, bringing the guys their burgers, greeting my next new table, and studiously trying to ignore the way Jed's eyes were burning holes through my clothes. My legs felt like they'd been licked with fire. Thankfully, rushing to and from the kitchen gave me a credible reason to be out of breath when I dropped off their check.

"I've got it," said Jed before Wade could even reach for his wallet. As he put his credit card on the tray, he looked up, "So, we're on for Saturday night, right?"

I placed a hand on my hip. "What, you thought I'd back out? I don't back away from a challenge."

Because we both knew the promise or "threat" of his kiss was a challenge.

He laughed, his left dimple popping, making my girlie bits all aflutter.

"Be right back," said Wade, excusing himself to the restroom with a smirk.

Jed's hand came up and tugged on mine, pulling me closer to the booth. I let him pull me till my knees hit the edge of his seat.

"I'm really looking forward to it." Our fingers were entangled, hanging by my side and out of view from my other customers, as he trailed his pinky along my outer thigh.

Screw Saturday! I wanted to straddle his lap and kiss the hell out of him right now.

"Where are you taking me?" I practically whispered.

"You'll see." His pinky finger swept softly over my skin, mesmerizing me along with his hazel eyes. "You'll need to wear some workout clothes."

"Workout clothes? The gym is not a sexy date, Jed."

He grinned. "Not working out." He squinted his eyes in thought. "Well, not really."

"It's not hiking, is it? I'm not sure if you're aware of this, but I'm not a big fan of strenuous exercise. I kind of loathe local pastimes like hiking and climbing mountains."

"Not hiking either." He grinned wider. "All strenuous exercise?" That pinky did another long sweep.

Face heating, I tipped my chin up. "Well...not *all*."

Lord in heaven. His hot look turned molten, practically incinerating me.

"Good to know," he growled nice and low.

Wade stepped up, saving me from embarrassing myself and saying something surely inappropriate like, *could I climb you?*

I stepped away and pulled my hand from his. "Nice to see you again, Wade." Then I turned to Jed, "Just text me the details. You guys have a good night."

I smiled and stepped away, stopping at one of my tables to check on them before hurrying back to the kitchen where I ducked by the dishwasher and caught my breath. Then I calmed myself down, rang Jed's credit card, then returned the receipt with a quick wave to him and Wade. My other table's food was about to come out so I had to hustle back to the kitchen. By the time I grabbed the platters for my other table and dropped them off, they were gone.

I bussed the table then picked up the credit card receipt, pausing when I saw a masculine scrawl at the bottom of the ticket. First, I blushed at the generous tip. Then I read the note at the bottom: *I need you to know that I REALLY want you to be on Team Jed. See you Saturday.* ☺

I couldn't help but walk on a cloud, giddy as a schoolgirl the rest of the night. Closing duties didn't even bother me a bit. I married those ketchup bottles, restocked the bar napkins, mopped down the kitchen station back line with a pep in my step and a song in my heart.

That song happened to be "Me Too" by Meghan Trainor, but no one knew that but me.

When I got home a little after midnight, I heard my phone buzz right before putting it in park. Aunt Polly had left the porch light on as always for me.

Jed: Did you get home okay?

My initial reaction was utter delight and a shameless grin that he checked to ensure I made it home safely. The second was that I was getting too caught up in this.

Me: I did. Thank you. Goodnight.

Jed: Night, Cola.

With a sweet, heavy sigh, I went inside and upstairs to bed, wondering what the hell I was doing.

Chapter Fourteen

-LOLA-

"Flirting is a fun part of the early dating phase." @kiss-n-tell
"Especially when the flirting is code for do me." @marlypants

I was perfectly prepared to *not* see Jed until Saturday. But I sure as hell wasn't prepared for what my eyeballs were going to witness that afternoon when Marly came tearing into my driveway like her ass was on fire.

"Marly's excited about something," Aunt Polly murmured with a glimpse out the living room window while she crocheted a polka-dotted pig toaster cozy.

I wandered out of the kitchen with a bag of Cheetos in my hand when Marly barged through the back door.

"Put that bag down, grab your shoes, and come with me."

Snapping her fingers for me to hurry up, she marched over and snatched my chip bag out of my hand, then tossed it on the counter. Hooking her arm through mine, she hauled me toward the door which still stood open.

"Wait, Marly! I've got orange fingers. Jeesh!" I squirmed out of her grip and went to wash my hands. "What the hell's going on?"

She bounced from foot to foot, her eyes wild with excitement. "I'm taking you to a show. Come on!"

"What kind of show is so dire that you can't keep your panties on?" I scrubbed my fingers clean under the kitchen faucet then dried my hands.

"Not telling. Hurry up, or we'll miss the best part!"

Aunt Polly's fingers froze on her knitting when she glanced up at Marly, squinting her eyes as if trying to remember something. "Oh, that's right. It's October." Then she smiled and went back to her crocheting.

"What is that supposed to mean?" I slipped on my Converse shoes at the back door. Aunt Polly didn't bother answering.

"Come on!" Marly grabbed my hand and dragged me out to her truck. Once buckled in, I said, "I don't suppose you're going to give me even a hint, are you?"

"Not even a teensy one."

I watched her bouncing in her seat, careening toward town, craziness in her eyes.

"I was about to take a shower and edit next week's episode," I grumbled like she'd put me out by dragging me who knows where.

To be honest, she had, because I was really looking forward to editing the last podcast recording. I wouldn't admit it to her, but listening to Jed's voice over and over while I edited out any audio hiccups was my newest obsession.

She didn't say a word, just turned up the radio blaring a fiery Carrie Underwood song— Marly loved her country music—as she drove straight down Main Street and turned left at City Hall, which was taking us back out into the middle of nowhere. I'd thought maybe there was something going on in the center of town, but she was headed back out past green fields. Then I saw it—the fire station.

"What in the world is going on?" I mumbled.

There was a beehive of activity going on next to the station as well as an audience in the open field across the street.

Marly giggled in that throaty, demonic way of hers as she pulled behind the line of cars parked along the road.

"Are those Cub Scouts?" I asked, staring at what had to be a troop of young boys and girls sitting in a semi-circle around two firemen in the grass next to the station.

A big guy I didn't know held up a fireman's mask while—yep, my throat went dry—Jed spoke to the kids, pointing out parts of the mask. Then the other guy lifted some sort of tank while Jed continued explaining the fire-fighting tools to them, apparently.

"What are we doing here? I'm not going to go sit with all the parents with their cub scouts on a field trip." A panicky note of embarrassment had made my voice squeaky.

Marly turned off the ignition and opened her door but remained seated while pointing to the field across the street. "Oh, those aren't parents."

"What are you talking about? Yes, they are."

"No, ma'am. You've been gone a while, and this right here is a little Green Valley tradition I didn't know existed back in high school." She pointed to the adults sitting in the field. "That is just about every mom and housewife in town. There may be a cub scout mom or two, sure, but apparently, this is a thing. Once a year, the cub scouts get a fire safety demonstration, and all the thirsty women of Green Valley come out to watch."

Marly slammed the door and pulled two folding chairs out of the bed of her truck, while I stared and observed the onlookers. Sure enough, they were all women. Maybe one or two dads. Some were sipping on drinks out of travel cups like they were on a beach watching the waves roll in. I climbed out of the truck.

"But what are they here for?" I glanced back over at Jed and the other fireman, now giving a lesson on using extinguishers, it seemed.

"You'll see." Marly laughed, carrying the two chairs. "Come on."

"I don't want Jed to see me here. What will he think of me stalking him like this?"

"Just trust me. You don't want to miss it."

But the thing was, when Marly said stuff like *just trust me*, it usually precluded some serious mischief. Like back when we got caught toilet paper rolling her PawPaw's house when we were twelve. We thought it was *so* funny, until we spent our entire Saturday morning peeling TP off the trees and the grass for hours while her PawPaw watched us from the porch, sipping his coffee and smiling. Or when we broke into her uncle's stash of whiskey at fifteen and were found passed out drunk in his barn with his goats. Or when we got caught skinny dipping in Bandit Lake by Sheriff Deputy Jackson James our senior year. That one was the worst!

"Trust me, she says," I mumbled but followed anyway. My curiosity was beyond piqued. "So, this is the Real Housewives of Green Valley?"

"Oh, yeah. They've all come for the show. And they aren't sipping on soda, mind you. That's afternoon cocktails to accompany the entertainment."

"Still don't see what's so entertaining."

"You will."

When Marly went to set up our chairs front and center, I yanked her arm and dragged her toward the back. "Not so obvious," I hissed.

Right as we took our seats, I then noticed a garbage dumpster parked on the other side of the brick fire station some ways into the neighboring lot on a slab of concrete. It was on the smaller side, not the big industrial kind. Some suited-up firemen were working around it, piling some lumber, what looked to be scraps from old furniture or something.

There was also a group of firemen in full gear loading onto the shiny fire truck parked right outside one of the three bays. There was an older engine in the second bay and an ambulance in the third.

About that same time, Jed and his partner motioned and said something to the cub scouts, leaving them under the watchful eye of Chief McClure, who'd been the only chief as far back as I could remember. Then Jed and the other big guy marched over to the firemen and geared up, too.

I thought my mouth was dry before. Jed unbuttoned and removed his short-sleeve uniform shirt, having a white T-shirt underneath. He pulled on the yellow protective coat and helmet one of the guys handed him, and then a siren went off in the firehouse.

The scouts had moved to the front of the lawn so they could watch what was taking place in the lot next door and from a safe distance. Jed hopped onto the firetruck and it rolled out, taking the short drive across the lot to the now burning dumpster. Apparently, they'd set it on fire while I was too busy ogling Jed. Flames licked high, as tall as a house.

My heart climbed up my chest and lodged in my throat. I was fully aware this was a safety demonstration and they'd likely done this a thousand times, but it didn't stop a flicker of fear from shooting through my veins. For the first time, I actually considered that Jed's choice of career was dangerous. I remembered the other night on our date and how he'd only shared the lighter, more humorous stories about his work. I wondered if that had been intentional, avoiding the more difficult topic of near-death experiences he might've had.

It was no mystery that fighting fires was a dangerous profession. But it just hadn't sunk in till this very second that when Jed was called out on a job, he was putting his life on the line. I wrung my hands in my lap, trying not to imagine what this might look like in real life. Or if this wasn't a controlled demonstration for the benefit of teaching the scouts fire safety.

I was relieved to watch the men working with quick efficiency, one climbing the ladder that extended from the truck, others assisting with the hoses, and all of them communicating effectively. The demonstration required them to work as a unit and tackle the fire from every angle of the dumpster.

One guy used the hose from the top of the ladder, while men helped carry the behemoth and maneuver it from the bottom. Jed and the others worked together to haul two other hoses around the fire, slowly dousing the flames. While my heart hammered, I was impressed at how well they worked together. It seemed like only a short time, but it actually took over thirty minutes for them to completely extinguish the fire to smoldering ash.

Marly was right. "Wow. That was impressive."

A pretty Black woman sitting in a chair in front of us half-turned to say, "You haven't seen anything yet."

She wore her hair in a bun, but wispy curls escaped to frame her face.

Leaning forward, I asked her, "That wasn't the whole show?" Because the poor guys looked exhausted. What more could they possibly demonstrate for these kids?

She turned back to me, her almond-shaped eyes twinkling with a mischievous glint. "You see the one on the end, supervising? With the axe?"

I caught sight of the tall, lean, dark-haired man near the same height as Jed standing off to the side. "Yeah."

"He's with me. So don't get any ideas, ladies." She gave us a smile, a dimple popping before swiveling back around and sipping from her water bottle.

What did that mean? I didn't come out here to ogle men or anything. Then I caught the expression on Marly's face.

"Why the hell are you grinning like that?"

"Just watch."

She motioned to the firefighters now climbing onto the fire truck to ride the short distance back to the station. The truck stopped along the side of the station, where the men stepped off and started stripping gear. And their undershirts that were soaked through with sweat.

"Holy cannoli," I whispered.

"You got that right," smiled Marly, all proud of herself. "Welcome to the annual man-meat show."

I was horrified and stupefied and in complete danger of swallowing my own tongue. I hoped there was a defibrillator in that ambulance just in case.

The shirtless models—I mean, firefighters—were sharing a garden hose on the side of the building, splashing their hair and faces. And of course, because of the lovely force of gravity, the water was sliding in tantalizing rivulets down their chiseled pectorals and abdominals as well as their muscled backs.

My gaze was riveted on Jed. *Good gracious almighty!* I was in so much trouble. Imagining what he looked like underneath his clothes didn't compare to the magnificent reality.

Some of the men continued to haul their gear back inside while others strolled over to the group of scouts, one carrying a charred piece of wood, telling them who knows what. There was so much skin and muscle on display, my breath had decided to up and vacate my lungs and not return.

After a moment of shock, I glanced around at the ladies of Green Valley, chatting or not while watching the firefighters move around and haul gear, displaying their muscular assets. Most of the onlookers, or ogle-lookers rather, were sauntering back to their cars, too. The actual moms of the scouts were strolling across the street to gather their kids.

I nudged Marly, whispering, "Let's sneak out of here."

She rolled her eyes. "Don't you want to go over and talk to Jed?"

"No, I do not."

The very thought of standing there and trying to explain why I was here toppled the most embarrassing moment of my life with Jed—aka locking my keys in my car—like a stack of toy blocks.

I stood and folded my chair swiftly.

"You know Jed?" asked the woman who'd been sitting in front of us.

When I did nothing but stare at her like a hare in headlights, she offered her hand. "I'm Sierra Betts."

"Hi." I shook her hand. "Lola Landry."

"Marly Rivers," added my friend/torturer, shaking her hand as well. "Yeah, she's dating Jed."

I shot Marly a look, which she ignored.

"Nice." Sierra laughed. "Jed's a good guy."

I nodded and swallowed hard, unable to do anything but agree. "He is."

Her intelligent gaze obviously caught the panic in my expression as I kept glancing toward the fire house. She seemed to understand that Jed and I weren't dating long enough that him catching me here would be anything but completely humiliating.

"Good luck to you, Lola." She folded her chair and walked toward the fire station.

"Come on," I hissed to Marly, speed-walking back to the car.

Right as we reached the street to take a hard left and escape to Marly's truck, Jed appeared from the side of the fire station where they'd been collecting gear. He was headed over to join the guy talking to the scouts when the most dreadful thing happened. He saw me.

Pulse plummeting, I ducked my head as if that would help and pushed Marly to walk faster.

"Lola!"

"*Shit.*"

Marly laughed.

"I'm going to kill you," I murmured before turning around to face the executioner, who in this case looked akin to a Greek Adonis rather than the grim reaper.

"I'll wait by the car," she called sweetly.

I would've protested further, but Jed was near the end of the drive on his side of the street. I glanced beyond his shoulder where the dark-haired, well-tanned, axe-wielding guy swept Sierra into a big hug, lifting her off her feet and planting a kiss on her lips. They looked so cute and natural together. That's because she belonged here. I didn't. I looked like a stalker. *Jeez*, this was embarrassing.

Swallowing down my dignity, I lifted my chin and walked across the street to where *shirtless* Jed waited with his hands low on the hips of his dark cargo pants and a knowing smile on his handsome face.

"Fancy meeting you here," he said when I finally reached him.

"Fancy that," I sassed back.

I tried monumentally hard to force my eyes to behave, but they were currently mapping the extensive breadth of his chest without my permission. As a matter of fact, they'd found their newest obsession, tracking the descent of a drop of water that looped around his navel and froze midway down his happy trail.

"What brings you here, Cola?"

I jerked my gaze back to his mischievous grin, contemplating ways to torture my best friend.

I was also debating whether leaning forward and licking him would be inappropriate. "Um, learning fire safety?"

His bark of laughter and dimpled smile detonated somewhere inside my chest and melted my insides into warm goo. Which, of course, drew my attention to his beautiful mouth and the fact that he intended to kiss me with that mouth on our next date.

"Let me guess," he finally said, amusement still prevalent in every word. "Marly?"

"So, I've been wondering if stretching her on a rack would be forgiven by local law enforcement. Do you think they'd give me a free pass, considering," I waved my hand at him and the surrounding scene behind him, "all this?"

"By this, you mean dragging you to watch a dozen firemen strut around without their shirts on?"

"So y'all do know that half of Green Valley's womenfolk are gawking at you from across the street, right? Only half of which are actual moms of the scouts? If that."

He nodded and exhaled a sigh, but that wicked smile remained in place. "Chief McClure said it's a local tradition, and the fine ladies of Green Valley also donate generously to our annual fundraiser, so we just do as we're told."

"Basically, this is a Magic Mike show, minus the actual lap dances, where you get your tips at a later time."

He edged closer, my eyes betraying me once again to dip down along his beautiful body, realizing that delectable drop of water had slipped down into the holy land.

"I'll give you a lap dance for free if you like, Lola."

Biting my lip, I forced my gaze up to his, noting the darkened look of lust glinting there. He lifted his hand to trail a finger along the underside of my chin, then the pad of his thumb swept underneath my bottom lip, pressing into the curve just below. I was completely frozen, thinking I was going to get that kiss before our Saturday date, internally flipping cartwheels at my great fortune and high-fiving Marly instead of planning her demise.

Without warning, he grabbed my hand and tugged me toward the fire station. "Come on, let me give you a tour."

"No, I can't." I pointed over my shoulder. "Marly's waiting."

"Hey, Marly!" he bellowed so loud a dozen heads swiveled toward us, including Marly's. "I'm gonna give her a quick tour!"

Marly nodded and gave us a thumbs up from where she was sticking the chairs in the bed of her truck.

Jed grinned down at me. "I just want to show you around real quick."

"Fine." I acted all put out while my gaze was still soaking in his shirtless loveliness.

And he damn well knew it. He led me through the open garage, one newer firetruck still out of the bay.

I tugged my hand free, feeling a little self-conscious, and glanced around. "So, where's your pole?"

Wincing at how that sounded, I peeked over at him. Sure enough, he was grinning like the devil himself.

"I mean, you know what I mean," I stammered, a blush heating my cheeks.

"Lola, if you want to see my pole, all you've got to do is ask. I'll show it to you anytime you want."

"Shut. Up." I playfully backhanded his abs which he flexed, reminding me how rock hard they were when my hand bounced off.

Chuckling, he said, "It's right over there."

Sure enough, there was a shiny silver pole toward the corner by the ambulance bay. Then he led me toward the door that opened into the firehouse. That's when my attention snagged on a plaque. I stepped closer, thinking it was some award or something. But it wasn't.

It was a tribute plaque to a firefighter who died in the line of duty. My heart dropped rapidly into my stomach and I suddenly felt sick. My emotions ping-ponged from unbridled lust to stark fear in a millisecond.

"Did you know him?" I asked, reading the dates. I was working in New Orleans when it happened.

"No. He was gone before I arrived here. But Forrest Winters, the federal fire marshal, sometimes comes around on poker nights and shares stories about him. They were best friends." Jed's voice had softened and sobered too. "He was a good firefighter. A good man."

"I didn't—" I cleared my throat, which had suddenly become rusty. "I hadn't given much thought to how scary your job is. How dangerous."

He stared down at me, his warm gaze caressing my face. He tucked a lock of my hair behind my ear.

"It is. It's an important job, though. I don't mind the risk."

I did. But did I have a right? He didn't belong to me. All I could do was nod, too afraid to say something else that would betray the emotions swimming inside me.

He smiled and took my hand again. "Come on, Lola. Let me show you around."

So he took me on a quick tour. He paraded me through a large main room with a giant flatscreen TV and cushy couches, some of the guys already changed and relaxed, watching ESPN.

"Aren't you going to introduce your girl?" one of the guys called as Jed pushed me down a hallway.

"Nope!" he yelled back.

Masculine laughter echoed in the TV room.

"Ashamed of me, are you, Jed?" I teased.

"Don't want those bastards flirting with you." He pointed to a door and kept pushing me past it. "That's the locker room, which is full of naked men right now so—"

I spun around, pretending to go for the door. "I'd love a tour of the locker room right now."

He hauled me over his shoulder like a caveman and marched on down the hall.

I squealed. "Put me down, Jedediah!"

His big hand was clamped over the back of my jean-clad thigh, and oh my, did I enjoy the feel of him gripping me possessively.

All of a sudden, I was slung off his back and tossed onto a mattress. He came down on top of me quickly, pinning me hard and caging me in with his big body. He scooped both hands into my hair, cradling my skull, and stared down at me.

"This is where we get some sleep when we need to," he whispered.

I couldn't speak. The sensation of having his hot, shirtless—and very hard—body on top of me stunned me stupid and speechless, apparently. His gaze swept my face, fixating on my mouth.

"I've fantasized about kissing this mouth so often," he whispered, voice low and husky, his thumb brushing across my lips now. "You just have no idea what torture is."

Immobilized by the soft touch of his fingers cupping my jaw and the gentle, promising sweep of his thumb, I managed to say, "Sometimes it's better just to make your fantasies a reality. The only way to alleviate that torture."

Kiss me!

"You don't say." Whiskey-brown eyes held me captive as he eased closer. The heat of his glorious chest radiated against me as he lowered his face, mere inches from mine. But before his lips brushed my mouth, he dipped his head lower, his nose grazing the underside of my jaw as he inhaled. Then those lips brushed my ear. "I plan to make that fantasy a reality once and for all."

I lifted my arms from my sides, resting my hands on his waist, fingers happily sliding over warm skin. I nearly moaned. Then he did, rocking his pelvis forward, the hard bulge in his pants pressing against my thigh and sucking all the saliva I had left in my mouth.

He lifted his head, eyes glittering darkly. His jaw clenched again as he closed his eyes.

This was finally it! He dropped his head closer, lips ghosting within reach.

"Saturday, Cola." His thumb brushed the crease of my slightly parted lips, grazing over my bottom teeth and tongue before he eased out and massaged the wet pad along my bottom lip.

Then he clenched his jaw again and suddenly lifted off me, hauled me back over his shoulder, and marched me back through the firehouse and downstairs.

"Bye, pretty girl," said one of the guys on a sofa, that big fireman who'd been teaching the Cub Scouts with Jed on the lawn earlier.

At least, it looked like him from what I could tell upside down. "Bye!" I waved.

Once outside and back on my feet, he steadied me since I was a little dizzy. And not just from being tossed around like a sack of potatoes.

The smoldering heat in his gaze made sensuous, dark promises when he repeated in a low, husky voice. "Saturday."

Then he turned and marched back toward the firehouse, making me watch him go. And I wasn't mad about it even a little bit. I stared shamelessly at the expanse of back muscle on display and the firm curve of his ass under those cargo pants as he swaggered off. Yeah, that man knew how to swagger.

A horn honking nearly made me jump out of my skin. I turned to see Marly laughing in the driver's seat of her truck. For once, I was extremely grateful for her shenanigans. Saturday couldn't come quickly enough.

Chapter Fifteen

-JED-

I was aware that I was nervous-tapping on the steering wheel, but I couldn't help it. For one, Lola was sitting in the passenger seat wearing black yoga pants, a sports bra, and a loose-fitting tank that barely went past her hips, torturing me with her amazing curves. And second, I was well aware that she hated physical activity.

She would do anything in freshman PE to get out of sports involving running. She even offered to clean and organize the coach's office, which always worked. She was a savvy negotiator even back then.

And though we wouldn't be doing any running, I didn't want her to be uncomfortable trying something physical that might make her feel awkward. On the other hand, I was dying to get there and get started just so I could get my hands on her.

"Not gonna tell me, are you?" she asked with a smile.

"We're here," I said, swinging us into the parking lot of Cage Erickson's gym.

"Wait. Is that the gym of that former MMA fighter Viking hottie?"

I arched an eyebrow at her. "Viking hottie?"

"My Aunt Polly's description. And I thought you said we weren't going to a gym?"

"I meant that we weren't working out. Not like you're thinking."

She hopped out of the car, scowling at the gym like it was the gate to hell.

"Come on," I laughed, reaching out my hand. "Trust me."

Still frowning, she took my hand. I led her around to the side entrance where Tempest told me to go. I didn't want to parade Lola through a gym full of buff guys while she was wearing that outfit anyway. I knew I had no right to feel this possessive of her, but it didn't stop my caveman instincts one little bit.

Opening the door for her, I let her go in ahead of me, not even trying to resist getting a good look at her glorious ass.

Shit. I looked away and thought of doing laundry and washing my truck. Otherwise, this lesson was going to get awfully uncomfortable trying to hide my hard-on.

Breathing deep, I waved to Tempest who was setting out the mats in this room she said was used for private lessons. She said Cage didn't mind us using it.

"Hey, guys! Good to see you, Jed." Tempest walked over, a bright smile on her face.

"Hey. So, this is Lola Landry."

"Hi, there." She reached out and shook her hand. "Nice to meet you." Then she clapped her hands together. "Okay, you guys ready to get started? I've gotta get back to Donner Bakery in an hour."

"Actually," said Lola, "I have no idea what we're getting started on. So that would be really helpful."

She didn't seem annoyed, but she crossed her arms and arched a brow at me to let me know she wasn't taking another step till she knew what was going on. Somehow, the fact that she hated surprises, or maybe it was the fact that I knew she hated surprises, made me want to laugh at her. But I didn't dare.

"Tempest is going to give a lesson in self-defense."

"Really?" She quirked her head to the side, her curly ponytail swinging against her shoulders. "I've never had one before."

I tamped down my simmering frustration at her response. She'd lived in New Orleans, which was far more dangerous than Green Valley. But that didn't mean there weren't dangers lurking around here.

"Well, you need it." My tone was a touch too authoritative, but I couldn't help it.

Lola propped her hands on her hips. "What is that supposed to mean?"

I squared off, keeping my hands at my sides. "Because someone I know sometimes locks her keys in her car and could find herself in an unsafe situation."

I hadn't told her or anyone else that I'd stayed up half the night after our first reunion when I unlocked her car door. I kept imagining all the most horrific scenarios of what could've happened if the wrong person came along to help her out of her jam instead of me.

We weren't riddled with criminals around here or anything, but a pretty girl needing a helping hand, and who happened to be overly trusting, might get herself into a situation she couldn't get out of. We had more than one motorcycle gang prowling the lonely roads of these mountains. Not all those guys were bad, but some were. I'm just glad none of the rougher elements of Green Valley stumbled across her at the near-empty gas station that day before I got there.

She opened her mouth to snap at me, then she stopped, seeing something in my expression. "You were worried about me that day?"

Not trusting myself if we started talking about that day—remembering the sleepless night it gave me after—I gave a quick nod then cleared my throat. "Besides, I made all my sisters take them, especially my younger sisters Bekah and Sam. Those two have a habit of finding trouble."

Lola smiled. "I know Bekah works at Green Valley Shine with Marly. What's Sam up to these days?" she asked, slowly following Tempest toward the mat.

"She's in her junior year at UT. Lives and works a part-time job in Knoxville."

"So big brother forced self-defense lessons on them, did he?"

"He did."

"And you don't think I can take care of myself? Look at these muscles."

She flexed her arm where a minuscule bicep muscle barely made a bump on her slender arm. I couldn't help but reach out and wrap my fingers around her bicep, enclosing it completely.

"Impressive," I said in all seriousness.

She laughed and wiggled away when I squeezed. "That tickles."

"You're ticklish?" My brows shot up.

"Oh, no, you don't, Jed. This lesson is over if you try to tickle me." She put her hands up in karate-chop fashion.

Now I was laughing. "No tickling. I promise." I crossed my heart. "Tonight."

She narrowed her eyes at me.

"Okay, you two, let's get going. I've got a new cupcake recipe I'm dying to try out back at the bakery."

Something squeezed inside my chest as I glanced over at Lola, readying herself on the mat, all serious and adorable.

"What do I do?" she asked, her eyes alight with learning something new.

This is what I loved about her. Even in a situation I knew she wasn't entirely comfortable in, she faced it with eagerness and optimism.

"First, let's talk about some basic self-defense knowledge." Tempest went on for a while about not making yourself an easy target, like avoid grocery shopping alone at night, make sure to park in well-lit places, walk with your head high and always on the alert, keep your keys with the pointy-end between your knuckles to use as a weapon if you don't carry pepper spray. When she'd finished, she said, "Okay, let's try the first move. I'll try it on Jed first, but this is the basic self-defense move when someone tries to grab you from behind. Jed?"

I'd attended these classes with my sisters, so I knew what to do. I maneuvered behind Tempest and wrapped my arms around her chest, then she quickly latched onto my arms, bent over, shifted her weight back, and flipped me onto my side on the ground.

"Oh! Jed, are you okay?" Lola looked actually stricken.

"Fine," I smiled, popping back up. "I've been knocked down a lot harder than that."

Lola shook her head. "I can't do that, Tempest. You've got some kind of superhero strength or something. Jed is so much bigger than me."

"Doesn't matter," said Tempest. "He's bigger than me, too. It's all about getting him off-balance and shifting your weight, using the strength of your legs to knock him down. You may not be able to flip him, but I'll bet you can knock him down. At least to the side like I did."

She nodded as she listened to Tempest, watching her slowly model the move without me one more time. Then she glanced at me.

"Stop smiling, Jed." That cute frown was back.

"Yes, ma'am."

"And no ma'aming me." She pointed a finger.

I nodded and motioned for her to turn around. "Let's give this a try."

"Don't grab me hard," she warned.

"What? You think an attacker is going to go easy on you?"

"Just go slow the first time."

"That's fine," said Tempest, "good idea. Just get a feel for it in slow motion, then we'll try it for real."

As soon as I moved up behind her, I yet again thought this might've been a mistake. Having her body this close was shredding my willpower. Then I zoned in on her reddish birthmark along the curve of her shoulder and neck. The one that I'd stared at and memorized when she would go to her locker below mine.

I brushed a finger along the amorphous shape, wanting to replace my finger with my mouth. It had a semi-roundness with a trail of reddish freckles behind it.

"What?" asked Lola, looking over her shoulder. "Do I have something on me?"

I shook my head, licking my lips. "I just remember this birthmark so well."

"You do?" she seemed confused, then she caught my gaze and had to recognize the heat simmering there. She huffed a laugh. "I always thought it looked like a slug. Called it slug-a-bug when I was little. That's why my Dad gave me that silly nickname."

"Funny. I never saw that."

"What did you see?" Her ocean-green eyes appeared endless, bewitching.

"A shooting star."

And she had no idea how many times I'd wished upon it. A wish that looked something like this, that felt a lot like this moment.

"Tick-tock, you two," said Tempest from farther off the mat. "Let's give it a go, Lola."

She snapped her head forward and I wrapped my arms around her. She grabbed my arms like Tempest had, then bent forward and did nothing to shift her weight, so all she did was press her ass directly back into my crotch.

"It's not working, Tempest!"

Oh, it was working alright.

"You have to step back with this foot and shift your weight, then pull him over," Tempest called from the sidelines.

I started laughing as she tried it again and again. By the fourth try, she actually managed to make me lose my balance and fall to the side, but I dragged her down with me. She landed in a sweet-smelling heap on top of my chest, both of us laughing. Till we weren't.

I had my hands on her hips and my eyes on her mouth.

My voice was husky with desire when I finally asked, "Is this good contact for a third date, Cola?"

She stared at my mouth, unsmiling.

"Not bad, not bad," said Tempest, clapping. "Now, let's try something else."

The next move required her to escape me when I grabbed her arm from the side, which she managed to master really quickly, slipping out of my grasp like a wiggle worm. It wasn't as artfully done as Tempest's demonstration, but still effective, which I found impressive but also adorable.

The last move was when you're attacked from the front, which required her to knee me in the groin to escape. Tempest taught her how to stabilize her attacker, me, by bracing my shoulders then using full momentum with weight on the back leg to knee upward. Of course, she was to stop before her knee actually made contact. I couldn't help but flinch, even in the slow-motion first round.

"Okay, now in real-time!" called Tempest from the side.

"What's wrong?" she asked, widening her eyes all innocently. "You nervous or something?" Blink, blink, blink.

"Cola," I warned, "don't even think about it."

"Or what?"

"You'll regret it."

She grinned as Tempest clapped her hands once together, signaling us to start. I lunged for her and grabbed her waist. She quickly maneuvered to plant the heels of her hands just below my shoulders and pushed to hold me away from her, then shifted and plunged her knee upward. She stopped her upward thrust barely in time, still grazing my balls. I fell in a heap and curled away from her, pretending she'd done serious damage.

"Oh, my God!" She was on her knees, grabbing my arm. "So sorry, so sorry! I stopped, but you—"

I rolled over and flipped her beneath me in a millisecond. Pinning both her wrists with one hand, I gave her a pitiful look.

"I warned you, Cola. You broke the rules."

"What!"

Before she could even register what I was going to do, I tickled her ribs with my free hand. She squealed and wiggled, arching her neck and laughing like mad.

"Say you're sorry," I demanded, barely curling my fingers into her ribs while she lost her mind.

"Sorry!" she screamed, roaring with laughter.

"I'm not sure if you're sincere enough." I curled my fingers again on the side of her ribs.

"I'm sincerely so, so sorry! Please, stop, please!"

I stopped, letting her catch her breath, which only made this position impossibly worse. I'd automatically pressed down with my body to keep her still. Feeling her sweet, soft body beneath mine was suddenly more agonizing than anything I could imagine.

Her panting slowed, green eyes fixed on my mouth. "Jed," she whispered.

"Yeah."

Her chest rose and fell, pressing into mine, speeding my pulse. "When am I gonna get that kiss?"

I lifted my gaze from her full, pink lips back to her eyes, black swamping the green. I wanted to kiss her so fucking bad, but it wasn't going to happen yet. I wanted her to crave it as bad as I did. I wanted her to feel the torture of burning, unfulfilled longing like I had back in school. And though I was sure nothing could make her want me as bad as I wanted her, I was going to torment her as long as possible.

I dipped my head lower, feeling the heat of her lips against mine. "Patience is a virtue, Cola."

"I've never been good at that virtue."

"I know." Then I eased up and helped her onto her feet.

Tempest stood there with arms crossed, smirking. "Session is over, guys. Good job, Lola. Even if the Neanderthal cheated by tickling you."

"Thanks, Tempest." She tightened her ponytail, and her cheeks flushed pink. "I doubt a real attacker would figure out that weakness of mine."

She laughed at the thought, but then a deep pang of protectiveness hit me at the idea of someone actually attacking her. Again. I'd known where my feelings were going ever since our day in Nashville, but I had no idea they'd taken hold so fiercely.

"You okay?" she asked, putting a hand on my arm.

"Yeah." I smiled. "Let's go grab some dinner."

We thanked Tempest and headed out the way we came while she locked up.

Once back on the road, Lola glanced down at her attire. "I hope we aren't going anywhere fancy."

"You're dressed just fine. But it may get chilly as the sun goes down. I've got a sweatshirt in the back if you want."

"That would be great."

I reached back and found my black zip-up hoodie and tossed it on her lap. Then I tried to focus on the road as I watched her slip into it. Another wave of possessiveness washed over me, loving having her in something of mine. Maybe Tempest was right, I was a Neanderthal. My thoughts kept wandering to very possessive places, and we hadn't even kissed yet. Not long to see what that would be like, though. If it came anywhere close to my fantasies, then Lola Landry was in serious trouble.

"So, how'd you like the lessons?"

"It was really fun, actually," she admitted with a cheery smile, glancing out the window as we wound up the mountain. "Don't tell Marly, though. She'll think I've finally fallen over to the dark side, enjoying fitness and whatnot."

"You'll have to admit it on the podcast."

She twisted her head to face me, a curly lock falling across one eye. "Oh, yeah." She tucked it back behind her ear.

"You forgot this was a podcast date?" I couldn't help grinning at the fact.

"Guess I did for a minute there." She huffed a nervous laugh and tucked her hands in the pockets of my sweatshirt.

Tension stretched in the silence, and I wasn't about to interrupt it. I was hoping Lola would take note that there was something more going on here. I knew it full well, but I wasn't sure if she did.

I pulled into the parking lot of Daisy's Nut House. Not many cars in between lunch and dinner, which is what I'd hoped. Daisy's was a hot spot for locals, but I'd timed it so that we might have a bit more privacy in the early afternoon.

"Fancy," said Lola with a cheeky grin.

"You don't approve?"

"I highly approve," she said before hopping out. "Daisy's is my favorite."

"I know," I mumbled under my breath as I got out on my side. She'd always arrive at school with a to-go bag of donuts, which had me frequenting the diner myself, hoping to catch a glimpse of her. Every now and then, I was lucky and bumped into her there on the weekends. Most of the time, I was too shy to approach her, so I'd just sit in a corner booth and stare at her taking an eon to choose a piece of pie to go with her take-out meal. She'd pretend she didn't see me, but I knew she did.

And here we were, now walking side by side into Daisy's together, her shoulder brushing my arm as we headed to the door. I held it for her, then I steered her to the booth in the back, preparing myself to make a little confession to her. Country music twanged around us, but like I'd hoped, it was pretty much empty this early.

"Hey, you two," called Daisy from behind the counter. "I'll be with you in a minute."

"No rush," I said with a wave as we settled into our booth.

"What's wrong?" asked Lola, her brows raised in question or perhaps concern.

"Nothing." I exhaled a heavy sigh, picking up the menu, frowning at it, then putting it back.

She laughed lightly under her breath. "Really? Because you seem awfully nervous all of a sudden."

I shouldn't be nervous about telling her. It wasn't anything I was ashamed of, and still, my heart drummed hard against my ribcage.

"Well, hello, stranger," said Daisy, smiling at me. "I haven't seen you in a while."

I smiled thankfully at Daisy, owner of this locally loved diner. Both for the fantastic food and doughnuts as well as the welcoming, hometown vibe of the place. "Been busy lately."

"Good to see you two together. So you finally decided to give it a go, did you?"

"What?" We both asked at the exact same time.

Daisy laughed and shook her head. "Oh, to be young and oblivious. What can I get you two?"

"Burger and fries, like usual. No mayo. And water."

"Alrighty. And you, missy?"

"Um," Lola had been looking at the menu but flipped it closed and said, "That sounds fine to me, too. But extra mayo, please." She grinned across the table at me.

"Comin' right up." Daisy sauntered off.

I leaned back and tapped my hand on the wooden tabletop, sighing heavily. "You're really not going to make Team Jed material that way, Cola."

"Oh?" She put on her serious, professional face, tucking her hands in her lap. "Let's just say that I *would* want to be on Team Jed, what would be the requirements?"

Folding my forearms on the table, I shifted forward. "First, you have to enjoy watching and attending football games."

"Wait a minute. I need to take notes." She opened an invisible notebook and poised her invisible pen over the tabletop. "Okay, ready. What else?" she asked in all seriousness.

I really wanted to drag her over the table and onto my lap so I could kiss the fuck out of her right then and there. Instead, I put on my own serious face and continued with my list.

"You have to agree to go grocery shopping with ornery grandmas on Friday nights."

Her lips creased her pretty face ever so slightly as she "jotted" down her notes. "Go on."

Daisy dropped our waters off. Lola flattened her palms on the table until Daisy swished back to the counter, then she picked up her invisible pen again. She was so dorky and cute I could hardly stand it.

"You'd have to love dogs."

"Yellow labs, to be specific, right?" Her lips tipped up in a sweet smile, breaking the veneer of pretending professionalism.

"Right." I took a sip of water, crunching on a piece of ice. "You'll have to come and meet him."

She blinked nervously then tapped her invisible pen on the table. "Back to the list."

"Right. So you'd have to enjoy Sunday barbecues and Saturday nights on the sofa watching a movie." I let my voice drop to an intimate level so that she understood those Saturday nights would be for us alone.

She blushed as she sipped her water. "What kind of movie?"

"Anything Avengers."

"Oh, you're a Captain America fan?"

"I'm more of an Iron Man guy, but Cap is cool, too."

"And what if your Team Jed partner doesn't care for the Avengers?"

"Has this partner actually ever watched an Avenger movie?"

Her eyes went skyward as she seemed to be trying to remember. "Maybe half of one?"

"I can't believe what I'm hearing. We need a movie night," I demanded with exasperation. "You can't discount the Avengers till you've actually given them a shot."

"Mm, maybe," she said, glancing away, obviously not sure she wanted to be alone with me on my sofa. She would be, though.

Daisy delivered our burgers, and we dove in, sitting quietly for a while.

"So, are you going to tell me?" she asked, wiping her mouth with a napkin.

"Tell you what?"

"Whatever it was you were thinking about when we walked in."

I glanced down at my plate and stuffed some fries in my mouth.

No. I wasn't going to tell her that tonight. I thought I could, but seeing her resistance to the idea of another date, a more private one at my place, had me skittish about opening up. But I could confess something else.

I ate the last bite of my burger, then leaned back in the booth.

Chapter Sixteen

-LOLA-

"My new boyfriend started talking dirty the first time we had sex. I don't know if I like it. What do I do?" @Jazzgirl
"Send him to my house." @marlypants

Charged silence. I'd never experienced anything like this. Not on the doorstep of giving a marketing proposal, not on that unfortunate ride in the elevator with my boss down to the lobby the day I was fired, not even in the wake of telling my Dad I was moving to New Orleans after college graduation. Nothing compared to the goosebump-raising electricity in the cab of Jed's SUV on the way back to my house. Thankfully, the drive was short.

When he unfolded out of the truck to walk me to the door, he wore that same hard expression he had after our first date, the man-on-the-warpath demeanor. I left his sweatshirt on the passenger seat and followed him to the porch.

I hadn't responded to his declaration at Daisy's. What could I say? *Hell, yes, I want you to want me!* That felt selfish when I knew this little affair could only be short-lived. I had heard from Optimum Media, and they'd said they'd be setting up interviews soon. If I got a job offer and the salary was competitive, I'd be a fool to stick around Green Valley. For what? For the remote possibility that my high school nemesis/obsession might turn out to be "the one"?

I had bills and responsibilities and a duty to my parents to make the right decisions for my future. I had a duty to myself to chase those dreams of being a top earner and securing my finances before I was thirty so my parents could finally retire knowing they wouldn't have to bail me out anymore.

I didn't want them to worry anymore. I wanted them to see me standing on my own two feet without the help of Aunt Polly. I didn't want Dad slyly sliding a hundred in my purse every now and then because he was worried I couldn't make it on my own. The guilt of being a burden was crushing. My bruised and battered pride was another problem. I wanted to be on top again, to show the world, and myself, that I was the success I was always supposed to be.

And then I turned around at the front door and saw the paralyzing magnificence of a hot-as-hell Jedediah.

"I really enjoyed our date," I practically whispered. I couldn't help it. My pulse rushed at a maddening pace, and I could feel the tension like a giant rubber band squeezing around my chest.

"I'm glad you did," he said, standing there stern and grave, fire sparking in his hazel eyes.

I waited, sure he would step closer and kiss me, but he stared a second more, then nodded. "I'll see you for the podcast then."

His voice was deep and dark, his shoulders tight and rigid.

My heart was sad and exasperated. "I guess so."

To my complete and utter shock, he turned and walked away. I couldn't do anything but stand there in a stupor watching him. He was really leaving without giving me the long-awaited kiss? But when he got to the stairs of the porch, he turned.

"Oh, yeah. I forgot something."

Then he came for me. Before I had a second to register the hungry look tightening his expression, his mouth was on mine.

Oh, my sweet, baby Jesus. Jed's mouth.

His fist was around my ponytail, tugging to get me where he wanted me. He slanted his mouth to go deeper, his tongue stroking mine on a guttural groan. I may have whimpered helplessly as I dug my fingers into his shirt, trying to pull him closer.

His hands slid to the backs of my thighs till he cupped my behind, then he lifted and pressed me to the door. His mouth devoured me with fierce possession, humming his approval when I wrapped my legs around his waist so he could settle right where I wanted him.

Squeezing my ass, he lifted one hand to my nape, his large hand wrapping the entire back of my skull.

"Fuck, Lola," he grated harshly, biting down my neck, nipping all the way over my tank top and one breast till he clamped his lips over my clothed nipple. Then his teeth, teasing it to a peak beneath the fabric.

Hissing, I fisted his hair to hold him there, damning myself for having clothes on. *Who invented clothes?* I rocked my hips, moaning at the friction of his hardness between my thighs.

Then he came back to my mouth, slowing down, sweeping his tongue and lips over mine, pinning me to the door with his ginormous, heavenly body.

I felt like I'd been dipped in turpentine, and he'd lit a match then tossed it on me. To say I was on fire seemed inadequate. I'd think we'd fallen into a hot pit of hell, but it felt way more like heaven. All of my imaginings of kissing Jed had never amounted to this explosive moment. Desperation, longing, and hardcore arousal swept me up with dizzying speed.

"Jed," I murmured, pressing my breasts hard against him, trying to get impossibly closer.

He cupped one breast, pinching lightly through the fabric, moaning into my mouth when my nipple hardened beneath his touch.

Then the beam of Aunt Polly's car flashed across the porch as she turned into the drive.

"Shit," I hissed as he lowered my feet to the porch on an agonized groan.

He pressed his forehead against the door just above my head, while I tried to wrangle my wits and simmer my libido. The only sound was of us both panting and the car door opening and closing on Aunt Polly's minivan.

"Lola—" he growled, voice husky and rough.

"I'll see you on Thursday," I said, peering over his shoulder at Aunt Polly grinning like a fiend and coming up the drive at a fast clip.

"Lola, wait, I want to—"

"Not now." I opened the door. "Later, Jed. Text me!" I yell-whispered, closing the door, then jerking it back open and pecking him fast on the lips before I slammed the door in his face.

I wasn't waiting around for the interrogation of a lifetime from Aunt Polly. I ran upstairs, very aware of my sweaty status. Both from the self-defense lesson and from the exercise on the front porch. Mostly the latter. Dropping my bag on my bed, I grabbed a towel from the linen closet and ducked into the bathroom. By the time I'd stripped naked and climbed into the shower, Aunt Polly was rapping on the bathroom door.

"Why did you send him off in such a hurry?" she yelled through the door.

"Can't hear you!" I scrubbed shampoo into my hair. "In the shower!" As if that wasn't obvious.

"So you and Jed are an item?" Even through the pelting water and the locked door, I could hear her excited enthusiasm.

"We'll talk later, Aunt Polly! So tired."

I'm such a liar. I was wiiiide awake. Like a bunny on Viagra. I was tempted to take care of myself in the shower after Jed had dialed my body up to incinerating levels with one kiss, but I'd rather do it in bed, when my legs didn't feel like they might give out beneath me.

Once Aunt Polly must've left her post in the hallway, I collapsed back against the cold tiles. That's when I realized I was trembling.

I let my head fall back, relishing the cool stone on my back and behind.

What had just happened?

His lips met mine then an earth-shaking explosion of lust flared between us. And now I was suffering aftershocks.

Slipping out of the shower, I toweled off then wrapped the towel around me, tucking it at my chest. After squeeze-drying my hair, I spritzed it with my detangler so it wouldn't frizz.

I tossed my clothes in the hamper and opened the door, listening. The downstairs television was on, so I tip-toed back to my bedroom, unprepared to talk to Aunt Polly about Jed. Because honestly, I had no idea what to say. Didn't know what to think, quite frankly.

Closing my bedroom door, I walked across the room to my dresser when a *tap, tap, tap* on my window made me wheel around, gasping and clutching my towel against me.

The light from the hallway just barely illuminated Jed in the second-story window.

"How in the—?"

I rushed over and threw up the window, terrified he'd fall off the roof and kill himself.

"What in the world are you doing?"

He ducked his big body through the opening.

"Your Aunt Polly's got a really strong trellis on the back porch."

Then he was standing in front of me where I had one hand holding up my towel and one lick of sense holding back my willpower.

"I needed to tell you something." His eyes dropped down my body, burning a laser-line through my towel.

I stared, speechless, unable to get my mouth to make words at the moment, because all I could think about was that there was just a scrap of terrycloth between me and his hands, his mouth. My brain was blaring warning signs, sketching out diagrams and spreadsheets to emphasize that if the one kiss had nearly made me orgasm on Aunt Polly's porch, then actual sex would likely undo me altogether.

I was shaking again, but this time because I was terrified. Of myself.

He took a step closer. I didn't move.

"I didn't want to text you. I tried to call you, but you didn't answer, and I couldn't leave till I told you."

"Told me what?" I managed to croak out.

He stepped even closer, his body heat enveloping me. He clenched his fists at his sides, his broad chest heaving more quickly.

"What I said at Daisy's was true." He lifted his hands slowly, sliding his fingers into my hair along my temples, cradling my cheeks in his palms. "After the podcast this week, I want to take you out again." He brushed his lips over mine. "And again." He slid his teeth across my bottom lip. "Not for the podcast. No audience or follow-up show. Just us. I want to see where this goes."

"I don't know."

He eased back a mere inch, still holding my face, firm but gentle. "You're telling me you've only been doing this for your podcast?"

"No. Not that."

"Then what?"

"I don't know." I shrugged, suddenly more aware of my bare shoulders. Apparently, so was he, his gaze skating across my chest then back up my neck. "It's just that my plan wasn't to stay here in Green Valley. Not that you're proposing marriage or anything," I let out a nervous laugh. He didn't crack a smile. Licking my lips, "I mean, I'm not looking for anything serious right now." Even as I said the words, they tasted like dirt and regret.

Rather than protest that I had the wrong idea, that he didn't mean he wanted anything serious, he spoke softly while his thumb ghosted across my bottom lip.

"You're always trying to plan every little step, Lola." A slow sweep of my upper lip, his hazel eyes molten. "Sometimes it's better to be in the moment, follow your instincts. Stop thinking and analyzing."

"I'm not very good at that," I whispered, realizing I'd clutched onto his shirt at his waist without knowing it.

He smiled so wide, that dimple popped.

"I know." He pressed his lips against mine, so softly, with a slide of his tongue across the seam of my lips before lifting away again. "Want to know what I'd do first if you agreed to my plan of having no plan?"

I nodded, swallowing against the impulse to leap on him like a wildcat.

The fingers of one hand caressed down my neck and the curve of my shoulder, trailing down my arm then back up.

"I'd drop to my knees and worship your sweet pussy with my mouth till you came."

I squeezed my eyes shut and moaned at that mental picture, heart hammering at Jed's naughty mouth. His trailing hand moved to my thigh, tracing the edge of the towel with a slow sweep. He dipped his head close to my ear, nuzzling his mouth against my neck, his whiskers feeling sensual rather than ticklish.

"Would you like me to do that?" he asked on a rasp, coming back to my mouth for a stinging nip of my bottom lip. "Let me get on my knees and beg you in my own way for a chance with you." He dipped his head and brushed his lips along the inner curve of my shoulder, rumbling low, "Let me lick you till you come, Lola."

Pure intoxication. His slow seduction and heady words pulverized any resistance I clung to. In that moment, I couldn't see one reason for not yielding.

Before I could respond, he sank to his knees and gripped my hips, his hold burning through the towel. "Tell me yes, and I'll show you how good it can be."

He moved his hands lower, his fingers tracing the edge of the towel on both my upper thighs, sending a pulse of heat between my legs.

"Yes," I said on impulse before my brain could talk me out of it.

He eased the flaps of the towel open and stared as he slid the tip of one finger along my slit. "Goddamn, Lola. You're so pretty and so wet, baby."

Then he scissored two fingers through my wetness and parted my lips before he circled my clit with his tongue.

"Jed," I gasped and reached back for my bed I knew was right behind me before I fell over.

He caught me around the waist and lifted me onto the edge of the bed, tugging the towel loose and unwrapping me. I fell back onto my elbows, watching him. I was too aroused to be embarrassed, the only light coming from the moon in the night sky. His eyes slid closed with a nearly pained look as he skated his big hands up the backs of my calves.

"You're so fucking beautiful, Lola," he growled against my inner thigh as he lifted both and rested them on his shoulders.

I clenched my hands into the quilt on top of my bed as he dipped low and opened his hot mouth over my clit, working it with his tongue.

Sucking in a hiss between my teeth, I arched my spine and dug my heels into his back, unable to stop from rocking up against his mouth. He groaned, the vibration adding another layer of pleasure. Then he dipped his finger inside me, pumping with shallow thrusts while licking and sucking me into oblivion.

"*Oh, God.*" I gripped a hand in his hair.

His chuckle rumbled against me, though he didn't let up for a second.

"Enjoying yourself?" I panted, staring down at him, working between my legs.

"You have no idea." He locked onto my gaze and didn't let me go as he finger-fucked me deeper and sped up the flicks of his tongue.

He somehow read my body, or perhaps it was my quickening moans, because he thrust in a second finger and sped up the pace right as I was climbing that wave. More like it came crashing down on top of me with tsunami-like brutal force and embarrassing speed. I clenched my jaw together as I came, trying to prevent from screaming and bringing Aunt Polly barreling up the stairs to see what was wrong.

He pulled his fingers out and gripped my thighs, groaning as my body trembled with the orgasm. He stayed put, lapping at me softly, steering away from my post-climax, overly sensitive clitoris. A spike of jealousy hit me like a bolt in the chest, realizing he'd perfected his moves on some other lucky woman. Or women. Then another wave of orgasmic endorphins washed through my body, and I forgave him quickly enough.

He climbed up my body and settled on top of me. Something about him being fully clothed pressed against my fully naked body was such a turn-on. He kissed me deep, stroking his tongue against mine, the taste of me on him sparking new desire. But what I wanted was to taste *him*. I wanted to make him unravel the way he'd done to me.

I shoved on his broad shoulders. He let me maneuver him on to his back, head on my pillow, as I straddled his thighs.

He shook his head, skating his big hands up and over the curve of my hips, dipping at my waist and mounding my breasts where he brushed his thumbs over my nipples till they peaked. I could've easily lost myself again in the mind-reeling pleasure, but I was on a mission.

"I have no idea what I did to deserve this, but the sight of you, Lola, right now?" He bit his bottom lip and grunted. "I could die a happy man."

"If looking at me makes you happy, then imagine how happy you'll be with my mouth on your dick."

"*Lola.*" He squeezed his eyes shut as I pulled down his workout shorts a little—thanking the inventor of elastic waistbands—and freed him from his boxer briefs.

I didn't waste time but went straight for the gold, sliding my mouth over his wide girth and straight down till he tapped the back of my throat.

He hissed in a breath, weaving his hand into my hair to wrap around the back of my head. He held gently, urging me on as he thrust up into my mouth with shallow pumps.

"Fuck, fuck, fuck, fuck, fuck."

It was my turn to laugh, but I didn't let up.

"Slow down. I'm going to come already. I don't want to come so fast. *God*, this is heaven."

I let him pop out of my mouth while I stroked him with my hand, gazing up with a devilish grin. "No mercy."

Then I took his sac in hand and gave it a good squeeze as I sucked him hard and deep.

His next groan was more growl than anything as he pumped up into my mouth on my downward stroke. Three more times, then he reached down and plucked me up like a ragdoll with his hands beneath my arms. I landed on my side. He wrapped his hand over mine around his dick and squeezed hard, stroking as he spilled onto my breasts and stomach.

His fierce expression and the sight of him losing all composure was the sexiest damn thing I'd ever seen. He fell back onto my pillow, panting.

"Don't move," he managed in a heaving breath. "One sec."

I grinned, reaching down to the end of the bed where my towel still lay spread out. He popped up and grabbed it before I could, then he pressed me onto my back while he wiped me clean, brushing over my breasts with infinite care and a possessive gleam in his eyes. Then he laughed. Like really laughed.

"What?" I asked, unable to keep from laughing with him.

"I swear to you that's not why I came through your window."

"Actually, you came on my bed. Technically, on my body."

He laughed harder before leaning over me and pressing his lips to mine. "And here I thought little Miss Plans-a-Lot couldn't surprise me."

Why that admission had me beaming from ear to ear, I have no idea. Maybe it's because I was the least spontaneous person I knew. And the fact that I'd shocked THE Jedediah Lawson with a killer blow-job had me preening like a peacock.

He hopped up after wiping himself off with the same towel, looking around the room.

"The hamper's in the bathroom," I told him, sliding off the bed toward my dresser. "Just set it by the door. I'll take care of it."

But then he opened the door and walked into the hall.

"*Jed.*" I whisper-yelled, going after him before glancing down at my naked body. "Dammit," I muttered, hurrying to my dresser and pulling on some panties and an oversized T-shirt.

By the time I rushed into the hall, he was coming out of the bathroom, his hair freshly slicked with water. "I used your toothbrush," he said, kissing me with minty breath and backing me into my bedroom.

"You did?" I tried to figure out if that grossed me out, but my face must've said it did.

He laughed. "Nah. I washed up and used my finger." He wiggled his index finger. "He's a multi-tasker."

And now I was blushing. "Hang on. I'll be right back, and then we'll see if we can sneak you downstairs."

I rushed back into the bathroom and brushed my teeth super fast, then crept out and leaned over the banister. Dang, Aunt Polly was rewatching *Schitt's Creek*. She could be up for a while.

Heading back into my bedroom, I found Jed with his shoes and shirt off, laid back on my pillows as comfy as you please. For a second, I was stunned stupid by the display of all that manly flesh I'd drooled all over at the fire station the other day. He was thickly muscled, rather than a lean, chiseled abdomen, which only made him that much more attractive. His physique was what one might call powerful.

"What are you doing?"

"She's not going to bed soon," he said, patting the place next to him in ***my*** bed. He smiled wider. "Come on, frowny face. Lay down with me a while."

Somehow, he looked more dangerous now than he did earlier, with a lusty fire burning a hole through my self-discipline.

"What? You're scared of me now?"

"Pfft. Don't be ridiculous," I said, still standing there.

When he arched a brow at me, I realized I *was* being ridiculous. There was nothing to be afraid of. Just a little post-orgasm chit-chat. Some might call it pillow talk, an activity generally reserved for lovers. But that didn't mean—

"Stop thinking so hard and come lay down, Lola."

Closing the door, I did. Crawling under the covers, I scooted in. When I went to lay down on my pillow, Jed wrapped me up in one arm, so I laid my head on his chest. Goodness, he had such a big, warm body. I tucked my free arm between our bodies, hesitant to wrap it around his waist.

He tugged on one of my curls. "Big bad, Cola. Scared of cuddling," he huffed on a laugh.

"I'm not scared."

Total lie, but the challenge made me wrap my arm around him anyway. And boy, was that nice.

"This was my favorite date so far," he said on a sigh.

I laughed. "I'll bet."

He curled his fingers at my waist and tickled me.

"No!" I wiggled to get away, but he stopped and pulled me even closer till I was half sprawled on his chest. "Why was it your favorite? Besides the obvious, of course."

"Besides the obvious," he murmured, squeezing my hip, "you finally seemed to relax and forgot that I was the guy who dubbed you Coca-Cola Lola back in high school."

His voice had taken a serious edge. The slow stroke of his hand over my hip and the intimacy of the moment gave me the courage to ask him something I'd always wanted to know.

"Why did you call me that? I thought," I stopped on a sigh, but was determined to go on. "I kind of thought we were friends back then, even when we were arguing over something. Until that day."

He stiffened beneath me and hugged me tighter. "We were. I was—" it was his turn to heave out a heavy sigh—"I was a damn fool, okay? Believe it or not, I was shy and awkward with girls. You were the only one I could ever really talk to. And I liked you. A lot." He paused. "Then I was embarrassed because you thought I was stupid."

"What?" I sat up on one elbow to look at him. "I didn't think you were stupid."

"You did, Cola."

I wasn't sure why but hearing him call me that name now had the opposite effect it did in high school. It was said with affection and tenderness that made me melty.

"You kept commenting on my F papers in English, and that last time, I just snapped." His expression was actually full of pain. "I never should've lashed out at you. It had nothing to do with you."

"You were upset about your failing grades. I, of all people, should understand that. I probably would've erupted into the stratosphere if it were me. I shouldn't have done that, I'm sorry."

He opened his mouth as if he wanted to say something else, but instead, he hauled me close again, higher up onto his chest. Even though I was half under the covers, it was the heat of his immense body and gentle heart that warmed me up inside.

"It was all my fault," he admitted softly, cradling my face in one hand and pulling me down for a soft, sweet kiss. "I had deserved your anger, and I was a complete idiot. I know it's far too late for any damage I might've caused, but I am truly, truly sorry."

I blinked back the tears that rushed up out of nowhere, not even realizing I needed that apology. It hit me with the force of a battering ram, knocking down whatever guard I'd kept in place between us. "It's okay," I said sincerely, pressing another kiss to his lips.

This one went deeper. He coaxed my lips apart and slid his tongue inside, stroking me with the softest kiss imaginable, apologizing with his mouth. And wow, did I like that.

Then he eased back and I settled back onto his chest. "So am I getting a ten on your date-o-meter?"

I laughed. "You'll just have to wait and see."

I thought he might bring up the earlier conversation and demand I give him an actual answer about his give-us-a-chance request. But the reality was that I didn't know what to do. If I turned my brain off, then I knew one hundred percent what I wanted.

Jed.

There was no guarantee I was going to get a job offer anyway. So I might as well enjoy my time while I was back in Green Valley, right?

That's what I told myself as Jed and I talked in the dark. I asked him about his grandmother and his dad and his sisters. He answered one after the other, creating scenes in my head of a rambunctious and loving family who I couldn't help but want to know better with how he laced each word with love and affection. Somewhere between talking about teaching his niece Zoe how to fish and his nephew Pete how to properly tackle in football, I drifted off to sleep in complete and utter bliss.

Chapter Seventeen

-LOLA-

"How do I tell my partner I'm ready for sex?" @Beebee
"Just tell them! Don't be afraid. Communication is key in all parts of a relationship."
@kiss-n-tell

The second I woke up, I popped up in sleepy disarray, remembering Jed was right next to me when I fell asleep. He was gone. Of course, he was gone. I'm sure he slipped out as soon as I nodded off. The pang of disappointment hit me square in the chest. I found myself rubbing that very spot before kicking off the covers and heading into the bathroom.

"Whoa, sista."

Falling asleep after sex-play with Jed and with semi-damp hair created a crazy nest out of my hair. No joke. A small family of swallows could've made a home of that mess. While brushing my teeth, I stared at myself, remembering last night. I rinsed my mouth and smiled.

Marly would be so proud of my boldness. She'd say I was channeling my inner-Marly, and she'd be right. I headed back to my bedroom to text her when I heard Aunt Polly talking downstairs.

It was Sunday. No way did she invite a friend over this morning. Sunday mornings were a sanctified day for her. Not for church—though she attended when the mood struck her and dragged me with her—but for the peace and quiet she demanded while reading the paper on the back porch overlooking the woods behind the house and the view of the Smokies in the distance. Aunt Polly was old school. Some things were sacred. Quiet Sunday mornings with her newspaper was one of them.

I shuffled down the stairs, frowning, when I heard her trill laughter from the kitchen. Then I froze in the entryway before I even saw the owner of the familiar baritone.

"The key is how long you whip the batter." He stood at Aunt Polly's stove wearing one of her aprons—the one with the red rooster wearing a chef's hat—over his workout shorts and T-shirt from the night before.

I stood there in sheer puzzlement as he flipped a pancake from the wrought iron skillet onto a fluffy stack on the counter. Aunt Polly sipped her coffee from the other side, watching him with little hearts in her eyes.

"Good mornin', sleepyhead," she said with a smile.

Jed turned in his bare feet, looking unbelievably endearing in my aunt's too-small apron. "Just in time, Cola." He flicked off the burner and set the skillet aside, taking his coffee and the stack of pancakes to the table.

"Sweetheart, you might want to run upstairs and throw on some sweatpants or something."

I was still staring at Jed, who'd taken up a seat in the nook near the bay windows as he forked sausage links and pancakes onto his plate. He was grinning like mad, ignoring me altogether.

"Lola, sweetheart." Aunt Polly walked over and turned me around to usher me out the door. "Go put some pants on," she whispered.

I finally glanced down at my bare legs, still in a state of shock. Hustling upstairs, I pulled on a pair of sweatpants, my emotions running amuck. At first, I thought...

Jed was in my house, cooking breakfast?

A swelling lump of elation bubbled up from my belly. Then...

Jed was in my house, cooking breakfast!

Damn him for letting Aunt Polly think we were sleeping together. Even though technically we *did* sleep together.

We hadn't even gotten to the lovers' part, and I wasn't sure if we would. Still, he shouldn't let on to her that we were carrying on or courting or whatever she was thinking right now downstairs until Jed and I had had a lengthy conversation about whatever it was we were doing. What if she told my dad?

"Oh, Lord," I mumbled, hurrying back downstairs.

Dad would be asking if I wanted a summer or winter wedding if he caught wind of this. First of all, he worshipped Jed, if that display of reverence and adoration at the Piggly Wiggly wasn't reminder enough. And second, he'd do anything to get me back in Green Valley for good.

But it wasn't in my *plans*.

I walked back into the kitchen like I had a man cooking breakfast every Sunday morning. Funnily enough, Aunt Polly was acting the same way. Like Jed was a regular fixture in our kitchen on Sunday mornings.

"Well, I can't thank you enough. Such a treat to have someone else cook breakfast for me." Aunt Polly poured syrup on her small stack.

"You mean Cola doesn't cook for y'all sometimes?"

I sat across from him and put my napkin in my lap. "I'm more of a baker than a cook," I admitted.

"Really?" His brows rose high.

"Why are you so surprised?" I forked three pancakes and three sausage links on my plate then reached for the syrup. "You expect all women to love cooking?"

"Not at all," he replied gently, smiling down at his plate as he cut into what looked like a fresh stack since I'd gone upstairs and come down. "You're just really good at baking, that's all."

"Oh." I blinked, feeling appropriately chagrined at myself for jumping to conclusions. "I can't cook. Not at all. Terrible at it. Right, Aunt Polly?"

Was I trying to scare him away or something? Maybe. I didn't know what I was saying anymore as I stuffed my mouth with a bite of pancakes.

Oh, my heavens!

I moaned at once, unable to stop myself.

He glanced at my mouth, a stain of pink burning his cheeks before he cleared his throat and said, "Well, I'm a terrific cook."

"Obviously, you are," said Aunt Polly. "I'll bet those sisters of yours taught you growing up."

"Actually, I'm more self-taught, believe it or not. I'll admit that Sally taught me her lasagna recipe. But when I moved back to help out with Dad, I decided Ramen noodles and frozen dinners just wouldn't cut it."

"I'm sure your dad appreciated it," she said with a smile.

"Yes, ma'am. Thank you. He did."

My curiosity was beyond piqued. Last night, we'd talked about so many things before I fell asleep, but not much talk of his father. Only that he has a physical therapist who still comes once a week, and Jed checks on him every night just to be sure he doesn't need something. I swear, the man was running for sainthood.

A vision of him with his head between my thighs last night had me thinking maybe not.

"Do you still cook for him?" I asked, forcing myself to eat without moaning in pleasure like a porn star.

"Every night."

"Guess that's why it's convenient that you live right across the street," I said.

"It is." He caught my gaze and must've seen something in my reaction, his brow pinching in the middle.

I halved another sausage link with the side of my fork, swirling it in the syrup. "He's a lucky beneficiary of your cooking skills," I admitted, forcing a smile.

He was so embedded in Green Valley. No doubt about it. My chest tightened for a second, but then Aunt Polly started talking about the upcoming Arts and Crafts Fair in Merryville, where we'd reserved a booth for selling her *Creature Cozies*. So I pushed all thoughts aside and regaled him with my master marketing scheme to reel in locals and use promotion code postcards to boost sales online.

I'd cleaned my plate and was wiping my mouth when Jed stood up and took my plate along with his and Aunt Polly's to the kitchen sink.

"Oh, no, you don't," said Aunt Polly. "I'll get the dishes. The cook doesn't have to clean."

"That's why I'm a pro at dish-cleaning," I said.

He chuckled as he stepped away from the sink, palms up. "Yes, ma'am. I hate leaving you with this mess."

"Not at all. It was a pleasure having you. You can cook breakfast any ole time." She winked at me, obviously giving the message that he was welcome to sleep over *any ole time*.

"I'll walk you out," I said, shoving him toward the hallway.

Once in the foyer, I opened the door and stood there awkwardly. He turned and took me in, smiling wide as he looked at my hair.

"I like this natural look you've got going." He tugged on a crazy curl.

"Shut up, Jedediah." I swatted his hand away. "I should be furious with you right now. I never said you could show the whole world we spent the night together."

He tilted his head in obvious confusion while planting his big hands on my waist and pulling me closer. "Your Aunt Polly isn't the whole world."

"Huh." I rested my hands on his biceps, admiring the strength of this man. "Until she tells my dad and it's all over. And we might've spent the night together, but we didn't *sleep* together."

"We did sleep together. Best sleep of my life, all snuggled up to your perfect backside."

My eyes must've bugged because he barked out a laugh before pulling me entirely against him.

"You know what I mean. We didn't have sex, and now Aunt Polly thinks we did."

"We'd better remedy that then. Don't want her getting the wrong idea."

"Seriously, Jed."

"What makes you think I'm not serious?"

I huffed out a sigh, still weighing all the pros and cons of dating Jed while I was back home. The pros were a giant mountain on the scale, but that one thing—the fact that I wasn't staying—tipped everything back the other way.

"Stop thinking," he said, leaning down and brushing a kiss on my lips. "Stop planning." He nipped my bottom lip. "Just let it go." Then he kissed me properly, one hand wrapping my nape as he devoured me on the doorstep. He groaned, stroking his tongue over mine before pulling back. "So sweet."

"That's the syrup," I whispered belligerently.

He smiled till his adorable dimple was showing, which made me frown again. "That's nothing but pure, sweet Lola." He pecked me on the lips and released me, then started backing away. "You work Tuesday night?"

"Nope. Day shift."

He nodded. "Can you be ready for six?"

"For what?"

"For me." His expression softened, a plea written in the vulnerable lines.

For *him*.

"Yeah." I cleared my throat and flipped my wild, messy hair, all nonchalant. "I can be ready."

He grinned wide. "Then it's a date. A non-podcast date." He winked and turned around, and I swear there was a lightness to his swaggering step.

I went inside and shut the door, leaning back against it, shaking my head at myself. "I'm dating Jed."

"Of course, you are," said Aunt Polly, crossing down the foyer toward her bedroom. "After all that noise you two were making last night, I'd say so."

"Aunt Polly!" I screeched as she disappeared down the hall.

All I heard was her chuckle as she shut her bedroom door. Then I hurried upstairs, realizing I had a new problem if I was actually dating Jed. And I knew the exact person to help me solve it. If my dang, hard-headed best friend would agree to it.

Chapter Eighteen

-LOLA-

"One thing to remember when dating is that you're opening yourself to new experiences and a new person. So be sure to open your heart as well as your mind." @kiss-n-tell

"W*hat* is going on?" gushed Marly when she walked into Donner's Bakery, where I asked her to meet me after work on Wednesday.

"What do you mean?"

Marly plopped down into the seat across from me and glowered. "For one, I caught you staring out the window with a super goofy smile on your face. And two, we have podcasting tomorrow. So you want to talk to me in person, but it's too serious to wait one more day." She pulled the plate with a slice of Jennifer Sylvester's famous banana cake in front of her and started diving in. "And, you bought me my favorite, so you're sweetening me up for something. Spill it."

She was totally right. After Jed took me to his place for a delicious dinner of Tuscan Chicken Pasta last night, we then adjourned to the back patio with coffee and dessert and played catch with his dog Joe. Then he promptly brought me home and walked me to the doorstep, where we shared a sizzling kiss. When he sent me on inside with a cheeky wink right as I reached down and grabbed his perfect ass, I knew he was trying to prove to me that he could control himself. That was also when I knew I'd definitely be dating Jed, and only Jed, while I was home in Green Valley. That meant I needed Marly's help.

"I have a proposition for you."

"Is he tall and hot and muscly?"

"Possibly," I said with confidence.

She snorted. "I can't wait to hear this." She stuffed another bite of cake in her mouth.

I pushed the iced mocha I'd bought for her across the table. "I need you to be me."

"Explain, please."

"For *Kiss-n-Tell*."

"Not an explanation. I'm already a cohost. What are you telling—" Her eyes bugged out and she gasped so fast she choked on her banana cake. I hopped up and pounded on her back.

Tempest glanced up with concern from behind the counter and started to walk over. "She okay?"

"Yeah. Just went down the windpipe." I kept pounding. "Thanks, Tempest."

Marly reached for her iced coffee and took three gulps, then set it aside, grinning at me with her now watery eyes all crinkled with giddiness. "You've got a lady boner for Jed."

"Marly," I hissed, eyeing Tempest at the counter, helping an elderly lady. So thankful she wasn't paying attention. "We're just having fun while I'm in town."

"I'll bet you're having fun. Has the fireman shown you his hose yet?"

"Marly."

"Taken you for a slide down his pole?"

I blushed and cleared my throat, smiling at the little old lady as she passed out the door behind us.

Marly gasped again and leaned forward. "You did, you cheeky monkey. Was he good in bed? Hells bells, I know he was. Something about the eyes. That gentle giant took you to pound town, didn't he?"

I couldn't help the maniacal laughter from bubbling up my throat. "What is *wrong* with you? Did your mother drop you on your head when you were little?" I cleared my throat and leaned forward to whisper, "We didn't go to *pound town*, but yes, I saw his happy trail." I blushed, even admitting it to Marly.

Since we'd been living apart for the past several years, we only texted and messaged every month or so to keep up. I'd actually missed her insanity, except when it came to sharing guy talk. I wasn't *quite* as open as she was. To Marly, there was no such thing as too much information. Or a filter.

"You've got to tell me. I've been rooting for you two since he dropped a book on your foot in tenth grade."

I stared at her a second, trying to remember. "The pre-calculus book?"

"I don't know. A big, heavy one. And I remember you were furious because how in the world did he get into that accelerated math class when you didn't, and he wasn't even making good grades in all his classes, yada, yada, yada."

I could barely remember that incident, but I did recall being jealous of him getting into a class reserved for juniors. Especially since I was a straight-A student, and I knew he wasn't.

"So, what's the deal?" asked Marly, sucking down the last of her iced coffee through the straw. "I get it you don't want to date other guys while you're schnoodling Jed. You want to convert our minisodes into full episodes? Change the theme of *Kiss-n-Tell* since you've got that big hunk of man meat now?"

"I don't want to change the theme. I want you to become the dater. Or datee."

Marly blinked, her expression blank. Not good.

"Oh, God, please, please, please, please! I can't change the theme now. My followers are on the rise, and that's marketing 101. Do *not* make a business change when your customer base is on the rise. Customer base equals social media audience in podcasting, so *please*, Marly. I need you to do this for me."

She made a production of sitting back in her seat, swishing her ponytail with a bit of sass, crossing her arms, and then eyeballing me.

"Do I get a raise?"

"You mean from nothing?"

"Yes. What do I get?"

"My undying love and admiration?"

"I already have that." She blew that off with a flippant wave of her hand.

"What do you want?"

She tapped her chin thoughtfully, knowing what she wanted already. I was sure of it.

"You have to babysit my babies when I go on podcast dates."

"What nonsense are you talking about?"

"My *babies,*" she squealed, bouncing in her seat as she slid open her phone. "Just look at my little darlings. I haven't even gotten to show you since you've been so wrapped up in Jed."

She was right. She'd told me about her neighbor's dachshund having puppies and that she was adopting two of them, but my brain had been elsewhere. She leaned across the table to flip through her pics, showing me at least a million of two furballs whose eyes weren't even opened.

"This is Scooter. He drags his little fat tummy across the floor. And this is Pooter, because, well, I'm sure you can guess. He's got a gastrointestinal problem."

"I'm still shocked you're adopting two puppies, Marly. You couldn't just start with one?"

"Nope. These brothers are super close. No way could I separate them, so now you're a godmother. Isn't that exciting!"

Her blue eyes sparkled with unrestrained delight. God, I was going to miss this girl when I moved. I pushed that aside. I'd worry about that tomorrow.

"Super exciting," I tried and failed to match her level of glee. "But do they really need a sitter when you go on dates? I mean, you don't even have to do long dates for the podcast. They can be short and close to home."

"Lola, obviously you've never had babies of your own."

"Obviously."

"I've already worked it out with my neighbor, Mrs. Martinez. When they're old enough to leave their mother and come home with me, she said she'll gladly keep them during the day while I'm at the distillery. But they'll need TLC when I get home. They'll have abandonment anxiety if I leave them at night."

"But they'll have each other."

"Lola Elizabeth, do you or do you not want me to be the new hot thing on *Kiss-n-Tell*?"

"Fine," I said, laughing. "I'll take over the dates again whenever I leave, or if this thing with Jed fizzles out first."

Marly stuffed a giant bite of banana cake into her mouth and chewed thoughtfully. I wasn't surprised when she finally swallowed and said, "So you're definitely leaving?"

"Of course. That was always the plan, Marly." Even as I said it, the anxiety of still not having heard from Optimum Media about an interview buzzed through my veins. In addition to the anxiety of having to tell my parents, specifically my Dad, that I was moving away again. *And* the stress of having settled so easily, so wonderfully, back in Green Valley and being faced with the heartache of leaving.

"So what if this thing with Jed doesn't fizzle out?"

"It will when I move."

"Who's to say it will?"

"Long-distance relationships don't work on a permanent basis. Minisode number five, remember?"

She pushed her empty plate aside and propped her elbows and forearms on the table, catching me with her serious face.

"Eventually, one person will have to move."

Marly sat back and shook her head, a smirk cutting her face into feline perfection. "You're a coward."

"*What?*"

"You heard me. A yellow-bellied coward."

I rolled my eyes, preparing to lay into her, when a group of teenage girls bustled in, laughing at something on one of their phones. The shop was too small for actual privacy.

"Let's go," I said, grabbing my purse and heading for the door.

Marly caught up to me in the parking lot as I speed-walked for my car. "I love you, Lola, but you know it's true."

"It has nothing to do with me. I like the guy." I whirled around by my car. "Okay? I admit it! I am in deep, deep like with Jedediah Lawson."

Marly grinned.

"But it won't go further than that because Jed is in deep love with Green Valley. A bond that can't be torn asunder."

"And you know this because you've talked to him about it?"

"No! Don't be ridiculous. I mean, we've only been on three dates, for Pete's sake. No, four."

"Four?" Her blue eyes bugged out. "When was this secret date?"

"Don't be so dramatic. It wasn't a secret. He just had me over to his house for dinner last night."

"He cooked for you?" Her devilish grin spread across her face. I just rolled my eyes. "Okay, four dates that were looooong overdue, and I daresay the sparks that fly between the two of you when you're together mean nothing, right?"

"He's got family here."

"So do you."

"I mean family who depend on him. Did you know that he takes his grandmother grocery shopping on Friday nights after her payday? And that he bought the house across the street from his dad, the house he grew up in, so that he can check on him every night? Every single night?"

Marly's smile dimmed, so I knew she was getting the message.

"And apparently he doesn't miss a single one of his nephew's pee wee football games. Also, he's a fireman for Green Valley."

"There are fire departments in Houston."

"But his family isn't. And cities have entirely different lifestyles than towns like Green Valley. He's happy here." My chest squeezed at the idea of dragging him away from a life he seemed to love. "And people need him here."

"Fine, then. He may not want to leave, and though I still think you should give him that choice, there's another option."

"We're not that serious for that kind of talk," I snapped back, one hand propped on my hip, then asked more quietly. "What's the other option?"

Because there was something deep inside me that wanted another option. In the off chance that this thing did indeed fail to fizzle.

She crossed her arms. "You could stay in Green Valley."

I stared at her and shook my head. "Marly. Do you even get me at all?"

I mean, for the love of God, I've even cried to her multiple times about how awful it is not to have that steady, weighty paycheck that guarantees my financial independence. And thus, my security. And achieving those goals I'd had in stone since I knew what an MBA was.

I went to school for marketing and business and there's not much opportunity for either of those in the vicinity of Green Valley. Perhaps in Knoxville, but that's even an hour away. Add inner-city traffic, and it could be closer to a two-hour commute both ways. Long commutes aren't my thing. When I lived in New Orleans, I took public transportation as often as possible. My duplex was only three blocks from our office, and I usually walked or took the bus or Ubered home when I stayed too late.

And this opportunity with Optimum Media—assuming they ever actually give me an interview—could literally be the job of my dreams. The progressive, growing, upward-thinking kind of company that values all ideas and is looking for hard-working and hungry young associates like myself. This could be the job to meet all of my girlish dreams of becoming a rockstar in the marketing world, dazzling clients, and climbing the ladder to executive success.

Marly dropped her defensive stance and stepped closer, gripping my shoulders and giving them a friendly squeeze. "I do know you. I know that you're one of the smartest people I know, brilliant beyond belief when it comes to business. But kind of a shit-show when it comes to personal relationships."

"Shut up," I chuckled and shrugged her off with a shake of my shoulders.

She arched a black brow at me. "Remember that guy, the one you dated your senior year at LSU?"

"Ugh. Warren. Why are you torturing me?"

"That creeper shouldn't have gotten to second base, and yet you let him move in and share your bed for three months."

"I hardly noticed." It's true. In or outside of bed, Warren was pretty forgettable.

"You had to move and change your phone number to lose him, if I recall. And that other guy you dated for nine months in New Orleans when you first moved."

"Timothy and I interned together, and he was the only person I knew," I defended myself. "It was easy to latch on to him."

"Except when he refused to unlatch from you. Didn't you say he used to sit on the toilet seat and talk to you about your day while you were taking a bath?"

"Yes," I admitted through laughter. "At least he was really good in bed."

"Until he revealed his secret foot fetish. He was always asking to paint your toenails."

"So what? He had a foot fetish. Plenty of people do."

"Not sure about *plenty*, but most normal people ask before they paint your toes while you're napping on the sofa."

"Ew. Don't remind me." I sighed heavenward, trying to erase that final straw that forced me to realize dating Timothy was a bad idea. "So I'm shit with dating."

"Ironic now that you're the dating guru."

"Not really. I'm the first-date guru. I've been on more first dates than anyone in history, and I'm amazing at it. It's what happens beyond date two where my judgment perhaps slips a little."

"Just a little." Marly held up her index and forefinger about an inch and squinted one eye, then she laughed and gave me another friendly shove on the shoulder. This was Marly's show of affection. "That's why I'm saying Jed is worth giving a go."

"I am giving him a go."

"I mean, see if it could be more."

"So I could fall for a guy I'd end up leaving? That sounds like a brilliant idea. And extremely painful."

Marly kissed her hand, then gave me a none-too-gentle slap on the cheek as she started to back away toward her car across from mine. "At least give his body a go, eh? See what riding that big cowboy is like?"

Then she started doing some sort of weird movements that looked like a half-fertility dance and a half-seizure.

"What are you doing?" I shouted on a laugh.

"Calling on the sex gods for you and Jed to bump uglies soon." She had finished it off with a twirl and an odd pelvic thrust, then a hip bump to the air and a shout. "Bam! That should do it."

I clapped. Not because it was remotely good, but because she made me laugh. She always could.

Then a shaggy-looking teen opening his car behind her shook his head and called out, "Better keep your day job. Not getting into Hollywood with that number."

Oops. Not a good idea, dude.

Marly spun and snapped back quick as lightning, "And you're not getting laid with that twenty-year-old junker."

He frowned and flipped her off before getting in his car and driving off with a squeal of tires. She tossed her hands to the sky, yelling at the fleeing car.

"Don't come at me, bro!"

"Marly." I pressed my lips together. "He was just a kid."

"Well, they need to learn to respect their elders." She opened her truck door and waved high in the air. "See you tomorrow!"

Tomorrow. My final podcast episode with Jed, which seemed to be the line in the sand he'd drawn for me. When I crossed that line, I could no longer fool myself into thinking this was *just a job*. Every date after that would no longer be for the podcast. It would be just for us.

Though I meant every word I'd said to Marly, I couldn't wipe the smile off my face just thinking about it. About him.

Chapter Nineteen

-LOLA-

"We did a poll and guess what? 93% said they prefer oral sex before penetration. So remember, folks, foreplay is your friend." @kiss-n-tell

"But what listeners really want to know, and I mean a helluva a lot of them are asking on the YouTube feed right this second," said Marly as she leaned close to the mic and gave us her best sex-laced, husky voice, "Did the end-of-the-night kiss push Jed to a ten on the date-o-meter?"

I felt Jed's gaze on me as I cleared my throat. "Indeed, it did."

"Whoop!" Marly's excited laughter filled my earphones, but all I really noticed was the big, warm hand wrapping around my bouncing knee. "Can we get more details than that, please?"

Glancing at Jed, I could've happily drowned in the whiskey-warm depths of his heated gaze. He wasn't smiling at all, and when he looked at me that way—the same way he did when I straddled myself above him in my bed that night—I could barely breathe. Add that to the way he smelled today—something cedar-ish and manly and delicious—and he was lucky I wasn't climbing onto his lap to take a bite of him.

"Pretty please?" pleaded Marly.

"I think not," I finally answered, still holding Jed's gaze. He sure as hell wasn't letting go of mine.

"How about you, cowboy? Will you give us something more than 'indeed' to satisfy our hungry and super-thirsty listeners?"

"I can tell you this."

His hand under the table curled around my inner thigh to cup the back of my knee, where he gave me a comforting squeeze. Though I was pretty sure he didn't quite understand the reaction my body had to his semi-innocent touches, because I felt that squeeze with a pulse of warmth much higher up between my legs.

"Your lovely and formidable host of *Kiss-n-Tell* really knows how to make a man feel good."

"That's what I'm talking about," crooned Marly. "So what does this all mean, you ask? Well, *Kiss-n-Tell* has a little announcement to make."

This was my cue. I'd written exactly what I wanted to say so that I conveyed the right message and held tight to my audience. Straightening in my seat, I pulled my note card closer.

"One thing Marly and I haven't touched on in any extensive way is what happens when that first date turns into a great second date. And the second turns into an amazing third." A gentle squeeze on my leg dragged my attention back to him. "Well, ladies and gentlemen, the answer is simple. You follow that trail and see where it leads, which has me in a bit of a predicament. The point of my podcast dates is to give a guy a chance, immerse myself in the date, and report back to you guys with fair and honest results. But I couldn't truthfully give another guy a fair shot on a first date right now. Not when my thoughts are...elsewhere."

"I'm curious," interjected Marly, "Jed, how would you feel about Lola continuing on her podcast dates?"

Another tight squeeze under the table. "I have to admit I'd want to pound the guy into the ground."

The aggressive, possessive vibes he was giving off only turned me on even more.

"Kind of what I thought," added Marly, "so tell them the big news, Lola!"

"Without further ado, our very own lovely and adorable Marly will be taking over on the podcast dates for now. Everything else will remain exactly the same. We'll co-host and record every week on YouTube, except I'll be switching into the driver's seat for the interviews."

"So there you have it, guys and gals." Marly beamed over her mic at us. "Cowboy Jed has swooped in and stolen our girl for the time being, but I can't *wait* to get into the saddle and take the dating reins for a while."

We closed out the podcast with our usual motto, then Marly pulled off her headphones and let out one of her signature cackles. "Now that was fun. Holy shit, Lola, did you see our views for this episode?"

After setting my headphones aside, I swiped my phone off the table and checked into my YouTube app. "Damn. Twelve hundred views while we were live? That's kind of insane."

"All due to him, I'd say." She gestured toward Jed, who was standing and removing his headphones.

"Marly, would you mind giving Lola and I the room for a minute?"

There was a deep undercurrent to that question that had my attention snap back to him. A rough, possessive tone in his voice. My lady parts quivered at the intensity of his hazel eyes and hard expression. Did I miss something?

"Sure thing, cowboy," sang Marly sweetly. "I'll pop downstairs for a snack."

She left and pulled the door closed.

"What?" I asked, actually a little scared of what I'd said that might've put that look on his face.

He came from around his chair, moving toward me slowly. I backed up on instinct and kept backing up until my butt hit the wall next to the door. He scooped his hand around my nape, tilting my chin up with his thumb as he pressed his body to mine. I whimpered, unprepared for the sudden assault to my senses.

He crushed his mouth against mine, sweeping in with an invasive stroke of his tongue. And I was totally okay with it, opening wider for him. His other hand curled into my jeans at the hip as he bit my lip before pulling a mere inch away.

"For now?" He said the words against my mouth softly but with a punch of power that had me pressing back into the wall. Didn't matter. He'd crowded me into a delicious cage of flesh and muscle that was all Jed. I certainly wasn't trying to get away.

"What?" I had no idea what he meant.

"You said," he started, with his hand at my hip, he wandered south where he cupped my vagina and rubbed the heel of his palm in just the right place, "that Marly will be taking over the dates *for now*."

"Uh-huh. What's the issue? I'm sorry, I can't think straight right now."

I rocked my pelvis forward, trying to get more friction. He altered his stroke, rubbing two fingers along the seam right over my clit.

"Oh, God, Jed."

He smiled against my mouth, but his words were dire, passionate, fierce. "I don't want you thinking this is just for now, Cola. I want you all in." He nipped my lip, leaving a slight sting. "Stop finding the out clause before we've even begun."

"I don't want out. Does it seem like I want out?" I clutched my hands in his hair, pulling him closer so I could get my mouth on his.

He let me. Briefly. When he pressed sweetly again with his fingers in the perfect place, I gasped and dropped my head back against the wall.

"Open yourself to me, Lola." My real name, not Cola. His gruff voice lowered so deep as he brushed tender words against my neck, painting a canvas of intimacy and desire. "I want you so fucking bad. I can't get you out of my head. I want to touch you, taste you, fuck you."

His hand went to the snap of my jeans, his other now clenched my hair.

"I need to feel you," he growled against the underside of my jaw.

In frenzied movements, I helped him unzip and push my jeans and panties down over my hips. His long fingers instantly slid along my wet seam.

"God. Damn," he whispered on a shudder, dipping one finger inside me before sliding back to my clit. "So wet for me."

I was partially aware of the moaning whimpers I was making as I clawed at his shoulder and the back of his neck, pressing him closer to my neck where he continued to lick and nip a line back up to my mouth.

"Look at me, baby."

I opened my eyes to half-mast, finding the green of his, a starburst against the hazel-gold. He lifted his hand to his mouth and sucked on the one he'd been stroking me with, then he pressed both his index and middle finger into my mouth, watching me suck and take them in all the way.

Hissing in a breath, he slid them out then stroked those fingers in a circle around my clit. "Open wider for me," he whispered against my mouth.

I did. Then he pumped them inside me at the same time that he crushed his mouth against mine. He groaned into my mouth, finger-fucking me in the perfect rhythm. He sucked on my tongue before pulling away to take light bites of my lips.

"Does it feel good?" he whispered darkly.

"So good," I breathed on another moan, thrusting forward to meet his every rub, wishing he'd just bend me over the podcast table and take me hard.

When I went for his pants, he wrestled both my wrists into his free hand and pinned them above my head. He shook his head.

"Not today." He maneuvered his thumb to press a brushing circle around my nub every time he thrust up inside me. "When I finally get to fuck you,

I'll need more time." He kissed me again, stroking faster in rhythm with my quickening thrusts. "I just need to see you come again right now. So I can make it through the day."

I squeezed my fists together above my head. "Well, you're about to," I mumbled before a jarring pulse of pleasure shot through me.

I dropped my head back again against the wall on a heavy groan, thrusting forward one last time. He went deep, and damn if it didn't feel so good as he kissed me again to drink down my moans. His own sounds of pleasure mingling with mine.

He waited until every orgasmic shudder had ebbed away before releasing my hands and pulling his fingers from inside me. He kept kissing me softly, licking his tongue along mine while he pulled up my panties and jeans, zipped, and re-snapped them together.

Then he spread those giant hands on my hips and kissed me. Long and deep, but soft and sweet. I let my hands fall around his neck, kissing him back drunkenly, reveling in this euphoric sensation of post-orgasmic bliss while Jed continued to shower me with affection. Hell, I could so get used to this.

When voices below announced Aunt Polly's arrival home, he pulled away with a sigh.

"And when I'm not thinking about all of those caveman things," he continued his train of thought from earlier, which I'd totally forgotten amid hormonal overload, "I'm thinking of talking to you and laughing with you and just being with you."

His confession was so genuine and tender. He squeezed my waist and pulled me tight against his broad chest.

"I want to be with you, without analyzing what it means or where it's going or rating it on some dating or relationship barometer. And I want you to be with me, too, in the same way," he whispered against my temple, his heart hammering hard in his chest, vibrating against mine. "Do you think you could do that, Lola?"

Forgetting all of my fears and plans, I nodded, my temple scraping against his beard. "I can do that, Jed."

He pulled away and gave me one of those big, dimpled smiles, sending off a forest of butterflies in my belly.

"Come to my house on Sunday."

"Okay," I automatically agreed, ready to agree to anything he wanted at this point. "What's happening Sunday?"

"Family barbecue at my place." He stepped back and pressed a final quick kiss to my lips.

Then he was out the door and jogging down the stairs.

"Wait." I popped my head out the door. "Did you say *family* barbecue?"

He stopped at the bottom and looked back, grinning like mad at what must've been my horrified expression.

"Get ready, Cola. You're going to meet the family."

Chapter Twenty

-JED-

"Where should I put this?"

Caroline's husband Thomas stood in my kitchen holding a Pyrex dish of macaroni and cheese.

"Put it in the oven. It's set on warm."

"Well, don't you look handsome?" Caroline sashayed in behind Thomas.

"Beer?" he asked, pointing out the sliding door to my back patio, eyebrows raised. Thomas was a man of few words. We got along perfectly.

"Yep."

He patted my shoulder as he passed by me.

"So, where's this girlfriend of yours?" asked Caroline, hiking two-year-old Tessa up higher on her hip.

Heat immediately flushed up my cheeks. "She's not my girlfriend, and I'd appreciate it if you'd refrain from calling her that in front of her."

"Why?"

"Because I'd like her to *be* my girlfriend, and I need y'all not to scare her off just yet."

"You're so paranoid," she said, rolling her eyes before plopping her diaper bag on my kitchen counter. "Take her, please, so I can put her bottles in the fridge."

"Come here, Tinkerbell."

She giggled as I scooped her into my arms. Immediately, she went for my beard as usual.

Though it was too short for her to get a good grip, she tried anyway.

"Ow!" I feigned pain and made a sad face.

She giggled and did it again.

"Ow!"

Giggle and repeat, till finally, I pretended to cry. That's when I felt the squish of two tiny,

cool hands on my cheeks. When I peeked my eyes open, she squeezed my cheeks harder.

"Unc Jay," she gurgled, the closest she could get to Uncle Jed at this point.

"That's right, Tink. Unc Jay's got you."

"Where's Dad?" asked Caroline, closing the fridge and moving the diaper bag on my breakfast table by the bay windows overlooking the backyard. "How's he doing this week?"

"Outside with Sally and the kids. Good. Aggravated as usual."

"Pfft. He's still mad about the nurse?"

I shrugged, poking Tessa in the belly to make her giggle some more. "Yeah, but until he gets his blood pressure back to normal, he's gonna have to deal with it."

"You know he's been getting Bekah to sneak him a dozen of Daisy's donuts on her visits, don't you?"

"I have not!" protested Bekah, stepping into the kitchen from the living room with Lola right behind her. "I only bring him a half a dozen."

My breath left my lungs. You'd think I'd get used to the effect of her walking into the same room as me by now. But I wasn't. Everything about her set my nerves on fire. Right now, I couldn't resist meeting her halfway across the kitchen. She looked so pretty, her curly hair piled in a bun, tendrils framing her heart-shaped face, green eyes wide. In denim shorts and a frilly, off-the-shoulder top, I had to stop myself from grabbing her ass when I hugged her with one arm.

Tessa squealed in delight, reminding me I was still holding my baby niece. When I pulled away, I didn't see she had a hold of Lola's bun.

"Ouch," Lola whispered as I tried to disentangle the toddler's wet fingers from her hair.

"Oh, shit."

"Sit," said Tessa, giggling.

"Aw, hell."

"Shut up, Jed." Caroline stood there, watching and laughing at me as I taught her daughter some new vocabulary.

"You wanna help here?"

Caroline's green eyes popped wide as she hustled across the kitchen. "I'm so sorry. I have no manners. Especially when my baby brother is embarrassing himself."

"Does that happen often?" asked Lola, tilting her head sideways as both Caroline and I tried to pry Tessa's sticky fingers from Lola's curly hair.

"No," said my sister, giving Lola a conspiratorial smile. "Which is why I just have to enjoy it when it happens."

"Thanks." I glared at her over Lola's head.

"There!" Caroline swept Tessa out of my arms, holding her wrist. There were at least four curly hairs stuck to her chubby fingers.

"Sit," squealed Tessa.

"No, no, baby girl. Don't say that." Caroline was still laughing as she walked her to the sink to wash her hands. "I'm so sorry, Lola!"

"It's okay."

I finally turned my attention back to her, horrified at what Tessa had done in a matter of seconds. Lola's beautiful hair was unraveled entirely, the bun hanging to one side, tendrils twisting every which way.

"I'm sorry," I said, staring at the mess Tessa had made. That baby girl was notorious for the wreckage she left behind.

"Don't worry." She felt the horrific mess of her hair. "Could I use a bathroom, though?"

"Yeah, of course." I led her out of the kitchen and around the corner, where I had a half bath right off the hallway. "Right in here."

She glanced up at me shyly and ducked inside. I took that moment to lean back against the wall and wonder why the fuck I thought this would be a good idea. She was barely in the door before she'd been assaulted by a drooling two-year-old. That was the youngest of my family.

No telling what the others would do. By the time she made it through them all, she'd be apologizing and remembering something she needed to do at home. Or worse, she'd just sneak out the back door and send me an I-changed-my-mind text.

The door opened, and she jumped to find me still there. "You didn't have to wait for me."

I gripped her shoulders to make sure I had her full attention. "This isn't exactly how I wanted your first moments with my family to go. Seriously, I'm *so* sorry."

She tilted her head back and laughed loud and hard, and I swear to all the angels in heaven, I felt it shimmer deep inside my chest, filling me with an unidentifiable joy I'd never felt before. When she braced both her hands on my shoulders and said in all seriousness, "Nothing to be sorry about," I knew I was so far gone, I was completely hopeless.

"I should cut this crazy mop anyway," she added.

I braced her with a hand around her nape, holding her still as I dipped my head for a luscious kiss. I kept it soft, gentle, just a little sip. Saving the best for later. Hopefully.

"Don't you dare," I warned her. "I love that crazy mop. The one thing you can't keep in control, Cola."

She nuzzled my beard with her nose on a soft laugh. "You know all my secrets, don't you, Jedediah?"

"Not yet." I traced the line of her pretty jaw with one finger. "But I want to."

"Jedediah!" yelled Caroline from the kitchen. "Are you actually going to watch the grill, or do I have to put Thomas on it?"

I grabbed Lola's hand and guided her back toward the kitchen. "We don't want that."

"We don't?"

"Thomas is a great guy. But the last time I let him watch the grill while I did an ice and beer run, I came back to charred burgers."

She laughed, squeezing closer as we made it through the kitchen, where Caroline was putting the garlic bread into the oven, and out to the covered patio. Dad was in a chair next to Sally, who was listening intently to whatever he was saying. That was pretty much the norm.

Sally was really close to Dad, her being the oldest and the one who helped him the most when he was widowed at a relatively young age with five kids to raise. Thomas and Sally's son, my nephew Pete, were taking turns throwing the ball with Joe. Bekah bounced Tessa on her knee next to my fourteen-year-old niece Zoe as they chatted away.

"Oh!" Sally jumped out of her chair, taking notice of us. "I'm Jed's oldest sister Sally." She offered her hand. Lola shook it. "Bekah has told me so many things about you."

"She has?"

"Told to her from Marly of course. All good." She turned to Dad. "This is Lola Landry. This is our Dad, John Lawson."

I bit back a smile as Lola shrank into me after shaking my dad's hand. He was an intimidating specimen. Almost as tall and as big as me, he may have lost some muscle over the years, but none of his presence. He still had a way of charming the ladies with his silver hair and beard, no matter their age.

"Pleasure to meet you, Lola. If you can stand sticking around, I'd be in your debt."

"Um, yes, sir. And why would that be?"

"Because my son needs someone else to dote on besides his competent father."

"Dad," chastised Sally, "Jed's just looking out for you."

"As I've said before, I don't need looking after. You've got that damn nurse here on a weekly rotation again." The accusation was for me.

"Physical therapist, Dad. Until Dr. Paulson clears you, he'll keep coming," I tossed back at him, not ruffled in the least.

Dad growled, which made Lola shift closer against my side. The fact that she was subconsciously seeking comfort from me made my chest tighten sweetly.

"Stick around, girl," Dad ordered Lola with a fierce glint. "He needs a woman so he'll stay out of my damn hair." Then he wandered off onto the lawn toward Thomas and Pete.

"His bark is worse than his bite," I whispered down to her.

"Hi. I'm Zoe." My teenage niece thrust her hand out for Lola cordially, but her fierce expression was the only warning she got before she asked, "How do you know my uncle exactly? And how long have you been dating?"

"Uh." Lola glanced up at me, but I didn't say a word. "We met in high school, actually. We've been dating a few weeks. A month?"

"About that."

Not quite a month, but somehow it felt like we'd been together forever. Her hand felt right inside mine, her body perfectly tucked against me.

"Well, I don't know if this is for fun or for real, but either way, be sure you're using protection."

"Zoe!" screeched Sally before I could even react.

"What? That's what Aunt Bekah told me."

"Rebekah Ann, what the hell are you teaching my daughter?"

"Your *teenage* daughter?" Bekah sipped her margarita in a Solo cup, still bouncing Tessa. "Everything she needs to know."

"She doesn't need *that* talk yet."

"Mom, please. I've known about sex since I was ten when you bought goats for the farm."

"Boys aren't goats," snapped Sally.

"Could've fooled me," murmured Bekah as Caroline picked Tessa off her lap. "They run around, butting their heads, and wanna eat and hump everything. They're basically goats."

"So I should go ahead and give Tessa the talk," added Caroline.

"Trust me," Bekah assured her. "She needs to know as soon as possible."

"Sit," squealed Tessa on her hip.

"Sit?" asked Bekah.

"Don't ask." Caroline sighed, giving me a look before wandering out to the lawn where Pete and Joe were both rolling around together.

"Let's check the chicken," I said, tugging on Lola's hand.

"Seriously, though," Zoe cut in, still wearing her stern face, "if Jed likes you, then I'm sure I will, too. Eventually."

"Come on." I chuckled as we made our way to the grill, where I'd been slow-cooking the chicken for several hours.

"Is her bark worse than her bite, too?" Lola whispered as we walked away.

"No. She'll tear you to shreds. I'm terrified for the first boy who tries dating her."

"I don't think her mom needs to worry so much."

"Not at all. If anything, the teenage boys of Green Valley need to beware of the force of that girl. They'll lose their balls for looking at her wrong."

She crossed her arms as I opened the lid and pulled my tongs from the hook on the side to turn the chicken one last time. It was almost ready.

"So she's gotten the defense lessons, too, I presume."

I shook my head on a laugh. "Not only did she finish every course Tempest taught, but she took up kickboxing."

"Well, I hope she isn't afraid I'm going to break your fragile heart or something."

A sudden riot of emotion swirled inside my chest, making that fragile organ in question thump quite a bit faster.

"I think that's exactly what she's afraid of." I couldn't help the intimate and heartfelt words from spilling from my mouth. I watched her reaction, afraid any small admission would chase her screaming from my house. And yet, there was nothing I could do about it.

My gaze wandered down her sweet, curvy body, those shapely legs on full display. My body hardened, but my heart softened. And my soul listened. This girl was exceptional, and every nerve ending in my body knew it.

I went back to flipping the chicken. "Besides, I'm Zoe's favorite."

"Why's that?"

"I think it started when I bought her a pony. Well, Cisco is a horse really."

"You didn't."

"Every little girl wants a pony."

"And you gave it to her."

"Why not?" I caught her shaking her head as she looked back at my family. "What?"

"*You.*" She tossed her hands up to gesture at me as if that explained things. "It's just not fair," she whined, tilting her head back to stare up at the afternoon sky.

"Life is never fair. You just have to make roses out of shit-hills most of the time." I flipped the last piece, then smiled at her. "It all works out. Now tell me what's not fair exactly."

She rubbed her hands down her cheeks in exasperation. "You cook. You take your grandmother grocery shopping. You take care of your dad. You make little toddler nieces all googly-eyed over you. You have all these crazy potential long-term-partner skills, and it's driving me crazy." She blew an errant curl out of her face.

I hooked the tongs on the side and faced her, holding her low on her hips. Then I murmured, "I've got so many skills, Cola. I can change a diaper. I mix formula bottles. I can even braid Zoe's hair into a fishtail."

She pouted, looking wholly put out. "You can't braid a fishtail. *I* can't even braid a fishtail."

Edging closer, I leaned down and whispered against her temple. "I've got other skills."

She hooked her fingers through the side-loops of my jeans, exhaling softly, her breath heating my neck.

"Let me show you."

"Tell me first."

"I want to taste you again. Hear you make those sweet sounds you make right before you come. I want to fuck you so slow," I whispered in her ear, "till you beg me to pound you."

"Merciful heavens."

"No mercy, baby."

"Here," said Bekah, poking her body in between ours and holding up a Solo cup for Lola. "I thought you might need this. This is my own concoction made with margarita moonshine. It's got an extra kick you might appreciate." She gestured toward the patio with a nod of her head. "Gran just got here."

Chapter Twenty-One

-LOLA-

"My boyfriend's mom is so different from me. I don't know if I like his family."
@YogaNut
"You're not dating his family. But also, different can be good. How boring would life be if we were all the same?" @kiss-n-tell

Meeting Jed's family was like falling into a vortex and being squeezed tight by fluffy teddy bears and sharp-toothed piranhas at the same time. Yes, I knew that metaphor didn't work, but that's the best way to describe the force of meeting such a rambunctious family.

I was used to my own family gatherings which—besides the Thanksgiving pilgrimage to my grandparents' house in North Carolina where all my weird cousins lived—was just me, Mom, Dad, and my kooky but kind Aunt Polly. This menagerie sitting at the two long tables under the patio was a combination of aggressive predators and passive prey.

I was well aware that I was prey today because Zoe pretty much spelled it out for me on our second conversation, where she expressed in no minced words how protective she was of her Uncle Jed and, more importantly, his feelings. If I weren't so terrified, I'd admire the man for acquiring that level of loyalty.

On top of sitting next to Gran the entire meal, who told me I needed to eat more carbs because while I had a *healthy width in the hips,* my upper body required *more packing*. She said all that with a laser look toward Jed, and I wondered if she thought I was competing against him on the football field. But then his youngest sister Samantha, who attended UT and had picked Gran up on her way in, told me to ignore her grandmother. She was only concerned that I wasn't strong enough to handle Jed in bed.

When I choked on my chicken, Bekah passed me my second margarita, and I nearly downed the whole drink in one swallow. Not to clear the errant chicken, but to numb my fracturing nerves. That Green Valley moonshine sure had the pleasant kick I needed.

To top it all off, I'd imagined Jed's father as this feeble man, hardly able to get out of his recliner. Not this strapping silver fox sitting at the opposite end of the table from Jed with the semi-permanent scowl only making him more handsome. It was like thinking, *I wonder what Jed will look like in thirty years*, then turning my head right and seeing him transport through time.

"Want some more chocolate pie?" asked Samantha, who was the sweetest of the family.

Besides Pete, Sally's son, who blushed every time one of his aunt's teased him or kissed his cheek or ruffled his hair. He was ten and absolutely adorable. His black hair and high cheekbones reminded me of a certain someone sitting at one end of the table. Pete would be breaking hearts in middle school in a few years.

"No, thank you. I couldn't eat another bite."

She popped up and took my plate before I could stop her, the rest of the family starting to pack up their things. Pete ran back into the yard to play with Joe while Sally recovered what remained of the three pies she'd brought with Zoe helping her.

"Can I help carry something?"

"No, I've got it," said Sally with a smile and a glance at her brother. "Thanks for hosting, as always."

"I'm happy to," he said, taking the remainder of the heavy-duty paper plates to the kitchen trash he'd set out on the patio.

In the span of one fabulous barbeque, it became alarmingly clear that Jed was the center of this family. Yet again reminding me that Green Valley was his home.

As if the fates heard my thoughts, my phone buzzed in my pocket. I pulled it out to see an email notification from Optimum Media. My stomach did a somersault.

I stepped inside the kitchen and quickly opened the email, reading their polite greeting and wish to set up an interview. I couldn't explain the utter joy coupled with the stinging pain I felt at that moment. I glanced out the sliding glass door at Jed hugging Bekah and Caroline goodbye before they traipsed off, hooking their arms through Mr. Lawson's and heading through the side gate.

I quickly replied to the email, graciously accepting the interview appointment in two days, all the while feeling a nauseating sinking sensation in the pit of my stomach.

"Something up?" Jed was carrying the trash bin back inside.

"No, nothing. Just work stuff."

"Podcast?"

I slipped the phone back in my pocket and looked around for something, anything, to talk about. "Smart move with the paper plates. No dishes to do."

Thankfully, he followed my quick change of the conversation. "With this crew? No way. Sally hosts Christmas, and she brings out the nice glassware. But Bekah and Samantha always end up doing the dishes because they don't contribute anything to the meal."

"Those are the rules? Bring food, and you're excused from cleanup?"

"Yep."

"I'll remember that then." I shook my head, confused at my own silly comment. I wouldn't be around for Christmas, at least I didn't think. "I mean, not that I'd be invited to Christmas. I don't know what I was—"

He had his hands cupping my face and his mouth on mine before I could stammer out any other objections. My immediate response was gluing my body to his and sucking his tongue into my mouth.

"Get a room," said Sally, coming in from the patio.

We pulled apart.

"This is my house." Jed glanced at her, smiling as he skirted by me to scoop some Solo cups off the counter and toss them in the trash.

"True. Guess we better get going then."

Caroline barreled through, grabbing the bottle Tessa didn't drink from the fridge and shoving it back in her diaper bag. Thomas walked in, carrying his daughter in one arm like a football and Pete sitting on his foot, arms and legs wrapped around his leg monkey-style.

"Anyone seen, Pete?" he asked, all serious as he tromped through the kitchen, dragging his weighted leg. "I wanted to give him a hundred dollars, but he disappeared."

"I'm here, I'm here!" he hopped off of Thomas's leg and did a jumping jack in place.

"Nope. Already gave it to Zoe." Thomas headed out the door with a two-finger salute to Jed.

"You did not!" Pete trailed after him, laughing.

"It was nice meeting you," said Sally, carrying two stacked pie dishes. "I hope we didn't scare you off."

"Not at all." I leaned against his kitchen counter and hugged my waist. "I enjoyed it."

"Uncle Jed, you're still coming by Thursday after work?" Zoe asked right behind her mom.

Jed had cinched two trash bags and had them both in hand. "I'll be there," he answered, blank-faced.

"Don't tell me you're braiding hair," I teased.

Zoe's brow puckered into a frown. "No, Uncle Jed helps me with my English papers."

"No way!" I shouted. "You tutor your niece too?" I realized right after that my disbelief might've come across as insulting in that he wasn't capable of tutoring, rather than there was one more thing added to Jed's resume for sainthood.

Something in the dead silence that followed hollowed out my stomach and replaced it with a stone of dread. Jed was tying the trash bag tighter unnecessarily, and Zoe's expression shifted from confusion to something akin to anger. They obviously misunderstood what I'd meant.

"I just meant—"

"Uncle Jed is the only one who knows how to help me." I felt the punch coming before it hit. "He has dyslexia like me."

I stood there and blinked, then blinked faster, wrestling with the avalanche of emotion swelling from my gut and trying to pour out of my eyes. I quickly turned away toward the sink as Zoe casually said, "Night, Uncle Jed." Then left.

"Night, Zoe." I felt his gaze at the dead center of my back, and I stood there, wishing he'd shoot an arrow straight through me and put me out of my sickening misery.

The trash bags dropped to the floor as the front door closed, and we were finally alone. I was afraid to make a sound, even to breathe, or the floodgates would open.

"Lola."

He used my real name, and that was all it took. I choked on a sob, cupping my hand over my mouth.

"Hey, hey. What's going on?"

"What's going on!" I spun and stepped back so he couldn't touch me. I couldn't handle him touching me right now. "You're dyslexic!"

"I know." He chuckled and gave me a self-deprecating smile that sliced right across my heart. "Don't worry. It's not contagious."

"Don't joke about this, you idiot!" I gasped, hot tears pouring as my mouth ran on without my permission. "Oh, my God. You're *not* an idiot. I'd never say that. But I did. I did! I called you Jockstrap Jed—" I sobbed again —"and everybody called you that, too. Because of me!"

My voice had taken on a squeaky twang I couldn't make disappear.

"Whoa, whoa, whoa." He looked genuinely concerned as he eased closer, hands out like he was trying to calm a wild animal. As much as I wanted to let him ease my agonizing and spiraling hysteria, I backed away, then turned and fled into the living room, where I paced beside his couch, looking for my purse.

"What are you doing?" he asked, following me, completely confused.

"I've gotta go, Jed. I've gotta go. I can't believe what I did."

I really must've seemed on the edge of a panic attack because I'm pretty sure I was already there.

"Baby, slow down." He grabbed me from behind, wrapping both arms across my chest and squeezing me firmly against his own. I resisted for two seconds before easing back into him. "Easy, Lola."

That made me cry even more. I lifted my hands to my face, my forearms crisscrossing his, then I just wept like a baby.

"Shhh." His mouth was in my ear as he rocked me against him, slowly from side to side. "Stop," he shushed me. "You did nothing wrong."

"I made fun of you because you were failing English. I called you that name," I whispered harshly, then I struggled to get loose, grabbing hold of his vise grip, but he didn't let me go.

"Do you remember why you made up that name?"

"Because I was a mean, hateful, spiteful skank."

"No." He chuckled into my neck. "Because I'd called you Coca-Cola Lola the day before. You were getting back at me, and rightfully so."

My jagged breathing slowed, but the tender sore still hurt—the one I'd made myself. "I remember being so mad at you that day," I admitted. "You told your friends I was a know-it-all."

"I know." He sighed, his giant chest spanning my entire back heaving out. "You'd noticed how many tests I was failing, and I refused to tell anyone why I was failing, so I deflected the attention away from me by dubbing you the four-eyed busy-body." He hugged me closer, whispering against the tender skin at the base of my neck. "It worked, and I was an asshole for it. Can you forgive me?"

"Me?" I twisted my head around since he apparently wasn't letting me loose. "I called someone with dyslexia, who I admired, a stupid jock in front of the whole class, and they laughed at you."

Bitterness dripped from every word coming out of my mouth.

He swallowed hard, his Adam's apple working. "That's on me. If I'd been able to face my disability then and maybe ask for help, then I wouldn't have hurt you. And you, in turn, wouldn't have hurt me."

"I never meant to hurt you." I gazed up over my shoulder into his hazel eyes that were sweeping over every inch of my face. "I don't think you're dumb."

His dimpled smile peeped out, and my bones melted. Good thing he was still holding me up. "I'm glad to hear that."

"I think you're really smart. And sweet. And kind. And strong and brave." I hiccupped on another sob. "I'm sorry for making fun of you." I swallowed the knot swelling again in my throat. "Do you forgive me?"

"Oh, Lola." His voice rolled deep and luscious. He dipped his head low as he unfolded one arm from across my chest to scoop away the neck of my shirt, exposing my birthmark. "I'm sorry for making fun of you." His mouth opened on my skin, then he whispered, "Do you forgive me?"

"Yes," I breathed. "I'll forgive you more if you keep doing that."

He swiped my shirt over my head and tossed it aside before I could blink. His mouth swept hot kisses down my throat as his hands tugged my bra straps down my shoulders. "Stay the night," he pleaded in a husky rasp.

I reached back to grab hold of his jean-clad thighs. "Yes."

Groaning, his hands mounded my breasts as he rocked his hips against my behind. His thumbs circled my nipples, drawing them tight before slipping them down to my jean shorts, unsnapping them furiously.

"You've been torturing me all day in these shorts," he growled, scraping his teeth along the column of my throat.

"It wasn't my intention," I mumbled, tipping my head back against his chest.

"I think it was."

I laughed, then sucked in a deep breath when he shoved my shorts and panties down my legs, then wrapped an arm around my waist and lifted me two feet over to the end of the couch.

"Jed—"

Before I could think or ask what he was doing, he was on his knees behind me, pressing a palm to the center of my back to lean me forward. I wasn't about to protest, already moaning at what I knew was coming. Right as my cheek hit the sofa cushion, his hot mouth opened on my slit.

"Shit." I went up on my toes, barely able to withstand the sensation of his lashing tongue, but he gripped the backs of my thighs to keep me in place, groaning as he worked me hard.

"I could lick you all fucking night," he grated huskily as he swept a thumb from my entrance to my clit, spreading the wetness from me and his tongue in a slick circle. "If I didn't want to get inside you so goddamn bad."

He stroked his tongue inside me. My spine arched on reflex. "That's right." That seemed to please him further as he set back to work. "Open for me."

When he widened my thighs, I went easily, having zero shame in giving him full access. The spiraling pleasure soared through me, catapulting toward the point of contact where his tongue flicked my clit.

"Fuck, yes," I muffled into the cushion, rocking back against him.

He slid the tips of two fingers through my lips, then pumped inside me. Clawing my hands into the couch cushion, my leg muscles tensed as I came with a sudden jolt and rush of inner spasms. I would've been embarrassed at how fast I came if it didn't feel so damn good.

He groaned with me, lapping softly around my sensitive clit. I slumped into the sofa, my whole body falling limp. I didn't move when I heard Jed stand and unbuckle his belt or toss his shirt to the floor or the crinkle of a condom wrapper.

"Can I just not move?" I was limp already.

"You're perfect where you are."

"You just do whatever you want," I panted. "I'll wait right here."

He chuckled, then his hand slid up my spine right as the thick head of his cock was *there*, spreading me further.

"Christ," he hissed, gripping my hip as he pushed in slowly, letting my body stretch for him.

My claws were back in the couch cushions, grabbing for purchase, but there was no holding on or preparing for the dizzying sensation of Jed's cock entering me for the first time.

I whimpered and lifted onto my elbows, pressing my ass back toward him, giving him more of me.

"Fuck, yes." Gripping my hips, he gave me slow, deep slides, knocking the breath right out of me with each sharp thrust at the end.

"More," I murmured, reaching back and gripping the wrist of one hand on my hip. "God, please *more.*"

He leaned forward and slid my arms up to cross above my head, his own larger ones enveloping mine. Our fingers were tangled, not quite laced, but gripping and grasping, desperate to clutch and hang on. It just didn't seem possible. Our bodies needed to move over and inside each other, our will not even our own anymore, instinct taking over.

He pressed his broad chest over my back, blanketing me in warmth and muscle and man, as he fucked me into a sweet stupor. I turned my head sideways and nipped his bicep just within biting range. He flexed.

"God. Damn," he growled, pounding me harder, all while cocooning me with his massive body and arms. "So fucking good. I knew it," he whispered close to my ear before biting my lobe, which only made my inner body contract in response. His rumbling growl vibrated from his chest into my back. "You're so fucking beautiful, Lola."

"So are you," I whispered, licking the reddish bite I'd just made on his bicep.

I had no idea sex could feel like this. I'd dated some guys who were pretty damn good in bed, but nothing felt like this. He wasn't just stroking me with his cock but touching me in places no one else possibly could. I'd kept men at a distance. Not because I was a commitment-phobe or because I feared intimacy, but because that level of affection had never appealed to me. Letting men in that far, that deep, felt messy and unpredictable and therefore uncomfortable. Hence, something I never wanted or remotely desired.

But, Jed.

He didn't feel that way. He was already deep in my psyche before our recent reunion. Since then, he'd slipped right under the covers, blindsiding me with fierce, unstoppable chemistry. The kind you know is a force all its own. It doesn't follow the laws of physics, but rather goes up and down, back and forth of its own accord, defying the every-action-has-an-equal-and-opposite-reaction rule. Because the reaction my body—my heart—was having to him wasn't of equal measure. It was mounting toward pleasure well beyond the norm, far greater than the expected. And my God, I loved it. I wanted it. Every damn drop.

"Jed, please," I whispered into his flexed bicep, giving him another nip with teeth as he ground into me with deep thrusts. "Make me come."

I needed that euphoria, that delirious edge of insanity, and Jed was driving me toward it with pounding precision.

"Whatever you want, I'll give it to you." He lifted off and out of me. I whimpered in protest at the near-painful loss of him. Then he picked me up and sat on the sofa, straddling my legs on either side of his lap. "Ride me." His voice was gravel-deep. "I want to watch you fuck me."

His jeans were still half on, riding low on his hips. He gripped the base of his dick, guiding me by the waist to slide down. Bracing myself on his flexed shoulders, I sank down onto him, both of us moaning with deep pleasure. I was so full, so aroused, breathless at the hot slide of him in and out of me.

He gripped my hips, fingertips digging into the flesh of my behind, and guided me in the sweetest tempo. I picked up pace then he leaned forward, that lock of hair falling in front of one eye as his mouth latched onto my nipple.

"Shit." I fisted one hand in the back of his hair at the nape, holding his head to my breast. "Yes, suck me like that," I whispered on a pant, riding him faster.

His big hands slid from my hips to grip my ass as he licked a line across one breast, down the slope between, and up the other to flick my other nipple with his tongue. Then he latched on and sucked me hard.

"God, yes." I rocked my hips in a circle as I came down, rubbing my clit against his hard shaft. "I'm about to come."

He fell back against the couch, resting his head on the cushion, his hands wrapping my hips as he watched me with a hooded gaze. Those molten eyes observed me with singular attentiveness, like a king admiring his spoils of war. And there I was, mounted and owning the most wonderfully erotic throne.

Without breaking eye contact, his eyes so dark they looked black, he slid his hand up to his mouth and licked the pad of his thumb before he lowered to stroke my clit in slow circles.

"Jed," I gasped, squeezing hard as I came, falling forward, my mouth opening on his neck.

I bit him, moaning through the orgasm as one of Jed's hands slid up my spine to my nape and gripped me there, the other still grasping my hip, holding me down.

He crushed his mouth to mine for a soulful kiss, then whispered against my mouth in a raspy command, "Hold on."

Then he gripped my waist and held me aloft, fucking me from the bottom, driving up hard and fast to the point I definitely had to hold on. His cock thickened further, then he hissed and held me tight, coming on a long groan.

"Fuck, fuck, fuck," he murmured against my neck, his dick pulsing inside me. "I think that tested the strength of the latex."

Though I was on the pill, I teased back, still panting, "Hope you didn't buy discount condoms."

He placed a suckling kiss right below my ear. "Only the best for you." Then another kiss on my jaw and another on my puffy lips. "Sorry I didn't make it to the bed."

I slid his lock of hair out of his eyes. "Do you see me complaining?"

He grinned. "That was..." He grinned wider.

"It was," I agreed, unable to hide my loopy smile either.

"Not sure if my legs work now, though. Can you carry me to the bedroom?"

"Ha. Ha. Very funny. I believe you better display your masculine prowess and carry me."

"That wasn't enough masculine prowess?" His eyebrows shot up.

"Maybe." I started to sit up, squeezing my thighs and inner muscles.

He sucked in a breath between his teeth. "You did that on purpose."

"Did what?" I did it again, squeezing hard, knowing he could feel me.

His eyes narrowed before he lifted me up and plopped me onto the sofa, bending my leg so he could pop my ass.

"Hey!"

He laughed as he headed to the hall bathroom to take care of the condom. All the while, I marveled that sex with Jed was aggressive, but also...playful. Who would've thought?

I glanced around, looking for my shirt. I found it and slipped it on without the bra, debating whether I should just get dressed and go home.

I mean, did he really want me to sleepover? Or did he just want to have sex?

While I analyzed the hell out of that, he'd washed up and returned in only his boxer briefs, which nearly made me choke on my tongue. I'd been so sex-addled, I hadn't properly taken in the beauty of this man. He wasn't all ripped abs and whatnot, but hard, thick lines and slabs of muscle honed from hard work and lifting actual heavy shit, not barbells in a gym.

I was still staring and admiring when he scooped me up in his arms and headed back toward the hallway.

"What are you doing?"

"As my queen commands. Carrying her to the bedroom lest she thinks my masculinity too unworthy of her."

I kicked my calves in a playful swing and smacked him on the bristly cheek, unable to hold in my giddy emotions.

He chuckled then tossed me on his bed. Pulling back the gray down comforter, he then shifted me up by the waist, landed beside me, and tucked us both under the covers. There was a lamp lit next to his bed. He reached over and switched it off, then lay sideways to face me, resting his head on his bent arm.

"Give me a few minutes, and then I'll take care of your pleasure again."

I laughed. "I'm pretty well-pleasured."

"Hmm."

His smiling eyes perused my face as I scooted closer to him on my side, tangling my legs with his, marveling at how good his ticklish coarse hair felt.

"When I can muster the strength, I want to fuck you again as soon as possible. If that's amenable to you."

"As long as I'm not asleep. REM is important."

"As important as sex endorphins?"

I rolled my eyes. "Way more important."

"I believe you've got your priorities mixed up, Cola."

"My priorities are always in perfect order." My mind went straight to that email from Optimum Media.

"What? You're not regretting it already, are you?" Actual fear shone in his eyes for a second.

"No. Not one bit. Guess I'm more tired than I thought." Which was true because I'd worked myself into a frenzy of anxiety about the family dinner. My body was finally coming down from a cliff of stress-induced mania. The nirvana level of sex might've had something to do with my rapid decline.

"Roll over."

I obeyed without hesitation. He slid a hand under my t-shirt and began scratching my back with blunt nails. The gentle sweep of his fingers made me want to arch my back and purr.

"Oh, my Lord, that is heavenly."

He chuckled. "Night, Cola."

"Night," I murmured into the pillow, drifting off to the soft caress of his magical hands.

Chapter Twenty-Two

-JED-

I woke to my raging hard-on pressed into the cleft of Lola's perfect ass. But that wasn't what really caught my attention, believe it or not. It was that her shirt gaped open just enough to reveal part of her birthmark. The one I'd admired and dreamed of kissing countless times as a shy teenage boy, too dumb to just explain to her how I felt. I wanted to tell her now. I was aching to, but I was fairly positive my feelings were much stronger than hers.

I brushed my thumb over her birthmark, remembering last night. Being inside her was better than all one thousand of my fantasies.

She moved, brushing her soft ass back against my cock. I groaned, unable to stop from leaning down and pressing a kiss to her birthmark, marveling that this was real, that I was actually kissing and touching Lola Landry. That she was in my bed. That we'd fucked last night. And that we were about to fuck again this morning. My cock jerked at the thought.

"Mmm," she hummed, rubbing her back and ass against me.

Sliding my hand under her t-shirt, I swept up to her breast, pinching her tight nipple lightly. She arched her spine, pressing her breast into my palm. I kneaded and pinched it softly, rocking my hard dick against her ass.

"Are you awake?" I murmured into her ear.

"I think I'm having a really good dream," she murmured in a sleepy voice.

"I'm about to fuck you hard into this mattress, Cola."

She just sighed when I slid my hand from her breast down over her hip, gripped her thigh, and spread her. I inserted my leg between hers, holding her open with a bent knee, then slid my middle finger along her pussy.

"*Christ*," I hissed into the skin of her neck, nibbling and whispering, "Like hot, wet silk."

She didn't say a word, her breathing coming quicker as she reached back to my hip, then tried to wrestle my boxer briefs lower. I lifted my hips till she was able to slide her slender hand inside and wrap her small hand around my dick.

Biting down onto her shoulder, I thrust into her hand right as I pumped two fingers into her pussy. "I need to get inside you." I licked a line up to her ear, nosing her thick hair aside. "I need to bury myself deep, Lola."

"I'm on the pill," she whispered. "Have you been tested since your last partner?"

"Yes. I'm clean."

"Me too."

Then she arched her spine, presenting her pussy for me to take. So I took her fast and hard like I wanted, driving in with one deep thrust.

"Fuck, yes." The feel of her bare, wet pussy squeezing tight around my dick was beyond heavenly. I gripped her bent thigh and spread her wider, lifting up onto my forearm so I could watch my dick disappear inside her. "Touch yourself. Let me see what you do to make yourself come."

She immediately slid two fingers into her own wetness and stroked back up to rub tiny, quick circles around her clit. All the while, I pumped into her faster. Deeper.

"Look at that," I growled. "How good my dick looks fucking you." I placed a suckling kiss below her ear. "Our bodies fit perfectly together." I scraped her with my teeth. "We were made for each other."

She moaned, trying to rock back and meet my pace, but my hips were moving so fast and hard, the *slap, slap, slap* of my thighs hitting her ass had me about to come already.

"You better come soon. I can't hold it long. You feel too good." I bit her again on the neck. "So wet and tight."

"Yes, yes," she hissed, her hips spasming.

I let go of her thigh and gripped her hip, thrusting deep and holding, my eyes rolling back in my head at the milking sensation of her orgasm around me. Before the pulsing of her climax had eased, I rolled on top of her, her head pillowed on my forearm, then I rutted like a wild animal, unable to stop myself.

I was a big guy and was careful of being overly aggressive or using my size ungently, never wanting to hurt someone by accident. I'd always been doubly careful when having sex, very aware of my ability to hurt a woman if I was too rough. And though I had zero thoughts of hurting Lola—far from it—a primal need to push deeper, to mark her permanently, somehow buzzed me into a near frenzy, pushing my need to dominate and fuck her harder.

"God, yeah," I breathed into the back of her neck, biting, suckling kisses along her shoulders as I pounded into her, my sac hitting her upturned pussy with each deep drive.

As my orgasm spiraled toward completion, I couldn't think beyond territorial words, like *mine* and *wife* and *forever*. The shock of it stole my breath as I came so hard the edge of my vision blurred. Pushing up on my hands, I arched my back as I pushed with all my force, burying myself as deep as I could.

"Oh, God," she whimpered.

"Yeah," I huffed after a long euphoric release, falling to my forearms and catching my breath. "Fucking fantastic," I panted.

I remained buried inside of her, wishing I could stay there forever.

Forever. That word again. My heart stuttered at where my brain was running away with itself. How could I have catapulted from mild obsession—okay, maybe more than mild—to dreaming of keeping her? Forever?

I kissed a line across her shoulders then pressed one to her temple.

Her mouth tipped up in a sleepy smile. "Now that was a fine way to wake up."

I laughed a little, my heart still hammering and my mind reeling at what I'd just discovered. Realized.

"I'm going to take a quick shower, then cook you breakfast."

I took a two-minute shower, needing to hurry and escape to the kitchen to clear my obviously deranged mind. Because what the hell was I thinking?

After toweling off and pulling on some sweatpants and a T-shirt from my dresser, Lola was up, pulling at the hem of her shirt, which barely covered her upper thighs, looking completely sexed up and adorable.

"Mind if I take a quick shower too?"

"Not at all. You can use one of my T-shirts if you want." I pointed to my dresser as I headed toward the kitchen, my chest filling with something buoyant at the thought of her taking a shower in *my* shower, using *my* towels, wearing *my* shirt.

My mind strayed to food, my stomach rumbling. My girl needed protein. Omelets. Wait, does she like eggs?

I backtracked to the bathroom, the shower already running. When I stepped into my bathroom, I thanked my former self for choosing glass doors on the renovated bathroom when I'd moved in. Because, holy fuck. The sight of Lola with her head tipped back, water running in rivulets over that creamy skin and full curves, her hair snaking in slick waves down her back, had me clutching my chest.

Strangely, it wasn't my dick that reacted the most to the sight of her there, but that hammering organ beneath my ribs, pounding happily at the sheer beauty of her.

Suddenly feeling like I was intruding, even though I'd seen it all more than once in the last twelve hours, I backed out and knocked on the door jamb.

"Hey, you like eggs? I was thinking omelets."

"Oh! Yeah! I love anything. All food." she called over the streaming water. "I'm easy."

"The fuck you are," I called back, peeking in.

She opened one squinty eye, the water still pouring over her face. "Jed."

"It took me like nine years to get into your pants. You ain't easy."

"Nine!?" She wiped the water from her face, her arms hiding her breasts. She turned sideways, seeming shy with her body, which only made me want to get in there with her. "That would mean you've been thinking about this since, what, junior year?"

"Not nine then."

"That's what I thought." She faced the showerhead, giving me a spectacular view of her ass.

"Eleven," I corrected.

She snapped her head over her shoulder. "You have not been—"

"Oh, yes, I have, Cola."

With that admission, I slipped out of the bathroom before stripping off my clothes, climbing in the shower and showing her how much pent-up lust I had for the woman.

By the time I'd chopped the onions and peppers, precooked the bacon, then folded it all together with spinach and cheese, she was shuffling into the kitchen in one of my white undershirts, her jean cut-offs barely showing beneath the hem. She was crimping her damp hair, looking shy and sweet.

Joe, who I'd let inside, trotted over to her, tail wagging like a madman. He whined till she leaned over and petted him.

"Aren't you a sweet puppy?" she crooned.

She murmured to him as I plated the omelets and brought them to the table. "Out you go, Joe." I opened the sliding door and let him out, tossing a dog biscuit in the yard from the box I kept on the shelf by the door.

She pulled her phone from her pocket and set it on the table before sitting. We ate quietly for a minute before she said, "This is really good, Jed." She shook her head on a little laugh. "Way better than my cooking."

"Only one person in a partnership needs to cook." Fuck, why do I keep pushing so hard? "Or," I added lightly, "they need a lot of surplus cash for take-out."

Her brow pursed into a serious expression. "I couldn't help but check out some of your books on the shelf in your room." I waited, wondering where this was going. "I saw that book *Dune*. From high school. Remember?"

Do I remember? Hell, did I ever.

"Yeah."

"How did you—I mean, if you had dyslexia, why did you want to read such a ginormous book? Back then, that is. You were still struggling with it then, right?"

"I'm always struggling with it," I admitted. "It doesn't go away."

"Sorry. I didn't mean to offend you."

"Stop apologizing. There's no need. And you haven't offended me. It has gotten better over time, since I force myself to read more now rather than avoid it. There is something to that phrase; practice makes perfect. Though I'll never be perfect, the more I read, the better I am at it, using some practice methods I learned." I chewed another bite of my omelet and sipped my orange juice. "I'd seen the eighties movie *Dune* once and loved it. I'd always wanted to read the book to discover the author's perspective, you know?"

She nodded. "Did you finish it?"

"No. Not in high school. I avoided reading as much as possible. Especially if I got frustrated. And I don't know. Maybe it was hormones or whatever, but I got frustrated quickly back then. Don't get me wrong. I could read, but lengthier texts were hard. Especially ones for subjects I didn't know anything about, like when I was at UT. But I still wanted to prove to myself that I could do it. I wanted to finish *Dune*."

"But you did eventually?"

A sharp nod. "After dad had the stroke, it took forever for him to hold a spoon and feed himself. But he did it. You've met him, so you can imagine that strong-willed man being dependent on Sally and me and my other sisters for things like feeding himself and taking a shower or putting on his clothes drove him mad. His stroke was severe, but he came back from it."

"He had help," she offered softly, having finished her omelet and leaned back in her chair, hands in her lap, steadily watching me.

"He did. But it was his own strength of will that brought him fully back. With the exception of using his cane and a slight lisp in his speech, he is the same man he was before the stroke. Learning from him, I sought help. There was an online counselor and program through UT, which might've helped me and my grades had I found them before I quit, but they taught me methods to help my dyslexia."

She swallowed hard. Her watery eyes and sweet smile made me even more proud. "And now you help your niece, Zoe." She paused, taking a sip of juice before adding, "But you knew in high school, right?"

I nodded.

"Dyslexia isn't anything to be ashamed about."

"I know."

"Then why didn't you get help then?" There was a desperate kind of look in her eyes. I knew she wanted to travel back in time and help that kid back in high school because that's who she was—always wanting to help others, especially when it came to school.

"It was hard after my mom died," I confessed, a sudden hush in the air at the mention of that old pain that never truly went away. Only dulled around the edges. "My dad was unexpectedly stuck with five kids to raise by himself. Sally was in high school and spent all her free time taking care of Caroline, Bekah, and Sam, helping with their homework, fixing lunches, getting them to dance class or soccer practice. I'd managed to latch onto my friend Wade whose mom hauled me places when I needed it, since we were already playing middle school football together."

"But Sally would've helped you, I'm sure she would."

"I know. I know now that I should've said something sooner, done something about it, besides make excuses that I was just 'bad in English' every time I failed a paper. But looking back at it as an adult is completely different than being in the moment and seeing the haggard expression on my dad at the end of every workday and to see him staring longingly at Mom's picture when he thought no one was watching. I couldn't lay another burden at his feet. I just couldn't." I paused thoughtfully. "Also, though I know you saw me struggling in our English class, I was always able to pass. I'm actually pretty smart, so I was always able to pull it off. And excel in math to bring up my GPA."

She winced. "I know you're smart, Jed." She swallowed hard.

"I didn't mean it that way." I softened my voice, not meaning to drag up all she'd said to the contrary in high school. I was truly over all of that. Had let it go a long time ago.

But I was suddenly coming to the realization that her mood had swung wide in the opposite direction from where we were when we woke up in bed together. She glanced away to gaze out the sliding glass door. Looked like a clear, beautiful day, and it had started in the most perfect way, but something pricked at me, telling me things were about to turn.

That's why I wasn't surprised when Lola glanced down at her phone and said, "There was something I wanted to mention to you."

"What's that?" I watched her closely, marking the nervous working of her throat and shifting in her seat.

"You know that I only plan to be in Green Valley for a little while, right?"

She glanced up, anxiety muting the care-free joy she wore a minute ago.

"Yeah." I knew it. And until recently, the thought of her leaving hadn't carved a gaping hole into my chest.

Her brow pinched, but she didn't say anything else. And it sure seemed like she had more to say. I wondered if this was where she cut this off, before we'd really gotten started. Lola didn't realize it yet, but this thing between us wasn't something you tossed aside so easily. I was well aware her dream wasn't to reside here in Green Valley. She wanted a big job in the big city. And I wasn't even sure I could ever ask her to give that up, but I sure as hell wasn't prepared to give her up if this was headed where I was pretty damn sure it was headed.

"Was there something else?" I asked cautiously, doing my damnedest to keep my voice level and calm.

Her green eyes rounded for a second as she seemed to consider my question. For far too long. Was she scared of this? Of us? Finally, she shook her head to answer me, but she was definitely biting her tongue on what she wanted to say.

"Lola, I told you I wanted you to give us a chance. And I meant it. Whether or not there's a job on the horizon down the line, I still want that."

She stared at her fingers in her lap, avoiding my gaze.

"Do you *not* want that?"

"No, I do!" She shook her head. A curl stuck to her lip. I wanted to reach across the table and remove it, then I wanted to kiss the fuck out of her and tell her she was mine. But that was ludicrous. She obviously wasn't anything close to that. Then why did it feel that way?

Her green eyes were wide with sincerity, and a little sadness, when she added, "I just worry that, you know, we might get a little attached and then we'd have to detach. And I'm just not excited about the idea of...all that."

Reaching across the table, I took her hand. "Why don't we worry about that when we have to?" I gave her a gentle squeeze. "If we have to." Then I stood and lifted both our plates. "Stop trying to plan everything three steps ahead, Cola."

I added some lightness to my voice, though I didn't feel it. Heading to the sink, I scraped off the scraps from her plate into the trash before rinsing and setting both in the dishwasher.

She appeared at my back, sliding her hand around my waist. "Didn't mean to ruin the morning." She sounded so despondent.

I closed the dishwasher and dried my hands before turning and pulling her into my arms, hugging her close. "You didn't." But there was a thread of tension stretching tight between us that wasn't there before.

I pressed my lips to her crown. "Do you work today?"

"Oh, crap! I took Mandy's shift." She spun away toward the table and grabbed her phone. "I totally forgot. She had some wedding shower or something, so I took her shift for her. I better get home and change. I don't even know if I have a clean work shirt. I wasn't planning to, uh, stay the night and all."

I followed her to the living room where she grabbed her purse then I walked her to the door, leaning against the door jamb.

"I'm glad you did."

Her tender expression sent a pinging vibration straight to my bones. "I am, too." She lifted up on her toes, hands on my chest, then kissed me quickly on the lips. "I'll text you later."

I sent her off with a light slap on her ass, hoping to come across playful and light and not at all as if I were freefalling toward inevitable doom. Because there was something she wasn't telling me, and right now, I didn't even want to know what it might be. I never was one to stick my head in the sand and avoid my problems, but I couldn't pretend that Lola up and leaving right now wouldn't leave a gash in my chest. I wasn't ready to let her walk away, like I did at graduation, because my feelings ran far too deep now to just open my arms and let go.

Watching her back out of the drive, I heaved out a sigh. "What a fucking morning."

After a night of the most fantastic sex I'd ever had, I had another round this morning. While buried balls-deep inside her, I realized something rather significant and horrifying and wonderful. I loved her.

I was in love with Lola Landry.

The euphoric feeling lasted less than an hour, only to be beaten down with the blow that she still considered Green Valley a pitstop in her career plan. That she may leave before I had the chance to tell her, to show her what she meant to me. What we could be together.

If she wanted to leave for a life in a big city, then I wanted it for her. I wanted anything that would make her happy.

I just really, truly, deeply wanted to be inside that circle of happiness with her.

Chapter Twenty-Three

-LOLA-

"Don't expect your partner to be perfect. You aren't. No one is. Just be honest and true."
@kiss-n-tell

"Do you have any purple alligators?"

"No, but we've got a purple raccoon," I told the elderly lady in her strawberry visor who'd gone through every available item on our table at the Merryville Arts and Crafts Show. "You can pre-order a custom cozy, and we'll ship it directly to your house."

"Hmm. Let me look through what you've got one more time."

Aunt Polly was ringing up another sale, and I wanted to tell Miss Strawberry Visor that we were running out of everything, so she better look fast.

We'd been here since ten this morning, and now close to one, we only had a handful of cozies left. Aunt Polly had been stocking up her bin for this particular show for two months. Fortunately, we had handed out all of the postcards with the website and Etsy shop info, and with only a few cozies left on the table, the bin now empty, it was a rousing success.

I was tired and hungry. And sad and grumpy. Jed and I hadn't been able to connect much at all this week. I either had a shift or podcasting to take care of with Marly. Our show this week had been on how to prepare for blind dates, a filler since Marly hadn't yet gone on her first podcast date. Jed had actually had to take his buddy Grizz's shift at the station—the big guy I'd seen him joking with at the fire station—and his dad needed to be taken to a doctor's appointment on another night. So after a blissful first weekend together, we hadn't even seen each other once.

The fact that so many people in his life depended on him had slapped me with the reality that he couldn't leave this place. He wouldn't want to. And what kind of person would I be to ask that of him?

The interview with Optimum Media had gone well. Really well. Or so I thought. I hadn't heard from them since, so maybe I was wrong. But they were an extremely impressive company. Yes, they were new, but they were expanding already after one year in business. And their clientele list included two large corporations in the Houston area with three more on the docket.

The CEO, Brett Marlowe, who did the interviewing himself, was genuine, pragmatic, and a listener. That last one alone told me he was a boss worth having. His ability to recognize that other people might have good ideas was probably why his company was taking off like a rocket. And I experienced serious excitement at the possibility of working for such a company.

Then my thoughts swiveled to Jed, and my mood plummeted. His texts weren't as flirty or as frequent this week which made me wonder if he already knew somehow. If he was already drawing away from me. A twisting pain wrenched my sour mood into feeling physically ill.

At the end of the interview, Mr. Marlowe informed me they had several interviews lined up and would get back to me as soon as they could. But at the end of the week, I hadn't heard a word, which made me wonder if perhaps the interview hadn't gone as well as I'd thought.

Maybe that was a good thing.

A shot of relief washed over me with that feverish little thought. If I didn't get the job offer, I didn't have to think about uprooting myself from home again, about that sad look on Dad's face, about Marly's tight-lipped but positive support, and about leaving Jed.

"I'll take the green bear cozy," came the familiar, deep timbre that immediately ignited a wave of fizzy tingles down my body.

"Jed," I whispered with a crazy grin as I looked up.

Heaven help me! How did this man become more handsome after a week of absence? My breath suddenly vacated my body, chest heaving, while I drank him in. Faded jeans, dark T-shirt, and navy-blue jacket, his black hair perfectly tousled, his face the finest thing I'd ever seen in my life.

His small smile widened as he reached across the table and took my hand, giving me a reassuring squeeze. And just like that, I felt like all would be right in the world. Nothing else mattered.

How had this series of events come to be my new reality? I'd gone from locking my keys in my car to a fake date for the podcast to more dates to the hottest sex under the surface of the sun to I want this man to smile at me like that for eternity.

"Hey, Cola," was all he said, which launched a gigantic smile on my face.

"Hey," I whispered nervously, but he squeezed my hand again to let me know everything was okay between us. At least, that's what I thought it meant.

"Well, hello there, Jedediah," said Aunt Polly, appearing at my side. "Come to give us a little support?"

"Yes, ma'am." He turned to his side and gestured toward the man I hadn't even noticed who was turning over one of Aunt Polly's newest creations I'd told her to try out. One for wine bottles. Rather than being shaped like an animal, these all had little bears stitched all over them with a skyline of blue mountains and the words Green Valley stitched at the top. We had sold them all this morning. Jed's dad was turning over our sample which we refused to sell.

"You make these for moonshine bottles?" he asked curiously.

Aunt Polly stepped around me to the other side of the table. "Well, if I knew the exact shape of the moonshine bottle, I'm sure I could."

"Dad, this is Lola's aunt, Polly Bridges."

Mr. Lawson finally looked up from his examination of our wine bottle cozy, and I swear I did not imagine a little shock in his expression before he displayed the widest smile I'd ever seen on the man.

He shot out his giant paw. "John Lawson."

Aunt Polly slid her slim hand into his and shook it. "Nice to meet you."

"A pleasure," he countered, holding her hand just a second longer than necessary.

Turning to Aunt Polly, I asked, "You mind if I take a quick break to chat with Jed?"

"Not at all, honey. You go right ahead." My aunt was actually blushing before she turned back to Jed's dad.

I nodded with my head back toward the cars parked in a field behind the line of tables and tents. Jed dutifully followed, lacing his fingers with mine as I led him around someone's RV. The second we rounded out of sight, he was on me. I curled my hand in his jacket and yanked him close while his mouth devoured mine.

A whimpering moan escaped my lips, which he answered with a deep groan. His hand slid into my hair, where he tugged not-too-gently, slanting his mouth and sweeping his tongue in deep. When I broke the kiss to bite his lip, he hissed and grabbed the backs of my thighs to haul me up against his body. I wrapped my legs around his waist with pleasure as he pressed me to the side of the RV and ground the steel pole in his pants along the seam of my jeans.

"Lola," he whispered with desperation.

My hands were everywhere, one finally finding its way up the inside of his shirt, where I scraped my blunt nails down his chest.

"Fuck, baby." He jerked his mouth out of my reach, still grinding his hips against me, teasing me with what he could give me. Fist in my hair, he held my head immobile, coming in for a gentle, tongue-sliding kiss. "I've missed you this week."

Rocking my crotch against him, desperate for more friction, I returned his soft kiss. "Missed you, too. So much."

That earned me a heart-stopping smile. "Come to my place tonight."

I let my head fall back into his hand, where he now cradled it against the RV's side. "I have to work." Rocking against him again, I whined, "I hate Bucky's. And podcasting." I traced the line of his beautiful jaw while I continued pouting. "And the fire station. And your dad's doctor."

He chuckled, holding my gaze, sliding the hand holding my thigh up to my ass where he gave it a good squeeze.

"All those things, huh?"

"All of them."

I avoided his eyes now, remembering the interview, and almost added it to my list of things I hated that had kept us apart this week. Then my pulse raced with more anxiety than lust.

His hand in my hair eased to encircle the nape of my neck, his thumb sweeping over my collarbone.

"Are you ever going to tell me?" he whispered gently, his thumb settling on my pulse at the base of my throat.

"What?" Yep. That panic was loud and clear in my voice.

He tilted his head, giving me a small, knowing smile. "What it is you're keeping from me."

No use trying to avoid it. I inhaled and exhaled a deep breath, staring at his suprasternal notch while I let my fingers explore this sexy part of him I loved so much.

"I had a job interview this week."

His body stiffened. And not in a good way. "Where at? In Knoxville?"

Shaking my head, I forced myself to be brave and look him in the eye. "It was a video interview."

He eased my body away from his, keeping his hands on my waist, still holding me tight. I couldn't look at him yet and needed to fill up the awkward and painful silence with something.

"I mean, I've had a ton of interviews since I was let go of my job in New Orleans, and none of them worked out. So no telling if this one will." I let out a laugh, but it was hollow and empty. Like me.

"It will," he assured me. "You're amazing. Unless they're complete idiots, they'll see that and offer you the job."

His words were kind and encouraging, while the tenor of his voice was achingly sterile. Like he said the words without his own permission.

Still not looking above his chin, I said, "That's sweet, but no telling. Anyway, I just thought I'd better, you know, mention it. Not that you said anything about us being serious or anything. I don't want you to think that."

He let loose a laugh that sounded jarring and unpleasant, finally hauling my gaze to meet his. Then I wished I hadn't. I'd seen that look on his face only one other time. That day on the bleachers, when I brought him snickerdoodles, he told me it was his mother's birthday and he missed her. It was a look of desperate longing. Was he already missing me in such a way before I was even gone? I wanted to say something, anything, to wipe that look off his face. It was devastating me one second at a time.

His voice was soft when he asked, "Where is this company?"

Clearing my throat, I told him in the same soft voice, as if I said it quietly enough, it might be less painful, "Houston."

"Texas?" His voice wasn't so soft anymore. It rang with disbelief and outrage. And hurt.

I planted my hand on the center of his chest, wishing reality wasn't intruding in on us yet again. "I'm sorry, Jed. Seems like we have bad timing again."

Rather than shutter away his feelings or let the evident simmering anger behind his eyes take hold and blast out at me, he looked out across the open field and parking lot of cars, then hauled me against his chest.

"Not bad timing." He pressed a soft kiss to the crown of my head, and the gentle gesture made me want to cry. "Everything happens as it's supposed to. If you get this job, we'll deal with it then."

"But, Jed—"

He angled my face up and took my mouth with a strong sweep of his tongue and a sharp bite on my lower lip. I wasn't sure if it was a distraction from the conversation or a punishment for it.

"We better get back," he growled, taking my hand and hauling me back between the cars toward our table and tent.

I wished I could think of something to bring us back to where we were when we first walked out here, but the news I'd dropped landed like a nuclear bomb. Though he held me tight and close, there was a definite thread of tension weaving between us now.

Aunt Polly and Mr. Lawson were smiling and laughing about something. Mr. Lawson had one hand on the table, allegedly using it as a crutch instead of his cane, but he seemed to be leaning in close to Aunt Polly, much farther than necessary.

Jed gave my hand a squeeze and a sideways smile. A bloom of relief burst in my chest. For a second, I'd thought he wouldn't look at me like that again. But he seemed to be back to himself again.

"Dad, you bought a cozy?"

Mr. Lawson was holding one of our customer bags.

"Took the last wine cozy. Polly here is quite talented."

Polly? Already on a first-name basis.

"You don't drink wine, Dad." Jed dropped my hand and sidled closer to him, hands in his pockets.

"Giving it to Sally."

"Mr. Lawson ordered some moonshine bottle cozies, Lola. That'll be something new for me to do."

Her beaming smile lit up her face, and so did the blush of color in her cheeks.

"That's great, Aunt Polly." I turned to Jed's Dad. "Thank you for the business. She loves trying new things."

"Bekah will love them. I'll bring the jug over this week, so you have the dimensions," Mr. Lawson told her with a wink.

Someone's phone buzzed, then Jed pulled his from his back pocket and frowned down at the text.

"Something wrong?"

"It's work." His fingers shot over the keyboard, replying to the text. He looked up at me. "Could you drop my dad off at home?"

"Oh, no. Is something wrong?" Aunt Polly asked.

"A brush fire that's already crowning on the eastern edge of the park." He was texting again.

Shaking my head, heart in my throat, I said, "What does that mean?"

He glanced at me, expression sober and grave. "It means I've gotta go. Can you take my dad?" His tone was urgent and gruff, one I hadn't heard before.

"Go on, son," said Mr. Lawson. "I'll call Sally."

"No, we'll take you home," Aunt Polly assured him.

Jed gave her a stiff nod, turned, and started jogging away. Suddenly terrified, I ran after him. "Jed!"

He spun right as I caught up to him and practically jumped in his arms. I planted a hard kiss on his lips. "Be careful."

"I will," he assured me, removing my arms and setting off again.

I watched him in a full sprint till he reached his SUV, then I walked back to the table.

"Oh, my goodness," Aunt Polly murmured while quickly packing away the table. "I hope they stop it before it reaches homes."

"Don't worry," said Mr. Lawson. "Those boys know what they're doing."

Even so, there was a tightness to his expression as he looked off into the distance where Jed tore out of the parking lot.

"Mr. Lawson, do you know what he was saying? What does crowning mean?"

His mouth was set in a grim line. "Jed has told me a thing or two. A crown fire is when the fire is spreading through the tops of the trees, independently from the surface fire."

The sinking sensation of bottomless fear threatened to overwhelm me. That fire was moving fast, is what he was telling me.

We packed up silently after that. I tried to keep my mind off the awful possibility that Jed could get hurt. Mr. Lawson muttered more reassurances on our drive home, but I didn't hear a word he said. This morning, I was a wreck thinking about telling Jed about the interview, but that didn't carry a candle of anguish and dread next to the thought of him in harm's way. If anything happened to him, I knew it would break me.

Chapter Twenty-Four

-JED-

Grizz, Maverick, and I were working on the burn out. Mav had joined the department just under a year ago and hadn't seen a fire this size, so I promised the chief I'd keep him close. We'd set a fire inside the control line to widen it so it would consume fuel between the edge of the fire and the control line.

So far, so good, but this fire was devouring the treetops at a remarkable speed. Several departments from surrounding areas, including Merryville, had joined us, but we'd kept to the side of the park closest to Green Valley.

"Chief wants us to bump up!" yelled Grizz, motioning to the line of men working the hoses off two trucks a half a mile away.

The bump-up method was more progressive, something we'd been studying but hadn't implemented. We'd build a fire line to contain a wildfire without moving back, giving the wildfire room to eat more wood. We'd keep the position by rotating a new crew.

It reminded me of when I played football, and the offensive line refused to back down to the most aggressive powerhouses of the defense. No matter if that defensive line felt like a mack truck powering through, we'd hold the line. The bump-up method was no different.

Already soaked through, my gear was suffocating in the heat of the blaze. I nodded then signaled to Maverick. We'd done a good enough job in building the burn out fire, trying to snuff out the wildfire's fuel, trying to contain it on this side of the road. If it crossed here, it would move up across the woodlands to several residences and one ranch just outside the park's borders on the north side of Green Valley.

Determined, the three of us huffed up the gravel road, hearing the calls of the men over the blaze. I took a minute to look up, noticing the wind had died down, the flames burning straight up rather than at a slant when we'd started. That was good.

I sent a quick thank you to the heavens and strode toward the front of the line across burnt brush so that Grizz, Mav, and I could relieve three of our guys on the hose. They'd moved the truck up into the burnt woods after they'd extinguished it here. Trucks from other departments had done the same, farther up the hill into the woodlands. We were lucky that most of these woods were relatively flat, only a slight incline.

"Got it," I yelled to one of our guys at the front of the hose, taking the lead.

Mav then Grizz were right behind me, helping to control the behemoth of a hose with a hundred plus pounds of pressure shooting like a waterfall up into the treetops. My muscles strained, but I panted through it, adrenaline still fueling me.

"Forward!" I called back.

We moved ahead about five steps in unison, parallel to the other hose to our right. The heat was insanely intense at this close range, even through our face shields, but the line held. Better, it was falling back a few feet at a time. For a blaze that licked up this fast and this hard, it felt like a miracle.

Whenever we had a fire this size to contend with, my top worry was the lives and homes at stake if we failed to contain it. At the moment, only one popped into mind as I strained my muscles with the powerful hose.

Lola.

The mere thought of a blaze running out of control and making its way to her Aunt Polly's sent a tidal wave of fear crashing over me. It was even conceivable that if this blaze ran away from us, it could reach that far into Green Valley.

I'd never felt fear like this before. A soul-crushing terror that could send me into madness. It was enough to renew my strength and determination against this fucker and snuff it out with my bare hands if I had to. No, that wasn't physically possible, but my love for this girl was a desperate, irrational thing wreaking havoc on my sanity.

I'd do anything to keep her safe. I'd do anything for her. Period.

A familiar, horrifying splintering drew my gaze up a split second before someone yelled, "Look out!"

Without a thought, I dropped the hose and spun. Grizz had already turned, but Mav was frozen, his gaze up. I tackled him around the middle and carried him a few feet into the ground as the burning tree cracked and fell.

-LOLA-

I WAS DOWN to sweeping the back line, having restocked the sugar caddies, the ketchups, and wiped down the tables. Tonight was ***not*** a good night at work.

I'd messed up two orders with the kitchen—my fault, not theirs. I'd ordered Bud Lights at the bar when the customers had asked for Miller Lites. I'd mixed up the credit cards on a table of women who'd all gotten separate checks. Getting the manager Harry to void the payments and start over had been delayed so long that my tip obviously suffered as a result of it. It was a really shitty night.

I could blame it on the full moon or some other such cosmic interference, but the truth was that my mind was only on one thing—the wildfire on the north side of Green Valley. Here at Bucky's, we were halfway to Merryville and well out of the way. And news came in about two hours ago that the fire had been contained.

I'd texted and called Jed at least twenty times. Literally. But he hadn't responded. Hadn't even read them. I was going to lose my mind if I didn't hear from him soon.

That hurt look in his eyes during our conversation today kept flashing to the forefront, causing a stirring of nausea that played on repeat throughout the night. Then my sadness would switch to fear, because where the hell was he if the fire was out. And why wasn't he answering my texts? I was an emotional wreck.

I'd taken a quick break from clean-up to text Marly and get Bekah's number. After I shot her a text to see if she'd heard from Jed and if he was alright, she texted back within minutes.

BEKAH: Yes, he's okay. There was an accident where one of the younger guys was almost seriously hurt. But he and Jed just had a few scratches.

. . .

I ALMOST SOBBED IN RELIEF. And worry. I thanked her for letting me know, then grew frantic, pondering why Jed wasn't responding. Maybe he was more hurt than she let on. *What had happened*, I wondered as I swept the last of the spilled fries, pickles, and lettuce into a dustpan and scooped it into the trash.

"All locked up, Lola. Let's go." Harold stood in the doorway leading down the hall to the office and the back entrance.

"Coming." I put the broom and dustpan back in the closet, washed my hands in the line sink then headed toward the back exit.

Mack was standing there at the open back door, his head tilted as he gave me a pitying look. "Rough night."

Not a question. He'd seen Harold hand me my ass after my third screw-up. Nodding, I left through the door first. Harold promptly locked the back door with his keys and gave us a quick wave over the shoulder.

"Have a good one." That was what I liked about Harold. He might be pissed and reprimand you quickly on the spot, but he didn't hold a grudge or keep the anger long.

"Night," I said.

"See ya." Mack walked beside me to my car, which was parked next to his truck. "Here."

He handed me one of Bucky's to-go bags.

"What's this?" I peeked inside, only seeing a styrofoam to-go box.

"Extra cheesy, extra meaty nachos."

I grinned up at him, though I felt like I was about to cry. "You didn't have to do that."

"Looked like you needed it after tonight."

Blowing out an exhale of fatigue and self-pity but most of all worry, I nodded. "I broke the record in how many fuck-ups you can do in one night and still keep your job."

"So what's goin' on?"

Mack stopped in front of my car, arms crossed, and gave me that big brother look. The patient kind that said he was listening, so I'd better spill it.

"Um, well, I think I screwed up."

He waited, giving me a slight nod to continue.

"Coming back to Green Valley is just a pit stop till I find a new job, ya know? And while I'm here, I hadn't planned on dating. I mean, not seriously, and nothing beyond the podcast."

Mack knew all about *Kiss-n-Tell*. Said he listened all the time, which always made me giggle. The idea of a giant teddy bear of a man who was happily married being entertained by mine and Marly's rants on the single life made me want to laugh.

"But you did, didn't you? Date someone seriously."

"That's just it. I mean, we've hardly been dating long at all, but it feels like we've been together forever. We knew each other in high school, and there's a little history there, but we went on a few dates, and I had a job interview for a company in Texas, and now...now, I...I just don't know." I looked at the Bucky's yellow neon sign and gulped down the sudden lump climbing up my throat.

"And now you have feelings for him, but you also want this job."

Snapping my gaze back to Mack, I mumbled, "Yeah."

Mack was one of those solid individuals you meet in life. The kind who said what they meant and meant what they said. Dependable. Trustworthy. The kind you'd turn to in a dire emergency, like a tornado warning or flash flood emergency or when your heart was splitting in two.

He lifted his giant paw and scratched the scruff of his short beard. "That's a tough one."

"But you have some advice, don't you?"

He turned those kind brown eyes on me. "My advice is pretty simple, and it ain't nothin' you haven't heard before."

"Which is?"

"Follow your heart."

That was pretty simple, and yes, I had heard it a hundred times before. Then he elaborated.

"Cut away everything else, Lola. Set aside your past, your future. The distractions, the obstacles, your plans, your fears. Just cut all of that out, then listen." He placed that big hand over the left side of his chest and thumped twice. "Let yourself feel. Then you'll know what to do."

"You make it sound so simple."

"It isn't, actually. Not at all. But if you do it right, as I said, you'll know what's right. What's best for you." Then he gave me a little shove in the shoulder toward my car. "Now get on home. It's late."

"Thank you, Mack." I shuffled my nachos to the other hand so I could open my car door.

He smiled and gave me a wave, then climbed into his truck. As usual, he waited for me to drive on ahead of him out of the parking lot before he followed.

I hated that Jed and I had ended our conversation like that today. But mostly, this icky feeling was because I'd spent most of the night tearing my hair out with worry. Today had reminded me yet again how important his place was here in Green Valley. How impossible it would be for him to leave.

Then my mind wandered back to the fire. Bekah said he was okay, but was he? I needed to see him to be sure. Not hearing from him, even by text, was driving me mad.

While my head spun with everything else—work, a job, leaving Green Valley—all I really wanted was to see Jed. Talk to him, laugh with him, climb into his bed. Climb *him*.

Suddenly, my pulse raced with want. Need. Rather than turn toward Aunt Polly's at the first intersection in Green Valley, I took a decided left with a buttload of determination and fortitude and, yes, a heavy dose of desire. I wanted to live in the now, not in my spreadsheet of plans. And not in fear.

My tires actually squealed as I rounded the curve onto his street, my emotions wreaking havoc on my ability to calm the hell down. But what was most surprising were the three words that kept repeating in my head, which were ridiculous. I shouldn't be thinking those three words about Jedediah Lawson. We'd only been dating a short period of time, and yet, somehow, my heart didn't give a good goddamn.

I pulled into his drive, grabbed the to-go bag, and hauled ass up to his porch. His Yukon was in the driveway. Thank God! He was here. He was alright.

Banging on his door, I hopped from foot to foot, knowing full well I looked and smelled like a grease pit, not unlike our first meeting. But I didn't care. I wanted to see him. I needed to see him. The desperation of my entire body—flesh, bones, blood, brain—ached to be near him. And I just couldn't stand it anymore.

Yet again, those three words popped into my head as Joe barked like mad on the other side of the door. I could hear him running away, his claws clacking, then coming back and barking and whining. There was no need for me to knock again, yet I did, my hands frantic to do something.

When I heard the sound of heavy footfalls coming across the floor, adrenaline shooting a spike of excitement through my veins, I couldn't even think straight. And when he flung open the door in nothing but a towel wrapped around his waist, his hair dripping from the shower that he'd obviously jumped out of to answer the door, the three words that popped out of my mouth weren't the ones I'd been contemplating and fearing and trying to ignore.

Instead, I held up the bag in my hand and said, "I brought nachos."

His hooded gaze swept over me, ignoring my weird greeting, taking in my heavy breathing, my most certainly wild eyes, and saw what I wasn't saying. Without a word, he grabbed my wrist and hauled me over the threshold. With a heavy slam of the door, he took my bag and tossed it on the little table in the foyer, grabbed me by the waist, and lifted me off the floor so he could slant his mouth against mine.

I wrapped my legs around his waist, my denim mini-skirt riding up my thighs when he pushed me against the wall and kissed me with greedy, aggressive strokes of his tongue. Moaning, I coasted my hands over his broad shoulders, down his biceps, across his chest, then back up again, trying like crazy to feel as much of him at once as heavenly possible. Like he might disappear if I didn't hold on tight.

"Jed," I whimpered, moaned, complained, begged, pushing all of my feelings into the one-syllable sound of his name, dredged up from that aching place inside. "You're okay."

I squeezed his shoulders, then he hissed. I pulled back, seeing a long red welt down toward his back. "Oh, Jed, are you—"

He crushed his mouth to me again, never saying a word, moving both hands down to my thighs, where he grabbed the hem of my miniskirt and yanked it up to my waist, completely exposing me. When he skated his fingers over the satin of my panties, he found me embarrassingly wet. He pulled back, watching me, still saying nothing, stroking me as I rocked into his hand, making desperate mewling sounds.

"Jed." This time, his name came out with a definite hint of the sadness swelling inside me, the regret and the concern I'd bore all day long, thinking I'd hurt him. That he might be out there injured in the fire. The emotions twisted together in a vortex that felt something like grief. Like goodbye.

He jerked the towel at his waist so that it fell to the floor, then slid my panties to the side. Grabbing hold of his dick, he rubbed the head through my slickness, just once, before pushing inside me. Nice and slow.

My mouth fell open, a sound of agonizing relief pouring out of my throat, while he thrusted in with shallow pumps until he was fully seated. He held me up and open by the backs of my thighs, his eyes sliding closed as he pressed his forehead to mine. His breath came out in a shaky gust, and then he started moving. Deep, slow thrusts with a jarring pound at the end when his hips were flush against mine.

Gripping his biceps to avoid his shoulder, I encouraged him, matching his tempo, grinding against him. "Yes," I whispered. "More, Jed. Give me more."

He obeyed. Holding me spread wide and pinned to the wall, he fucked me till I couldn't think straight. Normally, I'd need some foreplay or even some clit-play to reach orgasm, but I was barreling toward climax with irrational speed.

"Kiss me," I commanded. "I'm about to come."

The hot look he burned into me turned savage then his mouth devoured mine, invading with near-violent aggression as he pounded harder inside of me. When I came, he swallowed my moans, holding himself deep as I squeezed around his dick. Before my tremors had subsided, he went back to his punishing thrusts, his kisses rough in their dominance, his body a hot, steel wall, blocking me in. He bit my lip then buried his face against my neck on three final thrusts, each ending with deep, guttural grunts.

I held on tight while he pulsed inside of me. We clung to each other, panting. I couldn't verbalize what had just happened, and I was pretty sure neither could he. We'd collided with explosive need. The only thing that mattered was him getting inside of me, of feeling his hard body filling me up and pressing me into the wall, showing me with deep penetration rather than words exactly how he felt.

And I didn't want to use my words right now. Not about why I'd driven with desperate intent to get here so he'd fuck me like a madman. Because it was still there. That constricting band of vulnerability, of aching impermanence which had been the catalyst for our brutal coupling.

Rather than address what we should be dealing with, he lifted his head and pressed a slow, sensuous kiss to my lips. "Stay the night."

There was nothing else to say. "Okay."

"I COULD GET USED TO THIS."

"What? Late-night booty calls?"

After finally leaving his foyer wall, we'd adjourned to the shower, where we'd had sex again. Then to his bed, where we had sex a third time. He'd disappeared out of the bedroom after that. I'd heard a few beeps of the microwave in the kitchen. Three minutes later, he brought in a plate with the take-out nachos, nice and warm.

"No." We were naked and propped on our elbows facing each other, the plate in between us. "Eating nachos after hot sex."

I lifted a chip and scooped some salsa and sour cream that Jed had added to the plate. Right as I took a bite, a glob of sour cream fell on my boob.

I laughed while Jed's smile turned devilish. "Let me get that for you."

"Jed, don't—."

But he'd already launched himself forward and sucked it right off my boob, then proceeded to take a detour down to my nipple, where he gave me a quick suck before pulling away.

"Hey!" I leaned back, laughing and still chewing while covering my assaulted nipple.

"Mmm." He licked his lips. "Could definitely get used to this." He scooped salsa and sour cream onto his next chip and stuffed it into his mouth. "Sex nachos is now our thing."

"Thing?"

"A repeated event."

"So we'll do this again?"

"Often."

He grinned wide, and so did I, then we both suddenly weren't, because that indefinable timeline intruded like the drunk asshole who bumps the table when you're playing Jenga and knocks the whole tower over.

I lightly traced the edge of the angry, reddened scratch on his shoulder. "What happened?"

"A tree fell."

"A tree fell on you?!" I nearly launched off the bed, but he held me down.

"Not on us." He paused. "Thankfully." He heaved a sigh. "A branch caught the edge of us as we fell."

"How'd it happen?"

He explained how they were working as a three-man team, and the tree fell. Someone shouted, and he'd pushed him and a young firefighter named Maverick out of the way.

"So you saved his life," I emphasized.

He shrugged, a frown pinching between his brow. "We do what we're trained to do."

That might be true, but the honest truth here was that Jed was a true hero. Like all the firefighters risking their lives for each other, for the innocent people in the line of the blaze. Yet again, the importance of this man's presence rooted right here in these mountains reminded me that he couldn't really belong to me. Not in the long term.

But I didn't want to think about that right now. Eating one last nacho, I looked away over his head to the bookshelf on the wall behind him.

"Jed, you have quite the collection of sci-fi."

He moved the plate to the nightstand on his side and curled an arm behind his head as he looked over at the bookshelf.

"After I conquered all of the *Dune Chronicles*, I started reading more and more. Dennis E. Taylor, Peter F. Hamilton, Martha Wells. I really love their series. I've started to dive into fantasy, as well. Tad Williams is amazing."

I glanced at the giant books on his wall, feeling totally inept in understanding his disorder.

"I'm so sorry if this sounds stupid, but isn't it difficult to read with dyslexia?"

"It's not stupid." He turned his head towards me, reaching over with his free arm and hauling me against his chest. "It was difficult at first, like I told you before, but now I love reading. That's why when Sally told me that she saw Zoe struggling in elementary school like I used to, we immediately had her tested."

"And the reason you became her personal tutor." I trailed a finger up and down that line bisecting his abs straight up to his sternum. "And her hero." Just like everyone else's.

He chuckled. "Don't know about that." Then his expression turned thoughtful. "But, yeah. I didn't want her to go through what I did. And I wanted her to love reading like I do now. There's no reason someone with dyslexia should feel any less or shouldn't experience the same joy as everyone else with reading."

I swallowed the lump of emotion, of pride, in the compassionate man I was lying half on top of. Propping my chin on his chest, I stared up at him while his finger listlessly traced over my shoulder with my birthmark.

"You're something else, Jedediah Lawson."

"You are too, Lola."

Our voices were light, but the tension was heavy again. Like Lady Fortune simply would not be ignored, repeatedly intruding with reminders that this feeling was special. That this sort of connection didn't come along all the time. We gazed and petted each other a bit longer, then finally Jed broke the spell.

"Let's go to sleep." He reached over to the lamp and flicked it off. "Turn over, Cola."

I did, facing the other direction. He spooned close to me, banding an arm around my waist, and hauled me up against him. He continued to coast his fingertips over the curve of my shoulder and down my arm. The hypnotic repetition and delicious feel of his fingers on my skin began to lull me to sleep. My body went lax. But before I could drift off entirely, he pressed a kiss to the side of my neck and whispered words that would haunt me into my dreams.

"Life is fragile and fleeting. I learned that with my mom. When you find something good and beautiful in this crazy world, you hold onto it with both hands. And don't let go." His arm around my waist squeezed me closer. His lips brushed where my birthmark was, then he whispered into my skin, almost inaudibly, "That's how I feel about you."

I wasn't sure if he thought I was asleep or if he only felt brave enough to spill those words in the dark. But they seeped right into my skin—painful and poignant and so, so lovely to hear. I didn't want him to know I'd heard his confession in the dark, because then I'd have to admit that I didn't want him to let me go. The looming possibility that he just might have to making me press my lips tighter together and slip off to sleep without a word.

Chapter Twenty-Five

-LOLA-

"Why are teenage boys so dumb?" @zoebear
"Because they're made of 88% testosterone, 10% puppy dog, and 2% twinkie."
@marlypants

"Well, I hate to break this to the world, but teenage boys are stupid."

Marly and I both snort-laughed while I tried to come up with something kinder to say about teenage boys. I didn't want the entire generation of male teens who listened to this episode to feel maligned.

I was actually shocked when Zoe agreed to come on the show for a special minisode, *Teen Dating in Small Towns*. I'd fully prepared for her to tell me she wasn't interested, but I had the ulterior motive to prove to her I wasn't the witch she might've thought I was on our first meeting. And honestly, Jed cared about her so much that I found myself needing to know her.

After the first fifteen minutes on the show, I realized that Zoe may not have hated me on our first meeting as I'd originally thought. She just had one of those prickly personalities and the driest humor, which I knew would appeal to listeners.

"In their defense," I said into the mic, glancing at the video camera streaming this live to our YouTube channel, "teenage boys have to endure an overload of testosterone which probably contributes to a lot of their not-so-bright actions."

"I'd agree with you," Zoe added, "except that female adolescents are experiencing the same with estrogen, and I certainly don't act the fool like they do."

Marly grinned and leaned into the mic next to me, the laptop in front of us but off to the side. We'd never had a guest for a minisode and thought it best if all three of us were on the YouTube stream for this one.

"So tell us, Zoe," she said in her mock-serious tone. "What exactly is it that the boys do to get your attention that you find *stupid?*" She air-quoted the last part.

"For one thing, they insist on driving their giant trucks through the school parking lot and revving their engines. Please tell me how a loud engine is supposed to be impressive?"

"I hate to break this to you," I said, "but a lot of guys still do this long past high school."

"So some guys don't grow up?" She looked horrified.

"Nope," Marly and I answered in unison.

"What else?" Marly goaded.

"Well, there's this one guy I think is pretty cute in my math class. He asked me to come hang out at his dad's farm. We'd actually been talking a lot since I live on a farm, too. We seemed to have a lot in common."

"Sounds good so far," I encouraged, "then what happened?"

She rolled her eyes. "I get over there, thinking we'll—I don't know—check out his horses or something cool. But no. He takes me out to the pasture to watch him bushhog the field with his dad's big ole tractor."

"It seems to me he was trying to impress you with his tractor skills as opposed to his truck skills," I offered.

"Exactly! Neither of which is impressive to me. And also, asking me to go skinny dipping over at Bandit Lake for our first date is just disgusting."

My eyes went wide. "He had to ask you that as a joke."

"Nope. He was totally serious. And I actually thought he was cute up until he thought getting me naked in a lake was a good first date. Maybe all jocks really are dumb."

"Not all," I added, thinking of Jed. "Trust me."

"Who was this joker?" asked Marly, a bit affronted for her.

"No way!" I shouted. "If you say his name, her Uncle Jed will hunt him down and kill him."

Zoe smiled at that. "I don't want my Uncle Jed to go to prison, so let's keep names out of this."

"Good idea." I almost fainted at the thought of Jed overhearing this and throttling some teenager at football practice. I'd have to debate whether to edit that part out of the podcast episode, because he was more likely to listen to than watch the show today since I knew he was working.

"So tell us what you would find attractive if a boy you were interested in asked you out."

"Honestly, anything where we can actually have a conversation and get to know each other. I would love to just go sit at Donner Bakery after school and have a cupcake and soda or some coffee. It's really kind of sad because I thought the guy in my math class was going to show me maybe his dad's pasture and surprise me with a picnic lunch or something where we could watch the horses run and we could get to know each other."

Poor Zoe. She really did look put out that teenage boys were so utterly clueless.

"Well, maybe some of the guys will listen to this episode and learn a thing or two." I gave her an encouraging smile.

"Maybe so." She returned my smile, which I think was the first one she'd ever aimed at me.

Somehow it felt like I'd climbed a mountain and was rejoicing at the peak. I could see why Jed loved this girl so much, despite the fact she was his niece and he was sort of required to by blood and all. She was bright beyond her years and just plain fun to be around.

My phone buzzed in my lap just as Marly was winding the show down, thanking Zoe for coming out today and sharing her insights. My heart fluttered, hoping it was Jed. He'd been sending me double entendre texts all week from work. As a matter of fact, when it buzzed again, the hum zinged a bee-line between my thighs. I had a Pavlovian response to Jed's texts that weren't appropriate at the moment.

I leaned forward and closed out the show with our usual spiel, then Marly clicked off the recording, and we removed our headphones.

"That was awesome," I told Zoe.

"Yeah, you were perfect," agreed Marly.

I stood and opened my phone to find that I hadn't missed a text. I'd missed a phone call and a text. I'd always routed all my calls directly to voicemail whenever we were recording. Both the call and the text were from Optimum Media. My stomach plummeted.

I read the text: *Hi, Miss Landry. Please call us at your earliest convenience regarding the position at Optimum Media. Look forward to hearing from you.* The text was sent from the CEO himself, Brett Marlowe. The one who'd done the interview.

"What's wrong?"

I glanced up to find Marly and Zoe both staring at me with concerned expressions. For a second, I was definitely what Marly would call deer-in-the-headlights Lola, feeling as if my world was crashing down around me. I'd been living in this fantasy wonderland, enjoying this blissful life in Green Valley, and then this text reminded me that there was potentially a career and a world waiting for me outside these mountains. At least, I was pretty sure that it was. The president didn't text applicants to tell them they didn't get the job. That was his assistant's job, most likely. Or I'd have gotten a thanks-but-no-thanks email.

I swallowed hard, recognizing my erratic pulse ratcheting higher. "Nothing." I plastered on a smile. "Just got notified I forgot my cell phone payment." I laughed. Zoe looked relieved, believing me. Marly didn't.

"Well, this was fun," said Zoe, walking toward the door.

I held it open for her. "Thank *you*. I think listeners are going to love this episode." My voice sounded a bit too perky.

Marly frowned at me as I leaned in and gave Zoe a hug. Normally, I wouldn't have initiated the hug, but I was off-kilter. I wasn't usually a hug-initiator, and I wasn't sure Zoe and I were even on those terms, but amazingly, she hugged me back with a sweet smile.

"This was so much fun," she said, sounding for the first time like an actual teenager rather than an over-it twenty-something-year-old. "Thanks a lot, Lola."

"Let's hope we can whip those boys into shape," said Marly over my shoulder.

She laughed. "Let's hope. Oh, don't worry," She stopped me from following her toward the stairs, "I can find my way out."

She slipped down the stairs with another wave as Marly yanked me back into the room and shut the door.

"Tell me right now what the hell happened." Marly had her mean voice on.

"Um, so there's something I haven't told you yet." No reaction. I barreled ahead. "My friend Betty from college told me about a position opening at a media company. A really cool, progressive one, looking for entry-level agents. The salary and benefits were really good, but more than that, the company is top-notch. Mr. Marlowe, the CEO, is not only innovative, he actually listens to new ideas."

She crossed her arms. "When did you talk to him?"

"In our video interview last week."

A flash of hurt crossed Marly's expression. I could handle anything from her except that.

"Please, Marly, don't be mad. I didn't want to tell you unless there was a reason to."

"And now there's a reason to."

I looked at the text on my phone again. "Yeah."

She heaved out a sigh and marched over to me, planting her hands on my shoulders. "I'm not mad at you for chasing your dreams. I'm mad you didn't tell me about it."

"Chasing my dreams," I repeated. Funny that I'd almost forgotten about them in the last several weeks.

"Well, you better call them back!" she said excitedly.

"Right."

I pulled up the missed call and held my shaking finger over the call button. For a moment, I hesitated, knowing this call was going to change things irrevocably. Jed flashed to mind, and the knot in my stomach twisted tighter.

I pressed the button and waited. After two rings, Mr. Marlowe's executive assistant answered, then patched me through to him.

"Thank you for getting back to me so quickly."

"No problem," I responded breathlessly.

"I apologize for the delay in getting back to you. We did finish interviews last Friday, as I'd said, but then the team and I had a meeting about restructuring a few positions." He paused as if building up some sort of suspense or waiting for me to say something. When I didn't, he continued. "After reviewing your portfolio, our interview notes, and your new podcast platform, we decided that we don't want to offer you the entry-level position."

"Oh, I see."

He chuckled lightly. "I don't think you do. We've restructured so that we can offer you the creative director position, but we'd also like you to work with our senior account director as a brand strategist. Obviously, this is more than you probably bargained for, but we've also adjusted the salary to match the workload." When he gave me the annual salary figure, I tried not to choke on my surprise. That was almost double what I made at Clarks and Taylor. "The benefits package is the same. Your hours may be longer, but we'll compensate with time off for days you work overtime."

I was utterly speechless.

"I hope the silence is a positive sign." His austere and direct manner made him a great leader. It's something I could appreciate. "So, what do you think? Would you like to come and work for Optimum Media?"

"Wow." I laughed with sheer shock. "I-I don't know what to say."

"It's easy. Say you'll take the job."

Chapter Twenty-Six

-JED-

"You've got a shit bluffing face," Grizz told Mav across the poker table.

"So do you," said Chief McClure before he sighed and slapped his cards on the table. "I fold. Mav is on a lucky streak."

He didn't look like it with his arm still in a sling. I hadn't admitted to Lola how close a call it was when that tree fell. Mav had taken the brunt of the hit when the branch swiped my shoulder but broke his forearm.

"Lucky, my ass. Poker is all about strategy," growled Grizz.

"Are you going to bet or what?" asked Mav with a demonic grin on his face.

"Are those painkillers kicking in?" Grizz squinted across the table, studying Mav.

"I think it's called a winning hand," said Forrest Winters, who'd dropped in for Poker Night. "I fold, too." He slammed his cards face-down on the table.

I was listening, but my mind was elsewhere. As usual. Then, suddenly, a feminine voice cleared her throat from the entrance. And there she was. Lola stood there with a shy smile, holding a tray with tin foil on top.

"Hey," I said, jumping up and walking over, my heart reacting instantly to her presence. "What are you doing here?"

"I brought snickerdoodles." She held out the tray. "I brought enough for everyone."

"I definitely want some of your snickerdoodles," said Grizz with a not-so-subtle hint he wasn't talking about her cookies. He waggled his eyebrows. "Jed's always talking about how good they are."

"Shut up." I took the tray and set it on the counter. Grizz was already up and out of his seat to fetch it. "Go get your own snickerdoodles." Lola's expression of anxiety gave me pause as I turned her toward the door. "He's just clowning around."

"I know." But the edge of unease was still there.

Frowning, I took her hand. "Come on."

I didn't want these asshats watching us, and something told me whatever was on her mind, she needed to tell me in private. I guided her out into the garage and through the open bay behind the new fire truck that had been washed this afternoon.

Once out on the drive, I pulled her into my arms and kissed her properly. The night sky cloaked us with more privacy.

I'd missed her even though it had only been yesterday that we woke up in my bed together. Hell, I always missed her. She stiffened when I deepened the kiss, so I pulled back.

"What is it?" I circled my palms over her shoulder blades comfortingly.

"I, uh, I heard from Optimum Media."

Dread pooled in the pit of my stomach. I dropped my hands but remained right in front of her.

"And you're upset because they did offer the job or because they didn't?"

But I already knew. She wasn't just upset, she was nervous to tell me. That could only mean one thing.

"They offered me the job."

I nodded dumbly, fighting back the roar trying to crawl up my throat and hurl toward the stars. Toward a fate that had brought her back only to take her away before we'd had much of a genuine second chance at this. At us.

But it didn't have to be that way. It didn't have to end.

"Knowing you, you must've already made your list of pros and cons."

She snapped her head to the side to avoid looking at me. The light breeze lifted her unruly hair, her curls a chaotic mess even more than usual. It pricked me tenderly. And sadly.

"Am I right?" I asked, low and soft, afraid to ask anything at all. Terrified of her answers.

She shook her head with one sharp jerk.

Forcing myself to breathe evenly, I said softly, "Because you already know what you plan to do."

"I took the job." Her voice was strained, her eyes squeezed shut.

She didn't even think of talking to me about it. Not that I had any say-so over her life, but I did feel like I had an investment in her heart, that what we'd built in the past weeks at least allowed me a conversation. It seemed that's what this was, but it wasn't a conversation really, now was it? It was a statement of facts.

Deep down, I always knew that she'd be leaving Green Valley again. I just didn't plan on it happening so soon before I'd been able to make her fall for me the way I had for her. The fissure between my ribs began to expand. Still, this didn't have to end. There was always a way.

"When do you leave?"

She finally turned her head to face me, her eyes glassy. "Two weeks."

Gutted. Completely eviscerated. The pain was no longer a dull throb but sharp slices down to the bone.

"So soon." It was my turn to look away as I soaked in the fact that she'd be hundreds of miles away in two weeks.

"I'm so sorry, Jed. I honestly didn't plan on leaving so suddenly. But this opportunity, this job, it's better than anything I could've hoped for. The salary, the company, everything about it is literally my dream job." Her words were tinged with pain, so I knew she wasn't completely unaffected by this sudden change in our fates.

Glancing back at the fire station where my friends, my work brothers, were playing poker, I paced away and took a minute to soak in the idea of leaving all of this behind. It's true I'd carved a life here at home that I loved, but then there was Lola.

"Okay. So Houston." I exhaled a heavy breath, turning to face her. "I probably couldn't get things settled here for at least a month or so." Shit, I'd have to put my house up for sale. "Would you be open to renting a place together to save on money?" Panic streaked across her face. "If that's too soon to move in together, I can understand. I'm sure I could find something reasonable for just myself."

"*Jed.*" She shook her head, desperate determination in her voice. Horror, even. "You can't just up and leave Green Valley! Your father *needs* you. Zoe needs you. So does Sally. She's a single mom and depends on you as the man in her kids' lives. For that matter, all of Green Valley needs you." She waved a hand at the firehouse. By this point, a tear had slipped free down her cheek. "Your job is here. Your whole life is here!"

"But you won't be."

She was right. It would be painful to leave, but letting her go again would be the biggest mistake of all.

She shook her head, heartbreak in her voice when she said, "You can't leave here. I can't be the one who tore you away from every person who *needs* you. Who relies on you."

Then it started to dawn on me, my pulse picking up an erratic pace. Genuine fear settling in. "*You* don't need me?"

She swallowed hard but didn't answer, that look of despair frozen on her face.

"Are you saying that you don't think this—" I gestured between us, "—is going somewhere? That there isn't something here?"

She opened her mouth, then stopped and licked her lips before saying, "If I were staying, Jed, then yes, it would likely be going somewhere."

"Likely?"

"Definitely. But I'm not. This was why I told you I didn't want to date anyone. This right here!" She burst out into a sob on the last sentence but sucked it back in, letting the tears fall silently. "I won't be responsible for the reason you leave a family who needs you. We don't know that we'd work out, and then you'd have left for nothing. Uprooted your whole life and upset theirs for nothing."

It tore my chest open to see her crying, to see her hurting. Still, I was also quickly becoming aware that those tears were those of compassionate Lola, the girl who always wanted to help everyone else in high school, who was now looking at a guy whose heart she was breaking. Those tears were for me, because she didn't need me like I needed her. If she did, there's no way she could stand there and push me away. No possible way.

Unable to look at her a second longer, I paced away, burying my hands in my hair in frustration and fury. She doesn't love me. Not even fucking close.

"I just can't believe you won't even try," I mumbled.

"Maybe we could try long distance," she suggested weakly, obviously not believing it.

"Long-distance doesn't work," I said bitterly, still pacing in place. "I listened to that episode," I added sharply.

She was quiet then, but my anger was mounting. I didn't want stoic silence from her. I wanted her to fight. I wanted her to want me. To need me.

"And it's not even about that," I said, rage and hurt mingling together, pushing me to the edge.

"What do you mean?"

"It's the fact that it didn't even once occur to you that our relationship was worth saving."

"What are you talking about?"

"It was easy for me to see the solution when you said you were leaving. I'd have to quit my job, sell my shit, and go with you. But that idea didn't even occur to you once, did it?"

I stopped a few feet away and glared at her. She stood perfectly still, anguish on her face, unable to admit to me that she didn't think of it because she didn't feel for me the same way I did for her. I was fooling myself this whole time. Falling deeper and deeper in love with this girl, while she was biding her time and making plans to jet. What a fool I was.

"That's okay, Lola." I swallowed hard against the rock of agony and rejection lodged in my throat. "I know what's important to you. You go have a good life."

She made a choking sound at my hurtful, acidic words. I couldn't help but lash out, no matter how wrong I knew it was. Now she shifted to anger.

"I told you, Jed, that my stay here was temporary. Remember? I mean, what is it you want from me?"

The twist of fury and pain whirled inside my chest and pushed up my throat when I bellowed, "*You, goddamn it!*"

My voice was so loud it echoed through the bay and most definitely into the firehouse. Thankfully, no one came out.

She stared at me, the anger gone, only despair shining on her pale face as another tear slipped from those emerald eyes I wouldn't be gazing into anymore.

Tipping my head back to look up at the sky and anywhere but at her, the moon shone bright. Starlight blinked peacefully, a cool swathe of calm above us. The irony that it was such a beautiful night when my heart was breaking cut me a little deeper. It wasn't fair. This wasn't fucking fair.

Exhaling a heavy breath, I said in a quiet, solid tone. "It's always been you." Then I looked over at her, needing to hear the words to make it final. "Tell me, Lola. Do you want me?"

She shook her head, the gentle wind caressing her hair. "Jed, it's not that simple."

Perusing her pretty face, I wished like hell I'd had more time. "Yes, it is."

The pain was unbearably acute. I had to get away from her before I lost it. I closed the gap between us and cupped her nape, sweeping my thumb along the column of her slender neck, knowing this would be the last time. I couldn't chase her if she didn't feel the same for me, and that was the most agonizing realization of this whole conversation. Maybe if we had had more time, it would have been different. It would be too hard for her to let me go, the way it was for me.

I might be a lovesick fool, but I wasn't a fool. I couldn't move across the country on words like *it's not that simple*.

Pressing a kiss to her forehead, I whispered through a roughened voice, "Goodbye, Lola." Then I walked away.

Chapter Twenty-Seven

-JED-

"Fuck."

Wade set his draft beer on the table, staring at me with the most pitying look that I almost laughed. If I were capable of such a thing at this point. Three beers down in thirty minutes at Genie's Country Western Bar, and I was only mildly numb from the pain of what took place two hours ago at the fire station. When I walked back inside, Chief McClure had taken one look at me and told me to take the rest of the night off. I didn't argue.

I'd told Wade the whole thing, including the fact that I was in love with her. Something I hadn't told her. And wouldn't ever tell her now.

"I'm just so lost in her, Wade." And downed the last of my beer. "Truly and well lost. And now she's leaving."

"Y'all want another round." Patty, Genie's daughter, stepped up to the table and hooked her fingers through the handle of my empty mug. "Though you might want to slow it down."

"He doesn't need another one," agreed Wade.

"But I want another one." I gave her the sorriest ass expression I could manage, which probably hadn't looked much different than how I had since I walked in here.

"You better be driving," she said to Wade, narrowing her eyes.

"I am now." He sighed. "Don't worry. I'll take him home."

She nodded and headed back to the bar.

"So what'll you do now?" he asked me.

Chuckling, I asked, "What is there to do? She's leaving. She doesn't want me going with her. The end."

"I just can't believe it. After all that sad-ass pining in high school, when you finally get a second chance, and it's damn near perfect between you two, and you won't even fight for her."

"You mean, like you fought for Kristie?" He hadn't tried very hard to keep his fractured marriage together from what he'd told me.

"That's different."

"How? You loved Kristie."

"Loved. Past tense. That train left the station a year ago, but we were just hanging on for Jake's sake. Till we realized we were doing more harm than good there, too."

Patty set down another beer for me. "Y'all want something to eat?"

"Have you had dinner?" Wade looked over at me, sizing me up like he might be able to fix whatever he saw was wrong. And there was a lot wrong.

I scoffed at that ridiculous question then took three gulps of my beer.

"You should eat," he urged.

"Not hungry."

Wade huffed out a frustrated sound and shook his head at Patty.

I was staring at the thin layer of foam at the top of the beer, watching how some was clinging to the sides as the liquid wobbled every time I set the mug down.

"Though she did bring me snickerdoodles," I mumbled, realizing that I was a bit buzzed. "Could've eaten them. Don't want those now."

"What are you talking about?"

I glared at my best friend, who was now grinning at me like I was crazy. "They were pity cookies. Goodbye cookies."

"She brought 'em to the station?"

"Guess that was her way of easing the blow." I swiped the foam from my lip after my next gulp then snapped at him. "Well, I'm not eating them, goddammit!"

He held up his hands in surrender. "No one's making you eat her pity snickerdoodle cookies."

"Damn right. Shouldn't have baked the damn things anyway. It's just hurtful."

"How dare she?"

"Right? Like baking cookies was gonna offset breaking my heart." My palm went to the left side of my chest, rubbing absently.

"Jed." A little blurry-eyed, I looked over at him. His smile was sad. "Man,

I'm sorry. I truly am. And I know what you're saying. She isn't all in like you are. I get it. But still, do you think you can just let her go without trying a little harder?" He tapped the table with his index finger. "She might not be here for long, but you love this girl. I see how bad you've got it. Trust me. You can't just let her walk away."

His urgency and insistence gave me a mild flare of hope. I tried to think about what I could say to change her mind. Maybe we could try long distance? Fly down one weekend a month, maybe? Chief would let me set my schedule to switch shifts and get a three-day weekend here and there.

What about all the days in between? Texts and video chats? It could work.

Till she starts going out with friends from work, which of course I'd want her to, because I don't want her to be sad or lonely, then some dude from accounting or HR decides to tag along. And he looks all perfect in his expensive suit and charms Lola with his big brain. She'd tell me nothing is going on, and maybe there's not on her end—yet—but I'd get jealous and pissed off and act like a damn caveman about it. Then she'd end up confessing to the guy, and he'd say, 'oh, yeah. I'm definitely hot for you.' Then they'd bond over work. He'd bring her donuts and coffee for breakfast every morning, which she'd be too nice to refuse. And one night, she drinks one too many margaritas at their after-work bar, and that asshole kisses her, but the soul-crushing part is she kisses him back, then she calls me the next day after waking up in his bed and tells me she can't do this long-distance thing anymore. That it isn't fair to either of us. Meanwhile, I'd be searching for the tallest mountain in Tennessee to jump off of.

"Jed? Where'd you go?"

I shake my head, realizing that I can't do it. I can't fall more in love with the girl while she starts a new life and drifts further and further away.

"I just need to let her go." I drain the last of my beer.

Some sad-ass country song started playing, a few couples swaying in each other's arms on the small dance floor. I stared over, wishing I'd brought Lola here for one of our dates. I didn't care much for country music, but I'd bring her just to have an excuse to hold her tight all night long.

I didn't know the song or the artist, just caught the gist of some poor bastard who'd lost his job then lost his girl and couldn't find a reason to stay in this world.

Ah, hell. This was depressing as fuck. I needed to get out of here.

"Take me home, Wade." My head was spinning and my heart was hurting. "I just need to go home."

He pulled his wallet out. When I started to pull out mine, fumbling with my back pocket, he said, "I got it. You get the next time."

I didn't fight him. I didn't want to talk anymore, didn't want to think or feel anymore.

He tossed several bills on the table and waved to Patty as we cut through the few couples dancing to that sad as hell song.

Wade stayed silent on the road back to my place. He knew me well enough to know that I was done. But when he pulled up to my house, and I opened the door, he said, "If it's meant to be, it'll work out, man."

I smiled over at my best friend, or at least I thought I was smiling. I probably looked a little demented like that crazy dude Joker from the Batman movies. Funny thing about Wade. Even after an unplanned pregnancy and marrying the girl he loved only for both of them to fall out of love, he was an eternal optimist and a firm believer in fate.

A couple of weeks ago, I thought fate had stepped in too. What were the chances that my sister would tell me to go help a girl stranded at the gas station to get her locked keys out of her car and for me to go and see it was the girl who got away?

Coca-Cola Lola.

I'd almost tripped over my own feet that day, seeing her standing there, filthy from work and pretty as can be. To think of her now...the sting was too piercing. I couldn't even get on board with Wade's meant-to-be motto. So I just nodded and strolled—well, more like stumbled—up my driveway.

Joe was whining in the backyard, greeting me as he always did through the fence. "Comin', boy."

I dropped my keys on the foyer table but missed actually, so they clanked to the floor. Meandering in the dark to the kitchen, I let Joe in. He jumped up on me with paws on my chest.

"At least somebody loves me," I said, scratching his ears really good the way he liked.

He whined and hung his tongue out happily, panting and licking my face.

"Alright. Down, boy."

I bumped around the kitchen, getting him fresh water, sloshing it on the floor, and pouring way too much food into his bowl. I added a can of food to the dry and mixed it up like I did every night, making a hell of a mess on the counter, but I just didn't care. When I went to toss the can in the trash, I caught sight of the take-out box from Bucky's, and my stomach sank again.

Heading to the fridge, I pulled out a longneck and twisted the top, then downed a few gulps. Falling into a chair at the window, I stared out. Then up.

Yep. Still a perfectly beautiful night in the Smokey Mountains. Everything seemed right with the world. Except mine.

I set the beer on the table, knowing damn well I'd better stop now. I still had to work tomorrow. Life still had to go on. Without her.

Joe wolfed down his giant bowl of food in sixty seconds flat, or maybe not. I didn't really know. I couldn't tell the time right now. When he put his chin on top of my knee, I scratched his head again.

"Joe. Who am I gonna have sex nachos with now?" I huffed out a sad sigh, looking down at his concerned puppy eyes. "Nobody. That's who."

He licked my hand, trying to cheer me up. I wish that's all it took.

Against my better judgment, which was exceedingly impaired at this point, I drained the rest of the beer and slammed it back to the table, where it promptly tipped over, rolled across the table, and crashed to the floor.

"Back, Joe."

I pushed him away and leaned over to try and get the broken pieces, then my phone slipped out of my pocket. I went to reach for it, lost my balance, and stepped on it instead. Hearing the unfortunate crack beneath my toe, I stood back up.

"Aw, hell."

Not really caring anymore, I grabbed Joe's collar and hauled him out of the kitchen. "To my room," I mumbled.

He jogged on ahead of me while I bumped my way to my bedroom and fell onto my mattress, falling gratefully into a drunken sleep.

Chapter Twenty-Eight

-LOLA-

"Remember, when all goes to hell in your dating life, turn to family or a friend. Whether they hold you while you cry over ice cream or wine or straight tequila, you'll remember that you are loved." @kiss-n-tell

"Lola, baby. Time to get up."

Aunt Polly was wiping my face with a wet washcloth, which immediately had my puffy eyes opening. They were far puffier than usual after crying myself to sleep. I'd told Aunt Polly what had happened, refusing to call Marly when she told me to because I didn't want anyone yelling at me or anything. Thankfully, Aunt Polly had just held and rocked me in the bed like she had when I'd skinned my knee as a little girl.

"How are you feeling?" she asked, wiping my brow like a sick patient.

"Terrible."

It all came crashing back to me. The way it had ended with Jed last night. The agonizing look of pain on his face, in those eyes. And the reflection I'd felt deep down to my soul.

"Why does taking my dream job feel so awful?"

Aunt Polly set the washcloth in her lap and pushed my hair out of my face, tucking it behind my ear. "Because you're in love with a man who's here. Not in Houston."

My pulse jolted and my stomach somersaulted. "What?" My voice came out a bare whisper.

She continued to pet my hair, again soothing me like she did when I was a little girl, and I didn't mind it one bit. Right now, I felt that small and helpless.

"It's so obvious, Lola. That's the only reason this is hurting so much. Sure, I know you're the kind of person who'd rather deal with the annoying buzzing rather than hurt a fly. But this heartache you're feeling? It's way more than just hurting Jed's feelings."

Panic gripped me by the throat for a few seconds before I launched up out of bed. "I've gotta go see my parents." I went to my dresser and jerked open a drawer, then pulled on some jeans. "Tell them the good news."

Funny how sarcastic that sounded. Like it didn't even seem like good news to me anymore. Even though it's literally everything I've worked for, strived for. How could something so perfect now feel sour just by the mere mention of it?

Yes, I needed to go see my parents to remind myself what this was all about. They'd worked their bodies to the bone, ensuring I had every opportunity to make the best of my life and achieve the best career. And I finally had.

After disappointing them with my failure at Clarks and Taylor, I could share the good news that not only had I found a new job, but this one was ten times better with a high-paying salary I hadn't dreamed of having before I'd hit thirty.

"How about some breakfast first?"

She followed me out after I'd shoved on a sweater and my Converse shoes. "No, thank you. I'll just grab a coffee to-go and head over there."

It was Saturday, so Dad would be sitting on the back porch reading the news in the paper—yes, the old-fashioned way, from an actual paper. Mom would be having coffee quietly next to him, making commentary on what things she planned to do that day. Perfect place to surprise them with my exciting news, I thought, as I stared at myself in the mirror and brushed my teeth.

If I kept telling myself what great news this was, then I'd eventually feel it, right?

That's what I kept thinking as I grabbed a coffee in my travel tumbler then headed across town to my parents' house.

Driving the quiet streets this morning, I took a minute to soak in the views. The quaint scene of Green Valley's downtown buildings as I passed through to the other side where Mom and Dad lived. The picturesque winding of the country road, red and gold leaves fluttering from the haven of trees as fall rolled in. The misty mountains' breathtaking landscape in the distance that sheltered our little town with its majestic presence and beauty.

Tears pricked again. I'd miss this place. I had come back home primarily to find reprieve, to lick my wounds and heal, so I could get up and fight again. And just as predicted, Green Valley had done that for me. This place that I'd tried so hard to leave behind would never leave me. Not simply because of its inherent loveliness, but because of the people who lived here. Their faces flashed in my mind—Aunt Polly, Mom and Dad, Marly, Zoe. Even Mack.

Then there was Jed.

"Oh, God."

The sickening tumble of my insides at the mere thought of him again would have been enough to knock my knees out from under me if I'd been standing. I couldn't even sip my coffee, too afraid I'd toss it up in the bushes the second I got out of the car. I actually felt physically ill as I replayed his last words to me—the worst one of all being *goodbye*.

I swiped the back of my hand across my cheeks to dry my face as I turned onto our street. After dabbing my face with a tissue in the rearview then with my compact to try and hide the splotches, I marched up the drive with a peppy spring in my step, forcing a smile on my face.

Using my key, I let myself in the house, my heart pounding again at that familiar scent of home I'd become accustomed to. Why is it that no other place smells like home? It's like a blend of my parents and the things they liked, the things they cared about, suffused into a unique scent that could only be found in this twelve-hundred square foot space. I hadn't grown up with luxuries and excess, but I'd been given everything I needed inside these walls. Everything that counted. Security, kindness, encouragement, love.

They'd given me everything to become a well-rounded, successful adult. So I'd show them their efforts weren't wasted. That I was a daughter they could still be proud of.

I marched through the living area and to the door off the kitchen that led to the back porch. Mom and Dad were exactly where I knew they'd be, in their slippers and robes since it was chilly. Dad even had his little fire pit burning beside them. They both looked up in shock at me standing there.

"I got a new job," I said, injecting as much excitement as I possibly could. Then I promptly burst into tears.

Covering my face with my hands as I sobbed into them, I heard my mom pop up.

"Oh, Lola, honey. Come sit down."

She gave me a hug and rubbed my back, then guided me over to their porch table. When I managed to suck up the tears and wipe them away—again—I looked up to find Dad staring at me with that look of angry concern that protective men tended to get when something was hurting their women. I'd seen it on Dad, a time or twenty, throughout my life. And I'd seen it on Jed when I'd started to cry last night.

Of course, his expression also co-mingled with the anger of my rejection. I swallowed that painful reality down like a poisoned pill, switching gears to the *delightful* news I'd brought my parents. Yeah, I was now being sarcastic even in my own damn head.

"What job are you talking about, Bug?" Dad said as gently as a roused bear could.

"I got offered this great job," I went on, my voice a little squeaky. "This fantastic media company in Houston. Excellent salary and benefits. They loved me so much that they offered me a higher paying job than the one I'd interviewed for."

Then I crumbled in on myself and started crying again. Poor Dad was obviously uncomfortable, finally folding his paper and setting it on the table since he'd froze when I walked up and immediately had a meltdown. Mom ran inside and came back with some tissue, handing it over and scooting her chair closer to mine so she could rub my back, trying to console her hysterical daughter, who was apparently distraught from getting a fantastic new job.

Rather than ask me why I was crying like most clueless men, Dad assessed me for another ten seconds, then said, "I imagine Jed wasn't too happy about this new job."

I shook my head silently, wiping my face, in complete and utter amazement that there was still any liquid left in my body. How was that even possible?

"Lola, honey," Mom went on soothingly. "We know you two care about each other. Aunt Polly's been keeping us pretty well-informed of the goings-on over there. Surely Jed wants to try and make this work."

"He does!" I yelled. Practically shrieked. "But I can't let him pack up and leave Green Valley. You have no idea how important he is to his family. All the things he does for his dad, his sister, and nephew and nieces. It would be so selfish to take him away from that when I don't even know if this would last between us. We *just* started dating."

Those last words lingered in the silence, feeling oddly inaccurate.

"And you want this job more than anything," Dad says as a statement, not as a question.

It niggled at me, feeling wrong. Feeling like a lie.

Not *more than anything*, a whisper came to me.

"Let me ask you this," Dad said gently. "Why do you want this job?"

I finally pulled my gaze from my lap to his, feeling utterly confused but also loving my father for giving me a pragmatic direction to steer my brain for a second.

"What do you mean exactly?"

"Exactly what I said. Why do you want this job?"

Scoffing, I said, "Because it's everything I've ever wanted."

"Tell me what those things are," he demanded softly.

Blinking a minute, I said, "Money. Lots of money. And good insurance. Security that you and Mom don't have to pay for or have to worry about."

"Stop right there." Dad had his serious face on. "Do you honestly believe that your mother and I have lived sad, unfulfilled lives because we haven't had *lots* of money?"

"Of course not. You and Mom love each other. You have a good home." I gestured to the small house I'd been raised in. The one I loved, even with all its dings and creaks and cracks.

"Now answer this," he went on, his brow pinched. "Why do you think you need this job?"

"Because I can't work at Bucky's the rest of my life, mooching off Aunt Polly and worrying you and Mom to death." My voice cracked on the last part.

"Is this really what you've always wanted? This job in Houston?"

I opened my mouth to assure him that it was, but the words were stuck in my throat. For a solid minute, I couldn't do anything but try to answer him honestly. Finally, I was able to answer him with the truth. "It was."

"Was," he emphasized.

"Until I came back here and..."

"Fell in love," he finally answered for me.

Biting my lip, I nodded, sucking in a breath before more tears spilled.

He reached over and pulled my hand from my lap. Mom still rubbed my back silently, letting Dad handle my breakdown as usual.

"I have something to say, and I need you to hear it. Though this is a little tough love coming from your daddy who'd die for you, if need be."

I swallowed hard at the grim expression he wore. "What?" I whispered.

"All those things you said are true. But there's one you haven't mentioned. And that's your pride, Lola."

I stared wide-eyed at my father, who'd never even hinted at me not being perfect my whole life no matter what mistakes I made. Then he went on.

"You have it in your head that success means leaving Green Valley and getting the big job to show the world just how great you are. That's pride, my love. Not the good kind."

I winced, because he was right. My goals of leaving this town in my rearview mirror had always meant finding some brighter prize on the horizon. Where I could come home and say, look at all the things I did. It wasn't really all about the money as much as it was about being the best.

He softened his voice, but there was just as much strength in it. "Bug, your mom and I don't care if you have a fancy job in the city. We don't care if you *do* work at Bucky's for the rest of your life. But this is you." He chucked my chin. "Our brilliant daughter who always finds a way toward success. Just because you had it in that big brain of yours that success equals a big job and big money in a big city doesn't mean it's the only way. Sometimes, plans change. Sometimes, fate steps in and puts another path in your way." He squeezed my hand. "You just have to be brave enough to take the new path. One you hadn't planned on."

"And you think my new path is staying here? With Jed?"

"Doesn't matter what your mom or I think. What do you think?"

That single sliver of thought, of being able to stay here, overwhelmed me with a sense of relief I'd never felt in my entire life. Like the world was suddenly bright and perfect again after an awful storm. I could feel the anxiety draining away at the simple mention of me staying here.

"But what will I do with my degree?" I protested.

"You think the only possible way to use a marketing degree is by working for a large firm in a city far away?"

"Well, no, but it's not like there are any big media companies around Green Valley."

"No. But there are businesses here. And there are tons of people working remotely these days."

"Dad," I couldn't help but let a smile slip, "when did you learn terms like working remote?"

Because he certainly hadn't while working at the hardware store.

He picked up the paper and winked at me. "I may be your old fart of a dad, but I'm a well-informed old fart."

I laughed and leaned forward, throwing my arms around his neck. He hugged me back and whispered, "Success looks different for everyone, Bug. But one thing I can tell you for sure: it doesn't make you miserable and cry your eyes out. Find what makes you happy and don't let go, then you'll lead the most successful life of all."

Jed's words that night drifted back to me. *When you find something good and beautiful in this crazy world, you hold onto it with both hands. And don't let go.*

I gasped and sat up. "But I did let go."

Mom pulled me into a side hug and patted my back. "What did you let go, honey?"

"I'm so stupid, Daddy."

"No, you're not, sweetheart. You're just learning, is all. Making mistakes is the best way to learn what your heart wants and needs."

I squeezed him tight, then suddenly stood up, remembering Jed's awful expression when he told me goodbye. "I've got to go!"

I grabbed my keys from where I'd dropped them on the table.

"Well, stay for breakfast," Mom said, following after me through the house.

"Let her go, Ellen. She's got things to do."

Dad somehow knew what I'd done, though I wasn't sure it was going to be so easily fixed.

"No, Mom. I'll call y'all later!"

Then I took off running out the door and down the driveway. Once in the car, I snatched my phone out of my purse on the seat where I'd left it, then called Marly, frantic and panting, adrenaline firing through my veins.

Before she could even say hello, I cut her off, "I fucked up."

"I know." Her tone was one hundred percent aggravated arrogance. "I've been waiting for this call."

"You know about Jed?"

"Yeeep." She popped the last p like she was done with me.

"When? How? Who told you?"

"Well, let's see. My coworker, you might have heard of her, Jed's sister, Bekah? She got a call from Jed's boss, Chief McClure, who said Jed hadn't come into work. And wasn't answering his phone."

My heart plummeted, but I couldn't speak.

"Bekah and Sally tried calling and texting but got no reply. So Bekah high-tailed over there, thinking something awful had happened to him. Jed never misses work. Come to find out, he was still in his bed wearing his clothes from last night."

"What happened?"

"Apparently, he got lousy, stinking drunk because the love of his life—his words to Bekah—broke up with him."

"No!"

"Yep."

I felt physically sick at the thought of him drinking himself into a stupor over me. Marly rolled on as I started my car and backed out of the drive.

"He slept right through his alarm, and when Sally, who'd arrived by then as well, told him to get showered and dressed and get to work, he said no, he was taking time off. She told him he'd better clear it with the chief, but he said he didn't care if he lost his job, he wasn't going in. He wasn't working. He wasn't doing nothing till he was ready."

"Oh, my God."

"And furthermore, Miss Heartbreaker, his phone was smashed and broken on the kitchen floor next to a beer bottle. Thankfully, he had enough sense to keep his dog in the bedroom with him overnight, so he didn't get hurt. Drunk or not, I might've had to call the puppy police on him. And that would've all been your fault."

"My fault?! I didn't make him get drunk."

"I can't believe you didn't call me."

There it was. The hurt and injured bestie voice.

"I'm sorry, Marly."

"And I can't believe you broke up with Jed."

I bit my lip, too damn tired of crying. I needed to keep it together. "I'll be at your house in two minutes."

After hanging up, I pulled into her driveway right when I said I would and parked behind her F-150. Marly lived in the same small neighborhood as my parents. As soon as I parked, she appeared on the porch with her hands on her hips in a t-shirt and sleep shorts. But as I made my way from my car to the porch, her scowl and demeanor softened. By the time I reached her, she had her arms open.

I fell into them, all sobbed out, but the achy pain that had hollowed out my chest had me squeezing her tight and inhaling a deep, sad breath.

"I broke his heart," I mumbled into her shoulder.

"You broke yours, too."

I nodded my head into her shoulder, afraid I'd start crying again if I said it aloud. After a solid minute or two of her just hugging me, she pulled away.

"I don't know what to do." The wobble was back in my voice. "Marly, I really fucked up this time."

The weight of what had transpired between me and Jed last night pressed down on me. He'd all but said he loved me, and I'd told him basically it didn't matter. That my new job was more important. More important than him. I'd based all my decisions on a version of success and happiness that I'd been cultivating most of my adult life. And on my dumbass pride, like my Daddy said.

And the crazy thing was, my idea of ultimate happiness had changed the second I moved home to Green Valley.

Home. Yes, no matter where I went, this was still my home. Still the place that filled my heart with a contentment I would never be able to find anywhere else.

Even more so now. That sting I'd become familiar with since last night pricked again. "I need your help," I whispered to my best friend in the world.

"That's what I'm here for." She smiled, then turned around and opened her screen door. "Well, come on in. I've got a fresh pot of coffee so strong it could energize the team at NASA." She looked back as I followed her in. "Surely it could help two smart women figure out how to get one man back into your good graces."

"I want more than that."

She paused inside her living room and gave me a once-over, seeing how serious I was.

"I love him."

Her slack expression shifted into a bright, beaming smile. "I know you do." She turned and gestured toward her cushy, overstuffed purple sofa. "Have a seat at headquarters then. Looks like we might be here a while."

And we were. I needed to say more than I was sorry. I knew my course of action the minute Dad relieved me of my illusions about success and my stubborn pride. My plans shifted. I needed Jed in my life, but I also needed to show him what I felt. I owed him that.

"First things first," said Marly as she carried two steaming cups of coffee into her living room, "I want all the details on the sex. Bet it's mind-melting, isn't it?"

I rolled my eyes and sipped my coffee without answering.

"Well?" she urged. Marly indeed was a bit of a sex fiend.

I smiled over the rim of my mug. "Better."

"I knew it!" She fist-pumped the air. "Okay, okay. Give me the dirty details, and then I'll have proper motivation on how to win back your sex god."

For once, I had no problem recounting our dates and overnight stays, though I actually left out most of the intimate details and poured over how it felt to wake up in Jed's arms, to feel treasured and adored. To feel like I found my place of belonging.

By the time I got to sex nachos, Marly was on her third cup of coffee, having listened to me for what felt like an eternity of me confessing all of my feelings, all of the ways and reasons I was in love with Jed. And by the time I finished, I was sure I'd lost my ever-loving mind for even thinking of giving him up.

She suddenly hopped up and sprinted into her kitchen, opened and slammed a drawer, then ran back into the living room with a pen and pad in her hand and wildness in her eyes.

"I've got an idea." She bounced giddily. "And it's going to be epic."

Chapter Twenty-Nine

-JED-

I'd successfully avoided all of civilization for a solid week. Except for my dad, of course, who for some reason had remained blissfully silent on the whole ordeal. But he was ever-present. I knew that he knew because he'd come across the street to my place with a six-pack of Miller Lite under his arm the day after Bekah and Sally found me passed out in my bed at ten in the morning.

Not that I needed another drop of beer, but Dad's attempt to make me feel better touched me. We'd sat in silence on my back porch, having a few and watching the sun set.

Then he said, "Well, it'll all work out." And left.

Dad wasn't much of a talker. Never had been growing up. He was a man of action and few words, something I appreciated in the wake of Lola leaving me. He came over the next night with fried chicken take-out from Genie's. And that was how my slow road to recovery was going. Quiet meals with my dad. Just knowing he was there for me really had taken out the piercing sting of it all.

But every time my thoughts drifted to her pretty smile, her sweet face, and all the precious moments that wouldn't happen again, that cavern in my chest widened and deepened. Rather than go away, the pain morphed into a permanent throbbing ache. It might lessen over time, but I knew it would never go away. She'd made her mark, and it wasn't going anywhere.

I kept myself busy doing jobs around the house that I'd meant to get to and never had. I didn't want to be around anyone. Otherwise, work would've kept me busy enough. Solitary jobs at home helped keep my mind off things.

So I'd mended the wooden fence where a tree branch had fallen during the last storm, replaced three light fixtures to spruce up the place, and installed motion sensor lighting in the drive since it was pretty dark when I came home after late-night shifts.

I was painting the front porch when my phone buzzed on the bench. It had taken me three days to get it fixed. Grant had taken care of it since his company employed guys who could do that in their sleep. Still, it had taken me a few days just to get my ass in my SUV to go over to Knoxville. I was doing my best—and a damn good job, I might add—at avoiding all human beings.

That's why I huffed out a sigh when I saw Zoe's name lighting up my screen. I'd told Sally I needed the week and then I'd be fine, knowing she'd pass the message along to my niece and nephew that I was unavailable this week.

I didn't resent my family. I loved them more than anything. But dealing with my usual "uncle" jobs only reminded me why Lola was so adamantly against me following her to Houston. And hell, maybe she was right. Maybe it was a stupid idea to uproot my entire life for one person. At that moment, I'd thought only with that tender organ barely beating beneath my ribs. Now, with some space and clarity, I could see how crazy that might've appeared. You can't hang your hopes all on one person, right?

I rubbed my chest, and then my phone buzzed again.

Heaving a sigh, I laid the rolling paintbrush in the tray, wiped my fingers clean of the gray paint, and picked up my phone.

Shit. She wasn't texting. She was calling. She never called.

"*Hello?* You okay, Zoe?"

"No! Uncle Jed, you have to come over."

"What happened? Is it Pete?"

"No." She sounded like she was crying. "It's Cisco. When I brought him in from the pasture, he was limping, and now he's lying on his side. I think he got something in his shoe, or I don't know. You have to come over, Uncle Jed."

"Where's your mother?" I was already heading into the house to grab my keys. Sally should've called the vet.

"She had to go into Knoxville for some farming equipment or something. She stopped to have dinner with Sam and isn't back yet." Panic filled her voice. "I don't know what to do."

"On my way. Just keep him calm till I get there."

I grabbed my zip-up hoodie and jerked it on before jumping in the Yukon to head over. I wasn't an animal expert by any stretch of the imagination, but Zoe couldn't handle this by herself. In most ways, she already acted like a responsible thirty-year-old. In others, she was still a little girl and hearing that edge of panic in her voice had me hauling ass down the mountain.

Sally lived much lower in the valley than I did with a sprawling farm and pasture for Zoe and Pete's animals. If her horse Cisco was so badly injured he was laying down, then something was surely wrong. Still, I wanted to get there and be there for Zoe before I called the vet.

I swerved onto their gravel road and up to the house, slowing as I drew closer.

"What the hell?"

There were at least a dozen cars parked out on the lawn along one side of the house. Many that I recognized, including Wade's truck and Trey's Audi.

My birthday was a few months off, so what in the hell were these assholes doing? Was this some kind of breakup intervention? I sat in my SUV after turning it off, debating whether to start it back up and drive out of there.

Then Zoe appeared in the headlights in front of my vehicle. Smiling.

"Dammit."

I couldn't drive away from that smile, and she knew it. Exiting, I pocketed my keys and propped my hands on my hips.

"You're a mighty fine actress, Zoe Adelle."

"Joined the Drama Club this year, didn't I tell you?" she asked with a cheeky grin.

"You're trouble." I shook my head. "What the hell am I walking into?"

Frowning, I could hear some music playing in the distance.

"Come on, Uncle Jed." She took my hand and started hauling me around the house, glancing back at my paint-splotched shirt and jeans. "You could've dressed a little nicer."

"For a horse emergency?"

She laughed, steering me toward the back where apparently my best friends were throwing me a pity party with music and everything. The music was pouring out of the barn, which I could see was lit up from here. Tiki torches were framing the entrance to the barn, which was lit with white fairy lights hanging from the rafters.

"What in the world did y'all do?"

"Not us."

"What do you—?"

I cut off abruptly and stopped inside the entrance to the barn, taken aback by what I was looking at. The first person I saw was Wade...wearing a tuxedo. So were Trey and Grant. Grizz and Maverick were there, too. Candace wore a sparkly black cocktail dress, her arm hooked through Trey's, while she grinned at me.

Standing there, completely confused, I stared at the complete transformation of the barn into...into what? Ignoring my sisters, also dressed in fancy dresses off to my right, I tried to figure out what I was looking at because it was vaguely familiar. Tall cut-outs of ornate bridges and buildings framed the barn, hiding the stalls. Lamp posts were on either side, adding soft light to the space. Gold and black helium balloons were tied onto the posts.

A light flicked on, dragging my attention to the back where a giant cut-out of the Eiffel Tower was streaming with fairy lights right next to the banner with a painted script: *A Night in Paris*.

And my heart nearly stopped.

Frozen and aware that my chest was rising and falling dramatically, I scanned till I found her. Lola stood off to the left, wearing a short red, halter dress. Her curls were piled on top of her head, a few streaming along the sides. I had to blink a few times at how nearly identical she looked to the image burned in my brain from prom night.

Then she walked toward me and my joints stiffened. Every part of me went rigid, ready to bolt or push her away. I'd spent the entire week mourning the loss of her, trying to extricate her from my mind, and shedding all thoughts of any sort of future with her. And in that week, she hadn't once tried to call me or text me, so I assumed we were really and truly done. So I couldn't help the fact that my body went immediately on lockdown. By the time she was a mere foot in front of me, I'm sure I resembled a statue.

She looked at me with those emerald eyes, a myriad of emotions flickering behind them—regret, sadness, pain, hope.

I couldn't believe this was what I thought it was, so I stood there, saying nothing. Afraid it would vanish if I spoke and broke the spell. I was vaguely aware of the music now. An old song by Jewel was playing.

"I made a mistake." She gulped hard. "I've made a lot of mistakes." She stepped closer, but I didn't move. "I should've said yes to prom. I should've gone with you. I wanted to—" she gestured around us, "—go back to the first place where I went truly wrong."

My heart stuttered.

"If I hadn't let my own insecurities guide me—and my own pride," she swallowed hard, "I would've said yes, and things might've been different. But that's okay, because things worked out. We got a second chance."

She inched closer. Still, I didn't move, my blood rushing so hard I could hardly focus. I was afraid I might pass out.

"And this time, things were so perfect."

She smiled even as there was a pinch between her brow and a tear flaked right off her lashes.

"So perfect," she repeated. "Till I made another mistake. And I pushed you away. But then I realized that what I'd planned and what my heart wanted were two different things."

She lifted her delicate hand and placed it on my chest right over my heart, surely feeling it trying to pound its way out toward her. Right into her waiting palm.

"I love you, Jed," she whispered. "And I'm not going to make another mistake. I'm staying here in Green Valley, and if—" for the first time, she glanced away, another tear sliding down that beautiful, heart-shaped face, "—if you're still mad at me and need time to think it over, I'll understand. I'll give you some space, but—"

I crushed her body to mine and mouth to hers before she could say another word. I heard all I needed to hear. She didn't need to grovel at my feet or beg for forgiveness, and I sure as fuck wasn't waiting another goddamn minute to have her permanently in my life.

Ignoring the hoots and hollers, I curled my fist in her curls and slanted her head so I could go deeper. She bent to my will, moaning as I stroked my tongue inside her mouth. Banding my arm all the way around her waist, I held her tight. So tight. Not until I'd felt satisfied with a biting, bruising kiss did I finally pull away. But not far. We were both panting.

"You wore the red dress for me, didn't you?"

She laughed, lacing her fingers behind my neck, smiling so big it made my chest hurt with how beautiful she was.

"I did everything for you," she confirmed. "I'll do anything for you, Jed. I'm so sorry."

My hands slid along her waist to her back, and I pulled her till her body was flush with mine. "Hush now," I whispered against her temple. "Just let me hold you."

She called over her shoulder, "Marly, play that one again."

I glanced around at our audience, who were watching us, but also mingling and laughing. Marly ran over to a sound system by one of the Parisian lamp posts. The song restarted with the light guitar melody.

"Jewel?" I arched a brow down at her.

She pressed her body closer. "This song came on that night at prom and even then I'd wanted to dance to it with you."

I held her close and swayed, letting her have what she'd wanted, what she'd missed out on. Completely shaken that this was for real, I simply held on to reassure myself that she was mine.

Dipping my head low, I brushed my lips over that shooting star of a birthmark, marveling that I'd wished a thousand times for this to come true. And it finally had.

My dad was right. It all worked out. Speaking of which, I caught sight of him among my sisters, now talking to Aunt Polly wearing a pretty green dress. Not prom attire, but more like a chaperone. My gaze wandered the barn, completely transformed. This felt surreal, nostalgic, and totally brand new all at the same time. Thinking of prom, of our past, was bittersweet. Feeling her in my arms where she belonged was...perfect and right. I pressed my lips to the crown of her head.

She sang to the music, her cheek against my chest, about how she was meant for me.

"Same here, baby," I whispered down to her.

I cradled her close, thanking the stars or fate or heaven or whoever had a hand in giving this wonderful woman to me. Maybe it was even my mom.

We danced the next few songs without talking to a soul. Marly apparently had the good sense to play slow songs because I wasn't letting her out of my arms till I was good and ready. And that took a while.

We finally joined the others when Zoe started wandering the crowd, snapping pictures like the dance photographer. But Lola kept her hand in mine, our fingers laced together. I hadn't planned on letting her go anyway.

While Trey regaled us with some wild story about a blind date, I leaned down and asked in a low voice, "You really turned down that job?"

She grinned up at me. "Really and truly."

I clenched my jaw, concerned about that. I hadn't wanted her to give everything up for me.

"Get that look off your face," she ordered, tipping her chin up, expression serious.

"I didn't want you to give up your dream for me."

"I didn't." She shook her head and squeezed my hand. "You're my dream, Jed."

Closing my eyes, I hauled her up against me and buried my face in her neck. "I love you, Lola."

She pressed close, sighing heavily, and scraping her nails along my nape. "Have you had enough of the prom?"

"Ready for the after-party," I growled, my hand drifting down to the hem of her dress, where I trailed my fingers along the back of her thigh.

She tip-toed to whisper in my ear, "And sex nachos."

With that, I hauled her up off the ground and into my arms, then marched out of the barn.

"Hey! Where y'all going?" yelled Wade.

"We've got drinking games later," called Trey.

"Have fun!" I yelled back.

They laughed, then the music switched to a country song. I heard Wade yell, "Turn that crap off!"

Then Marly sassed something back, but I couldn't hear anymore with my strides long and fast, eating up the pasture toward the house.

Lola laughed, such a lovely sound that I'd missed terribly. "Marly loves country music."

"Wade hates it."

"Do you like the dress?" She switched gears.

"I'm going to show you just how much when we get home."

She curled her arms tighter around me, nuzzling the sensitive skin of my neck. "Yeah, Jed. Take me home and do all the bad things to me."

I almost stumbled. "You keep that up, and we won't make it out of the driveway."

"Fine by me."

"Why does my sister have to live so far away from my house?"

"Y'all only live like eight miles apart."

"Too damn far."

I opened the passenger side door and tossed her inside. By the time I'd gotten into the driver's side, she'd fastened herself in. I put the keys in the ignition and glanced over, her gaze eating me up with lust and longing. All of the bottled desire and yearning and hurt burst like a bottle-rocket. I reached over, yanked her seatbelt off, and hauled her into my lap.

Lola straddled me automatically, already unbuttoning my jeans and lowering my zipper. I hiked the skirt of her dress up her creamy thighs, all the way to her waist, moaning at the sight of matching red lace panties.

"You're trying to fucking kill me, aren't you?"

She pushed on my open jeans and boxer briefs. I lifted enough so she could free my dick. Lola was of the same frantic mind.

In! Now!

I grabbed hold of her ass, guiding her closer, while she pumped my cock once before lowering herself onto me. Zero foreplay and yet she was still so sinfully slick.

"Fucking right," I mumbled against her lips, thrusting up slowly as she sank down.

With one arm banding her waist, my other hand fisting her hair and guiding her mouth to mine, I pumped inside her. She rode me in the perfect rhythm, matching mine. After a few hard thrusts, I eased up, breathing hard against her mouth, tasting her sweet lips, staring into those heavenly eyes.

She was rumpled and breathless and soft and yielding. And mine.

"You're so beautiful, Lola."

She rode me slowly, sliding up and down in the same tempo of our easy sway on the dance floor, the sensation completely divine.

"You are, too, Jedediah Lawson."

I smiled against her kiss-swollen lips. I didn't even mind that she thought me beautiful, rather than handsome or some other masculine attribute. Then she started riding me faster, and nothing else mattered but the soaring ecstasy of feeling her shatter while I was inside her.

Easing back enough to slip my hand between us, I stroked my thumb over her clit, spreading our wetness in a slick circle.

"Come for me, baby."

Just like that, she did, with a sharp cry then a moan, pulsing around my cock so hard and fast that I couldn't hold back another second. I came right behind her, leaning forward and biting her exposed shoulder as I spent inside of her.

It felt so different this time. The euphoria doubled, tripled, as the afterglow of endorphins eased. It took me a second to realize what it was as I breathed in her skin, her head still on my shoulder, our bodies softening against and inside each other.

Nothing was waiting around the corner to take Lola away from me, or me from her. This marked the beginning of everything between us. I rubbed soothing circles on her back with my palm, luxuriating in this new realization.

Then she laughed against my shoulder.

"What?"

"Do you have any idea how many times I imagined us making out in your car back in high school?"

Smiling, I said, "No. Tell me more."

Leaning back to look at me, she said, "There's nothing else to tell. But high school Lola would've had a heart attack if she knew this was coming down the line."

Smiling, I kissed her pretty mouth, just a light brush. "High school Jed imagined way more than making out."

Her eyes widened, then she grinned. "Tell me more."

I twined a finger in one of her curls that had come loose. "He imagined sex with Cola countless times, in cars, on sofas, in beds, on floors, countertops." She laughed as I tugged on her curl and softened my voice. "Then he imagined a white dress and a church, a big house with a big yard, a couple of kids, and a dog."

Her eyes glazed over, dreamy and tender. She blinked rapidly, her smile melting away any lingering fears I might've had.

"Well, we've got the dog," she whispered against my lips. "Let's go work on the rest."

Then I kissed the hell out of my woman, the love of my life, and took her home where I didn't ever plan on letting her leave. Even though she didn't see this coming, this wasn't in her plans, it was always in mine. And she seemed pretty okay with that.

Epilogue

-LOLA-

"Dating is grand. But finding your HEA is even better.
Happily-ever-afters do come true, y'all."
@kiss-n-tell

One Year Later...

"Come on, ref!" my dad screamed at the football field.

"Dad, sit down." I laughed. "Why do you want to come to these things if all it does is raise your blood pressure?"

He winked at me as he settled next to Mom. "Because it's fun. I used to yell louder back in your day, Jed."

"Glad to hear it." Jed squeezed my knee from right next to me.

"Don't encourage him," I grumbled. "I still don't understand why he wanted to come. We aren't even in the championship yet."

"But we will be if they keep this up," said Zoe, snapping pictures from our front row seats on the bleachers in the Green Valley High School stadium.

"You mean, if your boyfriend takes us to the championship," added Sally next to her.

"Hush, Mom."

It seemed someone had been listening to *Kiss-n-Tell*, because the Green Valley quarterback had basically swept Zoe off her feet this year.

"Go, Cole!" she yelled in a very un-Zoe-like way.

"Smitten," Jed whispered next to me.

I shoved him with my shoulder. "Don't tease her."

His dad was quiet and focused on the game on our bench, sharing a bucket of popcorn with Aunt Polly. Those two had been dating ever since they met at the Arts and Crafts show. He'd even told Jed he didn't want him coming over and cooking every night because his "girlfriend" was coming over, which meant that Jed and I had many lovely nights at home together.

After I'd called Optimum Media, apologized, and told them I couldn't take the job, I'd decided to stay on at Bucky's. I wanted to see if I could put all my efforts into the podcast and the YouTube channel. Though I wasn't making a Clarks and Taylor salary, I was making a decent one now that I'd joined a podcast network.

The network caught the podcast and the attention from a travel agency based out of Chicago. Their marketing manager offered to hire me to travel to their honeymoon package hotels to rate and review them on the podcast. Of course, the trips were paid for, and I told them I could only do one a month. That was whenever Jed could work out his schedule to get a three-day weekend and go with me. There was no point in rating a honeymoon package if I didn't have my lover to experience it with. So far, we'd only visited one hotel in Boston, but we had the best time.

"Are you excited about New Orleans?" I asked him.

That was our next trip this month, and I was so excited to show him the sites. Especially since it was November, and the weather down south would be lovely.

"Are you hungry?" Jed asked, seeming uncharacteristically distracted.

"A little. Want me to get us some popcorn?"

"Actually, I brought us a snack."

Puzzled, I watched him pull out a plastic container with a lid from beneath Sally's feet on the other side of him. He set the flat container in my lap and lifted the lid.

"What did you do?" I asked, laughing at the pile of overly browned snickerdoodle cookies.

"They're not as good as yours," he said, a blush crawling up his cheeks above his trim beard. "Try that one in the middle. It looks the best."

There was one giant cookie in the middle that was less burnt than the others. When I lifted it, there was a blue velvet ring box. My hand holding the cookie started shaking. I was barely aware of Jed removing the box, handing the cookies to Sally, and bending onto one knee, slightly squeezing his big body there on the bleachers. Nor was I focused on all of our family turning to watch in breathless silence.

"Are you kidding me right now?" I whispered in complete and total shock.

He grinned up at me because I was already crying. "Lola Landry, I love you more than life itself. This is not a joke like you thought prom was, so please say yes this time and that you'll be my wife."

I launched myself at him so hard, I nearly toppled him on top of my dad sitting in the row below us. Thankfully, he had a good grip on the ring because I couldn't think past kissing him senseless.

"Yes, yes, yes!"

He laughed as everyone cheered in the stands. Not at the game but at us.

He tried to pull me back. "Give me your finger."

I straightened onto the bleacher bench and presented my left hand, wiggling my ring finger. As he slid it on, I whispered through happy tears, "It's so beautiful."

"Just like my girl."

Then his lips were on mine, and his arms were around me. We hardly noticed when an even louder cheer broke out across all of the bleachers, and everyone stood up as Green Valley's team made the winning touchdown. It was a wildly blissful moment for so many reasons.

That night, when we went back to his house and snuggled on the couch, he said, "You have to move in now."

He'd been begging me to move in with him just about every weekend, but I hadn't wanted to take that step till I had a little more saved in the bank so I could contribute to the house expenses.

"You're my fiancé, so you're moving in. I don't want to hear about bank accounts or half the rent or any of that."

"Fine."

"Fine?" He leaned up over me, where we stretched out together. "That was easy. All I needed to do was put a ring on your finger?"

I looked at the ring and smiled. I knew one thing about my pride. I would damn sure wear this ring and be his wife prouder than a peacock.

"Yep. I guess so."

He sighed with contentment and laid down again, both of us ignoring whatever was on the television as we started making all the plans for our happy life. I'd always been a solitary planner, mapping out the best path all by myself. But I was glad to admit that I was much happier making plans with my future husband.

And if any plans got derailed again, I just wouldn't care. I had Jed, and he had me, and that's all that really mattered.

Acknowledgments

First and foremost, I want to thank Penny Reid and Smartypants Romance for inviting Jed and Lola into the Green Valley world. Being on the SPRU team has been an amazing writer's experience from day one. And to Brooke and Fiona, you WOW me all the time. Keep being awesome.

My beta readers Lindsey Duga and Jessen Judice were *invaluable* in strengthening this story. Jed and Lola are so much more because of you two. Thank you both so much.

About the Author

JULIETTE CROSS is a multi-published author of paranormal and fantasy romance & the co-host of the podcast, Smart Women Read Romance. As a native of Louisiana, she lives in the heart of Cajun land with her husband, four kids, her labs, Kona and Jeaux, and kitty, Betty. When she isn't working on her next project, she enjoys binge-watching her favorite shows with her husband and a glass (or two) of red wine.

Find Juliette Cross online:
Website: https://www.juliettecross.com/
Newsletter: https://bit.ly/3HwQgXb
Facebook: https://www.facebook.com/juliettecrossauthor
Goodreads: https://www.goodreads.com/author/show/7795664.Juliette_Cross
Twitter: https://twitter.com/Juliette__Cross
Instagram: https://www.instagram.com/juliettecrossauthor/
Amazon: http://www.amazon.com/Juliette-Cross/e/B00MQ18Z1W/

Find Smartypants Romance online:
Website: www.smartypantsromance.com
Facebook: www.facebook.com/smartypantsromance/
Goodreads: www.goodreads.com/smartypantsromance
Twitter: @smartypantsrom
Instagram: @smartypantsromance

Also by Juliette Cross

BEAUVILLE SERIES:

- *Bright Like Wilfire* (May 2022)

STAY A SPELL SERIES:

- *Wolf Gone Wild*
- *Don't Hex and Drive*
- *Witches Get Stitches*
- *Always Practice Safe Hex* (June 2022)

VALE OF STARS SERIES:

- *Dragon Heartstring*
- *Waking the Dragon*
- *Dragon in the Blood*
- *Dragon Fire*
- *Hunt of the Dragon*

THE VESSEL TRILOGY:

- *Forged in Fire*
- *Sealed in Sin*
- *Bound in Black*

VAMPIRE BLOOD SERIES:

- *The Black Lily*
- *The Red Lily*
- *The White Lily*
- *The Emerald Lily*

DOMINION SERIES:

• *Darkest Heart*

• *Hardest Fall*

• *Coldest Fire*

Also by Smartypants Romance

Green Valley Chronicles

The Love at First Sight Series

Baking Me Crazy by Karla Sorensen (#1)

Batter of Wits by Karla Sorensen (#2)

Steal My Magnolia by Karla Sorensen(#3)

Fighting For Love Series

Stud Muffin by Jiffy Kate (#1)

Beef Cake by Jiffy Kate (#2)

Eye Candy by Jiffy Kate (#3)

The Donner Bakery Series

No Whisk, No Reward by Ellie Kay (#1)

The Green Valley Library Series

Love in Due Time by L.B. Dunbar (#1)

Crime and Periodicals by Nora Everly (#2)

Prose Before Bros by Cathy Yardley (#3)

Shelf Awareness by Katie Ashley (#4)

Carpentry and Cocktails by Nora Everly (#5)

Love in Deed by L.B. Dunbar (#6)

Dewey Belong Together by Ann Whynot (#7)

Hotshot and Hospitality by Nora Everly (#8)

Love in a Pickle by L.B. Dunbar (#9)

Checking You Out by Ann Whynot (#10)

Scorned Women's Society Series

My Bare Lady by Piper Sheldon (#1)

The Treble with Men by Piper Sheldon (#2)

The One That I Want by Piper Sheldon (#3)

Hopelessly Devoted by Piper Sheldon (#3.5)

It Takes a Woman by Piper Sheldon (#4)

Park Ranger Series

Happy Trail by Daisy Prescott (#1)

Stranger Ranger by Daisy Prescott (#2)

The Leffersbee Series

Been There Done That by Hope Ellis (#1)

Before and After You by Hope Ellis (#2)

The Higher Learning Series

Upsy Daisy by Chelsie Edwards (#1)

Green Valley Heroes Series

Forrest for the Trees by Kilby Blades (#1)

Parks and Provocation by Juliette Cross (#2)

Story of Us Collection

My Story of Us: Zach by Chris Brinkley (#1)

Seduction in the City

Cipher Security Series

Code of Conduct by April White (#1)

Code of Honor by April White (#2)

Code of Matrimony by April White (#2.5)

Code of Ethics by April White (#3)

Cipher Office Series

Weight Expectations by M.E. Carter (#1)

Sticking to the Script by Stella Weaver (#2)

Cutie and the Beast by M.E. Carter (#3)

Weights of Wrath by M.E. Carter (#4)

Common Threads Series

Mad About Ewe by Susannah Nix (#1)

Give Love a Chai by Nanxi Wen (#2)

Key Change by Heidi Hutchinson (#3)

Educated Romance

Work For It Series

Street Smart by Aly Stiles (#1)

Heart Smart by Emma Lee Jayne (#2)

Book Smart by Amanda Pennington (#3)

Smart Mouth by Emma Lee Jayne (#4)

Lessons Learned Series

Under Pressure by Allie Winters (#1)

Not Fooling Anyone by Allie Winters (#2)

Out of this World

London Ladies Embroidery Series

Neanderthal Seeks Duchess (#1)

Ingram Content Group UK Ltd.
Milton Keynes UK
UKHW011938210323
418937UK00005B/220